# TROUBLED WATERS

Hearts of the Children

Volume 1: The Writing on the Wall

Volume 2: Troubled Waters

Volume 3: How Many Roads?

Volume 4: Take Me Home

Volume 5: So Much of Life Ahead

# TROUBLED WATERS

A NOVEL BY

DEAN HUGHES

DESERET
BOOK

SALT LAKE CITY, UTAH

© 2002 Dean Hughes

All rights reserved. No part of this book may be reproduced in any form or by any means without permission in writing from the publisher, Deseret Book Company, P. O. Box 30178, Salt Lake City, Utah 84130. This work is not an official publication of The Church of Jesus Christ of Latter-day Saints. The views expressed herein are the responsibility of the author and do not necessarily represent the position of the Church or of Deseret Book Company.

DESERET BOOK is a registered trademark of Deseret Book Company.

Visit us at www.DeseretBook.com

This book is a work of fiction. The characters, places, and incidents in it are the product of the author's imagination or are represented fictitiously.

First printing in hardbound 2002.
First printing in paperbound 2009.

---

**Library of Congress Cataloging-in-Publication Data**

Hughes, Dean, 1943–
Troubled waters / Dean Hughes.
p. cm. — (Hearts of the children ; v. 2)
ISBN-10: 1-57008-861-6 (hardbound: alk. paper)
ISBN-13: 978-1-60641-173-5 (paperbound: alk. paper)
1. Mormon families—Fiction. 2. Salt Lake City (Utah)—Fiction. I. Title.
PS3558.U36 T76 2002
813'.54—dc21 2002009811

---

Printed in the United States of America
R. R. Donnelley and Sons, Crawfordsville, IN

10 9 8 7 6 5 4 3 2 1

*For William D. Hurst,*
*my dear friend and*
*father-in-law*

## D. Alexander and Beatrice (Bea) Thomas Family (1966)

Alexander (Alex) [b. 1916] [m. Anna Stoltz, 1944]
- Eugene (Gene) [b. 1945]
- Joseph (Joey) [b. 1947]
- Sharon [b. 1949]
- Kurt [b. 1951]
- Kenneth (Kenny) [b. 1956]
- Pamela (Pammy) [b. 1958]

Barbara (Bobbi) [b. 1919] [m. Richard Hammond, 1946]
- Diane [b. 1948]
- Margaret (Maggie) [b. 1953]
- Richard, Jr. (Ricky) [b. 1963]

Walter (Wally) [b. 1921] [m. Lorraine Gardner, 1946]
- Kathleen (Kathy) [b. 1946]
- Wayne [b. 1948]
- Douglas [b. 1951]
- Glenda [b. 1955]
- Shauna [b. 1959]

Eugene (Gene) [1925–1944]

LaRue [b. 1929]

Beverly [b. 1931] [m. Roger Larsen, 1953]
- Victoria (Vickie) [b. 1954]
- Julia [b. 1955]
- Alexander (Zan) [b. 1957]
- Suzanne [b. 1959]
- Beatrice [b. 1966]

# CHAPTER 1

Elder Gene Thomas leaned forward and looked into the font as Elder Russon lowered Johann into the water. Gene was serving as a witness, so he watched carefully to be certain that Johann's head plunged all the way under, and then he looked to make sure the boy's feet hadn't kicked up and broken the surface. But Gene was satisfied: Johann had been immersed.

Johann came out of the water sputtering a little. He coughed and then rubbed his hands over his dark hair, slicking it back from his forehead. He was looking at Gene by then and smiling. Gene nodded to him.

Johann Stahl was seventeen. He had started coming to *JMA*—German "Mutual"—with a friend of his who was a member of the Stuttgart Ward. Gene had met the boy at a youth outing and asked him whether he would like to take the missionary lessons. Johann had agreed, and he had responded positively to the lessons, but it had taken him a while to get up the nerve to ask his parents for permission to be baptized, and even longer for his parents to relent. The only disappointment now was that Elder Johns had been transferred and had missed the chance to attend. Elder Russon—Gordon Russon, from Logan, Utah—had been on his mission for only a couple of weeks, but Gene had wanted him to have the experience of performing the baptism. It seemed a good way to get him *begeistert*—"spirited"—right from the beginning.

As Johann sloshed up the stairs, he gripped his white trousers to keep them from slipping off his skinny hips. Elder Russon followed. He was tall and slender himself, and the only pants that had fit him around the waist were much too short. The two stepped on into the dressing room, but before the door shut, Gene heard them laugh. The sound echoed through the room, hollow, and Gene was embarrassed by the break in decorum.

By then Elder Bates, the district leader, had stepped to the front of the baptismal room. "We're going to listen to some music now," he announced to the small group of ward members. "As soon as Johann has changed his clothes, we'll confirm him a member of the Church."

Gene had been glad to see so many of the young people in the ward show up. They all seemed to like Johann. He was an unassuming boy, rather small for his age, and hardly the type to set the hearts of the young sisters ablaze, but he was funny and clearly popular. What concerned Gene was that the teenagers were all sitting together, and now they began to talk, rather too loudly, and some were laughing. Gene wanted this time to be quiet and thoughtful. For him, a baptism was the ultimate spiritual experience. It was the culmination of a missionary's work—a marker of success—but it was also sacred. He wished in a way that he had performed the baptism himself. He was certainly closer to Johann, and even more than that, he loved dressing in white, stepping into the warm water, feeling the closeness to someone he had taught. He had only baptized two people on his mission so far, and there was always a question of how many weeks or months might pass before it happened again—or whether it ever would. What bothered him even more was that he wasn't sure Elder Russon felt the same satisfaction. He was so new that he didn't know what it was to work for months just to find a solid investigator, and even though he seemed to like Johann, he hadn't watched the boy grow toward this day.

Gene sat on a folding chair near the front and tried not to think about the noise behind him, tried to concentrate on the smell of the water, the hint of steam in the air, even the little echo in the room—everything that said to him, this is what it's all about, to be here by this font. It was early June now, 1965, and Gene had been on his mission almost a year. He had been made a senior companion much sooner than most elders, and in a mission where baptisms didn't come easily, he'd had at least some success. But he tried very hard not to think that way. He had been blessed—he knew that—and it was wrong to take credit for things only the Lord could bring about. Still, it was nice to think that his name would appear in the mission newsletter that week as one of the few who had had a baptism. Sometimes President Fetzer published letters that were included on the weekly missionary report—especially those of the successful missionaries. He told himself he would have to be certain to write a good letter this week.

When Elder Russon and Johann returned, both with their hair wet and their faces shining, they seemed happy. Gene stood up and shook Johann's hand and at the same time hugged him briefly with the other arm. Johann sat down on the front row, between Gene and Elder Russon, and then Elder Bates introduced his companion, Elder Burnett, who gave a short talk on the Holy Ghost. He was a young missionary, only out five months or so, but one of the first to come through the Language Training Mission. His German was quite good, especially when he could prepare, but he spoke with an even, memorized tone that inspired little interest. The young people behind Gene were, if anything, noisier now than during the music. Gene glanced back several times and got a few embarrassed, even apologetic smiles, but the noise resumed each time. It was strange for Gene to think that these kids weren't that much younger than he was, and that not long ago he had been the one getting stares from his youth leaders.

Elder Burnett's talk was mercifully short, however, and then Gene had his chance to be part of all this. As he placed his hands on Johann's damp hair, he took a long breath, shut his eyes, and tried to draw in the Spirit. He felt the quiet come over the room, and he liked the closeness he felt to Johann, liked the feel of the other hands that rested on his own. He spoke slowly, carefully, called Johann by name, proclaimed the proper authority, then commanded: "receive the Holy Ghost." He paused and waited for the right words—although he had thought for a long time what he wanted to say. He wanted so much to feel that God was with him, that he wasn't just giving a little speech of his own. Still, the words that came were the ones he had prepared. He admonished Johann to use the Spirit to grow strong, to move forward in his eternal progress. He told the boy not to listen to Satan, to avoid the dangers of an evil world. He blessed Johann that he might marry in the Church someday and raise a righteous family.

It was a good blessing, but nothing new occurred to Gene even though he waited at the end for words of the Spirit. He found himself repeating some of what he had said before and then closing rather abruptly. Still, he felt good about Johann, good about the future of a young man joining the Church when young leadership was badly needed in Germany. He had been thinking all day about the possibilities: maybe Johann would serve as a Church leader in Germany someday; maybe this baptism alone would make all Gene's work worth the effort.

After the confirmation everyone in the room took turns approaching Johann to welcome him. The bishop hadn't been able to attend, but one of his counselors was there, with his wife and children, and the Young Men's MIA president, along with a few other members. The adults lined up, spoke to Johann one or two at a time, and then moved on. Then the young members came to him in a group, laughing, even teasing Johann a little, but everyone shook his hand, and Johann looked pleased. Gene worried that Johann's parents had promised to come—if they could—but hadn't. He hoped they wouldn't make things difficult.

Gene spoke to *Bruder* Schenk, the bishop's counselor, about ordaining Johann to the Aaronic Priesthood and keeping him involved with the priests quorum. By then, however, Gene was seeing something that worried him. Elder Russon was standing nearby talking to two of the teenaged girls in the ward. One was a pretty, dark-haired girl with vivid blue eyes. Her name was Giesela, and she was certainly the girl in the ward that missionaries noticed. She flashed those pretty eyes at any elder who looked her way. She had scared Gene on his first Sunday in Stuttgart when she had put her hand on his arm in a too-familiar style and welcomed him to the ward. Now she was giving her treatment to Elder Russon, and he was clearly enjoying it.

Gene was trying to talk to *Bruder* Schenk, but he could hear the other conversation. "Yes, I like it here very much," Elder Russon was saying in his LTM German.

"What do you like about Germany?" the other girl, one of the Dietz sisters, was asking, speaking slowly for Russon's sake.

"It's pretty," he said, but he was gazing at Giesela, laughing, and surely she knew what he meant.

"What's pretty? The Black Forest?"

"I don't know. I am not going there now." He was struggling for the right idiom, but he was certainly being clear about which girl had caught his attention.

"Don't you miss all the pretty girls in America?" Giesela asked. "We German girls aren't nearly so pretty."

That was enough. Gene turned from *Bruder* Schenk and stepped toward his companion. But Elder Russon was already saying, "German girls are prettier, I think."

"Oh, *Bruder* Russon, missionaries shouldn't look at girls. It's against the rules." Giesela was leaning toward him, trying her best to embarrass him with her closeness. But Russon didn't step back, continued to smile.

Gene had hold of his shoulder by then. "Elder Russon," he said. "Come here a moment." Then he tried to show his disapproval to Giesela without saying anything.

She gave the Dietz girl a little nudge. "I think *Bruder* Thomas is angry with us," she said. "We're laughing too much. He doesn't like to laugh." She had turned her beguiling smile toward Gene now.

Gene tried not to respond. "Come here, Elder," he said in English, and he moved him away a few paces. "Don't get in over your head. She's a little flirt."

"I know," Elder Russon said. "It doesn't matter."

"It *does* matter," was all Gene said for the moment, but after the elders had accompanied Johann on the streetcar to his stop and then walked to their own apartment, Gene tried again. "Listen, Elder, you have to be careful around some of the girls in the ward. They try to make you squirm. They think it's funny."

"They don't make me squirm."

"They should."

"Why? I was just kidding with them a little. Mostly, I was trying to use my German."

Gene was sitting at his desk, which faced the wall, between two tall windows. He had twisted around to speak to Elder Russon, who was sitting at the table in the center of the room. Now Gene got up, went to the table, and sat down across from his companion. "Giesela always goes after greenies. She knows that they haven't gotten used to how things are."

"For crying out loud, what did I do? I didn't say anything!"

Russon's voice had doubled in volume suddenly, and Gene realized he would have to be careful. Elder Russon had gone to college two years before his mission, instead of one, so he was the same age as Gene. He was confident, and clearly smart. He had been a psychology and pre-med major at Utah State, and had told Gene that he wanted to become a psychiatrist. He was sharp-looking, with horn-rimmed glasses and tightly cut hair. He had brought three expensive three-button suits, and two pairs of Florsheim shoes. Every morning, after he shaved, he dabbed on the Elsha he had brought with him, and the smell, to Gene, was much too strong.

"We're missionaries, Elder Russon. We can't act like teenagers. You can get into trouble really fast."

"Trouble? What are you talking about? Do you think I'm going to run off with one of those little girls? They're what—sixteen?"

"No. I don't mean that at all—although stuff like that has happened." Gene's eyesight had been getting worse lately, and that spring he had seen an optometrist and bought himself glasses, which so far he only used for reading. He took the glasses off now and set them on the table in front of him. "We have to have the respect of the members. We end up talking to them about really serious problems. Some of the elders even serve as branch presidents. If the members think we're kids, they can't trust us the way they need to. You can understand that, can't you?"

"I don't remember saying a single word that was inappropriate."

"You think German girls are prettier than Americans? What was that all about?"

"Just a joke. If we can't laugh with the members, I don't want to do this."

"You can laugh. But you can't flirt. The members see the difference. They know whether we're being nice guys, or whether we're acting like teenagers."

Elder Russon let his eyes close, rested his elbows on the table, and clasped the sides of his head. "Oh, brother," he whispered.

"Hey, look. We all have to find the line. It's something you'll learn."

"And what about lying? Will I learn that too?"

"What?"

Russon lifted his head and stared at Gene now, clearly taking him on, but Gene had no idea what he had meant. "I looked at the report you turned in last week. There's no way we worked sixty-six hours."

"Yes, we did. I kept track of our hours every day."

"So how do you count? All the hours we worked, times two?"

Gene was suddenly angry, and yet he knew exactly what Russon was talking about. "I don't figure it out right down to the minute," he said. He picked up his glasses and put them back on. "If we leave the door at nine in the morning and come back at nine at night, I count twelve hours and then take out lunch and afternoon study—or any other time we're not working. Most days we get in about nine hours, but this week we were over at Johann's until after ten, twice, and we had him at church, so all that time counted."

"And what about time spent hanging around the kiosk, over by the train station, eating chocolate and jawing with the other elders?"

"That was still lunch."

"Well, then, we took way more than an hour for lunch—and I'll bet you only subtracted an hour. And that was the same day we stopped by the bishop's house and talked to him so long."

"Hey, that's considered proselyting time. I had to talk to him about Johann."

"For about ten minutes. The rest of the time, we were just hanging around, playing with his kids and stuff."

"Oh, come on. Don't be so literal. Missionaries have to be on good terms with the members. That's how we get referrals."

"That's fine with me. I'd stay there all day, for all the good we do tracting. I'm just saying that you ought to tell it like it is when you turn in your report. I thought back over the days we put in last week, and I figured you exaggerated *at least* an hour, every day. We probably worked more like *fifty*-six hours than sixty-six."

Gene didn't respond. He sat at the table and looked at the plastic tablecloth. What he was remembering was how he had felt when he'd seen his own senior companions' reports. The hours always seemed a little inflated. Still, he had worked hard back then, and he was still working hard. "Look," he finally said, "I think most reports probably are a little—I don't know—*padded*, I guess. But that's the way everyone turns in hours. It's not a *lie*."

"It's not, huh? Very interesting. I guess a lot of little lies don't add up to a big one—not in your book."

Gene didn't say anything. He tried not to show any response. He had the feeling that the hours didn't mean much to Elder Russon. It was just his way of fighting back.

"But then, I hear you have big plans," Elder Russon said. "I guess you've got to look good."

"Plans? What are you talking about?"

"The mission secretary told me about you. He said, 'Thomas is a good guy. But he's bucking for zone leader or assistant to the president. He's a real politician.'"

"Elder Petersen said that?"

"Yup."

"He doesn't know me. I've never even worked in the same city with him. I've only met him a couple of times."

"I guess that's the word that's gotten around—from people who do know you."

"That's a bunch of *Quatsch!*" Gene said, and now his own voice was getting louder.

Russon shrugged, as if to say, "That's just what I've heard," but he looked satisfied, obviously pleased that he had gotten to Gene.

Gene looked away, trying to calm himself. The worst was that he felt a little "found out."

He had always believed that most missionaries thought highly of him, knew him to be a hard worker, but he also knew that he never saw the assistants to the president driving the mission Opel—looking so important—without imagining himself in the same position. On his first day in Germany he had realized who the big guns were. Within months elders had begun telling him he was going to get the job someday. What he knew, however, was that he shouldn't strive for such things. In high school he had wanted to be student-body president, and he had run for the office and won, but this was different. The measure of a missionary was his humility.

When Gene didn't say anything more, Elder Russon finally said, with some of the edge gone from his voice, "Look, it's no big deal. I'm the one who's messed up. Not you."

"What do you mean?"

Elder Russon leaned back in his chair and looked toward the windows. "I shouldn't be here. I never did want to serve a mission. I just gave in to the pressure. I'm probably just looking for things to be mad about. You're no worse than the rest of these guys."

"And what's that supposed to mean?"

Russon pushed his chair back and stood up. He walked to his bed, rolled the feather tick to one side, then stretched out. He was as long as the bed. He rested the heels of his big brown wing tips on the wooden frame, and then he put his hands behind his head and spoke with his eyes directed toward the ceiling. "All the elders are phonies, if you ask me. They're just a bunch of college guys playing a game. The sisters are the only ones who seem like the real thing."

"I don't think the elders are phony. They're just young guys trying to grow up really fast. It's not easy."

"Maybe so. But I don't like them. There's really no way I ought to be here. In fact, just so you know—I might not stay." He took his glasses off, then looked over and set them on the nightstand by his bed.

Gene knew this was a touchy moment; he couldn't say the wrong thing. "Elder, the first few weeks I was here, the only thing I could think about was how much I wanted to turn around and go home. I think a lot of guys feel that way at first."

"I'm sure that's true. But for most guys, it's just a matter of making the adjustment, getting used to everything. In my case, I really don't fit. And I don't see how I ever will."

"Don't make up your mind now. Wait six months. I can almost guarantee that you won't leave if you stay that long."

Elder Russon was still staring at the ceiling. He didn't say anything.

Gene waited a time and then he said, "Well, anyway, let's eat. Then we need to get back to work."

"And get our hours in. Everything's about *hours*. I'd like to know what that has to do with teaching the gospel."

"Elder Bentz used to tell me that if you work as hard as you can, the Lord will reward you for it. That's what today was all about—baptizing Johann. I think you'll feel the same way, once you've been here a while."

"Maybe if everyone told the truth on their reports, the Lord would reward them even more." He laughed, but there was more than irony in his voice. Gene heard the sadness, and he wasn't sure how to respond. So he got out some bread and cheese and marmalade, and the two ate. Then they went out for Saturday evening tracting—something Gene still didn't like. Russon was silent the whole time. He did his door approaches, but he sounded uninterested, stiff, and the people seemed to sense his distance. Gene found himself taking over the conversations quickly, and the elders were lucky enough to get into one apartment, even luckier that the middle-aged couple enjoyed talking with them. They had been in America, had thought of coming to Utah some time to see the national parks and then go on down to the Grand Canyon. They wanted to know all about those things, and Gene talked to them at some length. But when he tried to make an appointment to come back and talk more about the gospel, they were quick to say no. Still, if the elders had stayed on the doors, they would have had to stop sooner. This was time they could count, and it added the better part of an hour to their report. Gene was not exactly comfortable with that notion tonight—after listening to Russon—but he was still glad to get the extra time.

Later, as the elders rode home, Elder Russon remained silent. He was staring out the window at the rows of apartment buildings along the street, his head jiggling with the vibrations of the streetcar. Gene finally said, "They were nice people. Too bad they didn't want to know more about the Church."

Russon glanced his way and muttered, "Maybe you can go into business as a travel agent."

Gene didn't know exactly what Russon was thinking, but it was obvious that he considered the time a waste. Gene rehearsed his own little answer to that: he had broken down some barriers, made friends. Maybe the couple wasn't interested in the Church, but at least they had a better impression of Mormons now. Part of missionary work was public relations, just softening the way people around the world thought of the Church. What was wrong with that?

And yet, Gene knew something else. He had chatted longer than he might have, normally, mainly because he wanted that extra time. Maybe that was wrong. He wasn't sure. He just didn't like the idea of working with someone who was going to force him to think about that every time they entered someone's apartment.

Gene was a sound sleeper. Not much woke him once he was out. Elder Russon probably would have made it out the door had he not bumped a chair with his suitcase. The chair scraped across the floor, and Gene was suddenly sitting straight up, confused about what was happening. He saw the shadow, near the door, and even in the dark he knew that Elder Russon had his clothes on. "What's going on?" he said.

"Nothing. I'll see you."

The door was coming open, and Gene responded instantly. He threw back his feather tick, jumped up, and grabbed for Russon. He caught a handful of suit coat, then an arm, and he pulled. Russon spun, fought to yank his arm away, but he still had the suitcase in one hand. Gene drove forward suddenly, clamped both arms around Russon, and jerked him away from the door. But the suitcase clattered across the floor, and the elders stumbled in the dark and fell. They thudded onto their shoulders.

Russon was still twisting, trying to roll away. "You can't make me stay," he said. "I can leave if I want to."

"No. No, you can't. Not like this."

Gene hardly knew what he meant, but he wasn't letting go. He rolled onto Russon, knocked him onto his back, and fought to hold his arms down. But Russon thrust a palm against Gene's chin and pushed him up. Gene grabbed Russon's wrist and tried to force his arm back to the floor, but Russon pulled loose and swung at Gene. The fist struck hard, hit Gene's eye, but he didn't roll off. He was grabbing for the hand again, even as it struck a second time, hitting the same eye. And then Gene got hold of Russon's forearm. He pushed it down and held it against the floor. He had the guy pinned, but their faces were almost touching, their breaths coming hard.

"I'm going," Russon said.

"No." Gene kept holding on, breathing into Russon's face. He felt the pain finally, felt a thickness in his eyelid. And then he felt Russon's muscles relax, felt him give up. Gene waited, wondering what to do next. Finally, he hopped up, reached quickly for the light, and prepared for another move. But when the light came on, Russon was still on his back. He was staring blankly at the ceiling, the way he had that afternoon.

"I'll let you keep track of our hours," Gene said.

Russon's eyes finally focused on Gene. "What?"

"You can keep the report and put down any number of hours you want."

"Why?"

"I don't like it either. I don't feel good about the reports." Gene was still trying to get his breath. He was also staying by the door. He wasn't sure this was over.

"That's not the problem."

"It's one of the problems. What else?" Gene straightened out his pajamas, which were twisted around his body, pulling at his neck.

"I shouldn't be here. I never should have come."

"Do you believe in God?"

"Yes."

"What about the Church?"

"Yes."

"Then you should be here. I'm not sure I'm doing this right. Stay with me. Let's see what we can do together."

Russon didn't answer.

"Stay two more weeks, and then we'll talk it over again."

Elder Russon lay still for a long time. Gene was leaning by then, his back against the door. He touched his eye, felt the swelling. "Okay," Russon finally said.

"Get up and put your pajamas on. Go to bed."

Elder Russon sat up. "I can just leave again, as soon as you go to sleep. I would have made it last time if I hadn't hit that chair."

"I'll sleep in front of the door."

Russon shook his head, but he smiled. "You don't have to. I told you I'd stay two weeks, and I don't lie."

"Are you going to keep the report?"

"Yes."

"Okay. And you call it as you see it."

"I'll have to. You won't be able to see out of that eye."

Russon seemed to think that was funny, but Gene didn't see the humor. By morning, it might be swollen shut.

"What are you going to tell people?" Elder Russon asked.

"I ran into a door."

"Another lie?"

"It's almost true," Gene said, and for the first time, he smiled too. "Two weeks and then we talk again."

"Two weeks, and no promises after that."

"Okay."

# Chapter 2

Kathy Thomas was on a date with a boy named Marshall Childs. Her Grandma Bea had been trying to line her up for weeks, but Kathy had kept delaying. Now it was July. She would be leaving for college in less than two months, and she found herself wishing that she hadn't waited so long to go out with this guy. He had moved into Grandma's ward early that summer. He was six-three or so, which gave Kathy plenty of room to stand tall, and more than that, he was nice to look at. He had dark hair, sun-bleached in shades of brown, and he wore it longer than most guys she knew, looser. He had brown eyes that were shadowy, tranquil. What she liked most, however, was an ease she felt with him. He wasn't exactly quiet, but he didn't feel the need to be thinking up things to say every minute.

On top of everything else, he had taken her to the Paprika Café, on Twenty-First South. On her few previous dates she had gone to a movie or a school dance with other couples. This was a new thing to be sitting, like real adults, in an elegant dining room with nice linen on the tables, and the walls all hung with oil paintings, tastefully lighted. Kathy had ordered lamb with a curry sauce that was a little spicier than she liked, but everything was so classy that she didn't mind. The food had taken a while to arrive, and the two had chatted about their high school experiences, since he too had graduated in June, and about Marshall's adjustment to Salt Lake since he had moved from Phoenix. Then, while they were eating, he asked her why she wanted to go to Smith College. That had set them off on a chain of connected ideas. Kathy had told him about her desire to leave Utah for a time, to experience something new, and then about her time in Mississippi during Freedom Summer and her involvement in the march to Selma, Alabama. Marshall had listened and asked lots of questions but had never given much idea how he felt about the issues that concerned Kathy so much.

Kathy didn't finish all her lamb, which embarrassed her, since she knew how expensive it was, but Marshall said, "I can't let you leave here without eating the cheesecake."

"Oh, no, I couldn't. I'm really full."

"I'll order some for me, then. But you have to try it."

"Do you come here all the time?" Kathy asked.

"No. But my dad really likes the place. He brings my mom here. And once he brought the whole family." Marshall had already told Kathy that he was the oldest of seven children.

"That must have cost a fortune."

"I'm sure it did." Marshall was looking at the waiter, who was walking toward the table. Marshall ordered the cheesecake and then looked back at Kathy. "My dad always has enough money for the things he really loves—and he loves food. He's got this thing about teaching his kids to eat at nice restaurants so they'll know how to do that kind of thing when they get out in the world. But I have two little brothers who are five and three, and they made the people in this place *very* nervous. Scotty—the one who's five—dropped one of these goblets and broke it."

"Did your dad get upset with him?"

"No. Not really. He's pretty easy-going about things like that."

Kathy wasn't sure how to take all that. She couldn't quite picture the kind of family Marshall was talking about. "My dad doesn't like places this formal," she said, "even though my mom loves to eat out. He would look at these prices and say something like, 'I could buy a week's groceries for one of these meals.'"

"That's how people get rich. They don't throw their money around.

My dad's made good money in his life, off and on, but he never saves any. He likes to spend it too much."

Marshall seemed to know that Kathy's family was well off. She had actually hoped that he didn't. "What does your father do, exactly?" she asked.

"He's in on several things. But we moved up here so he could open a photo-finishing store. He's got one in Mesa, and another one in Phoenix. He's talking about opening up a lot of them, all over the place. But if I know him, he'll lose interest after a while and try something else."

"Does that bother you?"

Marshall had been leaning forward, his elbows on the table, but now his eyes came up, and he smiled. Kathy saw the ease again, and his white teeth. "No," he said. "I don't blame him. He does all right, even if we have some lean years every now and then. And he has a lot of fun. I can feel already that I'm sort of the same. I don't want to do one thing all my life."

"Do you know what you want to major in?"

"Yeah. I *want* to major in everything. I keep reading the University of Utah's catalog, and every class looks interesting to me."

"I know how you feel. I'm the same way. But I think I'm going to major in political science. And then I want to go to law school."

Marshall leaned back now, looked carefully at Kathy, as though trying to read who she was. She found herself holding her breath—because of the way his eyes were taking her in. "What are you trying to get out of life?" he asked.

"I'm not trying to *get* anything. I want to *give* something."

"Give what?"

That seemed an easy enough question, and yet she wasn't sure how to answer. "I want to make things better for the disadvantaged. I just feel that way too many people are suffering."

"So what do you want to do? Go to Africa—like Albert Schweitzer?"

Kathy had thought of that. But she wasn't sure she could live that way. "I don't know. Right now I'm more concerned about the way Negroes are treated in *this* country."

"Let me ask you something about that. If you hadn't gone to Selma, would it have mattered? Did it make any difference for you to be there?"

It was her grandpa's question—and maybe her own question to herself—but it didn't sound challenging. Marshall really seemed to be interested.

The waiter had arrived with the cheesecake. Marshall tasted it and then pushed the plate across the table. "I want to feed the starving masses," he said, "and I'm starting with you."

"Hey, I may be skinny, but I'm not dying of hunger."

"You're beautiful. You're built like all these new models."

Kathy was left without words, her breath gone again. It had never occurred to her that being so tall and thin was a good thing, and no one had *ever* called her beautiful. Still, she was almost certain that he meant it. "I'm not . . ." But she couldn't finish the sentence.

"You have those long lines that photograph so well. That's why models are so tall—because they make clothes look so great."

"But models know how to walk, and how to—"

"That was the first thing I noticed about you—how nice it is to watch you move."

Who was this guy? Kathy had never known a boy who could say things like that—certainly not without being embarrassed. But he was speaking as though it were just conversation, not flattery. "We'd better change the subject," she said.

"That's one powerful blush you have. I've seen fire engines that weren't that red."

"Listen, Marshall, you're way too smooth for me. This is maybe the fifth or sixth date of my whole life, and the guys I've gone out with usually have Clearasil spotted on their faces."

Marshall laughed. "That's all right. You're way ahead of me."

"What do you mean?"

"This is my third date. In high school I went to the junior prom and the senior dinner-dance, and that's all."

"You never had a girlfriend?"

"I had *dozens* of friends who were girls. But never a girlfriend. In my ward I was the guy the girls came to when they needed a shoulder to cry on."

"Okay. I'll go you one better. I've never kissed a boy. Not one."

He took a long look at her again, smiling all the while, and then he said, "You're turning red again."

"I can't help it. I shouldn't have said that."

"You're right. You shouldn't have, because I can't match you. It turns out, I'm *experienced* compared to you."

"So how many girls have you kissed?"

"Technically . . . none." He laughed, and for the first time he sounded really young, the pitch of his laugh higher than his deep voice. "But when I went to the senior dinner-dance, I walked my date up to the porch, and without any warning she grabbed hold of me and planted a big one right on my lips. I felt like I'd been *attacked*. She stole my innocence—and didn't even ask."

"It must have been awful." Kathy was smiling.

"Well . . . actually . . . it wasn't all that bad, you know. But she was a girl in my seminary class, and our mothers had fixed us up. She wasn't exactly someone I had picked out."

"And now it's happening again. You move into a new ward and some lady lines you up with her granddaughter."

He laughed. "Yup. It's the same thing all over. So far. I just hope you can keep your hands off me when I walk you to the door."

"I'll try." It was definitely time to let the subject drop. Marshall reached to take another bite of cheesecake, and then he pushed the plate even closer to her. She finally tried it. She had only eaten cheesecake once before, and it had not been nearly so creamy. She liked this. She used her fork to take a little more. Music was playing softly: stringed instruments, classical. She glanced around the room again, realizing how much she loved this elegance, but almost as a habit of mind, she reprimanded herself. There were so many families in the world who had never *glimpsed* such comfort, such beauty. They had never tasted rich foods, perhaps never even known the feel of a full stomach. There was something wrong about this much self-indulgence.

After Marshall had paid the check and left a three-dollar tip—which was quite a bit more than ten percent, the amount her dad always left—the two walked to the car. It was an old Ford station wagon, apparently a family car that had lost more than a few battles with the seven kids. Its only charm was that Marshall never thought to apologize for it even though he knew that Kathy's father operated a car dealership.

Kathy wasn't sure where she was supposed to locate herself on the wide front seat. She didn't want to "hug the door," as guys liked to say, but she wasn't about to slide up next to him, either. So she split the difference and then wondered what sort of message that was sending.

"So what about Selma? You never did answer me. Do you think you made a difference somehow by going there?"

The question again. "I do think it made a difference. There were thousands of us there. Any single person could have decided to stay home, and I guess it wouldn't have mattered much, but all of us together added up to something really important. It was a way of saying to the Negro people of Alabama, 'Not all whites are against you. Some of us will stand with you.'"

"And what did the white people of Alabama think about that?"

"Some of them marched with us. Not everyone in the South is against civil rights. I talked to a young man down there—a Negro—who told me he had lived in Chicago, and he thinks the prejudice in the North is worse in some ways, just not quite so open. But in Selma, we all came together. We weren't just trying to change things in Alabama. We were concerned people from all over the country, standing together for what's right."

Marshall nodded as if that made sense to him, but she couldn't read what he was feeling. Maybe he was as prejudiced as most white kids she knew—although few would admit it.

"I just think there are things that are basically wrong in our world," Kathy said. "A lot of people admit that, but then they wait for the problems to work themselves out. Only a few step forward and take a stand. I want to be with those people."

"What are you concerned about besides the rights of Negroes?"

"I don't like the way some people have to work so hard all their lives and still can't afford a decent house or an education for their kids. Then other people inherit wealth that they didn't earn themselves, and they're always well off, without having to do a thing."

"Aren't you one of those people?"

"Sort of. We're not really rich, I wouldn't say, but compared to a lot of people in the world, I live in splendor. So do you. But that's why I want to help change things, and not just live off my family's money." He was driving west, not toward her home, and she wasn't sure where he was going. Maybe just driving. "Don't you care about things like that?" she asked.

Marshall rolled down the window and stuck his arm out to signal for a left turn, but then he had to stop when the light turned red. "The signal lights on this car don't work," he said.

Kathy waited.

When the light changed, he made the turn and headed south on State Street, but he didn't answer the question. Instead, he asked, "Do these people want your help?"

"Who?"

"Negroes. Poor people."

It was a nasty little question, exactly the kind her grandpa would ask, and she responded with some anger. "That's like asking the good Samaritan if he's bothering some poor guy who's been beaten up and left for dead. When you see a need, you try to help—at least you do if you're a decent person. And you know what, the Negroes in Greenwood, Mississippi, where I went, they *loved* us. They treated us like royalty."

"Royalty?"

Now her temper fired. "We didn't *act* like royalty. I'm not saying that. And we didn't go there just to make ourselves feel good. But I know what you're trying to say—that we were sticking our noses in where we had no business. And that isn't true. We worked with the local people, and they appreciated it."

He looked toward her, rather longer than he should have while driving. "I didn't mean that," he said. "I'm just trying to understand. I've never stuck my neck out for someone I don't know—and I admire you for it. I'm trying to think whether it would be something I could do."

"Oh." She had done what she always did—popped off before she had listened. "I'm sorry. But everyone tells me I shouldn't have gone down there, and I guess I get defensive about it."

He nodded, seeming to accept her explanation. She liked him for that. "One thing has changed lately," she said, "and I guess I'm sensitive about it. Negro leaders—or at least some of them—are saying that they don't want help from white people. It seems like a slap in the face, in a way, being told by the organization we tried to support that we're not wanted anymore."

"But it's probably part of what they have to do," Marshall said. "I hated it when Malcolm X used to talk about his hatred of whites. I want to believe that Martin Luther King is right—that we can all come together—but Negroes probably do have to stop feeling dependent on whites."

"I'm sure that's right," Kathy said, but she was astounded. She hadn't expected Marshall to have an opinion. Maybe she should be asking *him* more questions.

Marshall continued driving south for a time before he said, "I'm going to take you to my favorite place."

"How could you have a favorite place? You just moved here."

"I found it right off. I doubt you've ever seen it."

"Where is it?"

"You'll see." He turned east at the next corner, and then he said, "Okay, here's what I want to do. I want to hear your life story. Start with how much you weighed on the day you were born, how many inches long you were, who the doctor was, and then work on from there. Don't rush. If we don't get finished tonight we'll get together again—as often as necessary."

"Are you serious?"

"Completely."

"You're playing games with my mind, Marshall. You're a very strange guy."

"No, I'm not. I just want to know every single thing about you. Nothing wrong with that."

It occurred to her that that was probably the loveliest thing anyone had ever said to her—although she was too flustered to think much about it. She felt the fondness in his voice, as though he had taken her hand, and his curiosity was like a caress. She laughed, feeling incredibly self-conscious, but she tried to comply. "I don't know how long I was when I was born. Probably about four feet. And I'm sure I didn't weigh much."

He didn't laugh. He asked, in a voice that brushed against her, "Just tell me what you were like when you were a little girl."

"I don't know. I was like most kids. I liked dolls and stuff, imagining, playing house."

"What about baseball?"

"No. I was always terrible at sports. But I didn't mind getting dirty. I remember that. I dug a huge hole in a vacant lot down the street—with three boys—and then we boarded up the sides and put a sheet of plywood on top. We had a little stairway and everything. It was supposed to be a clubhouse, but once we got it finished, there was nothing to do—just sit down there in the dirt."

"In Arizona we would have died of heatstroke if we had done something like that. But we still spent our summer days outside, even when it was 115 in the shade. I could play baseball all day long. I did, too."

"Were you good?"

"Not really. Not the way I wanted to be. I was going to be the next Mickey Mantle or Willie Mays, but I sort of hit my peak in high school. I could see by the time I was a junior that I had no chance to make it as a pro. I probably could have played for some junior college this year, but Utah and BYU weren't interested." He pointed at her, abruptly. "Hey, don't do that. You're getting us off the subject. We have to get back to your childhood."

"But if I'm going to tell you, you have to tell me, too."

"I know. That's the deal. Didn't I mention that?"

"No, you didn't."

"Yeah. That's how it works. But right now, we're doing childhood, and you just got me talking about high school."

Kathy realized they were heading up Little Cottonwood Canyon. She wondered where his favorite spot could be. But he didn't say. He continued to ask questions, and they compared their childhood days, their school experiences. Kathy remembered things she hadn't talked about in years. She told him about the time she had stepped on a nail and had to have a tetanus shot, the time she had caught nightcrawlers with her cousin Gene and wouldn't admit that she was scared of them, and the time as a five-year-old when she had gone to a birthday party in a pretty dress but had forgotten to put on her underwear. He told her about catching snakes and building a tree house, but he also described a touching little memory: the teacher he had fallen in love with when he was in fourth grade. The teacher had been young and pretty, and he had longed to let her know how he felt about her. So he had given her a valentine that said, "I love you bunches" and had bunches of flowers on it. She had hugged him and laughed and said, "I love you bunches too, Marshall," but she hadn't meant it, not the way he had. He said it had been all he could do not to cry.

Something was happening to Kathy—as though some string inside her chest had been plucked and was sending vibrations through her.

They reached the top of the canyon, the Alta ski resort, and he pulled his car into the big, empty parking lot. "What are we doing here?" she asked.

"Aren't you a skier?"

"Actually, I do ski some—very badly. But not usually in July."

"Oh. I'm from Arizona. I don't know how these things work. I thought we might do a little moonlight skiing. Maybe I messed up."

"You really are strange, Marshall."

"I deny that. Absolutely. Let's go out on the slope and see if anyone's skiing."

He got out of the car, then came around to open her door. She wasn't sure whether she should wait, but her mother had always told her that she was supposed to do that. When he opened the door, she immediately felt how cool the air was. "It's nice up here," she said.

"Ah, you're figuring this whole thing out."

"We just came up here because the air is cool?"

"That's half the reason. I'll show you the other half in just a minute. Come with me."

She was intrigued. They walked across the parking lot, their feet crunching on the gravel. Kathy could feel the breeze, hear it in the trees, and she could smell pine. She liked the fact that this wasn't a new place at all, but Marshall was making it seem so.

He led her past a chairlift and then on up the lower part of a ski slope. They hiked in silence until he stopped, maybe a couple of hundred yards up the hill. He let her breathe for a minute, and then he said, "Okay. Look up."

Kathy had glanced at the stars already, but in her curiosity about where he was taking her hadn't thought much about what was there. Now she saw the spread of stars, so thick in places that they were smudges on the sky.

"Wow," she said, her voice mostly breath.

"That's the other half. Sit down. Then lie back in the grass and look at it all."

He sat down, waiting for her, and then they both lay back.

"You're not about to make some fast moves on me, are you?"

"I just did."

He hadn't so much as touched her, but she knew what he meant. That string in her chest was twanging again. It was out of self-defense, just to say something, that she asked him, "So tell me, why do you like the stars?"

Marshall took his time before he said, "I used to watch the stars out in the desert when I was a kid. I got books about them and everything. I know a lot of the constellations. But most people say that the galaxy makes them feel small, and I don't feel that way. What I always think is that God really enjoyed himself when he made the universe. I can just see him saying, '*Look* what I did. Just wait until I put people down there. They're going to love this.'"

"Are you going on a mission when you turn nineteen?"

"Yup."

"Do you have a testimony?"

"Yup."

"Do you like to go to church?"

He laughed. "I'd rather look at stars," he said. But then he added,

"I like it sometimes. I had a friend down in Phoenix. We got interested in a lot of religious questions, and we had a teacher in priests quorum who had already thought about the same stuff. We used to go to his class and just fire away. He didn't have all the answers, but he had interesting ideas, and we loved kicking things around with him. That's when I first started thinking what a cool mind God has. Have you ever gone to an aquarium?"

"Yeah. In California."

"Just think about all the kinds of wild-looking fish God thought up. He's got to be the most creative artist who ever existed. And it's the same with insects and reptiles and plants—everything. He got started making things and just couldn't stop himself."

"I've thought about that. Exactly the same idea."

"Have you read *Silent Spring?*"

"Of *course*. Rachel Carson is one of my heroes."

"I thought you'd say that."

"Have you read it?"

"Well . . . yeah. A lot of it. If I ever got involved in any causes, I think I'd try to do something to protect our planet. Humans are ruining it. We've got to stop it before it's too late."

This was too good to be true. Kathy was sure she had floated off the ground. She tried to say something intelligent, not give a hint of what she was feeling. "At least Johnson is trying to do something about the junk all the cars are putting out—and about water pollution."

"I know. But we've got to change more than laws. People have to change how they feel."

"We can't wait for that. Factories are dumping chemicals in our lakes and rivers, and farmers use DDT without even caring what it's doing to the groundwater. Sometimes people don't wake up until you knock them over the head."

Marshall didn't respond, and that scared Kathy. Maybe she was sounding too harsh, too aggressive again. Maybe, if they talked long enough, they would clash—the way she seemed to do with *everyone*, sooner or later.

But after a time Marshall said, "Kathy, I like you."

"Really?"

"You're supposed to say, 'I like you too, Marshall.'"

"I like you too, Marshall," she said, with exaggerated fervor. "More than you can *ever* imagine."

"Ah, but you're wrong about that. I have an excellent imagination. I can picture you liking me *very* much."

It was a delicate moment, and one that Kathy didn't dare play with. She was quiet for once, and so was he, and they watched the stars.

After a time they went back to their childhood memories and even forged on into their teen years. They found out that they both liked jazz, that they had both sung in their high school choirs, and that they both played the piano. In fact, Marshall apparently played much better than Kathy. He had played with a jazz combo in Arizona and wanted to find a group in Salt Lake. He said he wasn't actually very good, but Kathy doubted that.

They talked about the future, too, and Kathy told him that she had read that Johnson was planning to build the troop numbers in Vietnam to 125,000. She wondered whether Marshall might have to get involved. He expressed no opinion about Vietnam, and she tried to worry about that, but she couldn't concentrate on her concerns with all those vibrations going on.

When they finally walked back to the car, way too much time had passed. It was very late, and that meant Kathy would have to deal with her parents when she got home. At the moment, however, what was filling her head was the wish that he would take her hand as they walked.

But he never did.

No wonder that girl in Arizona had made the first move.

# Chapter 3

It was summer holiday for Hans Stoltz. In the fall he would begin his final year of *Oberschule*. He was fairly confident that he would be allowed to enter a university after he graduated. He had finished the school year ranked number one in his class, and he had certainly gained the confidence of his teachers and his director. He didn't try to hide the fact that he was religious, but he made no special point of it, either. The great advantage of being such a good student was that it earned him respect even among those who considered religion stupid. Still, he had no close friends at school, and there was no one exactly his age at Church. Life was lonely. Since he had begun to go to church again, he had written his friend Greta almost every week, and he heard from her just as often. What he wished was that he could be closer to her, maybe see her once in a while. For the present, he wished that her letters would reveal some sign of affection, something more than friendship, but she seemed careful to avoid that.

All the same, Hans was much happier than his friend Berndt. Berndt had not been admitted to a university. He worked at a factory in town, doing accounting work. It was better than working on an assembly line, perhaps, but the pay was only slightly better, and the work was tedious. On Sundays he would complain to Hans, tell him how meaningless his life was, and how much he still longed to get out of East Germany.

One Sunday early in August, however, Berndt seemed changed. Hans could see signs of life in him, even if he appeared nervous more than happy. He walked outside with Hans, who pulled him away from the others, down the street to a place where linden trees hung over the walk.

Berndt stepped off the walk and faced Hans. "I know how to escape. I'm in contact with some people who know what they're doing. Do you want to go with me?"

Hans took a moment to think, but he knew he couldn't do it. "I don't dare take the chance," he told Berndt. "If we got caught, you know they would put us in prison. We're not children now."

"We're in prison already, Hans."

"That's what we said last time. But if we make the best of things, life doesn't have to be so bad here."

"That's what you say—because you think you're going to the university next year. What if they deny your application at the last minute, the way they did mine—then will you want to stay?"

Hans had certainly thought about that. But he was a better student than Berndt, and he had been so young when the two had tried to escape. The *Stasi* had never had clear proof that the two had tried to leave, but surely the agents who had looked into the case had no doubt. Still, they had probably put most of the blame on Berndt, who was older. "I don't know," Hans said. "Maybe things will gradually get better in this country."

"I don't believe that. I can see my life in front of me. It stops at a wall." His eyes seemed flat, unseeing, as if he were standing before the wall he was picturing.

Hans, of course, knew the feeling. But if he *could* graduate from a university in engineering, his life looked quite promising—especially if Greta were part of it. Hans's father, Peter, always told Hans that he would be needed as a leader in the Church. Hans felt no great longing for that, but he did like the closeness he felt to his parents and sister, and he knew now that he didn't want to separate himself from them.

"Hans, what if you knew it was a sure thing? Would you leave if I could convince you that I've found a way that can't fail?"

Hans knew Berndt—knew how confident he could sound—but he

also knew that Berndt hardly ever thought of anything but escape. It would be like him to overrate the certainness of someone's plan. "No, Berndt," he said. "I'm going to stay."

"That's fine. It's what I knew you would say." He looked down the street, then glanced back toward the church, where some members of the branch were standing, talking. "I need to ask you something else," Berndt said, even more softly. "You can say no again. You should say no, I think, but I need to ask."

"What is it?"

"Could you help us? Those of us who are going, we need one person to help—someone who will stay behind, but someone we can trust."

Hans felt his muscles tighten. He looked away from Berndt.

"I know what I'm asking, Hans. I would be putting you in danger, and you would have nothing to gain. Just say no, right now, and I won't ever mention this to you again."

Hans couldn't do that. He knew what this meant to Berndt. But he was thinking about more than the danger. He was thinking that he could lose everything he had worked for this last year. "I don't know, Berndt. I would have to think about it."

"No. Don't think about it. I understand. It's too much to ask of anyone."

"But what will you do—give up your plan?"

"We could go without help." He stopped, waiting for a couple from the branch to walk on by. "But it would mean the escape route would probably only be used once, and there are others who want to get out the same way."

"Why can't they help—the ones who want to go later?"

"That's the problem. They've been compromised. They were observed in the area and questioned. We think they're being followed. They can't try anything until they're no longer suspected. But if the rest of us wait, the escape route may be discovered. So those of us who are going soon tried to think who could help. I thought of you. But it was wrong of me."

Hans saw how deflated Berndt was. "I suppose, if you're certain it's really safe," he said, "something I can do without getting caught—I could help you."

Berndt considered for a moment. "No. Take some more time. If you do decide to help, I won't bring you in until everything is set up perfectly. If I think it's questionable in any way, I'll never tell you anything about it. If I come to you, I'll have a specific request, and I'll feel confident that it's something you can do safely."

"That sounds fine."

Two weeks passed and Berndt said nothing. Hans worried constantly, changing his mind a dozen times. He knew what his parents would say if they knew he was getting involved, and he knew that no matter how safe Berndt thought the plan was, if anyone investigated after Berndt was out, Hans would be a logical choice as an accomplice. If any guilt were traced to Hans, he would lose all hope for a future. But Berndt knew that and certainly wouldn't gamble with Hans's life.

On the following Sunday, Berndt whispered to Hans, "I need to talk to you right away. I'm getting ready to go, very soon."

Hans felt the words in his stomach, like a wave of nausea, but he said, "It's good. Why don't we walk a little, and you can tell me."

Hans often walked home alone, and he thought it might be good if he and Berndt walked away from the church now before his mother saw that the two were together. She and Inga hadn't come out of the chapel yet. They were probably waiting for Papa.

So the boys walked, and Berndt waited until they had reached and turned a corner before he asked, "Are you still thinking you might help us?"

"Probably. It depends a little on what you tell me."

"Let me tell you the plan, then, and explain what you would have to do. Don't make up your mind until I explain the whole thing. But remember, once you know, you're already in danger. So tell me if I should stop now."

"Go ahead. Tell me."

They were walking through a residential area with lots of apartment buildings. Berndt glanced up to see that windows were open on some of the lower floors. He whispered, "You know that people have gotten out by tunneling under the wall in Berlin."

"Yes. I know this."

"It's probably impossible to dig from this side without getting caught. But people I know have friends in West Berlin who have been digging a long and well-engineered tunnel."

"It's university students who do this, I've been told. They get help from engineers."

"I can't say anything about that. But it's a good tunnel, and some of our people helped them break through into a basement in East Berlin, just beyond the 'death strip.' Our group could use the tunnel and get out all right, but we need someone to go into the abandoned building and cover up the entrance so it won't be discovered before the second group leaves. If we don't try to get too many out at one time, perhaps many groups could use it. We could get hundreds out."

"Who will close the entrance next time?"

"I don't know. That won't be your concern. We're only asking you to help once. It's just a matter of putting some stones in place and covering them over with a thin layer of dirt."

"When are you going?"

"Are you going to do it, Hans?"

"Yes." But the word cost Hans more than he was willing to show. What he felt was that he had made the worst decision of his life, that he would pay dearly for it.

"We're going out Wednesday night."

"Do you really feel safe about this?"

"I do. These are smart people on the other side. It isn't the first tunnel they have dug. And the ones going out are just as smart. Every step in the planning has been careful."

"But I would have to take a train from Schwerin to Berlin, then back again, all at night. People will see me. Or if I missed a day of school, that would be the clearest indicator that I had been up to something that day."

"We've thought about all of that. And you're right. But we plan to drive a car. You could sneak out late, drive with us to Berlin, then use the same car to come back in the night, park it where it was, and go home. You'll miss some sleep, but no one will know you've been gone." He hesitated. "And yet, I know that's taking a chance. Someone, of course, could see you."

"I have no license to drive a car. I hardly know how."

"You know enough. There's no reason anyone would stop you, not unless you were to drive too fast."

"Berndt, it's what? Two hundred kilometers to Berlin?"

"No. Less than that. It's a two-hour drive, each way, and you'll be in Berlin less than an hour. You can do it in a night, no problem. You could tell your parents you're going to bed early, and then slip out. It's what I'm doing."

"The sun goes down late this time of year, and comes up early."

"There's still time."

"But—"

"I'm sorry. I don't mean to persuade you. I shouldn't do that."

Hans shut his eyes, tried to think. He needed to get out of this. "There's no one else who can do this—maybe someone in Berlin?"

"We haven't asked anyone else. It's possible we could still find someone, but . . . it won't be easy. It's you we trust."

Hans nodded. "Wednesday night, then. What time?"

The days that followed were the most frightening of Hans's life. He had taken big chances before in hopes of leaving the country, but he had always been able to imagine the joy of success. This time he had nothing to gain. But he wouldn't back out. Not now. And on Wednesday night, at almost two in the morning, he found himself standing in the doorway of an old warehouse across the street and a little north of where Berndt and his partners would enter the apartment house they would attempt to escape through. Hans was standing with Berndt and another man, whose name he hadn't been told. Berndt was watching the street, checking for any sign of patrolling police. Four of their group had already entered the apartment house, and now Berndt reported, "Two more just went in. We're next."

They were also the last two. Hans wanted them to hurry so he could do his part and then leave. But the plan was to wait two minutes and observe before making the next move.

The two minutes seemed ten times that long, but finally Berndt turned and wrapped his arm around Hans's shoulder. "It's time," he said. "Thanks for everything. Good luck. Wait another two minutes after we go in." He pounded Hans's back a couple of times and then stepped back.

"Good luck," Hans tried to say, but he had no voice.

The other man gave Hans's shoulder a pat, and then the two stepped from the doorway. Hans watched as they crossed the street and slipped along the front of the buildings, in the shadows. They were almost to the apartment building when Hans heard a voice. "Stop right there," a man shouted, the sound echoing down the street.

Hans flattened himself against the door and held his breath. For a few seconds he heard nothing, and then footsteps were coming, clapping on the paving stones. The same voice, this time breathless and much closer, boomed again. "Don't move. Stay right there."

Hans thought of rushing the guard. Or guards. Were there two? But he didn't move. He was too frightened.

The footsteps passed by him, and then he heard the same voice, speaking now, not shouting. "Where are you two going?"

Hans heard Berndt say, "Home."

"No one lives down here."

"We were taking the short way. We live close by."

"That's nonsense. This is not a short way to anyplace."

The steps had come to a halt, but Hans saw the beam of a flashlight, and then a second voice said, "Papers. Show us your papers."

At the same moment there was a whir of light, a clashing, metallic sound, and then only darkness. Hans knew without thinking that the flashlight had hit the street, and now he could hear scuffling, grunts. Instinctively, he jumped from his hiding place to help, but in that instant an automatic weapon fired, each shot like a cannon blast in the narrow street. Hans heard the screams—two voices—and he caught a glimpse, silhouetted by the muzzle flash, of bodies hurtling back, arms flailing. Hans stood stiff in the stillness that followed, only heard someone suck for air, and then he realized that he was not forty meters away, standing in the street. When he turned and ran, the sound of his own feet were like clapping hands, like firecrackers. He expected to hear the explosions again, expected to feel the bullets strike his back, but he was around a corner in seconds, and the weapons didn't fire. Maybe the border guards hadn't seen him in the dark, but he knew they had heard him. He had to stop making all this noise.

He charged up the street, then ducked into the doorway of an apartment building and tried the door. It was locked. He burst out and ran again and thought he could hear the sound of men running behind him. He ducked into an alley, knew that he could be trapping himself, but he sprinted until he saw something dark looming in front of him. He ducked behind the big objects, a couple of trash barrels, it turned out. He held his breath and waited.

But he heard nothing. Had the men run past the alley? Had they followed him or not? Maybe they had hesitated to leave the men they had shot. He didn't know what to do.

He waited fifteen, maybe twenty seconds, and then he ran again, on down the alley. He stayed up on his toes, trying not to make a sound. He was frantically trying to think how he could get back to the car. As he reached the street he glanced back, saw nothing, then peeked out quickly to see a Russian truck, coming fast. He jumped back, trying to think. He would be caught in the lights if the truck turned into the alley.

He ran hard for the trash barrels again, was only halfway there when he heard the truck rush on by without turning. Still, he kept going, back toward the street where he had first come in. He took a chance. He broke from the alley without checking first and raced across the street. He saw no one, but he didn't look. Another alley across the way reached through the entire block, and he ran all out to get to it. He still felt as though someone were running after him, but he kept going, turned from the alley, and didn't glance back.

But now he was on a major street, and he didn't want to be seen running. He slowed to a walk and tried to seem normal. He suspected that police would be coming from all directions, and they would begin to stop anyone they saw. He also knew that he had to cover about three blocks quickly and then drive away—and now he had to wonder whether cars in the area would be stopped.

Clearly, the sooner he was gone the better his chances were. At the moment any search that might begin was still unorganized. So he took a chance again, and he ran, hard. He watched for lights, for people, and once ducked into a doorway when a car came down the street. But it wasn't a police car, so Hans jumped from the door and ran.

When he reached the car, his lungs were heaving, and for a moment he couldn't find the key that Berndt had given him. It was in his jacket pocket, not his pants, and his relief was tremendous when he found it, got inside, hit the starter, and heard the engine kick in. He had had few chances to drive in his life, so he was thankful that Berndt had asked him to drive to Berlin. But in his haste, now, he was forgetting what he had learned—grinding gears, braking too hard, and losing track of the route Berndt had told him to follow to get out of town and back to the *Autobahn*.

Still, he had the good sense not to drive fast, and he was collected enough to locate a street he knew, one with a bit of traffic moving on it. With every minute that passed he felt a little safer, and finally he was out of Berlin, heading the right direction, back toward Schwerin.

Then it finally hit him. Berndt was dead. Surely, he was dead. He had been shot at close range, probably hit more than once. Certainly he hadn't survived that. Hans wanted to feel the pain, but it wasn't in him yet. He was still too frightened for himself. His troubles were only beginning now, not ended. The border guards may have allowed him to get away for the moment, but the *Stasi* would be looking for the tunnel, and they would be looking for accomplices. They would probably find the tunnel quickly, but they would search for conspirators for as long as it took. Hans couldn't help thinking that if Berndt and the other man were both dead, he had a better chance. If one of them lived, the *Stasi* would have someone to question—and that was something they did with cruel effectiveness.

The miles crawled by, but Hans made it back to Schwerin, and he parked the car where he had been instructed to leave it. He even managed to use his key and get back into his apartment. As he crept to his bedroom he heard his father's voice, asking, "Is that you, Hans?"

Hans merely said, "Yes. I'm getting a drink of water," and then he went to bed.

He didn't sleep, of course, and it was all he could do to behave normally at breakfast. But he made it to school without incident, and then the wait began. It was a couple of days before his parents heard the news that Berndt had been killed in Berlin. But it was all the talk at church on Sunday and the subject of a long talk by the branch president in sacrament meeting. The president was sorry for the loss, compassionate toward the Kerners, but there was also no question about the subtext of his talk: good members learned to be satisfied in the GDR. It was wrong to break the law, to challenge the authority of the government. Good members made the best of things, worked toward peace and harmony.

Hans talked to his parents, to the Kerners, to the other members about all this, always pretending that he knew nothing. The trouble was, the pain and regret were coming home to him by then, and it was all he could do not to show more emotion than seemed warranted. What he knew for certain was that he shouldn't have helped Berndt. He had assisted him to his death. He would know that forever.

On the following Tuesday, when Hans came home from school, two men in dark suits were in front of his apartment, waiting. He was frightened to see them, of course, but also a little relieved. This had to happen sooner or later. At least now he would find out what the *Stasi* knew.

"Are you Hans Stoltz?" one of the men asked.

"Yes, I am."

"We must speak to you. Is no one from your family home?"

"My sister could be there. My mother and father are both at work." He tried to speak in a friendly tone, as though he had no idea what they wanted.

"Let's go to your apartment. I suppose you know who we are."

"I'm sorry. I don't."

"*Staatssicherheitsdienst*," one of the men said. He was an ordinary-looking man of maybe forty, with brown hair and little color in his face. He seemed preoccupied, uninterested, as though he were merely going through the motions. The other man was even more extreme, hardly paying attention. He was tall, hunched, and considerably older. He didn't look at Hans—or at anything else.

In the apartment, Hans asked them both to sit down on the couch, and then he said, "So, what can I do for you?" He sat in his father's chair, across from them.

"Hot weather we're having, isn't it?" the shorter man said.

"Yes. And humid. I hope we have an early autumn."

"You attend the *Oberschule*, do you?"

"Yes, I do."

"That's lucky for you. You have a future. It's not like that for some of us." The man glanced at his partner, who made a little nod, as if to say he thought little of his own job. He still wasn't bothering to engage Hans's eyes.

"I would think that secret service work would be very interesting."

"Now and then. Mostly it's like this. They send us out just to ask a few questions."

"What questions?" Hans sat back, tried to look relaxed.

"They tell us you know this boy—what's his name?" He took his time pulling a notebook from his coat pocket. Hans was careful to wait, not to fill in any blanks for the man. "Berndt Kerner. Do you know him?"

"Yes. I've known him all my life."

"And I guess you heard what happened to him?"

"I heard that he was killed in Berlin. I talked to his parents on Sunday."

"Don't you know any details?"

"Only the rumors I've heard."

"What rumors?"

"Some people are saying that he might have tried to escape the country, but I doubt that's true. It's difficult for me to believe he would do something like that."

"And why do you say that?"

"He seemed happy the last time I talked to him. He didn't give the impression that he had any such plans."

"But our report says he tried to escape once before."

"He was accused of it. So was I. You know that. But all we did was take a day off from school and make a little holiday on the Baltic. People got the wrong idea from that."

"So that's what you say now, is it?" The younger man was showing more life. But Hans had known all along that the man's apparent lack of interest was only a pose.

Hans sat up. He tried to speak with conviction. "It's what I always said. It's the truth."

The man nodded, wrote something in his notebook. "And now you're saying that Kerner said nothing to you, never mentioned a plan to escape?"

"No. But then, even if he was trying to escape, I doubt he would mention it to me. We weren't really close friends. He's older than I am, and out of school. I give all my attention to *Oberschule* these days. I'm ranked number one in my class, you know."

"Yes, we do know." He stared at Hans for a long time before he said, "So that's going to be your story—that you had nothing to do with this?"

"My *story?*"

The man's eyes had changed. The carelessness was gone. "Where were you last week, on Wednesday night?"

Hans pretended to think for a moment. "Right here," he said. "I didn't go anywhere. You can check with my parents about that."

"Can anyone else verify that?"

"That I was here?"

"Yes."

"Only my little sister. I was here, doing homework, and then I went to bed. That was my whole evening." Hans glanced at the second man, tried to judge what he was thinking, but he still seemed to be paying no attention.

"What about the night?"

"What do you mean?"

"Did you get out of bed, travel in the night to Berlin, then back again?"

"I don't think that's possible, is it?"

"Of course it is."

"I wouldn't know. I don't drive."

"Who said anything about driving?"

Hans felt the shock of his own mistake, and he came close to losing his composure, but he took a breath, and then he said, "Is there any other way to get to Berlin at night? No train would get a person there and back. Late trains stop too often."

"So you've thought this all through, I can see. I suppose that means you drove there that night."

The tall man looked over at Hans, seemed to watch for a reaction. Hans was almost sure these men knew nothing, that they were only fishing.

"I told you, I was here. If you wait another hour or so, my mother will be home, and she can tell you."

A long silence followed. Finally the man said, "Don't assume this is over. If you were in Berlin, we *will* find out. You tried to escape our country once; you must know that you will never be trusted again."

"I know I was suspected once. But I've proved myself for many years. Talk to the director of my school, my teachers, my fellow students. I have nothing to answer for, nothing to fear." He looked the man directly in the eyes. "Trust can be lost, but it can also be regained. I have done nothing to break my trust."

"Yes, yes. And good liars are all around us. You very well may be one of them."

Hans wanted to tell him, "This is a government that makes liars of us all. There's no other way to survive." But, of course, he didn't say it. What he wondered, once they were gone, was why they hadn't pushed any harder. He knew that better interrogators could make things much worse for him, and it was that awareness that convinced him that the agent had been right about one thing: this was not the end of the matter.

# Chapter 4

Diane Hammond was sitting in her Uncle Alex's office, in Washington, D.C. The truth was, she was disappointed. She had expected something fancier. The building was plain and the office rather sparse. She had also been introduced to three or four congressmen, and they seemed as ordinary as the building. Now she was chatting with another one—whose name she had already forgotten. He was a sturdy man with stubby teeth and a receding hairline.

"Well, Jerry, you need to know," Uncle Alex said, "we brought Diane back here to see whether we could convert her to a better way of life. She's had a bad upbringing. My sister and her husband are both Democrats."

The congressman laughed. He was about to leave. Uncle Alex had walked with him to the office door and was standing next to him. Aunt Anna was sitting by Diane, the two on old wooden chairs, and Diane's cousin Sharon was in her father's big leather desk chair. At least the dark walnut desk looked new.

"Don't feel bad," the congressman was saying. "Democrats can worm their way into the best of families." He looked at Diane and grinned, but then he added, "Still, if your parents are anything like Senator Moss, from out in your state, they can't be too bad. Frank Moss is a Democrat I have great respect for."

Aunt Anna said, "He *is* a good man. And he's smart. Alex agrees with him at least as often as he does with Wallace Bennett."

Diane had been in Washington a couple of days and was going to stay for two weeks. Sharon had invited her to visit, and Richard and Bobbi had thought an inside view of Washington was too good an opportunity to pass up. Diane had liked the idea too, but now, with summer almost over, she was wondering whether she shouldn't have gotten a little more swimming and water-skiing in before school started. Uncle Alex and Aunt Anna were great people, and she liked her cousins, but Washington in August was not easy to take. The air felt like steam from a teakettle.

Conversations also seemed to turn, way too often, toward politics, and Diane was put on the spot. She had no idea what party she would end up supporting—if any. She had never been able to get herself to read or even to think much on the subject. She was seventeen, so she had almost four years before she would have to vote. She kept telling herself that maybe by then she would have a better idea how she felt about things.

"Back when I was growing up," Alex said, "almost all Utahns were Democrats. We've made some headway since then, but we've got eleven Mormons in Congress, and seven of them are Democrats, so there's still a lot of work to do."

"That's right. Republicans are a little hard to find *anywhere* these days." The congressman was smiling again, but he looked serious when he said, "I'll tell you one thing, Diane. In my home state of Michigan, George Romney's our governor. He's a Mormon, as I'm sure you know. I've never met a finer man. He would make a great president."

"*Republican* president," Uncle Alex added.

"Yes, but he's like me, *and* you—moderate on a lot of domestic issues and conservative on the economy. If someone like that had been running, we might have . . . well, never mind. Poor ol' Barry did his best."

Alex was nodding, and Diane knew what the two were saying. She had heard her parents talk about the way Goldwater had gone to extremes.

"Anyway, have a nice time with us, Diane. Are you going to come over and watch the House at work?"

"I think so."

"We'll bring her over," Alex said. "But there's not much for her to see today, is there?"

"There's nothing coming to the floor. But everyone has something to say about Watts. She can hear some speeches. Or maybe you can take her over to the other chamber and see if you can find Bobby and Teddy Kennedy. They're the guys everyone wants to meet when they come here—even the Republicans."

Diane actually did think she would like to do that, but she didn't say so. She only said, "It was very nice to meet you," as the congressman left, and then, once he was gone, "What did you say his name was?"

Alex laughed. "Gerald Ford. He's the most important Republican in the House, Diane. He's the new minority leader."

Diane didn't dare ask about that. She thought "minority" was a word people used for Negroes. And this man wasn't a Negro.

Sharon stood up. "Do we have to go watch Congress?" she said. "It's *soooo* boring."

Diane found lots of things boring, but she couldn't imagine that Congress would be. And then she found out. Very few congressmen were in attendance. Those who were there were walking around, talking in small groups, paying no attention to the speaker—some man who was droning on and on about the "underprivileged." Diane had expected something passionate, or had thought she might hear a debate, with all of Congress listening carefully, applauding for one side and then the other. But she saw no evidence of that during the fifteen minutes or so she sat in the balcony—with Sharon pleading the whole time, "Can we go now?"

Diane enjoyed church on Sunday even more than she did her excursions into the city. The Smithsonian buildings had been sort of interesting at first, but Anna took too much time reading all the little information placards. Diane had been excited to see the Hope Diamond and a few things like that, but a lot of the stuff was just not that interesting. At church, however—even though the chapel was a few miles away, in

Arlington, and not down the street—she felt at home. The place was stuffed, with three big wards in one building—something she hadn't expected—and most of the people seemed prosperous. Of course, her greatest interest was in the cute boys Joey introduced her to. She had never met so many really sharp guys in her life. They knew how to dress, and their confidence was obvious. A lot of them came from well-off families, and some of their fathers had important jobs in government.

After sacrament meeting that evening, as the sun was going down and the worst of the heat was finally diminishing, Diane sat with Sharon on a screened porch that looked out across the beautifully groomed yard. "Everyone thinks we have a gardener," Sharon said, "but it's about the only thing Mom really loves to do back here. She gets up at five o'clock every morning, while the rest of us are asleep, and she's always out there digging around until it's time to come in and kick Kurt out of bed."

"Doesn't he like to get up?" Diane asked.

"Who does? But he's the worst. Mom thinks we all need to do chores in the summer. She turns into this *German* mother—which she is, of course—bossing us around, telling us we have to get up early and do our work. Kurt stays up really late watching TV and everything, and then he gets in big fights with Mom when she tries to get him up."

A breeze had picked up and was brushing softly across Diane's skin, but she felt sticky, even after taking a second shower when she had first gotten back to the house.

"I'm worried about Kurt," Sharon said. "It seems like he's mad all the time. He's the only Mormon at his junior high, and I think he's ashamed to tell anyone that's what he is. He has a bunch of friends, and they all think he's cool."

"He is a neat kid. I like him."

"I know. And he really is cute. Girls call *him,* if you can believe it. So you'd think he'd be happy. But he wants to do everything those kids do, and my parents won't let him. He'd miss church all the time if he had a choice. On Sunday afternoons his friends are always going to movies or swimming, stuff like that."

"He's really nice to me."

"That's because he's in love with you. You're his *gorgeous*, *older* cousin. I'm sure you've noticed how much his buddies have been coming around this week. That's no accident. They all watch your every move—with their tongues hanging out."

Diane had noticed something of that sort, but then, that was part of her life. There was nothing she disliked more than boys *not* noticing her. At the same time, she sometimes wanted to talk and be natural, and it was hard when she was being stared at all the time.

The door from the kitchen opened, and Joey stepped out. He was eighteen now, and in just a couple of weeks would be heading back to Utah. He planned to go to the University of Utah and live in the family house in Salt Lake. He had a couple of friends who were going to be living with him there. The deal was, they were supposed to look after the house and yard. Sharon had already admitted she was skeptical about that.

With Joey was a boy Diane had seen at church that day: Kent Wade. He was tall, with light hair, almost blond, and strikingly dark eyes. Sharon had told Diane earlier that Kent had only had his braces off for a couple of weeks—just in time to head to Utah himself, where he would be going to BYU. What Diane saw were the results of those braces: straight teeth, wonderfully white, and a generous, wide smile.

"Hi, Diane," Joey said. "So what are you two doing?" Joey always seemed in control, cool, no matter what the situation. He had his hands in his pockets and was standing by the door, grinning. He had changed into chinos and a plaid, short-sleeved shirt. Kent was waiting at his shoulder, wearing a light-blue golf shirt.

"We're just out here talking. The air feels good."

"Diane, you remember Kent don't you? He was at—"

"Of course I remember," Diane said. She stood up and turned toward the boys. Now she was glad she had put on her bermudas and pink button-down. She had tried on three different tops after church, wanting to wear something casual that was still flattering to her shape. She had had a feeling Joey might show up with someone.

"Hey," Kent said. "So what kind of big things are you girls talking about?"

"I was telling Diane about our mom," Sharon said. "How she makes us get up early on summer mornings."

"It's so bad," Joey said. "We're going to start putting something in her milk—some kind of pill that will knock her out until eight o'clock, just once."

Kent was smiling, seeming amused, but at the same time paying no attention to Joey, just watching Diane.

"You guys talk for a minute," Joey said. "I'll be right back."

"Sit down, Kent," Diane said. She and Sharon returned to the little couch where they had been sitting. Kent sat across from them in an old metal lawn chair. "So . . . uh . . . how long are you going to be in Virginia, Diane?" he asked.

"Two weeks, total, but I've been here almost a week already."

He nodded. "Are you going to the White House and all that stuff?"

"We've been there already. I thought we might see Lady Bird, but she didn't bother to come out and say hello."

Diane could tell that Kent was trying to stop smiling—and having little success. "Did I tell you I'm coming to the Y?"

"Yeah. Are you excited about that?"

"I am. My grandparents live in Utah, in Lehi, so I've been there plenty of times. But I've never lived anywhere there are a lot of Mormons around. I think it'll be pretty cool."

"I guess. I kind of like it out here. Sharon tells me that the kids in the Church stick together."

"Kent wants to check out all the good-looking girls at BYU," Sharon said. "Out here, he's only got our ward to choose from."

"Did I say that?" But he was grinning again.

Joey had returned, but as he stepped onto the porch, he said, "Hey, Sharon, come here a minute. I need your help."

Sharon gave Diane a quick glance, as if to say, "Are these guys obvious, or what?" But she got up and followed Joey into the house.

Kent nodded. He didn't seem nervous exactly, but maybe a little self-conscious. "Maybe I'll see you out there sometime," he said.

At moments like this, Diane's instincts took over—and were usually right. She released a slowly expanding smile, and then she said, "I hope so, Kent. You need to find a way to get to Ogden some time. I could take you skiing."

"Hey, that would be so great. I know I could borrow my grandparents' car and make a trip up there—you know, maybe once in a while. My family goes up to Vermont sometimes, and we've skied up there, but I've never skied out west. I've always wanted to do that."

"I was up at Snowbasin almost every Saturday last winter. Or down to Alta or Brighton, by Salt Lake. We could meet there. That wouldn't be so far for you."

"Perfect. Really. Let's plan on it."

"Okay. I'll give you my phone number, and when you get to Provo, you can just call me and we'll set something up."

Kent glanced at the door, maybe to check whether Joey was about to show up again. "What about while you're here, Diane?"

"You mean you have ski slopes here?" This was the right time for her sly smile, the one she sometimes practiced before her bedroom mirror.

Kent was a little undone. She saw the lobes of his ears redden, heard him falter when he said, "Well, you know . . . I have *other* interests."

"What? Bowling? Roller-skating?"

"Right. Stuff like that." He winked, tried to be casual, but the red was spreading to his cheeks.

She loved that she could embarrass him. He had seemed so confident at church. Now he was as flustered as the high school boys in Ogden who came unglued when she toyed with them.

But he made a quick comeback. "I like movies," he said. "Maybe we could go to a show."

"I'd love that, Kent."

"What night?"

"I'm not sure. Let me talk to my aunt and find out what she's got planned this week."

"Great. Maybe I can check with you tomorrow, and we can choose an evening that's open for you."

Diane was actually thrilled at the idea. There was something very sweet about Kent, and Diane also knew, from Joey, that his family had a lot of money. What she didn't like was the quiet that followed. In the kitchen, a radio was playing, and she could hear the Byrds singing "Mr. Tambourine Man." She sang along for a moment, but she didn't say anything. She wanted to see what Kent would come up with.

Kent, however, was looking at the door again. Diane turned, expecting Joey and Sharon, but it was Uncle Alex. "Oh, hi, Kent," he said. "Where's everyone else?"

Diane said, "Aunt Anna is upstairs, I think, and the kids are watching TV. Joey asked Sharon to help him with something, but I'm not sure what."

Uncle Alex, who was still wearing his white shirt and tie, stepped closer and shook hands with Kent. "Aren't you going out to BYU pretty soon?"

"Yeah. In less than a month now."

Uncle Alex had been called to the stake high council, and he often attended other wards, but he still seemed to know everyone in his home ward. Diane was amazed that he could keep track of so many people. "Did you kids watch the news tonight?" he asked.

"No," Kent said.

"Things are still really bad in Watts. The place is burning up. The National Guard is in there now, which should get things under control before long, but I hate to think how many people are going to die."

Diane didn't really understand what was going on. Negroes in Los Angeles had been rioting. She didn't know why.

"There's a lot of looting, from what I've heard," Kent said.

"That always happens in situations like this," Uncle Alex said. "Everything just gets out of control."

"I'm not prejudiced or anything," Kent said. "I have some Negro friends at my school. But it doesn't make a lot of sense to me. Why do people want to burn down their own neighborhood?"

"I guess it depends on the neighborhood."

"But I would think some kind of house is better than nothing at all."

Diane had never gotten up. Alex walked over and sat down next to her, put his arm around her shoulders. But he was still looking at Kent, who also sat down. "I know. And Negroes know it too. In some ways, Watts isn't such a bad place, either. A lot of people have decent little homes there; it's not like a bunch of fallen-down tenements in Detroit or Chicago. But the frustration builds until it boils over. The unemployment rate in Watts is close to thirty percent. The crime rate is sky high, and—"

"Who made it that way?"

Diane felt her uncle's chest expand against her shoulder, but he waited, slowly exhaled, and then said, quietly, "I know what you're saying, Kent. But there's a lot of history behind what's happening in our country right now. There are very few things more destructive than hopelessness, and that's what a lot of Negroes—especially young people—are feeling. That, and anger. I don't know whether the police are as brutal as

Negroes claim they are, but I can't imagine that all the stories we hear are fabrications. Most of us were pretty smug when we thought that race problems were strictly in the South. Now we're finding out how bad things are in the big cities across the country."

"Uncle Alex," Diane said, "you amaze me, how much you know about everything."

"I wish I did *know* something. Anything. I spend my life trying to figure things out."

"Maybe so. But my mom has her mind made up about everything. You seem like you're working out your answers as you go along."

"The difference is, I have to vote on all these issues. I can't just ask what my party is going to do. I have to go home and explain myself—tell people why I voted the way I did."

Alex took his arm from around Diane, and then he leaned forward and put his elbows on his knees. "I had no idea how confusing issues can get. Some congressmen call themselves liberals or conservatives and then feel like they have to vote one way or the other on everything. But lobbyists are after us every day. And they feed us with a constant flow of information. And yet, the more I know about an issue, the harder it is to decide how I'm going to vote. And then, just when I get my mind made up, one of my colleagues in Congress sits down in my office and tells me that if I don't vote a certain way, he won't vote with me when I need him on my side. Or some rich businessman from back in Utah calls and tells me I'd better vote this way or that or he won't contribute to my campaign next time. I told myself I was going to come back to Washington and be my own man. But it's not as easy as it sounds."

"Maybe this sounds dumb," Diane said, "but why can't you just vote for what you think is right?"

Uncle Alex laughed softly, and he said, "That's a very good question, Diane. But when people think they're right, they usually have a hard time believing that any other point of view exists. So my constituents vote me in, and then each one thinks I should always do what he or she would do. Never mind that the opinion is split on every issue."

"But that's why they elect you—so you can look into things and make good decisions."

Alex leaned back so he could look at Diane. "They want me to get things done for them. They want to get money for state projects: dams and roads and federal buildings—all kinds of things. And the only way you get certain things into the budget is by supporting other people for the things they need. To gain any real power in Congress, you need seniority, but to get it, you have to get reelected, and to do that, you have to keep the majority of the people happy. So it's easy to say, 'Vote your conscience,' but it's not always something you can do."

"Are you discouraged already, Uncle Alex?"

He took some time, apparently thinking, before he said, "Yes. Somewhat. And I'm more of a realist than I was a year ago. But I do think it's a system that does work, after all is said and done. We end up with lots of compromise bills, but maybe that's better than letting any one group run off with the power. I just wish that some of our problems could be worked out. Dad always tells me that government shouldn't try to solve all the problems, and I know that's right, but I look at what's happening in our country, and I keep thinking we ought to be able to find a few solutions."

"Maybe colored people have to solve their own problems," Kent said.

Uncle Alex looked at him for several seconds before he said, "If that's true, then so do whites. And I think maybe the biggest problem we have in this country right now is hatred. I can't pass a bill to stop that."

Uncle Alex stood up. "Well, anyway, have a nice evening. Where do you think Joey ran off to?"

"Uh . . . actually . . ." Kent said, "I think he was trying to give me enough time to ask Diane on a date. But he must think I'm pretty slow. I already did that."

Alex laughed. "Thank goodness. I'd hate to think that I messed up your timing."

Kent was blushing again, this time having embarrassed himself, it would seem, but he laughed, and then he stood up. "Not at all," he said. "When I have a job to do, I usually get right after it."

Alex looked down at Diane. "You did all right," he said. "This is the guy I would have fixed you up with."

"Men!" Diane said. "You think you're so in control. Girls always know that you guys are catching on when you do exactly what we want you to." She glanced at Kent and showed him how a wink was supposed to look.

"Be careful, Kent. You may be in over your head," Alex said, and he walked to the door. "I'll see where Joey is hiding and send him back."

But Kent said, "Brother Thomas, I'm sorry about what I said. You know, about Negroes solving their own problems."

"What do you mean? Why would you be sorry about that?"

"I just think you have a good point. Hatred probably is the problem."

"What worries me now is that the hate is starting to come from both sides. I'm afraid Dr. King's message is getting lost in all the anger."

Diane was impressed, as always, by her Uncle Alex, and how deeply he cared about things, but she was also impressed by Kent's willingness to listen. It was the sort of thing her dad would have done. She had a feeling that Kent was more than just cute, that he really was a sweet boy.

Uncle Alex left, and some quiet seconds followed. Diane noticed the radio again. Sonny and Cher were singing "I Got You, Babe." Kent tried another wink, as if to agree with the sentiment. "Good ol' disappearing Joey," he said. "What a great friend."

Kent *sounded* cool enough, but the poor guy was blushing again.

# Chapter 5

Gene sneaked a look at his watch. It would be fifteen minutes before he and his companion could stop tracting and head to their district meeting. They had been knocking on doors all day, and fasting. It was a muggy day in late August 1965, and each hike up the stairs of these old apartments had gotten a little harder. Right now Gene felt as though he couldn't make it up another flight. But he couldn't leave early, either. All summer Elder Russon had been filling out the weekly reports, and he was a stickler. If they quit even a few minutes early, he would deduct that from their working hours for the day.

Most of the old buildings they were working right now didn't have intercoms downstairs, and the outside doors weren't locked. That made it easier to get to the apartment doors and look people in the face—which always seemed to help a little—but it also meant there was no getting out of the climb. Gene walked inside the next building and was relieved to get away from the outside heat. He stopped and leaned against the wall near the mailboxes. In a minute he would write down all the names he could get from the boxes, just in case the names weren't by the doors. But for a minute or two he wanted to breathe and feel the cooler air. "How are you holding up?" he asked Elder Russon.

"I'm beat."

"As soon as the district meeting is over, we'll all go to a *Gasthaus* and get something to eat."

Russon nodded. His skin was moist, even beaded up with sweat on his forehead. "Why do we have to wear suit coats in this heat?" he asked. "In some countries, elders get to take their coats off in the summer."

"That's in the tropics. If you think this is bad, wait until October. We have to wear hats from fall conference until spring conference. And that's something the mission is *strict* about."

Gene never knew what to expect from Elder Russon. The missionary reports were still an issue with him, but he also chafed at mission rules. He was a guy who longed to be alone, and sometimes he admitted to Gene that he wanted to get on his bike and ride away for a while. He also hated the idea of giving memorized lessons. He was convinced missionaries would do better if they talked to people naturally instead of bombarding them with questions that required set responses. Still, he had memorized his lessons perfectly, and he stayed with the wording even more exactly than Gene did.

"When it's cold, the hats are okay," Gene said. "I just hate dealing with the stupid things." But he didn't want to say too much and get Russon upset about one more thing. "Well, let's climb these stairs."

Elder Russon nodded and Gene led the way. He knew what Russon had been thinking. Standing in the hallway wasn't, strictly speaking, work. So Gene climbed rather vigorously, partly out of annoyance, and partly to give Russon a little of his own medicine. If he wanted work, Gene would give it to him. But at the top of the stairs they were both out of breath. Gene waited and drew in air for a time. He looked over at Russon, who was looking pale after the climb. Gene smiled. "If fasting is supposed to make you humble, I think I'm getting there."

"I think it's stupid," Russon said. "They shouldn't make us fast on work days. A lot of guys just slack off because they can't handle the heat and fasting at the same time."

Gene thought of the little speech he could give about the importance of having the Spirit with them as they worked, but he wasn't really buying it himself at the moment. He wasn't sure he felt anything but weakness and thirst. He believed a mission fast, from time to time, was a great thing, but he also knew he'd like the idea better once he had eaten. He tried to fill up his lungs with one big breath, and then he rang the doorbell. No one home. There were four doors on this landing, and he rang each one, then waited, but no one answered. "We could have saved that last flight of stairs," he said.

"We could save all of them—all the time—for all the good it's been doing us."

It was true. The elders had worked in Stuttgart all summer, and they had gotten nowhere since their baptism in June. The work really had seemed pointless at times. But Gene had the Schönfelds to remember, besides Johann. He knew that if he worked the rest of his mission and only brought those three into the Church, he couldn't feel too bad. He was hearing that the Schönfelds had callings in Ravensburg now, that both were making fast progress. They had written to him that they wanted to go to the Swiss Temple as soon as they had been in the Church a year. They were expecting another baby, and they wanted both their children sealed to them. "When you finally find someone who'll listen, it's worth it, Elder," Gene said. "It really is."

Elder Russon didn't respond. He merely stepped toward the stairs.

"Are you glad you stayed?" Gene asked.

Russon turned around and looked at Gene. "I guess so. But I still don't know whether it's for the right reason."

"What do you mean?"

Elder Russon reached a finger inside his collar and pulled at it. The collar was wet, and Gene could see where it had rubbed Russon's neck red. He wasn't the sort of guy who would choose, on his own, to wear a white shirt and tie, and his skin seemed to know it. "I'm glad I didn't give up. It would have been embarrassing to go back and face everyone. But I was hoping my mission would change the way I feel about a lot of things, and that's not happening."

"You've only been out three months."

"Six. I stuck out the LTM, and I hated almost all of that."

"Okay. But you've only been over here three. Just wait. Some good things are going to happen. At three months I was a mess, but I feel like I've grown a lot since then."

"One thing I will tell you," Russon said. He looked at Gene's chest, not his eyes. "You're okay. I couldn't stand you at first. But you're a good guy."

Gene wasn't sure what he should say.

"I hate the way missionaries put on such a big show, like they're so super righteous. But you've kept your promise even though it makes you look bad. I know it's killing you to turn in fewer hours than the other guys—especially when you and I both know we're working harder than anyone else in the district. But you've stuck to your guns about that."

"I think you're right about what we're doing. That's all."

"One thing I trust about you, too—when you bear your testimony, I can tell you mean it."

"I couldn't do that at first. I wasn't sure what I could claim I knew for sure."

Russon was looking toward the stairs but hadn't begun to move toward them yet. "I *believe* some things, but I don't *know* anything for sure. I don't think I ever will."

"Maybe we use those words too freely—'I know.' Maybe we ought to say, 'The Spirit has borne witness to me,' or 'I have faith that . . . ,' something like that. Germans have trouble with us claiming that we know things that they consider a matter of faith."

"But if we say, *Ich glaube*, it sounds like we're only saying, 'I think maybe it's true.'"

"I know. That's the problem. But I'm just telling you that we talk about 'knowing' so much that we make faith seem weak—and it isn't."

Elder Russon's eyes finally focused on Gene's. He seemed to give the idea some thought before he said, "Thanks. That helps me. That's good for me to think about."

The elders walked down to the next floor, but now it *was* time to leave for the meeting, so they continued on down, and even though it took all Gene's effort to pedal his bike, he liked the feel of the air moving over him, catching inside his coat and working its way through the fabric of his wet shirt. He needed to wear this shirt one more day, and the drying might help. He was suddenly feeling a lot better anyway—maybe because he would be able to eat before too much longer, but mostly, he knew, because of what Elder Russon had said.

The elders rode back to their apartment and dropped off their bikes, and then they walked down a little hill and caught a streetcar to the church. They sometimes biked across the city, but it was a long way, and the traffic could get frightening. Today, they probably didn't have the strength left to do it, and they still had to walk up a rather daunting hill to get to the church once they got off the streetcar. But they made the hike and were almost to the church when they spotted a black Opel. Gene knew the car. It was the one President Fetzer's APs drove. They were both good guys, and from what Gene had heard, were both first-rate missionaries. In June, the South German mission had been combined with the Bavarian Mission. Elder Durphey was from the other mission, and Gene didn't know him very well. Elder Russon thought that the senior AP, Elder Blair, was a little too slick, but Gene didn't think so. He was certainly confident, even "smooth," but that seemed his personality, not an act.

Gene had not expected the two to be at the meeting today. Maybe it didn't mean anything. Maybe they were touring the mission, sitting in on district meetings—or maybe they had needed to see Elder Bates. The only thing Gene worried about, although he hated to admit it to himself, was that they might give long talks and delay the end of the fast.

As it turned out, the APs did attend the district meeting, and they gave short talks, but the spirit they brought was good, and when Elder Bates asked the missionaries—eight elders and two sisters—to bear their testimonies, Gene felt something really powerful take over. When he got up to say something himself, he told everyone, "I'm ashamed of myself right now. I love the spirit I'm feeling, but all day long I've been wandering around wishing I didn't have to fast on a hot day like this." The missionaries all smiled, and most of them nodded. "I feel weak, but I feel strong, too. Really strong. I know this work only goes forward when we get in touch with the Lord—and stay in touch. I just wish I didn't have such a whiny attitude sometimes."

It was a good meeting for Gene. He came out of it ready to go back hard on the work—as soon as he ate. Everyone agreed to ride the streetcar together to a good *Gasthaus* they all liked, and that felt good to Gene, too. He only worried that the meal would take too long. Russon would dock the time off if they took longer than the hour scheduled for dinner.

Gene was talking to another of the senior companions, Sister Larson, and the group was heading for the door together when Elder Blair said, "Elder Thomas, could you stick around for just a minute? I need to talk to you." Elder Blair turned to his companion. "Elder Durphey, can you just sit in the foyer with Elder Russon for a minute?"

"Sure."

Gene told the other missionaries, "Go ahead. We'll meet you at the *Gasthaus*."

Elder Blair motioned for Gene to follow, and then he walked to the chapel, turned a light on, and sat down in the back pew. "So how are things going, Elder Thomas?" he asked. He turned and put his arm on the back of the bench so that he was almost facing Gene. Gene wondered how Elder Blair kept his clothes looking so good. He seemed to have at least four American suits, and missionaries weren't supposed to bring that many. Had he sent for more when he got called as an assistant? He was small, with dark hair that was always in place, as though it had been sprayed.

"Not bad. Since that baptism we had a couple of months ago, we've had trouble getting anyone past the first couple of lessons, but we do have one family that looks promising. They took the first lesson really well and said they would come to church this Sunday. We'll find out, I guess, whether they really mean it."

"Hey, don't talk that way. All that does is plant a negative thought in your mind. People who succeed don't let themselves think about failing."

Gene had come to question that kind of logic. He had heard way too much of it in the mission field. The fact was, no matter how positive his thoughts were, most people who promised to come to church came up with excuses when missionaries stopped by for them on Sunday. But that's not what he said. "Sure. I know I've got to be positive."

"You're a great missionary, Elder Thomas. One of our very best. Your German is excellent. You're a good teacher. And you're a natural leader."

"Well . . . thanks. I'm trying."

"When the mission president made you a senior at eight months and gave you a brand new missionary at the same time, he was obviously expecting big things from you."

Gene knew that, of course. But he didn't admit it. "The thing that matters to me," he said, "is that I've been involved in some good baptisms. That's what I want more than anything—just to see some more good people accept the gospel."

"That's exactly right. Don't think the mission president isn't aware of that couple you baptized down in Ravensburg, and the young man here in Stuttgart. Those are the kind of people who will build the Church over here."

Gene nodded. But he was wondering, what was this all about?

"I'm going to tell you something we normally don't tell missionaries. But the president gave me permission."

"Okay."

"We're getting ready for the next transfer—in two weeks. We haven't settled anything yet, but we're thinking about making you a DL. The president feels like you're the right man for the job." He smiled. "I'm not telling you where you'd be going—I'm not giving everything away—and I'm not saying for sure that it will happen, but the president wanted me to find out something before we take this step."

Gene's mind was spinning. This was incredible, to be moved up to DL when his mission wasn't even half over. It would be great to write his parents and tell them. And he knew without exactly admitting it to himself that if that happened he would be the logical choice at some point to become an assistant to the president. "What did you want to know?" he asked.

Elder Blair had stopped smiling. He looked solemn when he said, "Throughout your mission, you and your companion, whichever one you've had, have been right at the top of the mission for the number of hours you work. But lately, you haven't even led your own district. We can't figure that out. There's just no way we can make you a DL if you're not the hardest worker in the district you'll be leading. Has something kept you from working as much lately?"

Sooner or later, Gene had known that he would have to answer for this. For a moment he considered telling the whole story—that it was Elder Russon's idea, that Gene had had to go along to keep his companion in the mission field. But he couldn't do that. He was the senior, after all, and he wasn't going to pass the blame. The fact was, he had told Elder Russon today—and he had meant it—that the way they had been reporting was right.

"Elder Blair," Gene said, "I've never worked so hard as I have this summer, but I've been strict about how I count hours. I think a lot of missionaries pad their reports, and I don't want to do that."

Elder Blair began to nod and smile. "I told the president that's what I thought was happening. That makes me feel a lot better."

"I just think that if we're going to report work for the Lord, we ought to keep really close track of it, and not exaggerate—you know, just to look good."

"I agree with you. Couldn't agree more."

Gene felt exonerated, supported. For the first time he was really sure Elder Russon had pushed him in the right direction.

"There's no question," Elder Blair said, "that a lot of elders count everything they do. I think some of them even count their sack time." He laughed. "One time, in a stake conference, I heard a General Authority say, 'That's about as accurate as a missionary report'—and everyone laughed. It's just common knowledge that missionaries are too generous when they count their own hours."

Gene didn't know how to take that. Was he saying that the reports weren't accurate but that it didn't matter that much?

"So I admire you for keeping close track. But the fact is, if you're going to be a leader, you can't be giving the missionaries excuses for why you aren't meeting the mission goal. You just have to *do* it."

"The trouble is," Gene said, "there are only so many hours you can work, at least if you're also going to meet your study goal. When we're teaching a lot, it's easier to work a little later into the evening. But if you don't have lessons to give, there's a certain point in the evening where it starts to bother people if you're still ringing doorbells."

"There are a lot of things you can do, Elder—if you have your mind made up that you're going to meet that goal, no matter what. You can meet with members, for instance, and work on getting referrals. I don't think missionaries should hang around members' houses too much, but if you get acquainted, get their trust, and then ask for help, sometimes that's the best missionary work you can do."

"We do that sometimes, but the members get really tired of it. Missionaries have been harping on them for so long that—"

"Is that what you want me to tell the president, then—that you *can't* meet your goal?"

"No. I'm not saying that."

"Then what are you saying?"

"I'll work every hour of every day that I can. That's what I've been doing. But when I add it up at the end of the week, lately it hasn't been coming out to sixty-five." Elder Blair nodded thoughtfully, but the look of disappointment was almost more than Gene could stand. He had always lived up to what people expected of him—been the best at what he did. He wasn't going to let Elder Blair go back and tell President Fetzer that he had refused to make any promises. "But I'll do it, Elder Blair. No matter what it takes. I'll do it."

"All right. That's what I wanted to hear. And listen to me. Let up on yourself just a little. Okay? You don't need to make yourself look bad, compared to the others. If you're ten times more strict than everyone else, but you're working harder, what does that prove? You report fewer hours, but you don't really give a fair picture of what you've been doing."

Had Gene just heard right? Was Elder Blair saying the opposite of what he had said before? "The only thing is, I don't want to—"

"Elder, you can make yourself miserable if you sit down at the end of the day and question every minute that you stopped to look at the swans on the river. Most of the time, when you're out there, you're working or you're traveling to and from your work. No one says you can't stop to smell a rose along the way—or chat for a minute with the members after church. You have to be reasonable about the whole thing."

That sounded right. Elder Bentz had worked hard, but no harder than Gene and Elder Russon had this summer, and Elder Bentz had reported more hours. Maybe it really was Russon who was messing Gene up—making him look bad. "I think maybe I have gotten a little carried away with that kind of stuff," Gene said.

"Give it your all, every day. You'll meet your goal. I know you will. I did it for two years before I got this job. Nowadays, Elder Durphey and I put in *eighty* hours some weeks. And we study while we travel, so we get our study hours in too."

"I'll meet my goal next week, Elder Blair. I promise you that."

"All right. Don't be surprised, then, if you see an *Eilbot* in the mail in a couple of weeks. And you'd better be the best DL in the mission. I'm the one who's going back to Feuerbach to vouch for you."

"Don't worry. You can count on me."

Two weeks later the "speed letter" came—in mission stationery, with a bright red *Eilbot* sticker across it. Gene was being transferred to Esslingen, just a few miles outside Stuttgart, and a town that was known for having one of the most active, solid wards in all of Germany. It was the city everyone hoped to work in sooner or later. Gene got the letter on a Tuesday and would be leaving on Thursday. He would be district leader, the transfer said, and he would have a car: one of the mission's little blue VWs. He would have to write his parents and ask for thirty dollars more a month—to pay for his share of the car expenses—but he knew they would both be thrilled to hear about his new calling.

There were lots of things to do, and Gene kept busy for two days: "unregistering" with the city of Stuttgart, packing, visiting members to say good-bye. He even ran around and took a few pictures that he had always wanted to take. Elder Russon was mostly silent through all this. He had been that way for two weeks now.

Finally, on Wednesday night, after the elders had come home from dinner with a member family, as Gene began pulling off his shoes, he said, "You're upset with me, aren't you?"

Elder Russon sat down on his bed. He had already taken off his tie. He was now running his fingers over the sensitive skin along his throat. At least the weather had cooled a little. The nights were still way too warm for good sleeping, and the humidity was worse than ever, but a little rain had come, and the clouds were keeping the temperature down. "Why would I be upset?" he asked.

"You know why. Because I started doing the reports again."

"I don't care about that."

"Yeah, you do. You think I sold out."

Elder Russon had started unbuttoning his shirt. "We worked hard these last two weeks," he said. "Really hard."

"I know. But I gave us more hours than you would have."

"Two or three, maybe. I don't know. It's all about the same."

But it wasn't the same, and they both knew it. Gene knew that they had put in some time at the Bahnhof, making "street contacts" in the evening. It was something they could do, rather late, but Gene knew it was mostly pointless. There was no way to follow up on most of the people they stopped. In fact, he had the feeling that he just might be doing more harm than good, bothering people that way—and yet, it was time he could count. Gene also knew that he had gone back to counting all the hours of the day and then subtracting for meals and study—rather than to think back on wasted time. One day he had needed to get his bike fixed, and it had taken over an hour, but he had told the repairman he and Elder Russon were missionaries from the Mormon Church and then convinced himself that if they had made a good impression, that was a form of missionary work. What he had no question about was that he and his companion had worked harder than anyone else in the district, maybe anyone else in the mission, so he wasn't going to let himself feel too guilty about the reports he had turned in.

"You feel like I broke my promise, don't you?"

"Didn't you?"

"When this whole thing started, I told you that you should stay for two weeks, and that you could keep the report. After that, we just left it that way. But I don't think I promised that you would keep it as long as we were together."

"Look, Elder, you're a very good missionary. You work hard, and you try to do your best. You're heading for the top, and I don't have any doubt that you're going to get there."

"What's that supposed to mean?"

Elder Russon stood up and took off his shirt, then walked to the wardrobe and hung it up. Gene stood and pulled his own shirt off, all the while waiting. "I didn't know the mission field was like this," Elder Russon finally said.

"Like what?"

"I didn't know it mattered to missionaries so much to be put in leadership positions. And I didn't know we worried more about the hours we work than we do about taking the gospel to people."

"That's not true. That's what all this work is about." But Gene knew what his companion meant—knew all too well. He had not liked himself these past two weeks while he was "earning" his DL job.

"I just don't think hours ought to be the main thing we're thinking about all the time. It seems like we ought to ask ourselves, when we get up in the morning, what can we do today that might help us find someone to teach, and then, how can we do a good job teaching them?"

"That's what we do think about. But what can a mission president do? We've got almost two hundred missionaries over here, nineteen and twenty years old. If you just tell young guys like that, 'Please do your best,' what would happen? Missionaries would be sitting around their apartments all day. You have to give them a goal to get them going, to keep them busy. I know some of the time we put in isn't all that useful, but at least we're showing the Lord we're willing to work, and then we hope one of those contacts we make finally pays off."

Russon nodded, seemed to accept that, but he didn't say so. He sat down on his bed and pulled one of his shoes off, then cocked that foot over his knee and rubbed it with both hands. "I don't want to be a leader," he said. "I don't want to play the game. When I'm a senior, I'm going to work hard, but I'm not going to pad my reports, and I'm not going to make a big play to impress anyone. I'm just going to serve the best I can."

All summer Gene had told himself that that was what he had been doing. But he also knew how much it meant to him to be made district leader so early in his mission. He couldn't pretend that he didn't feel pleased with himself about that. "Don't sell yourself short, Elder," he said. "If you make too much of a point out of this reporting thing, all you'll do is send the wrong message. The president will think that you're not working—or that you're negative about everything."

"I am negative about some things. I hope I stay that way."

"Well . . . do it your way. Just don't make yourself miserable. You're not going to go home early, are you?"

"No. And I really do have you to thank for that."

"But you don't respect me, do you?"

"I wouldn't say that."

"Let me put it this way, then. You've been disappointed with me these past two weeks."

"Yeah. I guess that's true."

Gene nodded. "Maybe you're right. I don't know." He walked to the window. He could feel a bit of air coming in, but he knew it was going to be a hot night. He and Elder Russon had given two more lessons to the family that he had told Elder Blair about. It was an American couple, with two young kids. The husband worked for a company that had an office in Stuttgart. Gene really felt that there was a good chance they would be baptized. He hoped his replacement would do a good job with them, and that Elder Russon would help with the transition. Gene was going to a good city, and he was excited about his calling, but he wondered what he was giving up. Right now, being district leader didn't seem as important as it had when he had talked to Elder Blair. He knew he had disappointed Elder Russon; what he was trying to decide was whether he had disappointed himself.

# Chapter 6

Hans Stoltz was helping to set up a tent, but he was having little success with the stake he was trying to pound into the ground. The dirt was too loose and sandy, and rain overnight had left everything wet.

"I think you need a longer stake," someone said.

Hans knew the voice even though he hadn't heard it for three years. Greta. He looked up at her, saw her standing with her hands on her hips. He stood, but he wasn't sure what to say or what to do. She decided that for him. She threw her arms around him and said, "Hans, it's so good to see you."

"And you," he said. "How are you?"

"I'm happy, Hans." She stepped back enough to look into his face. She had changed a little. Her hair was longer and seemed lighter, maybe from the summer sun, and he hadn't remembered how pretty her skin was. He knew lots of girls who were actually better looking, but no face was so fond to him—after all these years of looking at her picture. He thought he saw the same fondness in her eyes. "This place is so beautiful," she said. "And you get to live here all the time."

Youth conference was on Schwerin Lake this year, just a few miles from Hans's home.

Members of the Church had reserved a cluster of campsites, and local members had lent their tents. Hans was part of an assigned crew that had been setting up the tents all morning. He would have been finished by now if this last one hadn't created such problems. But already the campers, young people from all around the GDR, were starting to arrive.

They would be coming in until evening, and the first activity would take place that night. Hans hadn't known when to expect Greta, but he was thrilled that she had already arrived.

He and Greta had written each other for years, but they hadn't seen one another since Hans had been fourteen. He was seventeen now, and Greta was eighteen. She was tan and fit, but it was her smile—a little out of balance and clever, as though she were about to wink—that he had always liked. She had graduated now, and she worked in a government office in Leipzig, but clearly she had also spent a lot of time outside this summer. "You look great," he told her. "What have you been doing to get so much sun?"

"My friend and I, we had a two-week holiday, so we rode our bicycles to the Erz mountains. We camped all along the way, had a wonderful time."

"Are you ready to camp again so soon?"

"I'm always ready." She was still smiling, still looking pleased, maybe even excited. "Just get me out of that ugly office where I have to work, and I'll sleep on a rock."

"Go check in with the sisters and find out where you're assigned. I'll be finished here before long, and then I'll come and find you."

"Good. Good. It's what I hoped." She picked up her satchel. "We can walk, maybe—take a good look at the lake."

Greta left then, and Hans finished his job. He piled boulders against the tent stakes, but the canvas still sagged. He hoped a wind wouldn't come up in the next few days. When he was satisfied he had done the best he could, however, he asked himself whether he should go look for Greta immediately or whether he should give her more time. He had never had a girlfriend, never gone on a date. In his branch were only a few girls his age, and he sometimes danced with them at branch parties, but they were not interesting to him. There were attractive girls at his school, and some of them had taken an interest in him at times, or at least seemed to, but he had never been comfortable with the idea of dating girls who weren't in the Church.

Hans held back for half an hour, stayed around some young men he knew, before he finally ventured into the girls' camping area. Once the conference was officially underway, he knew that section would be off-limits to him. He found Greta outside her tent, apparently waiting for him and clearly glad to see him walking toward her. She got up and took his hand. "Let's walk part way around the lake."

"It's huge. It would take—"

"I know. But let's hike a little, along the shore."

It was more than Hans could have hoped for. Her letters over the years had always seemed friendly, and nothing more, but now she was pulling him along as though her only interest was in spending time with him. "I'll show you a pretty spot up here," he told her. He moved alongside her and was disappointed when she let go of his hand. But he was surprised by how alive he was. For the last few weeks he had felt that he could never be happy again, not with his memories of Berndt's death, his regrets, his constant worry about being caught.

"What's happening in *Oberschule?*" she asked him.

"The director is letting me graduate with my class. I managed to make up the entire year I lost."

"That's because you're so smart. You're a genius in math, aren't you?"

"No, no. Not a genius. But it's easy for me."

"So you graduate next year?"

"Yes. If all goes well."

"What could go badly now? You certainly won't fail any classes."

Hans wanted to answer, but he didn't dare. Since his interrogation by *Stasi* agents, he had expected, every day, to be questioned again. He had no idea whether he was still suspected, or what might happen to him if he could somehow be placed at the scene on the night Berndt had died, but for these past few weeks he had felt as though he couldn't take a deep breath, never really fill his lungs, and he hadn't slept well. He would see it all over and over, in dreams, or played out in his mind while he tried to read or think of other things: Berndt's body folding, jolting backward. Hans would hear the short, blunt cry—two voices—unsure whether one had not been his own. He no longer asked himself whether the deaths had been his fault. He had dismissed the idea, rationally. He told himself that he had only meant to help; Berndt had asked him. But a more instinctive part of him had reached the opposite conclusion. He had been there, might have tried to help, but hadn't. He would always have to live with that.

So Hans didn't answer Greta. He merely walked along the path until it narrowed and ascended a rocky little hill. He let Greta go ahead. She climbed the hill easily, taking long strides. He liked her tan legs, the tone of her muscles. At the top, she stopped and glanced back at him. She was wearing a blue shirt, and she had tied the tails of it at her waist. He could see how slim she was. "Follow me," he said. "There's a place I want to show you."

Hans led her through some thick growth where there was no path, but when they broke out beyond the brush, they were standing on a ridge overlooking the lake. The extra elevation was just enough to give them a wide view across the dark blue water. They could see the bend along the west side, where the summer greens were set off against the blue.

"Hans, it's all so beautiful. Thank you."

"Don't thank me. God's the one who made it."

She laughed. "Well, true. But you brought me here to look at it."

"I know lots of places like this. I've hiked all the way around the lake before. I took my time and camped along the way."

Greta sat down and let her legs hang over the ledge. Hans joined her but was careful not to sit too close. He didn't want to assume anything.

"So tell me, Hans," Greta said. "Do you believe that now? That God made all this? Sometimes, in your letters, you seemed unsure."

"I *was* unsure."

"And what now? Do you know it yet?"

"I've had some good things happen in the past few months. I feel better about the Church than I did at one time—and better about God."

"What's happened?"

"I went back to church, for one thing, but it wasn't that so much. I started praying again, not fighting the Church in my mind. When I don't *try* to believe, just let myself feel whatever I feel, it seems as though God is there. Maybe it's just the way my parents have taught me to think, but it feels real to me."

"I want to tell you something that happened to me. But not yet. Right now I just want to look at this."

Hans smiled and nodded. He liked that she felt things, but even more, he liked her style. She wasn't like anyone else he knew. He had always wondered how much he really liked her, having only known her for a few days, and having only written since then, but now he felt the same surge of attraction he had known when he had first met her. He liked the energy he felt from her.

There were a few puffs of clouds about, but the sky was mostly clear, shading darker toward a place where the sky and lake seemed to blend. He could hear Greta breathing deep, as though she were trying to get it all inside her.

"What I want to tell you," she finally said, "maybe it isn't so important. But it means something to me. When I was little, my grandfather died. He was not in the Church, but he was a religious man, and he was opposed to the Communists. He would tell me to say my prayers, to trust in God—always things like that. I thought he was very old, but he was not yet seventy when he died.

"I don't know what this means, but I was asleep one night this summer, and I had a dream. I thought I was awake, in my bed, and I saw my grandfather standing by the side of me. He was wearing white—all white—but not a robe. It was a white shirt and white trousers. He stood by me, and then he walked all the way around the bed, as though he wanted to have a good look at me. He didn't say anything, and he didn't smile, but he seemed pleased to see me. And that was all there was to it. It felt good, you know, just to see him again so clearly, not just a memory or a photograph. And it seemed to say that he was all right. I want it to mean that he accepted the Church, and that he's sealed to my *Oma,* but I don't know that for sure. Maybe it was just a dream, but it felt so wonderful, and I've been happier ever since."

Hans understood. A year before he would have been annoyed by such talk, but now it sounded right. "I think that's all we get in this life," he said. "These little glimpses. What I always wanted was God to come into my room when I was wide awake and tell me what was true. It's what Joseph Smith was allowed to experience. But that was something special. Mostly, in this life, we're only granted a little vision like that—this chance to see your grandfather. It's enough to build your faith, not enough to replace it with knowledge."

"Sometimes big things happen. My mother was dying and our branch president blessed her. She was healed, right then."

"I know. But if you're me, you can explain that away. Her fever broke, or she was going to get better anyway—something. I can doubt everything. The more dramatic something is, the more I can make it seem nothing at all. But when God sends vibrations through me, just when I'm not expecting it, that lingers with me. My father gave my little sister a blessing, and he asked me to pray for the family. I didn't want to, but I did, and I felt something happen inside me. Then I felt it again when he blessed her. That's all it was, just something I felt, but it helped me more than anything ever had before."

"Faith must be very important," Greta said. "God wants us to learn it."

"I know. That used to bother me more than anything. Why did he want me to believe things I had no proof for? But if the smartest people were the ones who could understand truth most easily, what value would there be in humility? I've thought a lot about all this, and what makes sense to me is that the whole purpose of this life is to become more like God. That means we have to be meek. Maybe that's so we can have power in the eternities and still use it with gentleness."

Greta turned toward Hans and took hold of his arm with both her hands. "That's wonderful, Hans. What a beautiful thought." Hans felt a sense of joy, as though it had suddenly taken up residence there in his arm, just above the elbow, and was now seeping all through him. But then she asked, "How can you be so young and know so much?"

Hans didn't know what that meant. Was he just a boy to her? What he wanted was to make a closer connection. He wanted to tell her everything so they would have more to share, more common ground. "You heard about Berndt Kerner, didn't you?" he asked.

"Yes. He was your friend, wasn't he?"

"He was older, but yes, we were friends." But now he couldn't think what to tell her. It was always best not to put a friend in the position of knowing too much. If she were ever interrogated, it was better that she not have knowledge she would have to deny. So he only said, "It's been difficult for me, thinking about him. It's forced me to try to understand some things."

"My father told me that Berndt was trying to escape. He says there was a tunnel. Do you know if that's true?"

"Greta, I know many things—more than I should know. Do you understand what I'm saying?"

"You weren't going to go with him?"

"No. But there are things I know. I can't say what they are."

"I understand."

"When I was younger, I wanted to leave. Now I don't." That was only half his thought. He wanted to tell her, "I want to be where you are," but he didn't dare. What if she didn't think of him that way? He would sound so stupid.

"I could never leave my family," Greta said. "I could only leave if we could all go together."

Hans wondered what she meant by "we." Did she mean to include him? It didn't seem so, but he wanted her to give him some hint of what she felt—and then he would dare say more.

Hans and Greta sat by the water and chatted for almost two hours, and then they walked back to the camp. The talk had turned much lighter by then, and Hans found joy enough in her desire to be with him. The evening turned out well, too. The leaders introduced some games that were good fun, and afterward there was a big campfire. President Walter Krause, a counselor in the mission presidency, spoke. He was a warm, good-natured man, whom everyone liked. He told the young people that they were like no other group in the world. Because the members in the GDR were cut off from the body of the Church, it lay upon the shoulders of the youth to keep the gospel alive in this part of the world. They would soon take over as leaders, and much would be expected of them. Hans liked that idea. In years past he might have scoffed at all the importance being placed on the young members, but Hans was committed now, and he liked to think that even if his future in engineering might be limited by his religious beliefs, he could still play a significant role in the world by being a stalwart in the Church. He finally understood his father in that regard. But always, in the back of his mind, was the worry about the *Stasi,* about the possibility of going to prison, about his life—both in and out of the Church—being destroyed.

The next morning started with an early hike along the lake—to wake everyone up, the leaders said—and then the young people were divided into groups and were led in discussions. Hans was not in the same group with Greta, but he had walked with her on the hike, and then, after lunch, during free-time, they were together again. They spent some time at the lakeshore, close to camp. Some of the boys had gotten up a soccer game on a fairly narrow stretch of grass, and Hans and Greta watched. But after a time she said, "We need to do something. I need some exercise."

"Do what?" Hans asked.

"Let's swim out to that dock and back."

Hans looked out to the free-floating dock. It was well out in the water, five hundred meters or more. "Are you sure?" Hans asked her. "That's a long swim."

"I know. But I can do it. Can you?"

He thought of the night he and Berndt had tried to escape the GDR, out in the Baltic. That was the only time he had tried something quite so difficult, but he was pretty sure he could swim farther than most. "Yes, I can swim that far," he said. "In fact, I'll be there waiting for you when you arrive."

"Oh, you think so?" She was wearing a shirt and shorts over her swim suit, but now she pulled them off, tossed them aside, and ran toward the water. She dove in and began to stroke hard.

Hans wasn't worried. She couldn't keep up that pace for long. He pulled off his own shirt, ran to the water, and dove in himself, but he was jarred by the cold. He took smooth strokes, and it wasn't long until he caught up to her. "It's *cold*," he said.

Greta laughed. "You'll warm up."

She was working hard, stroking almost twice as often as he. He could have swum ahead, but he stayed next to her and liked the feeling that he was being protective. What he soon realized, however, was that the floating dock was farther out than he had thought, and surely farther than she had known.

Hans was warming from all the work, but little waves kept catching him at angles, making the effort greater than mere swimming in a pool. It all reminded him too much of that dark swim with Berndt, and he really wasn't sure he wanted to go all the way to the dock.

"It's a long way," he told her. "Do you want to go back?"

"I won't give up first. You'll have to." But she was breathing hard, and he wondered whether she was doing the right thing.

"You're stubborn, aren't you?"

"Yes."

So they kept at it for another five minutes or so. But their progress seemed painfully slow. Hans didn't like what he saw in Greta's face either. She was flushed red, in splotches, and she was breathing too hard. He kept watching her, wondering when to call the whole thing off, and then he saw her grimace. "Wait a minute," she gasped, and she stopped stroking. He turned toward her, began to tread water. He could feel her legs churning the water in front of him. "Are we halfway?" she asked

He looked toward the dock and then glanced back to the shore. "Yes. At least."

"We'd better keep going then, because—" But a little shriek broke from her. "My leg," she gasped. "My leg."

Her head sank below the water, and a burst of bubbles broke above her head. Hans reached for her, felt her arm, but couldn't get hold of it. She was sinking away from him. He let himself drop in the water and grabbed again, couldn't feel anything. He finally turned his head down, dove as best he could, and this time got to her, got his arms around her waist, and then pumped hard with his legs to bring her back up. There was a moment when he thought he couldn't make it, and the panic told him to save himself. But he didn't do it. He kept driving with his legs, pulling at the water with one arm. And then they broke above the surface and both gasped for air.

"My leg," she was saying.

He knew she was cramping, and he made an instant decision to get her back to the shore, not to take her toward the dock, even if it was closer. His instinct was to get to shallower water, not farther out into the lake.

Hans had taken swimming lessons as a boy, and somewhere in the advanced section of the course he had been taught the principles of life-saving, but he wasn't confident about any of that. Still, he told her, with some force, "Relax. Let me get you back." He was treading hard, holding her up, and he could feel her trying to help, but she was only making things worse.

He twisted her around, tried to take her in the life-saving hold, but she was still flailing about too much. "Just let me take you," he commanded. "Stop treading."

He felt her lie back, trust him, and he began to swim. The going was a little easier, with the wind, the waves helping, but it was a long swim, and Hans had never done anything like this before. He was still breathing hard from all the work to get her to the surface and hold her there. Now he was wheezing with every stroke. He told himself to pump with his feet, to keep afloat, and not to hurry, but his instinct was to flail hard, to try to get them to safety as fast as possible.

He kept glancing toward the shore, feeling that he was getting nowhere, wishing that someone would see what was happening and come to them. But he tried to yell a couple of times and got out little more than a grunt. He realized that it was up to him to keep his control, keep making headway, not to spend all his energy and take them both down.

He kept pulling, kept kicking. "We'll be all right. We'll be all right," he told Greta.

But she must have been in shock by then. She wasn't speaking, was only moaning, maybe from her leg, or from the cold.

Hans kept reaching, over and over, but his legs were wearing down. He had trouble keeping up enough motion to propel them. He could see that they were making some progress, but it was much too slow, and he began to feel that it wasn't possible, that he couldn't keep up the effort that long. "Help us, Lord," he said out loud. "Give me the strength."

It was Greta who answered. "I can help now," she said. He felt her lift, and he knew she had to be kicking her legs. For a few seconds he let his own legs rest, and then he drove harder than ever. And now he could feel the definite movement forward, the two working together.

They edged closer to the shore, moving better, but Hans's surge of energy was wearing out again, and Greta was grunting against her own pain, her leg obviously still hurting. Finally, however, a couple of boys saw what was happening, and they dove into the water and swam out. They reached Hans and Greta rather quickly, got on both sides, lifted them and stroked. By then Hans was getting little power from his own legs, but the two boys moved them ahead. The four finally reached shallow water, and all stood up, more or less at once. Other people rushed into the water and helped them to the shore, where Hans and Greta collapsed.

There was a flurry of activity for the next minute or two. Hans lay exhausted in the sand as friends laid towels over him, and finally a blanket from somewhere. He lay with eyes closed, breathing desperately, trying to bring himself back to life. It took some time before he could get himself to think of anything else, but finally he looked at Greta, who was covered too, her face almost purple. He wondered how she was doing. He could see her breathing, her chest under the blanket rising and falling in long pulls, and then she rolled onto her side and coughed some water out of her lungs. He sat up. "Are you all right?"

"Just rest a while," people were telling Hans, but he reached for Greta, took hold of her shoulder.

"Yes. I'm all right," she was saying. "Thank you, Hans. Thank you."

"We shouldn't have gone out there."

She coughed again. A girl was sitting next to her, holding Greta's head, and another girl was rubbing her feet and legs. But Greta struggled to sit up. She turned toward Hans, and he could see that she was crying. "I'm sorry," she said. "I got you to go."

She reached her arms around him. They were both kneeling, and she was clinging to him, sobbing. "We could have died. We almost died," she kept saying.

But Hans could think of none of that. She was holding him tight, her face on his shoulder, her tears running onto his neck, her body supple, touching his. He had never held a girl in his arms, never felt so close to anyone. It was all worth it, what he had just survived, just to feel her cling to him.

# Chapter 7

Kathy would be flying to the East Coast in the morning, staying overnight in a Boston hotel, and then taking a bus to Northampton, where her life at Smith College would begin. The Thomases had all gathered on Sunday at Grandma and Grandpa's house to wish her well, but tonight she was with Marshall. The two had spent a lot of time together lately, but sometimes Kathy wondered why. He was a nice-looking guy, and fun, really different from most boys she knew, but he was not someone she could ever be serious about. Life to him was a daily experiment. He was interested in everything and committed to nothing. Or almost nothing. He did seem serious about his mission, which was coming up the following summer. He remained curious about her devotion to certain causes, and she would sometimes find herself, when he questioned her, admitting to complexities she hadn't considered. That was good, to some degree, but it seemed his way to stay detached. She could never be serious about someone who stood behind the lines, watching, and didn't leap into the battle.

Tonight she and Marshall had spent the early part of the evening at Liberty Park. Kathy had prepared a picnic dinner—sort of. Actually, she had bought the chicken and potato salad at Harman's Kentucky Fried Chicken, and she had bought some cookies for dessert at Safeway. Kathy could cook if she had to, but it wasn't something she loved to do, and today she had had no time. Besides packing for school, she had been sorting through her life, boxing up most of it: her term papers and class notes, old science-fair projects from elementary school, piano lesson books, diaries. Glenda had been pleading to take over her room, but Mom was adamant that Kathy keep it for now. "She'll be back for Christmas and for summer next year," she had told Glenda. "And who knows, after this year, she may decide to come back and go to college here."

It was what Mom was hoping; Kathy knew that. Kathy was the first to leave home, and both Mom and Dad were having trouble with that. They admitted that they were worried about her, afraid of what she would become once she lived among so many people outside the Church. While Kathy had been boxing things that afternoon, her mom, Lorraine, had come in, looked around at the scattered reminders of a life, and then pulled Kathy up from the floor, held her in her arms, and cried. She hadn't said a word, but Kathy had understood—or thought she had.

Douglas was having a hard time too. He would walk into the bedroom, look around as if bewildered, and say, "Don't go tomorrow, Kathy. Stay until the next tomorrow."

Kathy was finding all this more difficult than she had expected, but she kept reminding herself of the other possibility. What if she stayed home and life continued as it was? She told herself she could handle the homesickness—and surely there would be some of that—for the sake of experiencing something new.

The picnic hadn't been as much fun as most of the dates Marshall and Kathy had been on. That was partly because Kathy was thinking of all the things she hadn't done, and partly because the weather was threatening and cool. It had been that kind of summer, with more rain than usual, but Kathy and Marshall had shared some nice experiences. They had heard George Shearing at Lagoon, and then gone back again the next night. They had attended an outdoor jazz concert, and Marshall had shown up in a classic black tux—borrowed from his dad, he admitted—and a blanket tucked under his arm, so they could sit on the grass. But they had also seen *Those Magnificent Men in Their Flying Machines* at the Motor Vu, with a tub of popcorn Marshall had popped and buttered, and a six-pack of bottled root beer in a cooler. Marshall could laugh like no one else Kathy knew—his low voice cracking into high-pitched yelps. He didn't seem to care at all that the movie was nothing but slapstick. It was not the sort of thing Kathy had ever liked, but she laughed so hard that night she snorted root beer through her nose—twice.

But tonight Marshall was quiet. The two ate their fried chicken and then took a drive up Little Cottonwood Canyon, as they had done several times that summer. But they didn't get out of the car, the air being much too cold in the canyon. Kathy also wanted to get back to finish her sorting and packing, a project that was taking more time than she had expected. She knew she would be up half the night.

When Marshall stopped his car in her driveway, Kathy did ask Marshall to come in. "I have a million things to do," she told him. "But if you don't mind sitting in my messy room, we could talk for a while."

"Sure," he said. "I'll hang around."

Wally and Lorraine were nuts about Marshall. When he and Kathy stepped into the family room to say hello, both got up. "We hope you won't stop coming to see us," Mom told him, and she hugged him.

"That's right," Wally said, and he shook hands with Marshall. "We feel like we're not just losing Kathy but all her friends."

The truth was, Kathy didn't have many friends. Dad was only going to miss Marshall, who was a polite young man with solid mission plans—exactly the sort of boy her father would like her to continue going out with.

Glenda and Shauna were lying on the floor watching the *Dick Van Dyke Show*, but they had turned to look at Marshall, whom they both adored.

"Don't worry," Marshall said. "I'll come by to see you. I promised Douglas we'd go fishing together sometime, and he'll never let me break that promise."

"He really likes you, Marshall," Mom said. "I thought he'd be jealous of you, taking his favorite sister away some nights, but it's been just the opposite. He loves you almost as much as he does Kathy."

"He's about the nicest kid in the world," Marshall said.

"I'm going to pack, and Marshall's going to stick around so he can sit on my suitcase when I try to shut it," Kathy said. "I'm trying to stuff my whole life into that thing."

"Don't try to take everything," Lorraine said. "Get back east and find out what you really want and don't want. I can send you a box of things, once you know a little better."

"That's just an extra bother."

"I know. But I don't want you hauling such a heavy suitcase. I worry about you getting from the airport to the hotel and then to the bus station." Lorraine stepped to the glass coffee table and picked up a candy dish full of pink mints. She handed the dish toward Marshall. It was a sort of automatic response. For Mom, part of having guests in the house was serving them. If Marshall stayed around long, she would show up with chips and dip or maybe ice-cream sundaes.

Kathy didn't admit to any concerns about her travel, but the truth was, she actually was a little worried. She had talked to Aunt LaRue that week, and LaRue had apologized, but she wasn't going to be able to meet Kathy in Boston. She was going to be involved in back-to-school faculty meetings all that day and couldn't get away in time to make the long drive across the state. Kathy had found that disappointing, but Lorraine had been frantic about it. She couldn't imagine how Kathy would manage the trip with no one to help her.

Kathy eventually pulled Marshall away from his admirers, and the two walked down the hall to her bedroom. He had never been in the room, and Kathy was conscious of the mess, but she knew it wouldn't matter to him. "Excuse the clutter," she said, all the same. Stacks of clothes and books and papers were still strewn across the floor, her desk, her bed. Kathy moved a pile of long-playing record albums, set them on her desk chair, and made room for him to sit down on the bed. And then she turned on the radio. She always listened to *Bowen and All That Jazz* in the evenings. What came on now was the sound of a muted horn. Marshall said, "Miles Davis. *Kind of Blue*."

Kathy actually knew that, but Marshall knew more about jazz than Kathy did, and she liked that. She could tell that he was smart, just by how well he collected information on so many subjects.

Kathy stared at a stack of blouses, still on hangers, that she had dropped on her bed that afternoon. She started going through them again. She *had* to make a decision about which ones she wanted to take. The fact was, Kathy liked to give the impression that she didn't care much about clothes, but she had always liked to have nice things. She had never been much of a shopper, but she could be a buyer in certain moods, and she owned a lot of nice blouses. She wondered how the girls at Smith would dress. LaRue had told her on the phone that girls weren't dressing up as much as they had in the past. Many wore pants, even jeans, to class now, and some looked really "Bohemian." "They go a little far, if you ask me," LaRue had said. Kathy didn't really like the idea. She hated jeans. Her legs were so long that she looked like she was on stilts. She hoped it was still okay to dress nice, like the girls she had seen in the college catalog that Smith had sent.

"Tell me which of these to take, Marshall. I can't take them all."

Marshall leaned over and pointed to the off-white blouse on top. "You've gotta take that one. You look great in it."

Kathy did like it. She started a pile of things she still needed to pack.

"You'd better take this blue one, too. You look *really good* in it."

Kathy smiled, and she added it to the pile.

"You know what? You'd better take them all. You look *breathtaking* in every one."

"You're no help. Why did I even ask you?"

"Hey, what can I say? I think you look great no matter what you wear."

"Yeah, right." But she didn't say the rest. They had been seeing each other once or twice a week for two months, and he had never kissed her, never even shown any interest in kissing her. He would hold her hand once in a while when they were walking together, but he didn't even do that during a movie or at times that might have been romantic. She never had any idea how he felt about her. Maybe she had found one more "buddy." She was eighteen—halfway to nineteen—and she had never been kissed. The idea of it was embarrassing. "I've noticed how breathtaking you find me. You can hardly keep your hands off me."

It was a blatant hint, and she felt stupid, but tonight of all nights, she wanted him to kiss her goodnight. She would probably never date Marshall again, maybe not even see him once he left on his mission, but if she could go with a guy two months without arousing any interest at all, then maybe she really was nothing more than a "stick," as the boys at Highland High had called her.

Marshall didn't rise to the bait. "Who's this?" he asked.

"What?"

"On the radio. What group is this?"

"It sounds like the Modern Jazz Quartet."

"Hey. Very good. What's the piece they're doing?"

"I don't know."

"'True Blues.'"

"I don't keep track of every cut on an album." Kathy was irritated. How could she say something that obvious to him and not get a response?

"You seem nervous tonight," Marshall said. "Are you scared?"

"About what?"

"About moving away. Starting a new life."

"I don't know. I am nervous, but I don't think I'm scared."

"This is a good thing for you, Kathy." He turned and leaned against the head of her bed. He was wearing a collarless knit shirt tonight, navy blue, and Levi's. He looked long, leaning back across her bed. She loved that he was tall, and she liked the cut of his face, his thick eyebrows. At the moment, however, she was seeing the good shape of his forearms, folded together.

"What makes you say that?"

"You need some room. You need to experience something new. I've never met anyone who's busting at the seams the way you are, just longing to take on the world."

"Is that good or bad?"

"It's Kathy."

How could the guy be so maddeningly neutral? "Don't *you* want to try something new?" she asked him. She was still staring at the blouses, too distracted to make a decision.

"Utah's still new to me. And next year I'll be leaving. I think a year here is going to be good."

"Do you know what you want to do?"

"What do you mean? Like what I'm going to major in?"

"Yes. But all the rest, too. What do you want out of college? Where are you going with your life?"

"Well, Mother, I'm still not sure." He grinned. He had such nice teeth. "You've been asking me that all summer."

"And you haven't ever answered me." Kathy found herself increasingly exasperated—with herself, with Marshall, with the clothes she couldn't decide on. She started folding the blouses, sticking them in her suitcase, almost at random. Maybe she would take them all and then bring back the ones she didn't want when she flew home for Christmas.

"I don't have any answers, Kathy. You know that. I'm going to take some classes—mostly required ones at this point—and I'm going to try to make a friend or two. Maybe I'll—"

"*Girl*friends?"

Kathy knew instantly that she had done something stupid. She was acting like a little girl passing notes in grade school: *I like you. Do you like me?* She folded one of her dressy white blouses, told herself it would be good for church, placed it on the top layer of her suitcase, and then pressed it down. She was running out of room, and she had a stack of pants she still had to consider.

She refused to look at him, but he didn't speak for such a long time that she finally glanced his way. He was smiling at her. "Kathy, I'm going to miss you."

"You've never made me feel that way."

"I don't know what to say to that. I would have asked you out every day of the week this summer, but I never felt like you wanted me around that much."

She *hadn't* wanted him around that much, but what she said was, "I wish I had known that. You're not an easy guy to read."

"Hey, I'm an open book. You're the mystery. You're the most self-contained person I've ever known. You don't need me. You really don't need anyone."

"You don't know that."

"'Kathy's Waltz,'" Marshall said. It took Kathy a moment to realize that he was talking about the number Brubeck was playing on the radio. He obviously saw more in the title than she did.

"Marshall, I don't know how to do these things. I've never dated anyone." She was still stinging from what he had said. She did need people. She cared about people. How could he not know that?

"Maybe you haven't learned how to give signals."

"What signals?"

"Like the ones you're finally throwing around tonight."

Kathy ducked her head, grabbed a blouse she had decided *not* to take, and began folding it. But she saw the bed move, heard it creak as Marshall got up, and then he was standing next to her. She still wouldn't look at him.

"I wish you were staying," he said.

She could feel him next to her, not quite touching, the warmth of him on her arm. This, of course, was one of those signals he was talking about; she had to do something. So she turned toward him, and that was enough. He took her in his arms and kissed her.

The kiss was longer than she expected, and he held her for a long time after. She loved the touch of him, the way he bent his head to hold his cheek against hers. And she loved, already, the memory of the kiss, the surprising warmth.

"I'd better go," he said, "or you'll never get packed."

"No. Please don't. Stay for a while."

He stepped back, tucked his hands into his pockets, and looked shy when he smiled. "Okay."

So he stayed for a while, but they didn't talk all that much. There wasn't much to say. She wanted to tell him that she wished, too, that she could spend this year with him, but she couldn't do that. She couldn't even say for sure how she would feel once he left, or even tomorrow. She had only been in love with him for a few minutes. How could she know what that would mean later?

When Marshall finally did leave, he kissed her one more time. And this time she cried. She cried half the night. What a mess she had made of things. She had finally found someone who cared about her, and she had only had an hour to enjoy the pleasure of it.

~

The experience at the airport the next morning was also worse than Kathy had foreseen. Her family went with her, and by the time she said good-bye, *everyone* was crying, even seventeen-year-old Wayne, who hadn't cried, at thirteen, when his finger had been slammed in a car door.

Douglas was confused and out of sorts, pleading with her not to go, and poor Dad seemed as though he would wash away. Mom kept saying, "We're okay, honey. Don't worry," but Kathy heard her whisper to Dad, "I feel like we'll never be the same. Our family is breaking up."

And that's what Kathy felt as the airplane lifted into a steep ascent and soared over the Wasatch Mountains. She had made a horrible mistake. Everything she knew was in the valley that was slipping behind her. A stewardess came to her, brought her a packet of Kleenex, and whispered, "Honey, I know how it feels. But you'll be okay. It just takes a little time."

That at least stopped Kathy from crying. She was not going to act like an idiot in front of all these people. But she felt numb all the way across America. She sat with a book open, pretending she was reading so she wouldn't have to talk to the man next to her, but she never read more than a paragraph without her mind wandering back to her family, her house, her valley, her *boyfriend*. She tried to muster up some excitement about her new life, but all the things she had told herself for the past couple of years seemed to have lost meaning, and she could only feel the absence of everything she cared about. Eventually, it was worry about getting herself to her hotel, once she landed, that distracted her enough to ease some of her pain. But a porter helped her with her suitcase and got her to a taxi, and at the hotel a doorman and then a bellman helped her to her room.

Then the door closed and she was alone again. She had imagined this night as exciting, with room service and her own TV, but it was a long, dull evening. She wanted to walk a little in Boston, but her loneliness seemed to take away the will, and she felt more fear in this big city than she ever had in Mississippi.

She was exhausted, but she didn't sleep well, and early the next morning she had to be up to catch her bus. Making the connection was no problem, but the long ride, with lots of stops in little towns, seemed endless. LaRue had promised to be at the bus station in Northampton, if she "could possibly make it," but the bus was half an hour late, and maybe LaRue had come and gone. All Kathy knew was that no one was there, so she took one more taxi, which dropped her off in front of Baldwin House, one of the "East of Elm" houses, just off the main campus. It was a Colonial red-brick building with ivy growing on the walls. She liked the comfortable front porch and the big fireplace in the "living room" downstairs, and yet it all seemed foreign, too formal, and rather intimidating. She had also hoped that by now—September—the summer heat would be over, but the humid air was coating her skin, beading up on her forehead, turning her hair into strings. She hoped she wasn't soaking through her blouse, under her arms.

There was some paperwork to do downstairs, and then she had to drag her suitcase up the stairs, but at least she was at the end of her journey. She had received word that she would share a room with a girl named Janet Stowe, from Hartford, Connecticut. When she unlocked the door and stepped in, she saw a dark-haired girl in jeans and a chambray shirt, with the tails out, standing at a chest of drawers. She turned around and smiled. "Hi. I'm Janet. I guess you're Kathleen," she said.

"Kathy." She set down her suitcase and stepped forward, shook the girl's hand.

"You're from way out west, aren't you? Wyoming or—"

"Utah."

"Oh, that's right. Salt Lake City." She pointed to a bed nearby. "I chose this bed. I hope that's okay. The other one is about the same."

"That'll be fine," Kathy said. She glanced around the room and felt a kind of gloom set in. Two beds, two desks, two chairs, and bare, hardwood floors—that was all there was, except for a big window and a nice view of a giant chestnut tree. She had been informed in the package of materials the college had sent her that she would be sharing a bathroom with everyone on the floor. The idea of that hadn't seemed so terrible at home, but the reality of doing that—and living in this room—was hitting hard now.

Janet helped Kathy hoist her suitcase onto the narrow bed. "My dad drove me up here this morning," Janet said. "I made him carry my bags up—and a bunch of boxes. I'm glad I didn't have to bring everything in one suitcase." She stepped back a little and stuck her fingers into her jeans pockets—a tight fit. She was rather big in the hips, and ample in other ways, too. "My parents are divorced. They don't even like to see each other. But it works out great for me. They both try to buy my love. Anything I want, I just drop a hint and end up getting *two*." She was smiling with perfect teeth—the kind that only braces could have produced. Kathy heard something in her voice—something "eastern." She sounded educated, more precise in her pronunciation than westerners, and yet, just under the surface was a certain crassness—the same tone Kathy had heard from the waitress at the hotel coffee shop that morning.

"So why did you get all dressed up?" Janet asked. At the same moment Kathy heard a scraping noise and looked around. Janet had struck a match. Now she was holding the match to a cigarette in her mouth. "I hope it doesn't bother you that I smoke."

It bothered Kathy a whole lot. Already the smell was filling the room. "Actually, it does. A little. In restaurants, when people smoke, it makes me cough."

"Oh, okay. No problem. I guess your parents don't smoke."

"No."

"I'll put this out." She walked back to the chest of drawers and stumped out the cigarette in an ashtray. "Don't worry," she said, "I don't smoke a lot. When I do, I can sit by the window and blow the smoke out."

Kathy didn't like what she was feeling. She wanted her own bedroom. She wanted to go home. How could she live with a girl who smoked?

"We've got to fix this room up," Janet said. "We need to buy some rugs and maybe dump these ugly curtains. They'll let you decorate the room any way you want—as long as you pay for it yourself."

"That's a good idea. Maybe I can ask my parents to send a little extra money next—"

"Don't worry about it. My dad took one look at this place and told me to do whatever was necessary to make it nice. He'll spring for it—and I'm sure my mom will say the same thing." She laughed in a deep, throaty voice. "I can double my money."

Kathy actually hated to ask for extra money, but that's not what she said. "I'll pay half. That's only fair."

Janet laughed again. "Great. I'll pocket the rest. Hey, if I were you, I'd change clothes. This room is kind of dusty."

"I'll do that." But she hated the idea of undressing in front of someone. She had always hated gym class in high school, just for that reason.

"You're *tall*. Are you going to fit in that bed?"

It was one more thing to think about.

It took Kathy an hour or so to unpack and arrange things, and all the while Janet kept asking questions—or going on at length about her own life. Kathy wanted to talk, make friends, but she couldn't seem to think. A kind of tightness was gripping her chest, actually hurting. She knew that if she were alone, she would be crying by now. She kept telling herself, "I'll be all right. I'll get used to everything." She knew she would even like Janet in time. She just had to make up her mind about that.

Late in the afternoon two girls from across the hall came by to introduce themselves. One was from New York City—a tiny, quiet girl named Becky Stein. She was dressed in a nice skirt and blouse, the way Kathy had been—and that relieved Kathy a little—but she seemed more sophisticated, older than Kathy. She admitted immediately that she didn't think much of the rooms. "For what we pay, you would think the college could do better than this," she said.

The other girl—Trisha Yost—was from Pennsylvania, near

Philadelphia. Kathy could tell that she was savvy. She told the girls that she had lived "everywhere." Her dad worked for a corporation that moved him around a lot. Kathy could see in the quality of her clothes—nice slacks and expensive shoes—that she had money. She was trim, almost too thin, and her hair, which was ratted high in a "beehive," could have been called "honey blonde," or something of that sort, but Kathy had the feeling that the color came from a bottle with just such a name on it.

The girls sat in the two desk chairs, and Janet dropped onto the floor. Kathy continued to fuss with her clothes, move things from one drawer to another, and hang up blouses she had first decided to put away. She was surprised how quickly she felt like an outsider. The other three seemed to connect in ways that Kathy didn't understand. Trisha and Janet had both gone to prep schools, and Janet had lived in New York at one time, which seemed to bond her with Becky. Kathy tried to think of something to say and finally asked what the girls' majors were going to be—but the question was dropped before it got around the room.

Janet said, "Hey, let's go see what's happening. Has anyone heard about any parties?"

"There's a reception here at the house later on," Trisha said. "And tomorrow they take us on campus tours. Then there's supposed to be some convocation thing at that big chapel."

"John M. Greene Hall," Becky said. "That's what people mean when they say JMG."

"Why don't we look around on our own," Trisha said. "There must be something going on. I keep hearing that the guys from Amherst are over here all the time."

"We'd better hope so," Janet said, "or we're going to have to go trolling on the streets. It was entirely my mother's idea to get me into a girls' school. She went here a thousand years ago, and she thinks it's still safe. I can only hope she's wrong."

"Let's do go look around," Becky said.

It was a moment of truth for Kathy. She didn't want to seem prudish and get off to a bad start, nor did she want to hole up in this little room, but she figured she was better off to let them know, from the beginning, who she was. "I'd like to look around. But I don't drink. So when you say 'party,' I guess that depends on what kind of party it is."

"Hey, no one's going to make you drink," Trisha said. "Just get a soda and have as much fun as you can—without help." She rolled her eyes. "You're a Mormon, aren't you?"

"Yes."

"I lived in California for a while. I knew Mormons out there." She looked over at Janet, who seemed mystified. "They're okay. But most of them are really uptight. We might have to teach the girl a few tricks."

Both laughed, but Becky said, "I don't drink either—not really. Maybe wine at dinner with my family, or something like that. But I don't drink beer at parties."

"Oh, brother," Janet said. "We'll have to make *new girls* out of both of you."

Kathy actually liked that—the way everyone was taking the whole thing as a joke. She knew she had to relax a little, show that she wasn't a little hick from out west.

The four walked down the stairs and along the way met some more freshmen who were all arriving ahead of the older students. The girls chatted and introduced themselves and then walked on outside. They strolled past some of the other houses, and everywhere girls were saying, "Is anything going on tonight?"

It was at the Davis student center, on campus, that Janet and Trisha finally got word of a place where they could find some sort of "gathering," as Janet called it. By then, however, Kathy had spotted a table where a girl was sitting. Across the front of the table was a white banner that read, "Students for a Democratic Society." Kathy could also see that some information was available. "Wait just a second," Kathy said. "I'm going to check on something over here."

She left the other three and walked to the table. "Is there an SDS group on campus?" Kathy asked the girl.

Most of the girls around the student center were wearing pants, but they looked classy. This girl was in worn jeans and a denim shirt. She had a button on her shirt that read "Stop the War." "Not yet," she said. "But we're trying to get something organized. There's a chapter at UMass, and one at Amherst. For now, we'll probably meet with those groups and start getting in on some of the action."

"What kinds of issues are you working on?"

"That'll be up to the group." The girl looked wary, as though she thought Kathy might be spying. "Are you going to school here?"

"I'm a new freshman."

"What high school?" The girl was smiling—surely, she didn't mean it—but it was the old question. Kathy knew she looked really young.

"I *am* interested," Kathy said. "I did some work in Mississippi summer before last."

"What kind of work? Are you talking about Freedom Summer?"

"Yes. I wasn't there the whole summer. But I was in Greenwood long enough to get knocked over the head and thrown in jail."

The girl was rather young looking herself, with big eyes and a loose braid down her back. Her eyes were huge now, and Kathy knew she had won instant credibility. The girl stood and reached out her hand. "My name's JoAnn," she said.

Kathy shook her hand, but JoAnn was looking away, and Kathy glanced around to see a guy in a flannel shirt, the shirttails out, walking toward them. He hadn't shaved for a time, but he didn't have much to show for it. When he smiled, however, he showed some dimples under the fuzzy beard. He really wasn't bad-looking.

"What's goin' down?" he asked the girl at the table.

"Hey, Robby, this little girl, who looks all of fifteen, got her head busted in Mississippi. She was down there for Freedom Summer."

"You're kidding me," he said. Or at least that's what he meant. He used stronger language—a word that embarrassed Kathy. He smiled and looked straight into Kathy's eyes, seemingly curious. The two were about the same height. "Where are you from?"

"Salt Lake."

"Hey, that's unbelievable. Do they have radicals in Salt Lake City?"

Kathy smiled. "I don't know how radical I am. I just think Negroes are being mistreated, and I went down there to see what I could do. I was also in the march to Selma."

"Hey, you can play on my team any time you want. I'm Robby Freedman. What's your name?"

"Kathy Thomas."

Kathy's roommates were apparently running out of patience. Janet walked toward the table, struck a pose with her hand on her hip—probably for the benefit of Robby—and said, "Kathy. Are you coming or what?"

Kathy turned, considered, and then she said, "No. Go ahead. I want to talk to these people a little more. I'll see you later, back at the house."

"Okay," Janet said. "I gotta hand it to you, you made the first move." She gave Robby a nod, as if to say, "Good luck."

Kathy knew she was blushing, but she turned back toward the table. "I've read a lot about SDS. I know the kinds of changes the organization wants to make in this country. I'm just wondering what kinds of things you plan to do this fall. Are you working on civil rights?"

"Not that much now," Robby said. "Black people are telling us they have to do it themselves. And that's probably right."

Kathy had heard Negroes called "black" lately. Some of the Negro leaders were saying that it was time to stop being ashamed of their color, time to embrace it. But the word still seemed disrespectful to Kathy. "I know that some Negroes, during Freedom Summer, were feeling like whites were taking over."

"You got that right," Robby said. "We're going to do what we can, but the leadership has to be black, and black people have to stand up for themselves. For us, it's all about Vietnam now. We gotta get that stopped."

Kathy knew plenty on that topic, but she didn't feel the passion for it that she did about civil rights. Still, she saw the connection. "A lot of the guys who are dying in Vietnam are Negroes," she said. "Rich white kids don't have to go."

"That's exactly right." She saw the intensity in Robby's dark eyes. "And we have no business over there. It's a civil war."

"It's worse than that," Kathy said. "The South Vietnamese have no real commitment to this war. America is fighting for *itself*—because this administration thinks our being there is going to stop Communism somehow. None of it makes any sense."

"You *are* on my team," Robby said, and she felt him leaning closer. "This country is about to blow. You saw what happened in Watts last month. That was not planned. That was just black people saying enough is enough. No more nonviolence. We're fighting back. And that's what students are going to do. General Electric and Ford Motor and the U.S. military have been running this country for too long. We're going to take it back."

Kathy nodded, trying not to show her doubt, but this kind of talk was a little much for her. She believed in Martin Luther King, in nonviolence.

"I'll tell you something, Kathy," Robby said. "I'm sure you're a liberal, but that's not going to do it. It's going to take *radicals* to turn this country upside down. What we're talking about is revolution. Nothing short of that is going to do it."

She nodded again, but only barely.

"So do you want to sign up? Do you understand what you're getting involved in?"

She didn't. She wasn't at all sure she should do this. But she wasn't about to walk away. "Where do I sign?" she said. If nothing else, she loved the way he looked at her.

# Chapter 8

Gene didn't want to accept what he was hearing. Brother and Sister Müller had been members of the Church less than two months, and now they wanted to have their names removed from the records. "I don't understand," Gene was saying. "What's the difficulty?"

Gene was district leader now, in Esslingen. It was December 1965. His companion, Mike Atkinson from Layton, Utah, had been on his mission for half a year or so. He was a good guy but not all that interesting. He seemed to find no humor in anything, nor any excitement. He went about his days without complaint, without moodiness, so he was easy, in that sense, but Gene couldn't think of much to talk with him about.

In November, Gene and Elder Atkinson had baptized the Müllers. They were a couple in their fifties whose children were all married. The Müllers had investigated the Church for at least six months before Gene had been transferred to Esslingen. He had started over with them, given them all the lessons, and this time made sure that they made their commitments and kept them. They had been happy on the night they were baptized, but now—a month and a half later—they were saying that they wanted out.

"I smoked too many years," Brother Müller said. "I just can't give it up. Last week I started again, and I can't go through quitting another time." He was sitting on a stiff chair he had brought in from the kitchen, his wife in another, next to him, and they had invited the elders to sit on their couch. The Müllers lived in a plain, square apartment house, the outside plastered with gray stucco—one of the many buildings put up in the early years after World War II. The living room was neat but sparsely furnished. Brother Müller was a hardworking man, an assembly line worker at a *Porsche* plant.

"We can start over, Brother Müller. What we'll do this time—"

"It's not *we*, *Bruder* Thomas. It's *I*. I'm the one who has to quit. You can't do it for me."

"I know. But we'll all help you."

"I don't want help. I've had enough help."

Gene heard resentment in Brother Müller's voice—something he had never noticed before.

"It's not just the smoking," Sister Müller said. "I paid the tithe, and you said we wouldn't miss the money, that we would come out all right. But it wasn't that way. We don't have a *Pfennig* now, and there's still a week left in the month."

Gene nodded. He had worried that he might have made tithing sound too easy. "Sometimes it takes a little time to make the adjustment," he said. "Satan is certainly going to tempt you right now. He wants you out of the Church. He wants you to get discouraged. But I know it's something you can manage."

There was quiet then. Gene could hear the big cuckoo clock in the hall ticking hard—drumming. Gene could tell that he and his companion had broken the Müllers out of a routine, a way of doing things, and they were frightened by the change. He felt sure that he just had to keep them active for a few months and they would be all right.

"Just take us off your membership list," Brother Müller said. "We don't want to do this. We've been *Evangelisch* all our lives. We never should have changed."

Gene knew he had to stop coming at them with arguments. He had to find a way back to the spirit they had obviously felt at one time. "Could we have a prayer about this?" he asked. "Could we pray now, and then take a week, and you could keep praying every day, asking the Lord what he would have you do?"

"No. We have already prayed, and this is what we feel is right. You aren't going to talk us out of it." Brother Müller was a lean man with gray skin and graying hair so fine that strands drifted around his ears like smoke. Sister Müller was more substantial, classically German, with reddened cheeks and an almost purple nose, the capillaries visible on her skin, like etchings. She had been feeding the elders at least once a week for months now, had seemed to cherish her time with them, but now she was looking down, refusing to engage their eyes, and Brother Müller was looking hard, even angry.

Gene's stomach felt sick. "You simply can't do this, Brother and Sister Müller," he said. "You've come too far. You can't let something as simple as smoking, or tithing, hold you back. I know you can—"

"There's something else," Brother Müller said.

But his wife was quick to say, "Don't mention those other things, Alfred. There's no purpose in it."

"What other things?" Gene glanced at Elder Atkinson. The elders had had inklings that something else was bothering the Müllers.

The clock was still drumming, and Brother Müller was looking resolved. He had always been someone Gene could influence, encourage—but all that seemed gone now.

"I will simply say this. The members aren't so wonderful as you told us they would be. You made it sound as though every member of your church was a Saint. And they all seemed that way to us at first. But now we know: they're merely the sort of people we've known all our lives. They can be unkind and short-tempered—all the things we've seen in our own church."

Gene had witnessed a little confrontation between Sister Müller and Sister Graff, one of the women in the Relief Society presidency. He had walked into the tiny kitchen at the church after a ward social, and Sister

Graff had been saying, "We must wash these forks again. They're *not* clean."

Nothing more had been said, but Sister Müller had tied her apron back on, quickly, deftly, and begun to run more hot water. Her face had been as red as her hands, and her jaw tight. Gene had tried to talk to her, but she had responded only curtly. It was the sort of thing Gene had seen many times—the Saints getting irritated with one another—but he hadn't considered it a serious matter. Was that the problem now?

"Brother Müller," Gene said, "people have little disagreements. They make mistakes. We're all human. But that doesn't mean the gospel isn't true."

Elder Atkinson said, "Even the best people say things sometimes, and then, later . . ." He had lost track of the structure of his sentence or couldn't think of the word he wanted in German. "They—"

"We expected more. You said the Holy Ghost would work on people, change them inside, and that's what we thought we saw in your members. But they are no better than others."

"They *try*. That's so much of the gospel—knowing what is right and striving toward it."

"They may try. We can't tell. But they aren't what you promised."

Gene didn't think he had promised anything of the sort. He tried to remember. He had talked to the Müllers about the Church's emphasis on family. He had talked about the influence of the Holy Ghost. He hadn't promised that the members would be perfect.

"Will you wait a little while—give this some time, and keep coming to church? I think you'll find that—"

"No. We've talked and talked, and this is what we've decided. Tell the bishop that we are finished."

"He'll want to talk to you."

"No. We don't want anyone else to come."

"Brother Müller, it isn't that simple. There are steps that have to be taken. He will have to talk to you."

"We'll only tell him the same thing."

But that was at least an opening. If Gene could get Bishop Knecht there, maybe he could lighten things a little with his good humor, talk them out of being so rash. He was such a good man; maybe they would respond to his wisdom, or at least his kindness.

"I'll talk to Bishop Knecht," Gene said. "But please, don't make a final decision yet. Could we pray now, before we go?"

"No. This is the way you make us feel guilty. We want no more of that."

What was he saying? Did they think Gene had browbeat them into joining the Church? Used prayer to do it? It was only a way to seek the Spirit.

But Gene *had* felt uneasy at times about the pressure he had kept on the Müllers. Maybe he had pushed them too hard, too fast. He wasn't sure. Still, the only hope he could see now was to get Bishop Knecht into their home.

Gene was anxious when the bishop didn't answer the door. He rang again, but almost at the same time, the door came open. "I need to talk to you," Gene said before Bishop Knecht could greet him.

Bishop Knecht was a pleasant little man who could speak his native *Schwäbisch* dialect like any street sweeper, but he could also give a powerful sermon in High German. "Yes, yes," he said, smiling a little, as though he were used to missionaries showing up with worry in their faces. "Come in. But I can't take long. I have a meeting at the church in thirty minutes, and I'm not ready." He was wearing a white shirt but hadn't put his tie on yet. He smelled of shaving soap.

Gene was suddenly embarrassed that he had been so abrupt. He followed Bishop Knecht down the hall to his little office. The Knechts lived in a house, not an apartment. It wasn't big or fancy, but it had a little garden area. Sister Knecht looked like any *Hausfrau* when she was out among her flowers, with her hair done up in a scarf and her rubber boots on, but she was a pretty woman who wore colorful dresses to church and espoused rather modern views in Sunday School. Bishop Knecht was more conservative, but he never seemed to mind his wife having her own say. Gene had never really seen him upset by anything.

He was smiling now as he sat in a leather chair behind his desk. He motioned for the elders to sit on the chairs across from him, and then he said, "*Bruder* Atkinson, how is it going for *you?*"

The question seemed a bit of a joke, as though he were saying, "I know your companion is upset about something. Maybe I would rather talk to you." Or perhaps, "If I don't speak to you now, I won't have the chance. *Bruder* Thomas will do all the talking."

"It's going well for me," Elder Atkinson said, nothing more.

"Bishop," Gene said, "the Müllers want to leave the Church."

Gene thought the news would create at least a bit of a shock, but the bishop nodded, seemingly unsurprised. "I've seen something coming," he said.

"It's the members," Gene said. "Someone has . . ." But he didn't know a German word for "offended" or "mistreated." He finally came up with "made them unhappy." "They told us our members are no better than people they know in their own church."

Bishop Knecht nodded again. He was a dark-haired man with a little asymmetric smile that never entirely left his face.

"I think it might have been Sister Graff," Gene said. "I heard her, after our ward party, speaking to Sister Müller. She told her the forks weren't clean, and she wasn't nice about it."

"People are people, *Bruder* Thomas. You know that."

"Certainly. But the Müllers expected more. And why not? The gospel *should* make people better."

Bishop Knecht smiled. "You sound rather harsh yourself, *Bruder*. Maybe the gospel should make *you* better."

Gene sank into his chair, let the air seep out of him. That's not what he needed tonight.

"I've known Sister Graff all my life, *Bruder* Thomas, and there is not a better person in the world. It's no easy matter, all the adjusting a new member has to do. Sometimes, when it seems a little too difficult, they look for excuses. Then a harsh word becomes a reason to go back to their old life. I've seen it many times over the years. Many times."

Gene sat up straight again. "That's just the problem, Bishop. We work so hard, get people ready for baptism, and after a few months they're lost. Why can't the members understand that? They *wait* to make friends. One member said to me, after I baptized a family in Ravensburg, 'I expect those people will fall away before long.'"

Bishop Knecht may have been in a hurry, but he showed no sign of it. He rested his elbows on his desk and looked at Gene for some time. "Yes," he said, "that happens. But this isn't easy for our members. Some investigators come to church only a time or two before they are baptized, and then, soon after, change their minds. The members *should* do more, *could* do more, but they have busy lives too, and frankly, they become skeptical."

"But why send thousands of missionaries all over the world if the members won't help?"

"That may be easy to say, *Bruder*, when you've grown up in Salt Lake City. But you have no idea what the challenges are here. The members give *much* help—more than you know."

Gene was sorry for the tone he was taking. He sat back and tried to think what he was feeling—and how he could explain it to the bishop. He finally said, in a gentler voice, "Bishop, I heard a few days ago that a boy I baptized in Stuttgart has stopped coming to church. And now the

Müllers. I've been in Germany half my mission now, and I've only baptized five people. Now I'm losing three of them."

"Were they *yours* to lose, *Bruder* Thomas?"

"What do you mean?"

"You said that *you* had baptized five people. You said that *you* were now losing three of them."

Gene saw the bishop's point, but he didn't like the inference. "You know I don't mean it that way. I'm just saying that missionaries work hard, and it's difficult to see the people we baptize fall away."

Bishop Knecht was maddeningly slow in his response, but he finally said, "Missionaries do work hard. They are young, and they give up a great deal to serve as they do. I certainly understand how you feel. I was a missionary myself, you know."

"Yes, I know."

"And I remember how it was. I worked hard and I wanted success. I measured that success by the number of people who joined the Church. But you tell me, *Bruder* Thomas, what's wrong with that?"

This was nothing new. Gene hadn't expressed himself exactly right, but he didn't need to be reprimanded tonight. "Bishop, I know what you're saying. All I'm asking is that you meet with the Müllers and see what you can do. And maybe you should talk to the members about giving new members more help."

"I've talked to the members many times, and I will continue to remind them. I will also meet with the Müllers. But right now I want *you* to listen to me."

"I am listening."

Still he waited. "You didn't come on this mission for yourself."

"I know."

"But do you? What is your goal—to see how many people you can baptize?"

"I want to think that I've done something important in Germany—

that all the work is worth it. If everyone I baptize falls away, it all seems so . . ." He knew no German word for what he wanted to say.

"What? A waste of time?"

"Not exactly. But . . . something like that."

"*Bruder*, it's the same struggle we all have. Following Christ isn't easy. But he doesn't ask us merely to do the work; he asks us to do it for the right reason. He doesn't measure our success the same way we do. You can love the Müllers, and you can try to help them, but you can't make their choices for them. And you can't measure the value of what you do by that choice."

Gene nodded. He wanted to leave now. His frustration was slipping away, and what he felt was sadness. Maybe his motivations weren't entirely pure, but what the bishop was asking of him seemed too much. Johann, the great young man he had baptized in Stuttgart, was slipping away, and Gene couldn't do one thing about it. Now the same thing was happening to the Müllers, the main source of his happiness in recent weeks.

"Let's see what we can do. I'll visit the Müllers, and I'll tell them we love them, that we care what happens to them. Maybe they will listen, and maybe they won't. You do the same. We'll try as long as they will let us. But finally, if they choose to leave the Church, we should feel nothing but sorrow for *them*."

Gene was suddenly embarrassed. The bishop seemed to know him better than he knew himself. He stood, and he could only think to say, "Bishop Knecht, I do love the members here. And Sister Graff has always been very kind to us."

"Yes, yes. But she's human, and so am I. So are you. That's the great problem: we try to make a perfect plan work with only mortals to do the job."

"I wish the Müllers could understand that."

"I think they do understand it. But they want to be loved, not just *converted.* If anyone can help them, it's you." The bishop turned to Elder Atkinson. "And you."

Elder Atkinson nodded.

The elders shook the bishop's hand and then left. It was a cold January evening, and Gene was glad to have a car. The heater on the VW was slow to react and was never quite adequate, but it was surely better than traveling around on a bike. Gene started the engine and then tried to think what he should do. "We have some call-backs in our tracting area we can check out," he told his companion, "but I was thinking, maybe we ought to go back to the Müllers right now. We could do what the bishop said. We could tell them how much we love them."

"I don't know. Maybe it would just seem like more pressure right now."

"*More* pressure?"

"You know what I mean."

Gene did know. He hadn't wanted to admit it to himself, but he had felt uneasy about some things he had done to get the Müllers baptized. When he had arrived in Esslingen, Gene had asked for commitments—nothing wrong with that—but he had sensed at times that he was outtalking Brother Müller, battering down his objections. And maybe he had made the man kneel with him at times to force the idea that certain questions could only have one answer. What Gene hadn't felt was the closeness he had experienced with the Schönfelds, the first family he had baptized.

"Maybe we should give them a little time, and maybe we could fast," Elder Atkinson said. He was tall, with legs that didn't want to be bent into a VW Bug. He was bending forward now, seeming to study his knees, as though he didn't dare say what he was really thinking. "You know, we could try to go back to them with the right spirit this time. That might help."

Gene took the words hard, knew what they meant. But he didn't say so. He merely drove back to the area where they had tracted that morning. One of the call-backs did work out. A young woman invited the elders in, and Gene turned the little introductory discussion over to Elder Atkinson. As he talked, Gene listened. Atkinson made a mess of German grammar, and he didn't project his voice the way he needed to, but there was something kindly about him, and the woman and her mother seemed to respond. They were clearly not interested in the Church, but they chatted with the elders for quite some time and wished them well when they left.

In the hallway, after, Gene said, "Good job, Elder. They're not going to forget the feeling you brought into their home." He didn't say the rest of what he was thinking, but they both knew what he meant.

It was too late by then to check out any more call-backs, so the two drove back to their apartment. Along the way they stopped at a little market that stayed open in the evenings. They had never found time to stop for an evening meal, and they were out of almost everything at home. They bought some wurst and cheese and bread, and a bottle of milk.

Near the door of the market was a little rack with newspapers on it. Gene stopped to look at the headlines. A small article was headlined "Nearly 200,000 American Soldiers Now In Vietnam." Gene read the first couple of paragraphs. A big battle had apparently taken place that fall at a place called the Ia Drang Valley. Estimates were that about two hundred Americans had died, but enemy losses had been over two thousand. General Westmoreland was predicting that with a "kill ratio" of that kind, North Vietnam would eventually give up the fight. That sounded hopeful, but Gene also thought of all the death. He wondered whether anyone he knew had died in Vietnam.

"Maybe the war will end before we get home," he told Elder Atkinson.

"My dad doesn't think so. In that letter I got yesterday, he said it would probably go on for years."

"Do you think we'll be drafted when we get back?"

"I don't know. So far, there's still a deferment for college, but I'm not sure how long that's going to last."

"I'm willing to serve my country," Gene said. "My dad did that, and in the long run, I think it made him a better man."

"Maybe so. But I want to get my education behind me, and I want to get married before I'm an old guy. If we go off for a couple of years to the service, that just puts college off again. Once a guy gets married, it's hard to finish up."

"Sure. But if Johnson runs from this fight, the Communists will push all the harder, somewhere else. Sometimes you have to stand up for things, whether it's convenient or not. Look what our parents' generation did."

"But this doesn't seem quite the same to me. I don't even know where Vietnam is."

Gene knew what his companion meant, but he was still feeling the things the bishop had said. He couldn't always think of himself first. There were things that were right to do, and Vietnam was one of them. If he was called to do his part, he had to be ready to sacrifice.

Still, it was all very hard to think about: war, life back in Utah, college. It was all from a time he hardly remembered. Nothing back home sounded the same anymore. He had gotten a letter from Marsha for Christmas, almost as though she wanted to reprise her impressive timing for her Dear John the year before. It had been a bare-bones kind of letter, with no news, no real content, but it had been a strange choice for her, to wait so long and then write a neutral little Christmas greeting. Gene had struggled with that for a couple of days, but the fact was, he no longer remembered Marsha, wasn't sure that he knew what he had seen in her.

What he did remember was the way she had always questioned his motives—the same way Bishop Knecht had tonight. Maybe Marsha had been right about him all along. He was trying to do his mission the right way, and he certainly did work hard, but time and again, his experience in Germany had been a sort of magic mirror to him, showing him who he really was. He knocked himself out each week to get his hours in, and even though he wasn't as strict at counting as Elder Russon had been, he certainly didn't stretch the count as much as he suspected a lot of missionaries did. He also tried, almost desperately, not to think about gaining positions of leadership. Lately, he had even told himself he was doing well, starting to get his head where it needed to be, but the bishop had seen right through him.

Before bed that night, Elder Atkinson said the prayer. He prayed for Brother and Sister Müller, and he did it simply. He seemed to believe that all this was in the hands of God and in the choice of the Müllers, that his own ego had nothing to do with the matter. Gene loved him for that, was glad to think better of him than he usually did. When he said his own prayers, he tried to do the same thing. He tried to think only what the Müllers would lose if they left the Church. But he wondered why he always had to work so hard to forget himself.

# Chapter 9

It was almost one in the morning before Kathy got her suitcase ready to close. She knew she was probably too excited to sleep, but she had to get a little rest before she caught the early bus. Since her first week at Smith College in September, hardly an hour had passed without her imagining this day when she would return home for Christmas break. She wasn't as homesick now as she had been the first month or two, but she had never stopped longing for her family, her comfortable room, her mountains. She hadn't really found a circle of friends she was entirely comfortable with. She liked Janet more than she had thought she might—or at least she did some days—but Janet was actually closer to Trisha, and Kathy spent a lot of time away from the house.

Kathy always wondered whether she was the one who excluded herself from other girls in the house, especially the three who were around her the most: Janet, Trisha, and Becky. Becky was Jewish, so it wasn't as though the others shared a religion, but Kathy's Mormonism seemed a deeper wedge. It wasn't that the girls discussed religion—they didn't—but Kathy found herself holding back, unable to express her honest feelings about a lot of things that seemed obvious not only to those three but to all the girls around the house. The girls spent a lot of time in the living room downstairs, and they lingered at the dinner table, served family style each night. Everyone talked constantly, loved to talk, and some were *very* smart, very up on issues of the day. God was a concept for them, a word like "nature," but Kathy knew no one who would have thought of kneeling down at night to pray. So Kathy didn't either—except when she was alone and knew that Janet wouldn't come crashing through the door. She lay in bed, instead, and said her prayers silently, but she felt the strangeness of that and wondered what the others would think if they knew.

It wasn't that Kathy was the conservative in the house. She was the one attending SDS meetings and helping to distribute leaflets at the student center. No other girl in Baldwin House would have been seen with the "radical crowd." Still, most were liberal enough to grant Kathy a certain respect for her political commitment, and when she argued about the war, about "current issues," she always held her own. Her separation had more to do with real-life choices. Almost all the girls were good students, motivated, eager to do exciting things with their lives, but they were also intent on having a good time. Kathy could hardly believe how much drinking went on, and how accepted it was to drink heavily on the weekends. Many of the girls seemed spoiled, used to having anything they wanted. Their interest in social justice was theoretical—all talk, it seemed to Kathy. She was too busy trying to "make a difference" to sit around and chat or play cards, or to worry about dating. Not many girls talked openly about sleeping with the boys they were dating, but it was understood, always implied by the racy comments they would make.

Tonight, with the break about to begin, Janet and Trisha had been going wild. Part of it was probably the excitement of getting away from the grind of school. The other inducement was certainly the wine they had drunk at a farewell Christmas party downstairs. Janet was not a great singer, but she always thought she was after she had had something to drink. Tonight she had been doing her James Brown imitation, belting out "I Feel Good" over and over.

Meanwhile, in a mellow voice, and a more accurate one, Trisha kept crossing the hall to wail the Byrds' song "Turn, Turn, Turn."

Kathy had finally put on a Simon and Garfunkel record, just hoping that "The Sound of Silence" would discourage Janet and Trisha from their own attempts, but now they were both joining in, and the combination wasn't pretty.

Janet had also been smoking nonstop—something she usually held to a minimum in their room. Kathy hated the smell and what it was doing to her clothes, but she never fussed about it. Janet usually kept her promise and blew her smoke out the window or went down to the porch where most girls smoked. Tonight, however, she was obviously out of control. "Hey, Kathy," she was saying now, much more loudly than necessary, "What time is your bus in the morning?"

"Six-twenty."

"You've got to be kidding."

"If I don't leave that early, I can't get home tomorrow."

"So are you going to bed right away?"

"Yeah, I hope so." She smiled. "But I doubt I'll sleep."

She meant that she was too excited, but Janet said, "No, I'll be quiet. Honest. No more singing. Although I do feel good." She suddenly yelped, James Brown style, and sang the line one more time, over the top of Simon and Garfunkel.

"You're fine," Kathy said. "I'll sleep on the bus in the morning, and on the airplane." The truth was, Kathy was never able to sleep sitting up. She knew she would be wiped out by the time she reached Utah.

"Trisha and Becky are coming over. We're going to exchange our presents. We'd better do that now. Then you can get to bed."

Janet left and came back with the other two, who were laughing hard about something Kathy hadn't heard. Trisha and Becky were each carrying a wrapped gift. Kathy got her own out, from her closet, as did Janet, but Janet had to apologize. "Hey, I didn't wrap this yet, but I'm not going to do it now, just in time for Becky to tear the paper back off." She hauled out the gift in a shopping bag, and then everyone sat on the floor and leaned against the beds. At least the floor was covered with a pretty Persian rug now—one that Janet had picked out and paid way too much for. Kathy had paid her half and had felt the pinch ever since.

Becky had also shared in the wine, but she looked dragged out, tired, not full of silliness like the other two. Janet was wearing cutoff jeans and a Smith College sweatshirt, no shoes, but Trisha still had on the pretty cranberry-colored dress she had worn to the party. The girls had decided a couple of weeks back to draw names, since they were stressed about the money they had available for Christmas. Kathy and Becky were on rather strict budgets. Janet and Trisha spent more than they received every month, then called home to beg for more, but they were both getting warnings from their parents that enough was enough.

Kathy had bought Trisha a Barbra Streisand album. It wasn't a very imaginative gift, she thought, but Trisha seemed pleased when she opened it. Janet put it on the record player immediately and sang along, filling up the room with an intentionally nasal version of "People."

Janet had bought Becky a set of hot curlers, which was a bit of a joke since Janet had borrowed Becky's and somehow managed to burn out the heating unit. But Becky's gift was even funnier, since she had bought the same thing for Janet.

When Trisha handed her gift to Kathy, she said, "I hope this isn't stupid."

"What is it, a training bra?" Janet asked, and the girls all laughed—Janet so hard that she had to wipe tears from her face. Kathy's flat-chestedness had been the subject of plenty of teasing all fall.

When Kathy opened the package, what she actually found was a book. It was Theodore White's *The Making of the President, 1964*. She was ready to tell Trisha thanks, that she had wanted to read the book, but by then Janet was already saying, "Oh, yawn."

"No," Kathy said. "It'll be fascinating. I almost bought this when it first came out, but I didn't think I had time to read it. Now, I'll read it on the airplane."

"You did say you wanted to sleep," Janet said. "The book should help."

"Shut up," Trisha told her. She grabbed a little pillow from Kathy's bed and threw it at Janet, who put up her hands and knocked it down, but for once in her life she didn't toss it back.

There was quiet for a moment, except for Streisand. "People . . . people who need people . . ." Then Trisha said, "Kathy, you're just so hard to buy for. The only thing I know you love is books—and you're interested in politics. So I thought that might be the right thing."

"Am I that weird?" Kathy asked. "Is that what you all think of me?"

"Hey, we all like to read," Becky said. "We're *Smithies*."

"That's right. I like to read D. H. Lawrence novels," Janet said. "All the dirty parts."

"But it's not weird to be interested in politics, is it?" Kathy asked. "A lot of the girls in the house talk about that kind of stuff."

"It's a yawn to me," Janet said.

Becky had been sitting with her legs folded under her, but she slid them out straight now. "There's nothing weird about *politics*. But you have to admit, some of the people you hang out with are teetering on the edge of *strange*."

Kathy knew what Becky meant. Most of the girls in SDS had read Betty Friedan, who, in *The Feminine Mystique*, had asked women why they wanted to look like Barbie dolls. A lot of them were now going around in hiking boots and men's shirts. The guys in SDS were growing their hair over their ears, like the Beatles, and wearing faded jeans. The truth was, Kathy didn't like that look, but she didn't say that. "People in SDS don't want to wear some middle-class 'uniform,'" she said. "They don't spend their money on clothes."

"Don't give me that," Janet said. "I think some of those guys buy new jeans, pay ten dollars for them, and then wash them a dozen times before they wear them."

"Yeah, and rip holes in the knees," Trisha added. "Tell me that's not a uniform."

Kathy knew there was something to that, but she admired her SDS friends more than she did these three girls. "Have you ever heard Robby Freedman give a speech?" Kathy asked.

No one responded. No one even looked at her.

"He's *powerful.* You ought to listen to him sometime. I don't care how he dresses. It's his ideas I care about."

"I'll tell you what I like about him," Janet said. "It's the way he looks in those tight jeans he wears. Now that's something I can get excited about."

Kathy decided it was time to give up. It was late, and Janet wasn't ever going to listen to Kathy's opinions, not seriously. "Well . . . I've got to get to bed," she said.

"You know you like his body and not just his mind," Janet said.

"He's not bad-looking," Kathy said.

Janet laughed. And then Trisha said, "Kathy, you can't have it both ways forever. You're going to have to choose."

"Choose what?"

"You don't drink, don't smoke, don't go to bed with the boys. And that's fine. But the people you hang out with don't think that way."

"They don't care about that. They're just happy to have my support when it comes to the work we're trying to do."

All three girls laughed. "Don't give me that," Janet said. "Robby Freedman may want your heart, but he wants your body, too."

"Not *my* body," Kathy said, and she tried to laugh. "Who wants a stick?"

Janet laughed, but she also uttered an expletive that would have shocked Kathy a few months before. She hadn't even heard boys in Utah speak the way some of the girls did here, and worst of all were her SDS friends. They used the one word she found most repulsive as though it were a noun, verb, and every form of modifier. She saw no reason why they felt they had to do that, but she had heard so much of it that she didn't wince the way she had at first.

"Kathy," Janet said, "you know so little about yourself, you shock me sometimes. Don't you know how sexy you are—with those long, long legs?"

Kathy hadn't noticed any guys falling into her path.

"You put off this aura," Becky said. "You're like a child, with that innocent face of yours, and yet you have this distant, sophisticated style. You're a mystery, and that's *intriguing* to guys. They look at me and I'm just this shrimpy little thing—like someone's little sister."

Aunt LaRue had told Kathy something similar once, but Kathy had never bought it. She had thought her aunt was merely trying to make her feel better. Kathy hadn't found time to hang out with LaRue as much as she had expected to that fall, but they went to church together every week, in Amherst, and they usually got together every other week or so, just to have dinner or chat for a while. LaRue was less than happy about Kathy's involvement with SDS, however. She supported some of the causes SDS fought for, but she thought that school should come first, and she had had some bad experiences with the radicals on campus. She found too much anti-intellectualism in their attitudes. She kept warning Kathy to be careful about what she was being drawn into.

The fact was, Kathy had thought she would get away to college and "find herself," but at this point, she was more confused than ever. She didn't really fit with anyone, not even LaRue. She knew that some of her "movement" friends smoked marijuana, and she kept hearing talk of LSD. She had heard some of them refer to Timothy Leary's "research"—his idea that certain drugs could open a person's mind and expand awareness. Leary had been fired from Harvard, arrested, released, and then arrested again—all for his use and distribution of LSD—but he was still seen as a kind of hero among some of her friends. That was hard for Kathy to imagine; drugs frightened her. Still, she saw the hypocrisy in people who used alcohol regularly and then looked down on those who used drugs. It was all part of the same kind of behavior, as far as Kathy was concerned.

"By the time you graduate from this place, Kathy," Janet said, "I suspect you'll either be smoking dope, wearing tie-dyed shirts, and sleeping with Robby Freedman, or you'll be more like us—drinking on weekends and not afraid to have some fun. There's no way you can stay the way you are—this sweet little Utah girl who thinks she's also a radical."

"I don't think that's what will happen," Trisha said. "I think she'll run away. She'll go back to Utah, marry that cute Marshall guy, and start popping out babies—just like all Mormons do."

Kathy didn't say anything, didn't choose to argue. But she wondered. She didn't see herself in any of those images, but she had the feeling that her friends had a point. She was probably going to change. It was hard to walk so many delicate lines and keep her balance.

The next day was arduous. Kathy had no trouble getting up, since she had never really reached a state of deep sleep, but the bus ride was agonizing. She tried to read the Theodore White book, and she did find it interesting, but her eyelids wouldn't stay open. Still, when she tried to sleep, nothing happened. The flight was a little better, as she gradually caught a second wind, but by the time she landed in Salt Lake and got to her feet, her knees ached and her legs felt weak. It was her excitement that carried her off the plane and into the terminal. The whole family was waiting, and there were a few minutes when she felt as though she had arrived in the celestial kingdom. Douglas clung to her as though he would never let go, and Wayne, who was usually cool about such things, dropped all pretense and hugged Kathy as he never had in his life. "I've missed you, Sis," he said. All the while, little Shauna had hold of Kathy's legs, and Glenda was reaching around her waist, from behind.

Eventually Kathy hugged Wally and Lorraine, told them how much she loved them, and then they all began to walk toward the luggage area. Kathy felt more at home than she ever had in her life, and the idea crossed her mind that maybe she *should* stay here—if not now, at the end of the school year. She had gotten away and experienced something new;

maybe now she could be happy at the U. Marshall would probably be leaving on his mission by then, but he would return there, and even though he had only written twice, he did seem eager to see her during the break. So at least he hadn't forgotten her entirely—not yet, anyway.

Dad had a new car, a pretty blue-green and white Olds 98. He drove Ramblers to his dealership, but he always kept a bigger, grander car around. Everyone piled in, with Kathy in the backseat with Douglas and Wayne, and the two little girls up front with Wally and Lorraine. Douglas was still clinging to Kathy. "Please don't go away again," he told her. Kathy held him close. She had missed Douglas more than anyone else.

"Do you think you've changed at all?" Dad asked. "I can't see any sign of it yet. Except your hair."

She had worn one of the outfits she had taken with her, and so she must have looked much the same, but she had let her hair grow all fall, and it was certainly longer, straighter, than they had all been used to. "I don't think I've changed much," Kathy said, but she wasn't sure about that. She hadn't felt quite like the same person lately.

But Mom asked, "Where did you get the sandals?"

"At a little shop in Northampton. They're really comfortable for traveling."

It was the right answer, but she also knew the sandals were part of the "look" of her radical friends, and her mother had probably made the connection. Still, it was a strange thing to mention, almost as though Mom were watching for something—some sign of "trouble." Or maybe not. Maybe Mom just thought they were cute sandals. Kathy wasn't going to fight with anyone this trip home. She just wanted to bask in all she was feeling, have a great time with her siblings, play with Douglas, and see her friends.

When they reached Country Club Drive, Kathy loved seeing all the familiar surroundings, and then she liked walking into her house. Nothing had changed there, and everything she looked at seemed a symbol of who she had always been. In her room she picked up a picture of herself on her baptism day. In the photo, she was standing with her dad, both of them dressed in white, her hair not yet wet. Her dad was holding her tight against his side, and she, lanky even then, had wrapped one arm around her dad's waist. It seemed to her that life had been much simpler then; she longed for more of that feeling now.

She started to unpack but lost interest quickly, set her suitcase on the floor, and told herself she would do all that in the morning. She walked out to the TV room and watched the ten o'clock news with her parents. She liked seeing the familiar faces: Dick Nourse, Paul James, and funny Bob Welti doing the weather—and all in color now. The news stories were mostly local, and not of great importance to her, but Nourse did say that President Johnson was considering a Christmas pause in the bombing over North Vietnam, with the hope that the action might lead to a peace treaty. Wally didn't say a word, and neither did Kathy, both probably aware that this was not something they should discuss, but then Nourse read a story about *Gemini 7* nearing the end of a fourteen-day mission. *Gemini 6* had also gone into orbit during the mission and had maneuvered itself into a position close to the other spacecraft, where the two had remained for a few hours.

"I think we're going to make it to the moon," Dad said. "This is a big step toward that."

Kathy reacted almost automatically. "I don't know whether that makes a lot of sense, Dad. We have so many problems down here, what's the point of spending all that money to get to the moon?"

"We can't ever stop exploring," Mom said. "I think that's something *you* told me, when Kennedy first announced he wanted to go to the moon."

That was true. Kathy had always believed in the space program, loved the idea of it. But she had heard Robby Freedman give an intense speech about the way poverty was allowed to endure in spite of Johnson's promises, while the government spent its money on bombing Vietnam and sending men on pointless expeditions, all to get to the moon ahead of Russia. She had changed her mind that night. "I just think we need to deal with the most important things first," Kathy said. "Going to the moon is a cute stunt, but what does it really accomplish?"

No one answered, and Kathy hated the silence. She told herself that she wouldn't start again. She wasn't going to do this.

Dad waited until a commercial came on, and when he spoke, she could hear that he was being careful. "I know where you're coming from, Kathy. I do sometimes wonder whether the space program isn't mostly about symbolism. But those kinds of symbols can be important. Our country needs something to believe in with so much going on that's negative."

Kathy said, with equal care, "Maybe so. But it all seems a little too calculated—like Johnson wants to keep us looking to the skies instead of thinking about the problems we have in our cities."

Dad looked pleased—maybe just to hear his daughter criticize a Democrat. They were sitting on opposite ends of the couch, but now he turned toward her. "That might be true, Kathy, but I can't believe how much the government wants to take over everything these days. I think Johnson wants to get socialized medicine started with this Medicare plan, and he's trying to get the federal government involved in education. It's just a lot more federal red tape, if you ask me. Then he pushes through this so-called anti-pollution bill. Now the government wants to tell the automobile manufacturers what kind of engines they can put in their cars. That probably sounds like a good idea, but it's going to cause all kinds of trouble. Cars are going to jump way up in price. It won't be long until a regular guy won't be able to afford one."

Kathy couldn't believe it. "Dad," she said, "we can't let cars continue to spew out all the junk that's going into our air. Look at what's happened to Los Angeles. The whole country is going to be like that before long.

Someone has to stop it. You know the auto companies aren't going to do anything until they're forced."

"You'd be surprised. Carmakers sell the people what they want. If customers want their air cleaned up, that's what they'll demand. That always works better than having the government try to decide what's best."

"Oh, come on, Dad. People don't care. They just want their big gas-guzzling cars, and they'll keep right on breathing air so full of garbage that it kills them. Look how many people still smoke, no matter what the surgeon general tells them."

Kathy knew what she had done even before her father looked away from her. Her old impatience had returned, her tone of superiority. She thought of apologizing and trying to start over, but it was too late. She knew what her parents were thinking: she's still the same old, know-it-all Kathy. But she really wasn't. She wasn't the little girl she had been. She had gained so much perspective in the past few months. She waited until the sports news came on, and then she said, "Boy, am I tired. I'm going to bed." She got up and walked to her father, kissed him on the cheek, and said, "I love you, Dad."

"I love you, too," he said, but the damage had been done. She heard it in his voice. And when she kissed her mother, she saw the disappointment in her eyes. She had longed so much to be home, but she hadn't even made it through the first hour without the old tension returning. Kathy told herself she was just tired; she would do better from this point on.

Marshall called the next morning—which pleased Kathy immensely. He seemed genuinely eager to get together, so they made a date for that night. She was even more pleased when she saw him. She had forgotten his shy way of looking at her. The picture she had of him at school was cute, but the photo made him look like a model, not like the gentle guy he was. What she felt again was his goodness; he was a boy without a lot of hang-ups or drums to beat. It was as though he had taken a look at life and told himself, "I like it. It's good enough for me." She knew she needed more of that feeling herself.

"I just thought we'd get something to eat," Marshall said as they walked to his car. "So we can talk."

"No trip to Alta?"

"Hey, they've got snow up there this time of year. My old car wouldn't make it."

"I thought you were going to start skiing."

"Actually, I did. Or at least I've gone a couple of times." He smiled. "But I have to catch a ride when I go."

"Plenty of girls at the U are probably happy to take you along with them."

"Yup. That's what I love. Ski bunnies. I only started skiing so I'd have an excuse to hang around the lodge and check out the good-looking girls in their tight ski pants."

He may have been making fun of the idea, but she wasn't so sure it wasn't true. He had come to Utah without connections, and during the summer the two of them had been each other's little world, but now he had probably found lots of other girls to take out. It made her wonder, once again, whether she had made a mistake in going east.

But he gave her all his attention, asked her everything about Smith, about herself. When she asked him about his life, he told her that he had been shopping around for a major. "Nothing bowls me over as the thing I want to do all my life. I think I'd be some sort of scientist if I were smart enough, or maybe a musician if I could actually make a living at it."

"I wouldn't think about making a living first," Kathy said. "I'd follow a passion and see where it leads."

They were eating at the Hot Shoppes, downtown. It wasn't as fancy as the Paprika, but Kathy had ordered fish and chips, with lots of lemon and tartar sauce, and liked how relaxed she felt with Marshall, who was eating a big, dripping hamburger with lettuce and tomato. He ordered a hot-fudge sundae for dessert, with two spoons, but Kathy couldn't bring herself to eat much of it. She was already too full.

Marshall was concentrating, making sure he got a good mix of ice cream and chocolate, spooning it in and then letting it melt in his mouth as though it was, after all, the main point of what he was doing at that moment. He looked up, however, in response to Kathy's advice, and said, "Passion doesn't pay the rent. At least my passion wouldn't."

"Oh, darn. I was hoping you were *very* passionate by now."

It was the most flirtatious thing she had said in her life—maybe the *only* flirtatious thing she had ever said. She felt herself reddening. But he only smiled a little and didn't seem to feel a need for a comeback. She loved him for that, and maybe hated him, too. She fumbled to think of something to say and mentioned school, which led them back to more talk about Smith and about Kathy. And after a time, maybe to make a gentle point, she told him about Robby Freedman and the Students for a Democratic Society.

"What exactly does this SDS group do?" he asked.

"It started in Michigan. A guy named Tom Hayden was probably the main thinker in the group. He helped write a declaration of their purposes that they called the Fort Huron Statement. It's about the materialism and apathy in America. The only problem is, there's hardly time to talk about any of those basics anymore. Vietnam has taken over everything. There's no way this nation can create a decent, fair society until we get ourselves out of that mess. That war is just so *deeply* wrong."

"What do you mean 'wrong'?"

Kathy took a breath. She never knew whether Marshall was innocent or crafty. "It's hard to know where to start," she said. "Everything about this war is evil. All this talk about fighting for freedom is a joke. We're fighting to take freedom away from the Vietnamese people. We're an immense power attempting to thrust our will upon a tiny country."

"Won't the people be better off if we do?"

"Do you really believe that?"

"I don't know. I'm asking what you think." He spooned some more ice cream into his mouth.

"But what do *you* think?"

"A lot of people are saying that if we don't stop the Communists in Vietnam, all of Southeast Asia will fall to them."

"That's ludicrous, Marshall. How can you listen to that kind of stuff? Communism isn't one big system. We ought to talk about 'communisms.' If we left the countries in that part of the world alone, they would be no threat to us—or anyone else."

"But isn't that just the opposite of what you said before? It sounds to me like we're *not* doing this for ourselves. Aren't we trying to help a little country protect itself? Don't we have to show that kind of leadership in the world if democracy is going to survive?"

"Marshall, I can't believe you're naive enough to believe that. The people we're supposedly protecting have no commitment at all to this fight. General Westmoreland keeps talking about 'winning the hearts and minds of the people.' Why do you think we have to win them over? It's because their hearts are with Ho Chi Minh."

"Maybe the peasants don't even understand what—"

"See! You say we're fighting for democracy, but you don't believe in it yourself. We have to tell those stupid peasants what's good for them. Right?"

Marshall looked at the table for a long time. Kathy held her breath. What had she done now? She could hear the voices in the room, the clinking of plates, utensils, a man calling to a waitress, 'Miss?'—but time seemed to hold. Marshall had surely had enough of her now.

"At some point, I'll probably have to go over there," he finally said, in a soft voice. "I'd like to believe that my country wouldn't be dropping bombs on people without a good reason."

She tried to change her voice, to show that she cared about him. "You don't *have* to go. Guys are starting to say no. Did you read about all the demonstrations in October? Those were sponsored by SDS. We had a hundred thousand people out to those marches, and a lot of them were guys who are planning to file for conscientious objector status or just refuse to go. Marshall, this war is immoral. If you don't want our country to do something that's wrong, take your stand. Don't go."

"Were you there for the march?"

"I couldn't go. A lot of our people went down to New York, and I wanted to go—but I just couldn't." He nodded, and she felt the embarrassment. She had been in college only a month or so when the demonstrations had taken place. She had still been uneasy about spending the money and taking the time away from school. But now she wished she had gone. She knew she shouldn't talk so tough if she wasn't willing to do her own part. "If we can keep building on our movement," she said, "the day will come when Johnson won't be able to fight his war. There just won't be enough men willing to go."

Marshall shrugged. "I can't refuse," he said. "If I get drafted, I'll go. What I worry about right now is the quota on missionary deferments that the Church agreed to. Only two guys can go out each year, from any one ward."

"Is that going to be a problem?"

"It might delay me some. But the stake can adjust and send three from one ward and one from another—that kind of thing. My bishop says he's pretty sure he can work it out so I can go next summer, or at least by fall."

Kathy hadn't thought about things like that for such a long time. It was right of him to worry about his mission, but why was he buying into this line about stopping Communism?

"Marshall, do you really believe in this war?"

"I'm not sure. But I believe in my country."

"That's what all those Nazis said who put Jews into the gas chambers."

Marshall took a long look at her, but he didn't say anything.

It was a very bad moment, and one Kathy regretted. She doubted she would ever see him again. But he let the subject go, and he treated her well. He even talked quite pleasantly after that, and at the door, he kissed her—just not with any passion. She saw him a couple more times while she was home, and what evolved was a quiet standoff, with little talk of things that mattered to Kathy and only a little kiss each time he said good-bye.

It was a painful time for Kathy. She had longed to see him all fall, had hoped for so much more. The night before she was to return to college, she found herself trying to find a way to apologize, to bring something back. But Marshall only said, "You're good for me, Kathy. I like to think; I just don't like to make my mind up. You force me to decide what I believe."

She didn't want to *force* him. She wanted to love him. And she wondered what was wrong with her that she couldn't just do that. Even more important, she was certain he could never love her, and she felt the loss. He was such a good person. He had taken Douglas fishing twice already and had promised to take him again in the spring. It touched her so much to think about that. Why couldn't she accept what she liked about him and let the rest go?

When she boarded the airplane the next morning, the best thing, she realized, was that she wouldn't be so homesick now. She had less to miss in Utah than she thought she had. Christmas day at Grandma and Grandpa Thomas's had been an ordeal for her. She had spent the entire time avoiding arguments and listening to amazingly simplistic comments from her uncles and aunts and cousins—and especially her grandpa. They were all such good people, and she loved them all. She just couldn't talk to them.

# Chapter 10

"Come with me. There's someone I want you to meet," Kent Wade said. Diane was meeting lots of cool people. She would be enrolling at BYU in the fall, and it had to be good to make a few acquaintances before she arrived. She and Kent were at the Junior Prom, and Diane was thrilled. The theme of the prom was "*Enchanté,*" and everything really was enchanting. She and Kent had started the evening by attending a Four Preps concert. Diane could hardly believe that she had actually seen the group in person, had heard them sing "26 Miles." And now she and Kent had been dancing in the Wilkinson Center ballroom, with a silver ball sending off soft, whirling reflections in the hazy light. The boys were all dressed in tuxedos or dinner jackets, the girls in elegant long dresses, and the Scotsmen, a genuine "big band," was playing dreamy music. It was so grown-up, nothing at all like high school.

Since Kent had moved to Utah, Diane had seen him several times. He had driven to Ogden twice in the fall, once just before his return to Falls Church for Christmas, and then, in the winter, on three different occasions, he had met her in Salt Lake and they had gone skiing. He had also called her once a week or so, and they had talked way too long, considering what the long-distance bill must have been, but he didn't seem to worry about that. Now he had asked her to the prom, just as Diane had hoped he would.

Diane could hardly believe how different Kent was from other guys she knew. He had a quality of self-assurance about him that Diane loved, yet there was something sweet in the deference he paid to her. He seemed a bit in awe, always mentioning how pretty she was, seeming to feel lucky just to be with her.

Kent loved BYU, and Diane could see why. She felt how different it was from other places. She had gone to a dance at Weber State earlier that year with a guy even older than Kent. That had been nice, but it hadn't been as grand, and something about the students here appealed to her. They weren't all *that* different, but there was a wholesomeness—even though she hated that word—that made for an atmosphere she hadn't experienced before. No one said much about the Church, as such, but Diane liked the spirit she felt. Every guy she met had been on a mission or was planning to go—that became obvious—and even some of the girls talked of going.

The students also talked about their wards: one guy mentioned that he had met his date by being assigned to home teach her. He joked about counting the evening as a home-teaching "visit." But that was all just part of the world they lived in. Church and school were the same thing, and Kent said that's what he liked. Diane liked the idea too. At Weber or the U, or at Utah State, the clubs and fraternities seemed to dominate life, and there was way too much drinking.

Kent had been leading her, her hand in the crook of his arm, but now, to get through the crowd, he took her hand and tugged her along behind him. "Gib!" he called out.

A big guy who looked as though he had never worn a tux before, and didn't want to now, turned away from his partner and looked toward Kent. "Hey," he said. "Kent."

"I want you to meet someone," Kent said. "This is Diane Hammond, from up in Ogden."

"Holy cow!" Gib said. "If I were you, I wouldn't let the guys around here even *see* this girl. They'll all be after her."

Diane liked that. She let her smile shine. What she knew was that Gib was right about how she looked. She had bought a pink dress with a lace overlay, and she knew exactly how good her blonde hair looked, cascading down her back over all that pink. Diane had paid to have heels dyed the same color as the dress, and she was wearing white gloves and carrying a little silver case to hold her lipstick and mascara. Kent had picked her up in the afternoon and driven her to Provo, and then she had gotten ready at Kent's sister's apartment, taking over two hours on her hair and makeup. The plan was for her to stay overnight and go to church with Kent in the morning, and then he would drive her back on Sunday afternoon.

Everything had been perfect so far. She had worn a cute lavender pants outfit on the way down, and they had stopped at Bratton's Grotto on the way through Salt Lake City. Kent had suggested lobster, which Diane had never eaten. It was the most expensive item on the menu, and Diane had always been told to be careful about that, but she had also learned to take the boy's lead, to select something in a price range he chose. Kent had made it easy this time. "I want you to try the lobster," he had said. "It's great. They fly it in, fresh every day."

Kent's sister, Sandy, had turned out to be lots of fun, and she had helped Diane get her hair just right. When Diane had finished her makeup and stepped before a full-length mirror, Sandy had gasped. "Diane, don't come near me at the dance," she said. "The comparison is sickening. You're the prettiest girl I've ever seen." And then she had planted an idea: "You'll be homecoming queen if you come to BYU. Or Belle of the Y."

It was a marvelous thought. Diane was going to enroll at the Y; she had made up her mind about that already. Maybe she really could win one of the queen contests.

Kent was still laughing at Gib, who hadn't raised his jaw since he first looked at Diane. "I think you're right," Kent said. "I'm not going to bring her down here again. While I'm on my mission, I think I'll hide her away in a cave somewhere."

Gib's date finally said, "Hi, I'm Lauren James. Gib is breathing a little too hard to introduce me right now."

But Gib wrapped a big arm around Lauren. "Not true. Not true," he said. "What I meant was, next to Lauren, you're the prettiest girl here."

Lauren was rather a big girl, nearly as tall as Gib in her heels. She was wearing a powder-blue satin dress, with a scooped neckline, almost a little too low for BYU standards. But the outfit seemed just a little too dainty for such a strong-looking woman. Still, she was pretty, with brown hair, teased rather high.

"Gib plays football," Kent said. "He's on the freshman team this year, but when he gets back from his mission, he's going to be one of the starters on the offensive line."

"Wow! That's great," Diane said, but she felt as though she had sounded a little too high-schoolish. She really didn't want anyone to know how young she was.

"Diane's uncle is Alex Thomas, the congressman," Kent said. "She took a trip out to see her cousins, and I met her out there in Falls Church."

"And where did you say you live?" Lauren asked.

But it was Kent who answered. "Ogden. Both her parents are professors at Weber State." Diane wasn't exactly sure that her mother was considered a "professor," since she only taught part-time, but it did sound important. Diane was just happy that she didn't have to trot her mother out to say something that would humiliate her.

"So where do you go to school? Weber?" Lauren asked.

"No. I'm coming down here next year."

Lauren smiled. "I was afraid of that."

"Well, I want to get some more dancing in," Kent said. "I think you can understand why."

Kent took Diane in his arms and whisked her away. He was a good dancer. He held her tightly to him, danced smoothly, strongly, with nothing timid in his motion. "We've had this big thing down here all year," he told Diane. "President Wilkinson doesn't like all these 'fad dances.' You know, the Monkey and the Frug, stuff like that. Almost every day there's a letter to the editor in the *Daily Universe*, saying we shouldn't be doing them—either that, or that they don't hurt anything." He looked down at her and laughed. "The only thing I know is that when I dance with you, I want to hold you in my arms."

Diane knew all the latest dances—had never thought much about it. But she had to wonder, maybe they weren't the right thing for Mormon kids to be doing.

But now Kent was letting go of her again, so he could introduce her to another friend—as he had been doing all evening. They all seemed to be fun people, though—most of them seeming rather prominent on campus. Diane thought Kent made a little too much of a point of her being "the congressman's niece," and yet, she rather liked the reflected light. High-school kids didn't care much about whose uncle was in Congress, but these students were clearly impressed. And almost everyone commented on how beautiful she looked.

When the prom was nearing its end, Kent found Gib and a couple of other friends, and the four couples drove in two cars to a place called the Wooden Spoon. They ate banana splits and laughed at all the funny things the guys, especially Gib, kept coming up with. Provo wasn't much of a town, really, not as big as Ogden, and not with as many nice stores—except for Clark's—but BYU, in a way, *was* Provo. Almost everything was on campus, and the students lived in dorms or nearby apartments. Quite a few of the students were not from Utah. She was sure that Weber State would not be nearly as fun, with most of the kids living at home and merely commuting to campus each day.

Eventually Kent drove Lauren to her apartment, where Gib walked her to the door and took a couple of minutes before he returned. Then Kent took Gib to his place in Helaman Halls and drove Diane to his sister's apartment. "I know it's late, but why don't you change, and we'll just go for a walk on campus. It's such a pretty night."

That was perfect. Diane was way too excited to go to sleep—even though it was after one o'clock—and for the first time in her life she didn't have to report home by a certain hour. She liked Sandy, but she wasn't in any mood for girl talk. She wanted more time with Kent. She wanted him to kiss her. He had given her a little goodnight kiss on their second date, but after skiing, there had not been a good chance. Now she hoped for something a little more than a quick peck. She knew she was completely safe with him, that he wouldn't "try anything," the way Scott, her first boyfriend, had sometimes done. But she wanted him to hold her and kiss her, and frankly, she wanted him to say something about a future together, after his mission.

So Diane changed into a third outfit, even though she was embarrassed to let Kent see how many options she had brought with her. She just hadn't known what they would end up doing, and she had wanted to look good in any situation. What she wore now was much more casual: tan bermudas with Keds, a white button-down-collar shirt, and a brown cable-knit cardigan. She was glad to see that when he returned, he had also changed clothes. He was wearing Levi's and a BYU sweatshirt with a cougar across the front. She liked the fact that he knew the right details: his white socks and penny loafers, the oxford-cloth button-down under the sweatshirt. And he had definitely put on some fresh Elsha; she loved the smell of it. Lots of guys at the Y were still wearing crew cuts, but it wasn't the latest look, and Kent knew that too. He wore his hair quite short, parted, and merely combed over, with no little waves. Everything about him was *so* cool.

"Let's just walk over to campus," he said when she met him at the door. He reached for her hand.

The apartment was a couple of blocks south of campus. They walked hand in hand under the big sycamores and maples. Lots of cars were still moving about. It hardly seemed as late as it was. On the south edge of campus, they climbed the long stairs, and then they walked toward the Wilkinson Center. All along the way, they talked about Diane coming to BYU: what she might major in and where she might want to live. "I know most freshmen stay in the dorms," Diane told him, "but I don't think I want to do that. I wonder if I could maybe room with Sandy. I really like her."

But Kent told her, "I don't think you should. That's too much pressure. Every time you went out with some guy, you would wonder whether Sandy was sending me a report."

That sounded as though Kent was thinking of the future, maybe expecting her to wait for him, but he had never said that. The idea scared Diane a little, and at the same time she liked to think that he felt that way.

Eventually, Kent found a little stone bench, and the two sat down. The air was cool, but Diane was warm from the walk, and Kent sat close and put his arm around her. "I don't like to think of you down here next year," he said. "We've joked about it, but the truth is, guys are going to be hovering over you like vultures. You'll be going out every night."

"You mean you care about that?"

"You know I do."

"Actually, Kent, I have no idea how you feel about me. We haven't really seen each other all that many times."

"That's only because I couldn't get up to Ogden very often. I would have been with you all the time if you had been here. It's probably good you weren't. My grades would have gone down the drain."

"Maybe not. Maybe I would have been going out with all those other guys you keep talking about."

"No. I would have stood in front of your door and fought them off."

"What about next year? Are you going to go off and leave me to the wolves?"

"I don't want to. I ought to make Gib stay home and camp in your front yard. Or maybe I can hang a sign around your neck that says, 'Private Property. Hands Off.'"

She turned toward him, gave him a little punch in the ribs, and then looked up into his eyes. "So you think you own me, do you?"

"Oh, no. I didn't mean that." She had only been teasing, but she could tell that she had embarrassed him. "I really do think you should date. No one has a right to ask a girl to sit around and do nothing while she's in college."

Diane slid back a little. Light from atop a nearby pole was shining across Kent's face, so she could see him clearly. "Kent, I think we need to talk a little about this. You're giving me lots of hints, but you've never really told me what you think of me. Are we getting *serious?*"

"*I* am, Di. I've never been so serious. I'm scared to death that you'll get married while I'm gone. All I ask for every night, when I pray, is that you'll still be here when I get home, and you'll give me a chance—no matter how many super-cool guys have been dating you while I've been gone."

"Kent, I'm only seventeen. I'm not going to get married before you get back."

"You don't know that. I've seen lots of freshman girls drop out and marry some RM they meet the first year they're here. It happens all the time."

"I don't want to get married that young."

"That's what everyone says until they see that engagement ring."

Diane laughed. She touched Kent's face. "You really pray about me every night?"

"And every morning. I think of you all day long. I keep wondering how I could have met the most beautiful, perfect girl in the world. Sometimes I even think about dropping the whole idea of going on a mission, just so I won't lose my chance with you."

"You wouldn't do that though, would you?"

Kent shook his head. Then he looked down, taking hold of both her hands. "I shouldn't have even admitted to you that I think about things like that. I don't want you to know what a bad guy I really am."

"Kent, I could never think you're bad."

He looked into her eyes. "Diane, I really do have this burning testimony now. I didn't so much before I came out here, but at the Y, you can't help getting serious about the Church. I have a religion teacher who brings up this really interesting stuff. He makes you think about everything. My testimony's gone from about a three, on a scale of ten, to something like *eleven*. I don't have any doubts at all anymore."

"That's so cool, Kent. I've always wanted to marry someone who was just really faithful and could lift me higher—because I know I'm not as spiritual as I ought to be."

"If you come down here next year, you will be."

"I guess. But I need someone in my life who never lets me slip at all. That's one of the things I can feel in you—that you'll always be like that."

"Diane, does that mean you've been thinking about us being together in the future?"

She let her eyes drift away from his, thought she really shouldn't be too forward quite yet. "Kent, you're the neatest guy I've ever met. That's all I know. I guess we'll find out about the future as we go along."

"Oh, man. That's more than I thought you would ever say. I feel like I'm floating on a cloud right now. I really do." He bent forward.

Diane turned her head a little and waited, let her eyes go shut. His lips touched hers, and then his arms slipped around her. It was a long, lovely kiss, but it didn't feel lustful, the way Scott's kisses had. When he moved back from her, he said, "Diane, I'll never ask you to wait for me. That wouldn't be fair. But I am asking you to wait to get married. Wait for those two years, and keep some piece of me in your heart. Go ahead and compare everyone else, and let your heart decide. But give me a chance to be in the finals—you know what I mean? Don't pick the winner until I get back."

"I won't, Kent. I know I won't. Right now, I feel like you're filling up my whole heart, and there won't be room for another boy to get so much as his little toe in."

Diane was not entirely satisfied with the image, and she began to laugh at herself, but at the moment Kent's lips were coming her way again, and she didn't get her head turned in time. Their noses bumped and then slid on past, not as smoothly as she might have liked, but the kiss was just as good, just as long, and maybe a little less "BYU approved" than the first one.

---

The next morning Diane got herself out of bed by seven and worked on her hair and face again. Kent was coming to pick her up for nine o'clock Sunday School. After that, they would drive back to Ogden for Sunday dinner with the Hammonds, and then Kent would stay for sacrament meeting before this whole perfect weekend was over.

Diane had also brought a church outfit—with Sunday School, not sacrament meeting, in mind. She wore a simple dress, beige with a round neck, no collar, and a little brown belt. Her only adornment was a gold circle pin. She simplified her hair, too, letting it fall, without so much curl in it.

Maybe she only imagined it, but Diane had the feeling in the Sunday School class that several of the girls were "all eyes" when Kent came in. And the looks they gave her seemed somewhat less than a sister in the gospel might exchange. But then, maybe they were just tired. Everyone had been out late the night before.

The talk in the class was about the nature of the priesthood, according to the scriptures. The teacher was an intense, older-looking guy who had served his mission in Norway. He kept quoting someone named

Bingham: Bingham says this, and Bingham says that. Diane finally asked Kent, "Who's this Bingham?"

He whispered back to her, "Nephi Bingham. Haven't you heard of him?"

"No."

"Oh, man. You need to take a class from him when you get down here—if you can get in. He talks about stuff most people never even *think* about. It's just so deep, it blows you away."

Maybe so, but Diane couldn't figure out what the teacher was talking about. She had lost the whole idea somewhere along the way. But she was still watching those girls out of the corner of her eye—the ones that kept ogling Kent. She thought she heard the word "blonde" in their whispers. She wanted to turn around and say, "Yes, it's my natural color. Where did you buy that 'auburn' tint you're trying to pass off as the real thing?"

"This is so amazing," Kent whispered. "Bingham has got to be one of the smartest guys in the Church. It's like for the first time, I finally understand what the word *spirit* really means."

Diane had missed that somehow, but she was glad Kent got it all. He could maybe explain it to her someday, or even better, he could teach it to their kids. She couldn't think of anything neater than having a husband who could give really thoughtful family home evenings. Her own parents were smart, but family home evening, when it actually happened, was usually a bore. Her mom and dad thought it was interesting to raise a lot of questions no one could really answer, and then kick the idea back and forth between the two of them while Diane and Maggy had to wait the whole thing out and wonder what was on TV.

After church, Kent gave Diane time to pack her things, and she put her tan bermudas on again, with a red shirt, no sweater. She didn't want him to know that she had actually brought another pair of long pants. Besides, she had been tanning already this spring, and her legs looked great in shorts.

The drive back was the best part of the whole weekend for Diane. Kent was driving a Plymouth he had borrowed from his grandfather, with a big seat that allowed her to sit close to him. Everything had been said now. They really were girlfriend and boyfriend, and she had committed to "be there" when he got back from his mission. She had always thought it would be fun to wait for a missionary, to mark off the days on a special calendar, to write him every week, and to feel his spirit as he wrote back all the great things that were happening to him. She had heard there was a club at BYU, with all the members waiting for missionaries. That was going too far, she thought, but she did want to let people know about "her missionary."

They held hands most of the time as Kent drove, and they chatted affectionately, like "steadies." They listened to the radio and even sang along with certain tunes, but when the Righteous Brothers began "You're My Soul and Inspiration," Kent looked at Diane as though he had forgotten all about the highway. She thought she would dissolve, just ooze right into the seat covers. And then Kent gripped her hand tight and, as the Righteous Brothers continued to sing, said, "Diane, I need to say it. I love you."

He put his arm around her, and she snuggled closer to him. It was the most natural thing in the world to say, "I love you too, Kent."

He gave her shoulders a squeeze, held her for a long time, and when she glanced toward him, she saw that tears were running down his cheeks. "I've never said that to a girl before."

"I haven't either."

"To a girl?"

They both laughed, but he hugged her tighter and said, "I've never been this happy in my whole life."

"Me too."

Diane's only worry was that "technically" she probably had said it once before. She was pretty sure she had told Scott Laughlin that she loved him. But she really didn't think that counted, since she had been so young and all, and Kent would never know anyway.

That night, after sacrament meeting in Ogden, Kent stayed for a while, and the two sneaked off to the family room and kissed a little more. But then he had to go, and Diane felt the pain. She realized how hard it would be to see him leave for his mission. Her lovely weekend was over, and now she had to go back to high school for another couple of months and only see Kent once in a while. He promised to drive to Ogden as often as he could get the car, and she promised to find a way to get to Provo, if she possibly could, but when the semester ended, he would go home—and the next time she saw him, he would be on his way to the mission field.

Diane walked him to the car, kissed him good-bye, and then ran back to the house and on to her room. She lay on her bed and cried.

It was maybe ten minutes later that a knock came on the door. "Can I come in?" Bobbi was asking.

Diane didn't want this, but she called out, "Sure," and then she sat up.

Bobbi stepped through the door and then leaned backward against the door frame. "Oh, honey," she said, "you've been crying, haven't you?"

Diane nodded.

"Do you miss him already?"

She nodded, and the tears started again.

Mom walked over to her, sat down close, and put her arm around her shoulders. "I know that feeling." She laughed a little, which Diane couldn't understand. "After I met your dad, he went to sea, and I didn't know whether he would ever come back. How would you like to deal with that? Kent's going to be back here in a week or two. I could see that in his eyes."

"Do you like him, Mom?"

"He's a nice young man. He's just very young. A mission will be good for him."

What was that supposed to mean? He was the most mature guy Diane had ever known. Why was Mom always so condescending about everything?

"So what happened this weekend? You two seemed to go from 'dating' to 'love birds.' I could see it the minute you walked into the house this afternoon."

"It was all so *perfect*, Mom. I hardly know how to tell you."

"It's all that 'good spirit' down at the Y. How can a girl resist?"

Diane pulled away and stood up. "Mom, it's really *special* down there. Why are you always so sarcastic about it?"

"I'm sorry," Mom said, and she laughed. "Anyone who went to the U feels a certain responsibility to knock BYU once in while. It just goes with the territory."

"But Mom, you don't know what it's like. The kids down there really get serious about the Church. They take religion classes from these brilliant men, and—"

"Oh, yes. Nephi Bingham."

"Why do you say it like that?"

"Never mind. I'm sorry."

Diane had no idea what her mother was implying. Kent had been *changed* by his experience at BYU. It was too bad Mom had never gone there.

"Honey, I do think some of the religion professors start to take themselves a little too seriously, and they throw around a lot of philosophic language that actually complicates principles that don't need to be made *profound*. They're just simple and true."

Diane didn't know. She only knew that Mom could spoil the best things in her life, over and over.

"Honey, I think you'll love BYU. I'm glad you're going there next year. Just don't lose your balance. There's a thin line sometimes between righteousness and *self*-righteousness. And don't get *too* serious with anyone—including Kent—*too* soon. You need to graduate from college, not drop out after a year or two to get married the way so many girls down there do."

"I don't want to get married really young," Diane said.

"Famous last words," Bobbi said, and she laughed. She got up and walked to the door. "I just hope you'll stick to your guns on that," she said as she left the room.

Diane was furious. Mom had ruined everything. She had made Kent sound childish, and religion seem foolish. Maybe the best thing about going to the Y would be getting away from Mom.

# Chapter 11

Hans was leaving school on an April afternoon when he saw *Direktor* Knorr in the hallway. "Excuse me, Hans," the director said. "May I speak with you a moment?" He stepped to the side of the hall, as did Hans, and then he leaned close and whispered, "I had two *Stasi* agents here today, asking about you."

"Really? What did they want?" Hans *was* surprised, but mostly because so much time had passed and he had begun to think that the *Stasi* had forgotten him. Had they learned something new? Had the car finally been traced? Had someone else, besides the two who had been killed, known that he was involved?

"They wouldn't say what they wanted," Knorr said. "But they had lots of questions. I told them you were our best student. I assured them that you are loyal to your country. It's all true, isn't it?"

"Yes. Yes, of course." Students were walking by. Hans could see that all of them were watching as they passed. It wasn't the normal thing for the director to talk this way, whispering in the hallway.

"Hans, you can't let me down. I've vouched for you all along, kept you in school. Without me, you never would have been accepted to a university. If you're involved in anything that you shouldn't be, they will blame me."

"Don't worry. I'm not doing anything to get you in trouble."

"They were persistent, Hans. They kept asking all about you, your family, your former attempt to escape the country. They wanted to know whether you drive a car. I told them you don't. That's true, isn't it?"

"We have no car. When would I have a chance to drive?"

"That's what I told them. But why would they ask?"

"I don't know."

"These things don't happen by accident. There's some reason for it."

"*Herr Direktor*, I've done nothing wrong. I promise you that." But even as he said it, Hans knew that his definition of "wrong" was not the same as the one used by the *Stasi*.

The director glanced at a group of younger boys, sixth-year students, who walked by, chattering and laughing. He nodded to them, waited a moment, and then said, "I've never taken such a chance for a student—for anyone." He stared into Hans's eyes. "I hope I'm not being a fool." Then he walked away.

Hans walked on out to the street and down to the corner where he caught the streetcar to his home. He took his usual seat, toward the back, alone, and as the car rattled along he wondered what to expect. The *Stasi* surely had some reason to suspect him, and the agents weren't likely to give up. In the past month or two he had begun to feel some relief, had actually felt a degree of optimism that the cloud over him was lifting, but now he knew better. There would be no end to this. He was not likely to escape the relentlessness of their pursuit, and once they had him, he would lose everything.

When he reached his apartment building, he checked the mailbox before he climbed the stairs. He was pleased to find a letter from Greta, although it reminded him that he had told her nothing of his troubles. What if he were put in prison? That would surely end any hope for them to be together. Once he got out, he would have no future—nothing he could offer a wife or a family.

Hans had received his acceptance to attend a technical university in Magdeburg. But now he wondered about that, too. Those kinds of decisions could be reversed by local officials. Even if they found no conclusive proof against him, they could cancel his acceptance merely on the basis of their suspicions. He didn't believe the *Stasi* had any hard evidence against him, but as he had done hundreds of times before, he tried to think of everything that had happened, tried to think of any way he could be traced. In the middle of the memory was an image: Berndt being thrown through the air, the life already gone from him. And then, as always, his thoughts turned from himself to Berndt's parents. He saw them every Sunday at church, knew how much they were grieving. He wondered what they would think of him if they knew that he had been there. They had every right to ask why he had helped—why he hadn't tried harder to talk Berndt out of going.

Hans opened the apartment door with his key, but he found that Inga had come in ahead of him. She was sitting at the kitchen table doing her homework. He greeted her, but he couldn't bring himself to tease her, laugh with her, as he normally did. He merely walked on to his room, sat on his bed, and tore his letter open. He unfolded the pages and felt some pleasure in seeing Greta's handwriting, all crimped and crooked—ugly, really—but so familiar now. The first paragraph was funny. She joked about her work, how boring she found it, and what a donkey her boss was. The next paragraph came without warning:

> I have exciting news, Hans. The last thing in the world you would probably expect from me. I've fallen in love. Completely in love. I don't know whether you ever met Jürgen Krammer. He was at youth conference in Schwerin last summer. I thought he was strange, and not very handsome. I knew he took an interest in me, but I laughed about it. I even joked about his funny nose, with a little bump in the middle. Well, I like that nose now. He wrote to me, and then he came to see me, and I'm not sure what happened. I fell in love, and he did too. We're not engaged yet, or anything quite that serious, and we couldn't marry right away if we were, but I think

> something will come of this. It's not easy to find someone who's in the Church, and I like him very much. He's funny and smart, and he has a decent job. I'm happier than I have been in a long time, and that's the best. I hope something so good will happen to you someday, when you're older. It's so hard to find someone just right, but it can happen if you hold out hope. I suppose, now, I'm proof of that.

The letter continued with news and talk of the weather in Leipzig and reports on mutual friends. Nowhere was there an apology, or even a hint that Greta knew this news would hurt him. Hadn't she known what he felt for her? What did she mean, "when you're older"? Had she always thought of him as too young for her?

Hans put down the letter, and he knew the truth: she had never loved him, never even thought of him that way. They had been friends, pen pals, and nothing more. She fully expected him to be happy for her. Hans felt all remaining hope seep away, as though it were exhaling with every breath. He thought of cursing God the way he had done at times in the past, but he was quick to tell himself that it wasn't God who had let him down. He had made his own stupid mistake, always assuming feelings from Greta that simply hadn't been there.

He wanted to be angry, to toss the letter across the room and shout out his hatred for the girl, but he couldn't even muster any anger. The letter was too innocent, too friendly. She expected him to write his congratulations, and he would do that. But for the moment, he only stared at the dull wall of his bedroom. Once more things had worked out wrong. Once more he had to live in fear of his own government, and once more his future was in the hands of powers he couldn't control. And now his picture of a better future—a life with Greta—was not just gone but shown for what it had always been: a childish illusion.

Hans couldn't move. He had homework to do, but he couldn't do it. Nothing else mattered enough to get him off his bed, so he lay back, looked at the ceiling instead of the wall, and felt the emptiness. He thought of praying, but he could only wonder why he had asked over and over for bread and received rocks—one rock after another, all his life.

His mother came home after a time and eventually came to his room. He had left the door open a crack. She pushed it open a little more and said, "Good evening, Hans. Doing homework?"

He didn't look at her, didn't respond. After a moment, she said, "Are you tired?"

"Yes."

His voice was like an echo from a cave, and he knew she heard it. She stepped all the way in. "What's happened?" she asked, sounding frightened.

"Nothing. Not really. I'm just tired."

"Tell me, Hans. Please."

He had never told his mother what he felt for Greta. He didn't know whether she could understand, and he didn't want to talk. He hesitated for a time, and then he tried to choose the simplest words he could. "I got a letter from Greta. She has a boyfriend now. A Mormon."

"Oh, Hans. I'm sorry."

So she did know. She came to the bed and sat down. She touched his hand. "These things happen," she said.

"I'm younger than she is. It's what I should have expected." But this hurt him more than he wanted. He was struggling not to cry—he absolutely would not do that.

"Did she know how you felt about her?"

"I suppose not."

"She didn't say she was sorry?"

"No. She was happy. She wanted me to know."

"Hans, that's so difficult. I loved an older boy once, much older than

I. He wouldn't even treat me like an adult. He teased me about being a child. It almost broke my heart."

Hans knew the story. He didn't want to hear it again.

"It was your father, you know. He finally paid attention to me."

"I know. But Greta plans to marry this man."

"Maybe. Maybe not. Shouldn't you at least tell her how you feel about her?"

He had thought of that but had known immediately how selfish it would be. It would only hurt her, and it would change nothing. "No," he said. "I can't do that."

"Listen to me, Hans. You don't know what will come of this. These things can pass as quickly as they appear. If it's supposed to happen, it will, and they will marry, and you will find someone else. Something good is coming in your life. It's just a matter of having faith."

Hans had learned something about faith in the past couple of years, but he didn't believe in anything quite so simple as his mother did. He didn't think that everything always came right in the end. Some people had sad lives, disappointing ones, bad marriages, early deaths—all sorts of misery. There was no reason to assume that his life would take another turn at some point. Maybe this was his test, to live a heavy, sad life, and to be faithful all the same.

"When your father left Germany, I thought I would never see him again. It was the worst time of my life. I loved him so much, and he was gone. He wrote to me, but he promised nothing. I knew he felt something for me, but I was sure he would find a pretty American girl and forget about me. I was such a skinny little girl, not very pretty, and I had never had so much as a nice dress to wear. I would picture the American girls, like movie stars. I had rarely seen a movie, but I had seen Rita Hayworth, and I thought he would find a girl like that, who was so beautiful and so desirable. There seemed no hope that anything good would ever come to me. We were so poor, so frightened, so beaten down. And then a letter came, and Peter said he was coming back to me. I was just this skinny, ugly little girl, and he had chosen me. He was coming back. So it can happen, Hans. Things can happen. They can turn out all right."

"You were never ugly, Mama. Papa tells the story another way. He says that you had eyes the size of plums. He got to America and could only think of you."

"That's what he says now." She laughed. "But he thought I was only a little girl at first, and that's the truth. He lived with my family for a long time before he even noticed me—and I tried everything I knew to make him look."

But there were so many differences in Mama's story. Papa had noticed her before he left, and he had found no one else in America. He hadn't written to tell her how happy he was to have found a lovely girlfriend he wanted to marry. And Mama didn't see the most basic truth: the fact that things had worked out for her didn't mean the same would happen to him.

"You'll find someone, Hans. If it isn't Greta, it will be someone else. But someone will love you, and you will love her. God wants all that to happen for you. I know he does."

"Not everyone finds someone, Mama. It's not always like that."

"I know. But it will happen for you. I make you that promise."

It was a silly promise, and yet Hans couldn't resist the feeling it gave him, the bit of hope. But the numbness was lifting, and the pain was setting in. He was feeling far too much, and he didn't want his mother to know it. "I must do my homework," he said.

"It's good. You do that. I'll make dinner. But believe in my promise, if nothing else. I can't bear to see you hopeless."

She left, and Hans tried to measure his own trust. He found himself wanting to accept her promise, even let it comfort him, however illogical it seemed. But he didn't want to put his hope in Greta any longer. He didn't like illusions. What he also knew was that his mother had no idea what kind of danger he faced from the *Stasi*. All the same, he couldn't let all that paralyze him. For now, the most important thing he could do was get up and do his homework.

~

Hans was quiet at dinner. He didn't know what his mother had told Papa about Greta, but he hoped more than anything that the subject wouldn't come up. As it turned out, it didn't, not while everyone was at the table, and Inga ate rather quickly and asked to be excused. She never ate very much, but she studied harder than Hans ever had at her age. She would be twelve in another month, and she seemed intent on proving herself, showing the other kids at school that she was just as smart as they were—smarter—even if she did attend church. Hans had heard her say as much.

When Inga was gone, Mama said, "Hans, I told your father about Greta."

"I'm sorry about it, Son. But she was older than you. It's not common for girls to notice younger boys."

It was a typical statement from Papa. Did he really think that Hans would feel better, having heard the obvious? "I know," Hans said. "It doesn't matter."

"Of course it does," Katrina said. She had gotten up and was taking dishes to the sink.

"Let me mention something else," Peter said. "I know you took Berndt's death very hard. He was your friend, and I understand that. But death is something else we have to learn to accept in this life. I've watched you since then, all winter long, and you seem to have lost some of your will. This can't be good for anyone. It doesn't help Berndt now, not even his parents, and it doesn't help you."

"I've kept up my studies. I've—"

"Hans, you always turn to your studies. But you have to turn back toward life. You can't take things so hard. When I was your age I had seen more death than you will ever see. I had watched close friends die all around me. Everyone I knew in the army died, and I was left. It was a terrible time, but I had to find myself again and come back to life."

"I know." Hans was finished. He wasn't going to say any more. But then he did. "The deaths around you were caused by war. They weren't your fault."

Some seconds passed while the words sank in. Then Papa said, "Berndt's death wasn't your fault, Hans."

"It might have been. I'm not sure."

"Did you say something to him? What do you mean?"

Hans hardly had the strength to tell the story, and yet he wanted it out of him. He had lived with it inside too long. "I was there that night. I wasn't trying to escape. I went with him to help. I saw him die."

"Oh, Hans," Katrina said. She came to him, wrapped her arms around him from behind, and pressed her cheek to the side of his head.

"What were you doing there?" Peter asked.

"He asked me to drive him there—he and another man. I was supposed to cover up the entrance to the tunnel—so it wouldn't be found, and others could use it later."

"And you weren't going with them?"

"No." But the irony struck him for the first time. His chest seemed to convulse, and a sob broke from him. "Because of Greta. Mostly. I didn't want to go."

"But it wasn't your fault, Hans," Mama was pleading. "How could it be your fault?"

"I should have talked him out of it. I knew how dangerous it was. Or I should have helped him fight off the guards."

Peter, in his usual way, was waiting, considering. Hans had no idea what he was thinking. "Maybe you should have tried to talk Berndt out of it," he finally said, "but he wouldn't have listened. He was going to keep trying until he got out—that or have it end this way. And as to fighting the border guards, you would only have gotten yourself killed. They had weapons; you didn't."

"But I should have tried. I watched him get shot. I watched him fall. And then I ran."

"You had to run."

"I know. I know everything. I've thought about the whole thing so many times. But I keep seeing him fall, in my mind, and every time I do, what I *feel* is that I let it happen."

Katrina sat in the chair next to Hans. She kept her arm around his shoulders. "Why didn't you tell us?"

"It was stupid for me to go. I took a terrible chance. I've been interrogated by the *Stasi*." He made an instant decision not to tell them about the agents coming to his school. He didn't want them to worry as much as he knew they would.

"Why did they talk to you? Do they know something?"

"No. Someone would have picked me up by now if they really knew anything. They only knew I was his friend."

Peter nodded and then, for a time, stared at the table. "Something more to worry about," he finally said, and Hans saw the agony that he had wanted to avoid—placing this concern on his parents.

"I'm sorry," Hans said. "I'm so sorry. Berndt needed help, and I thought I had to do it, to be a friend. But if I had said no, maybe he wouldn't have gone."

"That's not true," Mama said. "They would have found someone else. They would have tried it, sooner or later. You know they would."

But Hans wasn't sure. Maybe no one else would have been foolish enough to help them.

"I want to tell you something," Peter said. "You know part of this story, but not all."

Hans waited. He wanted something that would make a difference, that would help, but he couldn't think what his father could say.

"You know that we named you after a boy I fought with in the war. You know he died. But I've never told you how he died." Peter continued to look at the table, telling the story without looking up. "I was sick. I couldn't have lived much longer. We had gone through so much in the cold, without enough food, and I was at the end of my will. It was Hans who kept me alive. He wouldn't let me give up. When we got a chance to escape the trap we were in—at the port in Memel, in Lithuania—Hans was helping me to a ship when an artillery shell struck a building next to us. A wall collapsed on top of us, but most of the force hit him. I found the strength to get him to the ship, but he was the one who died, after all he had done to keep me going. He saved my life, Hans, and he died doing it."

"That wasn't your fault either, Peter," Katrina said.

"I know. But it felt like my fault."

"Your father left the army then," Katrina said. "He walked away and refused to fire another weapon. That's how he ended up on our farm. We took him in."

"Hans, things happen. One man dies and another lives. We never know exactly why. But the worst thing we can do is waste away because of it. Then two lives are lost. We have to do our best with the life that has been granted to us."

"Did you feel that way at first?"

"No. It took me some time."

Hans nodded.

"You can learn from me, Hans, from my experience."

"I'll try." But Hans wasn't sure. He hadn't told his parents everything. That night in Berlin, as he had hidden in the doorway, he had heard the guards running. But they had not seen Hans. An impulse had come to him, the thought of charging the men, knocking them down, giving

Berndt time to run. If he had done it, followed his instinct, and sent the men sprawling on the street, there might have been time for everyone to get away. Not a day had gone by since Berndt had been killed that Hans didn't think of it, ask himself why he hadn't done it. The truth was, and he knew it, he had been stopped by his own fear. That's what his father didn't know, and that's what Hans had to live with.

# Chapter 12

Kathy was nervous and surprisingly self-conscious, but she stood in front of the doorway and thrust a sheet into everyone's hand, almost forced each man to take one. She had marched in a couple of protests that spring, but this was the first time she had confronted people so directly. The fact was, she was nervous, but she wasn't going to let anyone see that she was.

"What's this?" a guy asked her. He was not as tall as she was, not strongly built, but something in his voice—an annoyance that bordered on anger—frightened her. She continued to hold the paper in front of him, the edge pressing against his chest. "It's a *real* test—the one you should have taken today. It asks you how much you know about Vietnam."

"Yeah, and I'll bet it's not at all one-sided. Right?"

"Just read the questions and try to answer them. You'll learn a lot."

He was pushing by her. He did finally grasp the paper, but he wrinkled it up in his fist. "I'm sick of you people," he said. He tossed the test at a trash can, missed, but didn't bother to go pick it up.

Inside the building, on the University of Massachusetts campus, undergraduate males were taking a test mandated by the federal government. It was supposed to measure the students' actual learning. Those who got low scores and were also low in class standing were supposed to be made eligible for the draft. The government was running out of draftees, with so many young men in college. The 2-S deferment for students was still in effect, but Johnson wanted to start drafting students who were not buckling down. This test, being given all across the country in

May 1966, was the first step in finding out which students ought to be drafted.

Some of the young men accepted the SDS version of the test with apparent interest, and one even stopped, read some of the questions, and then said to her, "This is good stuff. That's what they should have been asking in the other test. I'm a psych major, and that test they gave us was all full of math and physical science. No one's going to do well on the stupid thing. I think that's what Johnson wants to prove—that college students are all a bunch of draft dodgers."

"Of course," Kathy said. "He wants a huge pool to draw from."

"Well . . . keep up the good work," the guy said, and he walked away.

She glanced back to thank him and at the same time extended a test to someone else coming out the door, but this man shoved her hand away. "Hey, keep it," he said. "I happen to love America. I'm not a *Commie*."

"Then go sign up for the army," Kathy said. "Quit hiding away here at the university."

He had been walking on by, but now he stopped and grabbed Kathy's shoulder, pulled her around. "Hey, little girl. I'm in ROTC. I'll be going to Vietnam as an officer—and my life will be on the line. What kind of danger are *you* going to face?"

"It takes guts *not* to go," she shouted at him as he walked away, but that made him laugh.

She turned back to the door, but she heard a voice behind her—quiet but intense. "Don't do that." She turned to see Lester Franklin, one of several black activists who were helping out today. "Treat them with respect," he said. "That's the only chance we have." He stepped away and extended a test toward a young man who shook his head and brushed by him.

Dee Dee Harris, another of the black students, was laughing. She whispered to Kathy, "Don't mind Lester. He's from the South."

Kathy was busy, but a few minutes later, when the last of the crowd had apparently exited, she told Dee Dee, "Lester's right. I shouldn't smart off to people. It doesn't do any good."

"I don't buy that," Dee Dee said. "I'm tired of being polite. Lester marched with Martin Luther King—the *Laaawwwd* himself—down in Birmingham. They both still think bowing and scraping and pleading is the way to change this country."

"It's not bowing and scraping. Dr. King doesn't do that. I was in Greenwood, Mississippi, during—"

"I know all about that, Kathy. I've heard your story. But you heard what Stokely Carmichael said when he went back there this spring. We're tired of saying 'freedom.' Now we're saying 'black power!' And that's what it's going to take. I'm not just talking about the South. It's worse up here in a lot of ways."

Lester had returned. He smiled, glanced at Dee Dee, and then looked at Kathy. "Is Dee Dee trying to set you right?" he asked. He was small, trim, and neatly dressed, with tight lips that gave him an earnest, devout look—until he smiled. He was a freshman, like Kathy, but his big smile made him look even younger.

"You're the one telling people what to do," Dee Dee said. She wrapped her arm around Lester's shoulders, then kissed his head, like a mother. Kathy thought Dee Dee was beautiful, with her huge dark eyes and bronze-tinted skin.

"I'm sorry," Lester said. "I shouldn't have said anything."

Dee Dee grabbed the back of Lester's neck and gave him a little shake. "Hey, that's all right. You don't have to be afraid of this girl. She may be white, and ten feet tall, but she don't scare me." Dee Dee had used an exaggerated southern intonation for this last phrase, but her diction was normally not only northern but a bit too pure, almost British.

"I don't scare *anyone*," Kathy said.

By then, Robby Freedman was using a little loudspeaker system to call people together. Kathy walked with Lester and Dee Dee, and they joined the crowd. Most were campus activists who had been handing out the alternative tests, but fifty or sixty others had come close enough to listen. What Kathy didn't like was the way Robby looked. She thought it would be smarter for the protesters to dress like other students, but Robby was wearing a khaki army-surplus coat and a red bandana around his head. He had also been letting his hair grow long.

Kathy knew that Robby loved these moments, and she understood why. She found him electric when he spoke. She loved his voice, his intensity. But today he began slowly, almost gently. "I love my country," he said. "We all do. We're here because of that. We love what America is *supposed* to stand for. This country was founded on the idea of equal opportunity, of fairness to all people. It was supposed to be a place where no king, no dictator, ruled over the masses of common people."

"That's all gone!" one of the guys from SDS shouted.

Robby looked down, waiting. He let the pause reach the crowd, silence them. Some people who had been standing at a distance moved a little closer. And then in a plaintive tone, he whispered into the microphone. "Yes. We are losing all that. We're losing our way. We have become the very thing we were never supposed to be."

There was no shouting this time. His sadness seemed too real for that. Kathy felt it. She was well aware that Robby understood how to move a crowd, was good at it, but she also knew how deeply he did care.

Now his voice built in volume, took on a professorial tone. "Dwight Eisenhower saw our problems coming. He feared what he called the military/industrial complex. He dreaded the day when a nation *needed* war—needed it economically. He feared a day when generals could join with businessmen, wage war, and in the process fill their own pockets." His voice raised another notch as he said, with force, "We pretend to care about the people of Southeast Asia, pretend that we're protecting them from the evils of Communism. What those poor people need, more than anything, is protection from *us!*"

This last had been almost a shout, but then he paused again. He let the SDS members shout, "Right on!" let their voices die out, and still he waited. He softened his voice again as he finally said, "We, the people, have become we, the powerful. America takes what it wants from this world, uses it up, wastes more than it conserves, and then leaves the crumbs for the starving nations. What is it we're offering the people in the Vietnam villages—something better than they have? No. As always, we are enriching the corrupt leaders of so-called South Vietnam, and we're killing the peasants, killing their little children with napalm, defoliating their jungles with Agent Orange, encircling them with barbed wire, and telling them that it's all for their own good."

This was what the nation needed to know. Kathy felt the sting under her eyelids, looked at Robby through a blur of tears.

"We *must* stop this war!" he shouted. "This *sick*, immoral war. We, the common people, the young people, must say no. When Johnson has no soldiers he will have no war!"

The SDS crowd roared, and out of the noise a chant emerged. "Hell, no, we won't go! Hell, no, we won't go!" But Kathy looked at the students on the perimeter—the curious ones who had only come to hear what Robby would say. They were not chanting. Some were even shouting back. Kathy wondered if any of the students had been moved at all by what Robby had said. What was the point of holding these rallies if Robby was only preaching to the choir?

Robby looked out toward those students as though he wondered the same thing. "Some of you took Lyndon Johnson's test today. Were you asked to do any math problems that calculated the sick philosophy of a 'body count' war? The French tried to defeat Ho Chi Minh by killing the people of Vietnam, and they finally had to admit that a ground war in Asia was impossible. The North Vietnamese will fight forever. We are sending our boys to do the impossible. Even if the war were just, it would—" He stopped, looked up to his left, and then cringed, stepped back.

Kathy looked in time to see a large rock hurtling toward Robby. But it didn't reach him. It dropped into the crowd, and Kathy heard screams, saw someone go down.

There was a pause for a second or two as everyone held, waited. Then someone shouted, "Get an ambulance!"

It was Lester who got into motion first, as though he knew about such things. "I'll call," he yelled, and then he took off running for a nearby building.

"Who is it? Who's down?" people were asking, but Kathy was turning to see whether more rocks might be coming. The students in the distance were standing, watching, their hands in their pockets or their arms folded. She couldn't see who had thrown the rock. Most of the guys back there wouldn't have done such a thing, but they didn't look overly worried, either.

"Make room," someone was yelling. "Give him air." The crowd surged backward and Kathy moved with it. Then she looked to see Robby, who had raised the microphone again.

"You won't stop us that way," he shouted. "You can break our heads, but you can't break our spirits. We'll fight, and we'll die if we have to, but we're going to *stop* this war."

The shouting started again, both the cheers from the SDS people and the insults from the onlookers. Kathy heard a deep voice bellow, "You're a bunch of traitors!"

Kathy heard a siren not long after that, but it was another five minutes before the ambulance reached the site. By then, she knew more. A guy named Rusty Campbell had been hit in the back of the head. He had been knocked out, was conscious now, and was bleeding badly.

That was all rather abstract until she worked her way around the crowd and stood where the gurney passed. She saw Rusty, a red-haired boy she knew from SDS meetings. His face was ashen, his eyes distant. And then she saw Phyllis Peters, Rusty's girlfriend. She was holding a wadded T-shirt in her cupped hands, and blood was dripping through her fingers. All Kathy could think was that someone really could die. Someone would, sooner or later.

❧

An hour later Kathy was sitting in the backseat of a car in front of Robby Freedman's house. When the rally had ended, almost everyone from SDS had walked from campus to the rented house where Robby and some of his friends lived. A few had gone to the hospital, but most had gathered to wait for word about Rusty. That hadn't taken long. Rusty had needed some stitches, and he had a concussion, but he would be all right.

Kathy had carpooled to Amherst that day with three girls from Smith. She had hoped to leave once the news had come, but the other three wanted to stick around. By then, someone had gone for beer, and the original plan—a little after-the-demonstration celebration—had been resurrected. The girls told Kathy that they wouldn't stay long, but she knew better, and a worry she had been feeling for at least a week began to reach the panic stage. She had intended to catch up on her reading every night for a long time, but she was putting in way too much time at planning meetings or standing in the student center distributing leaflets. She had to study tonight, probably all night.

Fortunately, Kathy had brought her textbook, since she had suspected that something like this might happen. She tried to use the time to read a chapter on cell biology, but she was distracted by the sounds coming from the house. A Bob Dylan album was blasting from the open doors and windows, and inside, Kathy could see people dancing, drinking. Certainly some would be smoking marijuana. It all made her uncomfortable. She was keeping her head in the book, however, when she realized that someone was standing at the car door. She looked up to see Robby. He opened the door and bent low. "I can't believe it. You're studying."

She was embarrassed. She didn't always like Robby, was bothered by his self-absorption, but she knew she also cared about his approval. "I've got a test in biology in the morning," was all she said.

"Come on inside. I'll teach you some biology you won't forget."

She looked away. This was Robby at his worst, and she wanted nothing to do with him when he was like that. He smelled of alcohol.

"You don't like me, do you?" he asked.

"Not when you talk like that."

He was smiling. She loved the dimple under his beard but wished he would shave so she could see what he really looked like.

"Hey, this was our day. Now it's time to feel it. All that garbage they're trying to feed you in school is part of the whole thing we're fighting."

"Robby, that's stupid. Biology is biology, and I need to pass it to graduate."

"Why graduate? That's just more of what's wrong with our system. Who decides what we learn? It's certainly not us."

"If college is all wrong, why don't you drop out?"

He laughed again. "I'd rather be on campus than anywhere else. That's where I can make things happen."

"And you need the money your parents keep sending you. If you drop out, they're going to say, 'Get a job.'"

He didn't answer, only smiled. "Kathy, all you are is a little do-gooder. You know how to *think*, but you don't know how to *feel*."

She looked directly into his eyes for the first time. "I loved what you said today, Robby. It was true, and it was strong, and I respected that it came from your heart and not just your head. I felt that as much as anyone did."

He allowed a long, dramatic pause while he looked into her eyes.

Then he nodded. "Every time I think you're hopeless, I find something new in you."

Kathy needed to change the subject. She felt herself blushing. "How's Rusty?" she asked. "Have you heard anything more?"

"He's fine. And I'm glad he took a rock in the head. It was the best thing that could have happened today."

"Are you serious?"

"Hey, we'll be on the news now."

Kathy thought of Phyllis's bloody hands. "It makes me sick to hear you say that," she said.

"Think about it. We didn't hurt anyone. And Rusty will be okay. But those *patriots* showed themselves for what they are."

"They'll call it a riot on the news, and blame it on us. Violence only—"

"Violence is the only thing people really understand. When we beg the government to stop the war, the big boys just laugh at us, but when there's war in the streets, Johnson has to pay attention. What do you think the black movement has taught us?"

Kathy didn't believe any of that. It was more of the big talk that a lot of people in the antiwar movement loved so much these days. She didn't say that, though.

"Think about it," he said. "And we'll keep talking. You're what? Nineteen now?" She nodded. "You've come a long way this year. I'll give you another year, and you'll be right where I am. You'll drop all your Mormon idealism, wade in, and get yourself dirty." With that, he walked away.

Kathy went back to her biology, or tried to, but after a few more minutes she saw Lester walk from the house. She rolled down the car window and yelled to him, "Are you leaving?"

Lester walked over to her. "Yeah, I am. I don't belong in there."

"You don't drink, do you?"

"No. But it's not that. I just don't fit. Dee Dee's in there talking about the 'black revolution,' and everyone's listening to her like she's some sort of prophet."

"At least she's found some white people who are on her side."

"Yeah, but after Selma *lots* of white people were with us. Now—since Watts—there's all this backlash going on. All we've done is take everyone's mask off. Turns out, northerners are just as prejudiced as southerners. Everyone wants to talk about 'law 'n order,' but it's just code language for 'Keep those niggers in their place.'"

"I'm afraid the same thing is happening with Vietnam. The polls are saying now that most people think the war is a mistake. But they still don't want to withdraw. They think it's un-American to agree with us."

"That's the problem. If we get people mad enough they'll dig in their heels, and this war will only last longer."

"But it's so frustrating when people won't even look at the facts."

"I know what you're saying. But the people in there"—he pointed to Robby's house—"they want to burn the country down and then start over, and I don't see what good that's gonna do. Good people need to change their hearts. That's what we gotta work on."

"How do we make that happen?"

"The sit-ins worked. We brought attention to our cause without showing all this anger and hatred. People said to themselves, 'That ain't right. It's gotta change.' We can still do that. I honestly believe there are more good people than bad. It's what I learned from Dr. King."

"It's what I learned from my church."

He nodded, and he didn't say what Dee Dee had once told her. He didn't tell her that he couldn't respect a church that kept the priesthood from blacks, but Kathy wondered whether Lester was thinking just that.

Kathy took her biology test the next morning after about two hours of accidental sleep. She hoped that she might pull out a C somehow. On the following Sunday, as usual, she drove back to Amherst, this time to go to church with LaRue. She liked the fact that a few students were in the ward—mostly from the University of Massachusetts and mostly grad students. They were open-minded people, and some even expressed their reservations about the war.

What was difficult for Kathy was that much of the ward was made up of local people who assumed the war was all about fighting for democracy. She was almost sure she could convince them otherwise if she could teach them a little history, but she never really got that chance.

On this particular Sunday, she left sacrament meeting fuming. The speaker, a man from the high council named Washburn, had been talking about the devotion of the early Saints—and tied that into the great purpose of America and its divine destiny. The truth was, Kathy's mind had been wandering from the talk when she tuned in enough to hear him say, "If you ask me, these young people today who speak out against our country ought to be sent to live somewhere else. Then they might appreciate the liberty they've always taken for granted. When I had to put my own life on the line, back during World War II, at least I didn't have to wonder whether the folks at home would support me. It's a shame what's happening now."

Now, in the car on the way home, Kathy was telling LaRue what she thought of all that. "I love that guy's logic. The great thing about America is our liberty. So anyone who uses that liberty to express an opinion different from his ought to be shipped away."

LaRue laughed quietly. "Kathy, it's hard for men who fought in World War II. They just can't imagine anyone refusing to support our soldiers."

"I don't have anything against the soldiers. They didn't think this war up. But what's the guy arguing, that everything our government ever does is right?"

"No. Of course not. He'd probably be the first to complain about high taxes—and it would never occur to him that he was being 'disloyal' to say such a thing."

"And that's supposed to make sense? He can complain when he disagrees, but people who are against the war aren't allowed the same *liberty?*"

LaRue was driving, watching the narrow road. There was a "Sunday driver" in front of them, an older man doing about twenty miles an hour. "What's this guy doing?" LaRue asked, sounding rather impatient, but she didn't try to pass. She simply slowed a little more, and then she said, "Kathy, Brother Washburn is no philosopher. If you expect consistency from people—including yourself—you're going to wait a long time."

"Okay, fine. He can sit at his dinner table and spout his ideas all he wants, but he has no right to get up in church, talk politics, and assume that everyone will just nod and say amen."

"I'll bet more did than didn't."

"That doesn't make it right. If I had gotten up there and explained my reasons for opposing the war, even in the most religious terms—which I *could* do—I'd be in major trouble. The bishop would be calling me in to tell me to keep my mouth shut."

"I know. I'm sure that's true. Although our dear bishop would be very nice about it."

"And you don't *care?* What's going on with you, LaRue? Since when did you become such a conservative?"

The car in front of LaRue's finally turned off onto a little side road, and LaRue had to come almost to a stop before the old driver made his turn, but once he did, she gradually accelerated. Kathy and LaRue had been traveling this road all year, and sometimes LaRue scared Kathy, she would drive so fast. It was a beautiful drive now, in May, with the trees deep green and the white bark of the birches glistening in the late afternoon sun. Maybe that's why LaRue didn't speed up quite as much as usual.

"Kathy, when I was in college—which wasn't as long ago as it might seem to you—I almost went nuts about things like this. For me, it came to the point where I started missing church a lot, telling myself over and over that I wasn't going back. But I couldn't do that. The Church was too much a part of me. So I had to ask myself what to do about the fact that so many Mormons had different opinions from mine. I—"

"It's more than that, LaRue. They all think alike, and they're all so sure they're right. People who don't know the first thing about an issue already have their answer, waiting and ready."

"Kathy, that's the way most people are—not just Mormons. That's something you have to learn to live with—either that or go crazy."

"I think I'll choose crazy."

LaRue laughed. But then she asked, "What did you hear from your own leaders at your rally over at UMass this week? Was it in-depth analysis, or wasn't it mostly slogans?"

LaRue had a point, but Kathy was in no mood to admit it. "Maybe at a rally you have to make things kind of simple. But people in our group know a *whole lot* about the war. They read. They discuss. They wrestle with all the questions."

"Some do. Some are just tagalongs. You know that."

Kathy found herself a little softened by the accuracy of the description. She thought for a time before she said, "LaRue, we're sending our young men halfway around the world to push our system off on people who don't want it. That's not right. It doesn't take a lot of brilliance to understand that."

LaRue was smiling, which was infuriating. "Think about that for a minute," she said. "Is it really *quite* that simple?"

"Basically, yes."

"Basically?" She was still smiling.

"We agreed to let the South Vietnamese hold a free election, and then we stopped it because we knew we would lose. Explain to me how that fits into our idea of 'liberty.'"

"Kathy, I tend to agree. But there are arguments on the other side. The Communists are not a bunch of sweethearts. They're infiltrating the south, intimidating people, scaring them into submission. President Johnson has a pretty solid group of advisors, most of them left over from the Kennedy administration, and they really feel a need to take a stand somewhere, establish the idea that the United States won't sit by and let this kind of Communist expansionism continue."

"But the Vietnamese people resisted the French, and now they don't want us in their country—not in the south any more than in the north—except for the corrupt puppet government we've set up. Most of the people want to be left alone, and they'll fight us forever rather than let us take over. So what is this great moral stand we're taking? We're the expansionists."

LaRue was driving into Northampton, entering the long main street that curved up the hill toward campus. "Look," she said, "some very smart people believe that Russia and China are watching to see what we'll do in Vietnam. If we retreat from our commitment, and let South Vietnam fall, maybe the next test will be in West Berlin or South America."

"Fine. I think that logic is circular and wrong, but I can respect a person who holds that opinion. And those people should respect *my* opinion. What bothers me is that I didn't get any respect from brother what's-his-name today."

"Kathy, if he smoked, you'd be the first to tell me that we ought to be forgiving and kind. There are all kinds of things people do that aren't entirely right. I know one young woman who sometimes gets sarcastic and nasty with her own grandfather—and she has an aunt who's been known to do the same thing to the same man. What kind of terrible women are they?"

Kathy was the one nodding now. "Okay. I know. But at least after I do it, I'm sorry. I think that guy—"

"Brother Washburn."

"I think Brother Washburn is convinced he gave a great sermon. And if I told him where I disagreed with him, he'd denounce me for being un-American and a lousy Mormon."

"But that's the great thing, Kathy. You're bigger than that. You're deeper, more compassionate. Right?"

LaRue smiled, and after a few seconds, Kathy did too. "Right," she finally said. "I'm wonderful. That's what I like about myself."

They both laughed.

"Kathy, you know me," LaRue said. "I've been arguing with people all my life—and I have strong opinions about all sorts of things. But maybe I'm finally getting old enough to find out that something I believe with all my heart at a certain age turns out to be something I disagree with a few years later. You and I both need to learn not to take ourselves quite so seriously."

"I know that. I always know—right after I pop off and say something I shouldn't."

But that night when Kathy tried to work on a paper that was due that week in an English lit class, her mind kept wandering back to the conversation. She wondered why she always ended up at odds with everyone. Robby thought she was a "little do-gooder," and yet a lot of the members of her ward would probably think her antiwar activity was wrong. LaRue was patient with her, but that very patience was maddening. Some things were worth fighting for, and she and LaRue had fought together in Mississippi. Now LaRue seemed to be saying, "Let everyone have an opinion. One idea is as good as another." But what about the idea that black people were inferior to whites? Was that an acceptable worldview? And what about the attitude that the Vietnamese needed Americans to tell them what form of government they should have? Was that as valid as any other point of view? Kathy didn't think so. LaRue's philosophy, at least the way she had been talking that afternoon, would lead to never taking a stand about anything. Maybe Lester was wrong too. Maybe at times the only right thing was to be as offensive as possible—to shock and trouble and annoy people until they started to think. Hadn't Christ upset a lot of people?

But the thought of Christ was subduing. She couldn't really picture him spouting off the way she sometimes did. She knew, in fact, that she ought to be trying harder to be like him.

# Chapter 13

The weather in Augsburg had been hot all week, and dreadfully humid, and then, on a Tuesday afternoon, heavy clouds moved in, and a hard, steady rain began to fall. Gene was glad he had a car. Life on a bike wasn't so bad when the weather was nice, but rain made things miserable. The best thing these days, however, was that he and Elder Howard, his companion since he had been transferred to Augsburg, were teaching a young family, and today they were picking up their two children, a little girl named Helga, who was six, and a nine-year-old boy named Joachim. They were great kids, with big eyes and funny round faces—and Gene loved to go to Primary with investigators. It was a perfect time to relax, play with the kids, and at the same time feel that he was using his time well.

Before the elders picked up the kids, however, they stopped off at their apartment to grab an early meal. Right after Primary the elders were scheduled to give a lesson to the Schotts, the parents of the little children. Gene wasn't sure when he and his companion would get another chance to eat.

The elders lived upstairs in a little two-apartment building. Two other elders lived downstairs. Gene stopped at the mailbox and checked the mail. He had a letter from his mother, and the mission newsletter had come. Elder Howard took the newsletter, and Gene opened his mother's letter as he climbed the stairs. She and the kids had returned home to Utah for a while, to get away from the humid heat in Washington. She talked about loving Utah, and how much she missed it. Kurt was worrying her, she said, still hanging out with kids she didn't like. She was glad to get him away from his friends in Virginia for a few weeks. She wondered whether Gene could write Kurt and encourage him in some way. Gene was tempted to write and chew him out. He didn't know exactly what the kid was doing that was wrong, but there must be something to it if his mom was so upset.

"Elder Thomas."

Gene had walked into the apartment, reading, and had sat down on his bed. He looked up at Elder Howard, who was sitting on his own bed, opposite Gene. There had been something strangely hesitant in his voice. He was skinny, slow-moving by Gene's standards, and not exactly a powerhouse missionary, but he was a nice enough guy, and Gene liked him.

"I have some . . . I don't know . . . I guess bad news for you."

"What are you talking about?"

"The mission president called a new AP. It's Elder Wayment."

Gene stared at his companion, trying to accept the possibility. "Let me see that," he said. He stood and reached, and Elder Howard handed over the newsletter. But there it was on the first page: Elder Wayment's picture. He was standing with President Fetzer and Elder Banks, the other AP, and he was grinning, looking happy, as though he deserved the position.

"I know you were expecting to get that position, but—"

"I've never said that." Gene was angry. He wanted to rip up the newsletter and throw it in Howard's face. The guy had been out on his mission six months and thought he knew the score now, but he had no right to say something like that.

"I know. But everyone kept telling you that you were going to get it. You must have thought you would."

"Wayment's a good elder. He'll be fine." But Gene was thinking what this meant: another seven months left on his mission, and now, no chance to make AP. The timing would be all wrong when Banks went home. The president always called his assistants when they had around six months left. This was supposed to be Gene's time.

"Maybe you'll get to stay here for a while now. We can baptize the Schotts."

"That's right. That's great." Gene walked back to his bed and sat down. He tried to read the newsletter. He looked at the reported numbers from the different zones and saw that his zone was ranked third this week, which wasn't great, but it was the highest of those that hadn't baptized. But so what? Where would that get him?

"I've heard a lot of elders talking about it. They not only thought you'd get the position; they thought you deserved it. Wayment's kind of a climber."

"That's no way to talk," Gene said. "I'm sure the president prayed about this a lot before he made the call. Wayment must be the one the Lord wanted."

"Do you think it always works like that? To me, it seems like a lot of the guys who get positions aren't necessarily the best missionaries—and they're sure not the most humble."

Gene wanted to scream at Howard, to tell him to shut his mouth, but he didn't know why. All he knew was that the disappointment was setting in deeper with every second. He had pictured himself driving around the mission, directing zone conferences, doing interviews, working daily with the mission president, being in on all the decisions about programs and transfers. He had always loved to think of himself going to the airport to pick up new shipments of greenies, teaching them on orientation days.

"Well, anyway," Howard said, "don't feel bad. At least you made zone leader."

"What's that supposed to mean?"

"I'm just saying—"

"Do you think that's the only reason we're here—to strive after *positions?* That stuff doesn't matter to me. The only thing I want to do is baptize some more good people before I go home. The APs almost never get a chance to do that."

But Gene's voice had started loud and gotten louder, almost hostile, and Elder Howard was looking shocked. "Okay, okay," he said, and the whole thing might have dropped. But Howard was sounding angry himself when he added, "Everyone in this zone was saying the same thing—that you've been gunning for the job your whole mission."

Gene felt something go off inside him. He wanted to take them all on—Howard first and then the rest of the zone. He actually came off his bed, reached toward Elder Howard, and was about to grab him by the shirt, when he stopped himself just in time. He stood, staring at him for a moment, and then he said, "Just shut your mouth, all right? Just shut it and keep it shut."

"Lay off, Elder. I'm not putting you down. All I'm saying is—"

But Gene was losing it. "I told you to shut up," he screamed. And then he bolted for the door. He had to get away before he knocked the guy on his back. He slammed the door behind him and ran down the stairs, taking three steps at a time, but Elders Graham and Doxie were down by the mailbox. "Hey, we just saw the news," Doxie said. "Too bad, Thomas."

"Shut up!" Gene was shouting again. "Where do you guys get off, accusing me of something like that? From now on, if you've got something to say to me, say it to my face."

"What?"

Gene pushed open the door and went outside. He was about as far away from his companion as he was supposed to go, but he wanted to take off, just take off and run. He wanted one full day away from all these guys, this whole mission thing. He was so tired of it all. He stood on the front step for a moment, breathing. The rain had let up a good deal now, but he could still feel fine little drops touching his face, his hair. It felt good. But then Howard stepped out the door. "Elder, what are you doing?"

"Leave me alone."

"That's just the point. I can't leave you alone."

"Oh, back off." And suddenly Gene was walking toward the VW, pulling the keys from his pocket. He needed a few minutes. What could that hurt? So what if he got into trouble? That might be a nice change. He had never done anything wrong in his whole life. Gene Thomas—the responsible one.

He opened the car door, jumped in, and slammed it. Howard had run to the opposite side, but the door was locked. Gene turned the key and started the engine just as Elder Howard grabbed the handle. At the same moment, Gene popped the clutch and shot backward, spraying wet gravel. He swung the car back and around, shifted gears, and blasted out of the long driveway. In his rearview mirror he could see Howard, gesturing, shouting. Gene didn't care. He was going to have a few minutes to himself; that's all he wanted.

He drove hard through the streets of town, and he headed for the *Autobahn*. When he broke out of the city traffic and onto the highway, he floored the gas pedal. The little bug didn't exactly jump ahead, but it gradually picked up speed. There was no speed limit out here, and Gene wished he were driving a big car, even just his old "Vickie" from back home. He wanted to see what it felt like to pass the hundred-mile-per-hour mark. He wanted to take a chance—some kind of chance. He wanted to be *bad* for once, for a lousy ten minutes in his life.

Wayment was a jerk. That's what he really thought. He was a pusher, and he always reported a ton of hours, but he didn't have the depth of a slice of baloney. He was all show, all slickness, all talk. And now Gene would be out knocking on doors another seven months, and Wayment would be cruising around the mission acting like a big shot. Gene had set out to be quarterback, back at East, and he had gotten the position by the time he was a junior. He had set out to be student-body president, and he had won it by a landslide, and now, for two years, he had planned on this, worked for it, prepared for it. He didn't care whether he was supposed to want it or not. He *had* wanted it. And there were no second chances.

The VW was winding tight, the whine like a scream, but Gene kept his foot pressed all the way down. The left window never would close tight, and there was a whistle of air through it now. What he wanted was more power, some way to push this little car up another notch—that or blow it all to pieces. "You're such a *jerk*, Wayment!" he yelled. "Why *you?*"

But it was God he was really disgusted with. So he let loose. He screamed, trying to break the windshield with the force of his own voice. "You know what he is! You know it! How could you do this?"

He was breathing hard, crying finally, and he knew he had gone too far. He felt the anger drain away and the shame begin to take over. He kept going for a time—maybe ten minutes—but his tantrum was over.

He spotted an off ramp and took it, then crossed over the highway and started back toward town. He drove back into the streets of Augsburg, but he was almost back to his apartment when he realized that he would have to face the other elders in a few minutes, and he wasn't ready for that yet. He would have to apologize, make things right with them, but even more, he had to resolve some things in his own head. He had little more than half a year to go now, and he had to find a way to deal with things the way they were, not the way he had thought they would be. So he pulled off and parked by the side of a street near a walkway along the Lech River. The rain had let up even more now, only a mist still in the air. He knew a bench there, and he wanted to sit for a time and think this all through.

But when he reached the bench, two girls, maybe sixteen or seventeen—one of them quite cute—were sitting where he had wanted to sit. They were wearing jackets, and one still had her umbrella up. It was a long enough bench, however, that he walked to the end, brushed the water away as best he could, and sat down as far from the girls as he could. And then he turned away, looking toward the river and the quaint old bridge that crossed it. He knew he had to pray, but he wasn't ready yet.

What he had been doing was wrong, of course. He had known all along it was wrong. He had been telling himself for two years that no matter how much he wanted the position, his purpose in being a missionary was not to be AP; it was to serve in whatever way the Lord chose. It was to seek out the honest in heart and try to bring them to the gospel. Why did he have to keep relearning that?

Gene thought of Marsha. It was she who had first challenged him to do things for the right reasons, and perhaps, without her, he never would have raised such questions now. He longed to triumph over himself, to prove to her—as much as to himself—that he could do it. What he wished now was that he could find the genuine humility he saw in some people. He had seen it in his father, who worked so hard, had grown so prominent, and yet seemed unimpressed by the positions he held. And he had seen it in his grandmother, who spent her life doing good and didn't know or care whether anyone noticed.

Gene finally began to pray. He gripped his hands together and described to the Lord how ugly his behavior had been over the last hour, how wrong he knew it was. He laid it all out, partly to see it himself; he described his jealousy, his greed, his need for attention, his lack of spirit. He was beginning to ask the Lord to help him through his final months when he heard a voice next to him. "You're not from here, are you?"

He turned and saw the cute girl with the short blonde hair looking at him, smiling. "No. I'm not."

"I think you're from England, and my friend thinks you're an American."

"American," he said. He knew he had to leave now.

"German boys don't wear suits like that. And they don't sit on benches in the rain."

"Americans don't either—usually," he said. "But it's stopped now, hasn't it?" He stood up.

The girl was smiling as though he had said something clever. "Are you in the army?"

"No. I'm a missionary."

This caused both girls to laugh. "I doubt that," the second girl said, the one leaning around the blonde girl. She had brown hair, matted from the rain, and too much lipstick.

"I *am* a missionary," he said.

"Then why do you look so sad? Aren't missionaries supposed to be happy?"

He looked at the blonde girl, who had gradually stopped smiling, perhaps in response to his own expression. "Perhaps I'm not as good a missionary as I ought to be," he said. "I wish I were."

"You can make a visit to my house anytime," the brown-haired girl said, and then she ducked back, hiding her face behind her friend. Both giggled.

Gene hadn't really thought of himself as "alone" until now, hadn't even thought as much about mission rules as he should. He had been too wrapped up in what he had to think about. "I must go," he said.

"Aren't you going to teach us to repent?" the blonde girl said, her dimples appearing. The other girl was laughing hard now, still hiding her face.

"I think you're nice girls," he said. "But you *should* be more careful. You don't know what kind of man I might be."

He walked away. He had seen a rather solemn look come over the blonde girl's face, as though she had actually listened.

He got into the car and drove back to the apartment, then slowly climbed the stairs. He was halfway up when the downstairs apartment door opened and Howard came out. "I'm down here," he said. "I didn't think I should stay alone."

Gene nodded.

Reality was back, and suddenly Gene realized what he hadn't done. "Do we still have time to go get the kids for Primary?" he asked.

"I don't know. But the first thing you have to do is call Munich. President Fetzer told me to have you call the instant you came back."

"You called him?"

"What else could I do?"

"I don't know. But you could have waited just a—"

"They told us the first day I got here, if anything like this ever happened, call the mission office immediately."

Gene nodded. Maybe a little anger came back, but not much. He was in trouble now, and he knew he deserved it.

~

The following morning Gene was sitting in President Fetzer's office in Munich, where the mission headquarters had been moved the previous winter. Augsburg was not too far from Munich, so when Gene had called the night before, the president had only talked to him briefly. "I want you to come here in the morning, Elder," he had said, firmly. "You and your companion drive over. I want you to account for every second you were alone."

"All right. What time should I be there?" Gene had asked. And then he had spent a long night, rehearsing what he would say, trying to imagine what questions President Fetzer might ask.

And now here he was, sitting across from President Fetzer's big desk, waiting. The president was scribbling some sort of notes on a sheet of paper. He had looked up only long enough, as Gene had entered, to say, "Just a minute. I'll be right with you."

But now he set his pen down and took a long look at Gene. "Elder Thomas, do we have a problem?" he asked.

"Well," Gene said, "I guess so. I left my companion for about an hour—or maybe a little longer than that. I broke the mission rules."

"Tell me what you did while you were gone."

"I drove my VW on the *Autobahn* about as fast as it would go, and then I turned around and came back."

"That's it?"

"No. I stopped and sat on a bench by the river—because by then, I wanted to pray. There were a couple of teenaged girls sitting at the other end of the bench, but when they started talking to me I left."

"Nothing improper of any kind happened—is that what you're saying?"

President Fetzer was a nice man, likable, and even when he was being stern, there was some hint that he liked Gene, thought the best of him. He was a slim, neat man, with well-trimmed hair and a sparkling white shirt. The scar on his upper lip always made him look as though he were smiling, even when he wasn't. Gene wasn't as frightened as he had expected to be. "No. I didn't do anything wrong—except maybe drive kind of fast. But I know I shouldn't have taken off. I've never done anything like that before, and I'll never do it again."

These were some of the words he had tried out in his head the night before.

"Tell me this. Just how fast will one of those mission VWs go?" Now he did smile.

"I had it up to about a hundred and twenty K. I think that's about seventy miles an hour, isn't it?"

"Was it shaking all over?"

"Yeah. Kind of."

The president leaned back, crossing his arms over his chest, and the smile disappeared. "Okay. I know what you did. Do you want to tell me why?"

"I got mad at my companion and the elders downstairs, and I just wanted to get away for a little while." He hoped that would be the end of it. He didn't want President Fetzer to know how hungry he had been to gain a position.

"You must have been *very* angry."

"Yeah. I guess I was. But it passed away pretty fast. I feel stupid about it now."

"You don't seem like the kind of elder who flies off the handle like that. You've always been one of our strongest missionaries."

"President, I don't remember ever doing anything like this in my whole life. I'm not sure what got into me."

"Maybe, for the first time in your life, you didn't get what you wanted." Gene ducked his head. Howard had apparently told him what the conversation was about. "Do you think that could be right?"

Gene took his time thinking over what he wanted to say. He raised his head slowly, looked the president in the eye. "Yes. I think that's exactly right. I've been spoiled all my life. I like to win. When I read the newsletter yesterday, I guess, to me, it seemed like I lost."

"It came down to you and Elder Wayment. I'm sure you know that."

"Well, no. I didn't know, but—"

"Of course you knew."

"Not really. People kept telling me I would get it, and I guess I wanted it pretty bad, but I didn't know what you were thinking."

President Fetzer leaned forward and put his elbows on his desk. He had his suit coat off, was wearing only his white shirt and a deep-blue tie. "There are a lot of things to consider when I choose someone for a position like that—but for me, the biggest thing is trying to get an answer from the Lord—what *he* wants me to do. When I get an answer, I don't always know the reasons. I don't pick the best missionary, necessarily—

based on my own observation; I pick the missionary the Lord wants me to call."

"Sure. I understand that."

"When you look back on your mission someday, what you're going to care about are the people you helped bring into the Church. The rest of it really doesn't matter very much."

"I know. I've had some good baptisms, but not very many, and some of those have fallen away already. Sometimes it feels like I haven't accomplished very much."

"Then why in the world would you want to be up here in the office when you have several good months to find more families?"

Gene nodded. He gripped his hands together. "I couldn't sleep last night," he said. "And that's what I kept thinking. All I really wanted was not to have to tract anymore. I was just looking for a way to end my real mission early, and that doesn't make sense."

President Fetzer laughed. He leaned back again. "Listen, Elder, I served my mission here too. I know what it's like. I used to ask my companion, 'What's wrong with these hard-headed Germans?'—and I'm one-hundred percent German myself. It's a tough place to serve. But you've got the best months of your mission ahead of you."

"I know. That's exactly what I've been telling myself all night. I didn't sleep at all."

"So what do we do about this little incident? You've broken one of our most important mission rules. I've had some sad things happen while I've served in this position, and every one of them would have been prevented if missionaries hadn't found a way to slip away from their companions."

"I assume you'll release me as zone leader," Gene said. "I don't know what else you'll do. I hope you don't send me home. What I'd like the most, though, is to stay in Augsburg. I like the ward, and we've got a good family we're teaching. When we met them, they didn't believe in God. But they're changing. I think they might be ready to accept the gospel."

President Fetzer picked up his pen, fiddled with it for a time, but didn't say anything. When he set it down, he said, "How would you like to spend the rest of your mission? What's your goal now?"

"I don't want to be a leader. I just keep letting positions like that get me mixed up about what I'm trying to do. I want to spend the last seven months of my mission working as hard as I can."

President Fetzer nodded. "I like that. I'm glad that's what you're feeling. But here's something you have to remember, Elder Thomas. You don't decide those things. I do. And the Lord helps me make the decisions. I asked you, and I'm glad to have your opinion. I even like your opinion. But if I feel inspired to send you somewhere in this next transfer, keep you as a ZL or take your position away from you entirely—even make you a junior companion because I can't trust you after what you did yesterday—I expect you to go and do what you're called to do."

"I understand that."

"But aren't you wondering what I will do?"

"I'm still hoping I get to stay in Augsburg a little while, but otherwise, it doesn't matter. I feel like I've messed up my whole mission. Most of the time my heart's been in the wrong place. These final months, I want to see if I can't make up for some of that."

"That's good, in a way. But Elder, don't be too hard on yourself. So much of life is trying to get your heart right, and no one is as pure as he ought to be. I'm not going to make you a junior companion, and I'm not going to punish you. You've been one of our best missionaries—no matter what you say about yourself—for almost two years. I'm not going to let this one mistake ruin all that. But don't even *think* of letting it happen again."

"Oh, no." Gene smiled.

President Fetzer smiled too. "I don't know what I'm going to do with you in the long run," he said, "but for right now, you get back to Augsburg, and you continue on as zone leader. Above all, see what you can do with this family you've been talking about."

"Thank you. I will."

Gene felt a lot better than he had on the way to Munich. But he wasn't satisfied with himself. He had made a vow, but he knew very well that the test was still to come.

# Chapter 14

Kent Wade was leaving on his mission, but before he entered the Language Training Mission in Provo, he made a last trip to Ogden. He and Diane ate at the Utah Noodle Parlor, where they had the jumbo shrimp—butterflied, battered, and fried—that were the specialty of the house. Afterward, they drove up Ogden Canyon. She thought of taking Kent to South Fork and the bridge that she and Scott had taken their magical "rides" on, but it didn't seem quite right, so she had him turn at Huntsville, where she showed him President David O. McKay's house, and then had him drive onto the point that extended into Pine View Reservoir. They parked and walked down to the shore. It was a warm evening in August 1966. They took their shoes off, and Kent rolled up his pants a little, but Diane didn't need to lift her skirt. She was wearing a favorite miniskirt, probably for the last time. She knew she would never be allowed to wear it at BYU, where she would be going in less than a month. She hadn't been able to resist, however, showing Kent how good her legs looked, brown from a whole summer of sunning.

Later, the two sat on the beach and watched the last of the sunlight disappear, the orange glow wobbling on the easy waves. Kent was on his way to Argentina and would be studying Spanish at the LTM. It would be strange for them both to be in Provo but unable to visit each other, but Kent had heard that the missionaries were allowed, on P-Day, to get around the city a little. "Maybe we could accidentally bump into each other somewhere," he said. "At the Wilkinson Center, or something like that. Accidents do happen, you know."

"Would that be a good idea, Kent?"

His smile faded gradually. "Probably not. It might just make things worse. It's going to be tough to be so close to BYU and not be able to do all the stuff I did last fall. I can't stand to think about all the guys chasing after you." He took hold of her hand.

"I'll just be a little freshman. No one's even going to notice me."

Kent laughed. "Are you kidding? The guys scout out all the new girls. You'll get caught in a stampede."

The truth was, Diane liked to think that might happen, but she didn't want to say that to Kent. She knew she wanted to date, plenty, but she also knew she wanted to date Kent again when he got back. Right now, she couldn't imagine meeting anyone she would like more. "Don't worry about that, okay? Just be the best missionary in Argentina, and know that I'll be counting the days until you get back."

"Do you mean that?"

"Of course I do." She touched his hair, more blond than before, after a summer of sun, and looked into his dark eyes. Then she gave him a gentle kiss. "I love you, Kent. You know I do."

"I don't seem to know anything anymore—except that *I* love *you.*" He kissed her, then turned toward the water again and pulled her close to him so that she was leaning against his side. "All my life I've been planning on my mission, but right now I wish I didn't have to go. I know that's the wrong way to feel, but I'm really scared. I don't know what it's going to be like in Argentina—and mostly, I want to stay here and just keep going to the Y and be with you. It would be so great to be there together."

"No. You wouldn't be happy with yourself if you didn't go. And we're both too young. It's better this way."

"Not if I lose you."

Diane turned a little, so she was looking at him. "But don't you think that things have a way of working out for the best? If we're meant for each other, we'll end up together."

"I don't know if I believe that, Diane. I see too many terrible marriages—even divorces."

"Don't you think that happens when couples don't try hard enough, or when they get off the path and start doing things they shouldn't?"

"Maybe. I don't know. But my cousin married this guy who turned out to be a real jerk. He treated her rotten. They were divorced after just a few years."

"You would never treat me that way."

"Just give me that chance, okay? I'll treat you like a *princess*, every day of your life."

"Don't worry, Kent. We'll have our chance. We'll make each other so happy." She nestled close to him again. She worried that her words were a little too close to a promise, but she really didn't want him to worry. She was going to write to him every week—she knew that for sure—and she would absolutely never commit to another guy until Kent was home and they had had another chance to be together.

"I'll never love anyone else but you," Kent whispered in her ear. "Just remember that every day I'm gone."

Diane didn't promise the same, but she felt it. When he kissed her again, she let herself melt against him, and then they cried together. This would be their last night together for such a long time.

Two weeks later, Richard and Bobbi drove Diane to Provo and then helped her carry her things into the King Henry Apartments. Most freshmen girls lived in Heritage Halls, but Diane's friends at BYU, including Kent's sister, Sandy, had told Diane she would like an apartment better. The only problem was, she and Janet Torgeson, her friend from Ogden, had signed up as roommates at a beautiful new apartment building, and then Janet had decided at the last minute—or her parents had—that she couldn't afford to go. So Janet was staying at Weber State and Diane would be assigned to some roommates—all people she didn't know.

The apartment was designed for six girls, with a kitchen, a living room, and two bedrooms filled up rather tightly with three beds in each. Diane had driven down fairly early and, as it turned out, was the first to arrive. The apartment manager told her that one of the bedrooms would be occupied by three girls who had lived there the year before, older students who weren't likely to arrive for another day or two, but Diane would be sharing her bedroom with two other freshmen.

Diane was excited, doing fine, until she looked at her dad as he was about to leave. His eyes had filled with tears, and she could see him swallowing, trying to control himself. She went to him and hugged him. "It's going to be so lonely at our house, sweetheart," he said. "It's hard to think you've grown up so quickly."

"I'll be home a lot, Dad—probably more weekends than you'll even want me."

"Come home *every* weekend, if you want. And if you can't find a ride, I'll come down and get you."

"Be careful what you promise," Bobbi said from behind him, and Diane's first thought was that her mom was probably happy to get rid of her. But then Diane saw the tears on her mother's face, and she was caught off guard by the emotions that set off.

"It seems like only a few days ago you were the size of little Ricky," Bobbi said. Ricky was with his grandma in Salt Lake so he wouldn't drive everyone crazy while they unpacked the car. "It's so hard for me to let you go."

Diane was amazed to hear her mother say such a thing. The past two years had seemed to stretch on forever. She had longed for nothing more than this day. But as her parents began to edge toward the door, Diane could hardly stand the thought of being left alone in this empty apartment with its ugly orange couch and chairs, and little else. She followed them to the car and hugged them again, and by then everyone was crying, Dad the worst of all. By the time the car pulled away—the miserable old station wagon Dad was going to drive until it rusted into dust—Diane was ready to run after her parents and tell them to repack the car.

She walked back up the outside stairs to the second floor. Then she stepped inside the apartment but left the door open, just in case someone would come by and she could say hello. She decided she had better start organizing her things. That would occupy her and make her little section of the bedroom seem "her place." But she opened her suitcase, glanced around, and was suddenly in tears again. How could she live here with five girls she didn't know?

Diane slipped to her knees and prayed. She asked for strength, and she felt buoyed up a little when she stood again. She made herself stay busy, but it was more than an hour before her first roommate arrived—and that wasn't much help. The girl came with her parents, and the whole scene was a repeat of her own farewell—only worse. The family had driven down from Wyoming—Star Valley. The father didn't cry, but he couldn't say a word. He held his hat in his hand and stared at the ground like a kid who had just sold his pet calf at a Future Farmers of America auction. The mother fussed and worried and complained about being crowded together with so many other girls, and in the end she gripped her little daughter and cried as though she were lamenting a death in the family. Then the two little sisters did the same. By then, Diane was actually doing somewhat better. She wanted to say, "Buck up, kid, the first hour is the worst: I've been there. I know."

When the family walked out and the roommate staggered back in, damp and red from her eyes to her neck, she lay on the couch in the living room and cried some more. Diane decided to leave her alone for a time. But finally she returned to the living room and said, "If I were you, I'd start unpacking. It gets your mind busy."

"I will. And I'll be all right in a couple of minutes. I know I'm acting stupid."

"I'm glad I got here first. You didn't get to see me blubbering in the bedroom. By the way, my name's Diane. Diane Hammond."

The girl sat up. She was short, with stout legs and colorless hair that looked as though it had been thought up in the fifties—curled a little and down on her shoulders, with a little wave in her bangs. She was rather sweet looking in her little traveling outfit—a striped top, beige and brown, the brown matching her slacks. Diane suspected she was the smartest girl in her high school and *loved* to read. Maybe it was her glasses that gave that impression. They were shaped like cat eyes, with a line of "jewels" at the corners. No one had worn those things for years.

"My name's Julianne Horsley." She pronounced it "Julie-Ann." She looked at Diane as though for the first time, and then she said, "I *just knew* I'd end up with a roommate like you. I'm going to watch you get ready for dates every night of my life while I sit here and study. You're my big sister all over again. The curse continues." But she laughed, and suddenly she looked a lot better. She had a nice smile, sort of long, with turned-up corners. Diane didn't say it, but she thought she could work with the girl. If she helped her fix that hair a little, hid her legs, and maybe accidentally stepped on those glasses—so she'd have to get some new ones—she'd get some dates.

"I'm not going out every night," Diane said. "I'll have to study twice as hard as most people just to pass my classes. Besides, I'm waiting for a missionary."

"That'll last about three weeks."

"Hey."

"No girl like you is going to stick it out for two years."

The girl had a mouth on her. But Diane sort of liked her feistiness. "I didn't say I was going to *sit home* and wait," Diane said, and she winked. "I'm just saying I'm not going to get serious with anyone."

"Maybe not. But every RM who meets you is going to get serious—*instantly*."

"I've got an idea. Why don't you start unpacking? I liked you better when you were bawling for your folks."

They were grinning at each other now. "Okay," she said. "I'm just glad you admitted that you cried too."

The third roommate didn't arrive until after noon. She had driven in from Van Nuys, California, with her older sister, who helped carry in her things and then took off to her own apartment. The new girl took a quick look around, did a once-over on Diane and Julianne, and said, "Hi. I'm Terry Turner. Is that not the ugliest furniture you've ever seen in your life?"

Those were the words, but her face seemed to say, "Isn't this fun? I'm away from home."

She was a pretty girl who filled out her skirt and blouse in all the best places, but maybe in some of the wrong ones a little, too. She had straight blonde hair, lighter than Diane's, but clearly she had improved on the color the good Lord had chosen for her. Diane took note of that.

The girls introduced themselves, and then Julianne said, "You're sharing a bedroom with us."

"We don't have our own rooms?" But Terry was still smiling, as though the idea was rather appealing.

"It'll be just like summer camp," Diane said. "We can sit up all night in our jammies and talk about the cute boys at our junior high."

"I like you, Diane. You only *look* like someone I wouldn't like." She was *still* smiling. Diane was pretty sure Terry wasn't nasty. She was just a smart aleck. "Now answer me this question: Where do the boys live?"

"Half of these apartments have boys in them," Diane said.

"A lot of the boys live down in Helaman Halls, on the other side of campus," Julianne said. "A boy I know from Afton lives there."

"What's Afton?" Terry asked.

"It's a town in Wyoming. That's where I'm from."

"Don't worry. That wasn't your fault. You'll overcome it in time."

Julianne laughed. "It's not so bad," she said. "You're from LA, I assume."

"How did you know that?"

"I've seen you before. You're all over Wyoming in the summertime."

"I see I've been put with a couple of smart-mouths," Diane said. "What happened to the sweet little BYU girls I've always heard about?"

"They didn't have the sense to avoid the dorms," Terry said.

The next few days were crazy but fun. The other three roommates were older—a senior and two juniors—and fit the BYU image a little more than Terry did, but they were really nice. They were all from Holbrook, Arizona, and had grown up together. Carol and Susan Huff were sisters—both small and dark haired—and Annette Poulson, Susan's best friend from high school, was a little taller, a little lighter in complexion, but still almost interchangeable. The best thing was, they were pleasant, could cook, and weren't the type to be noisy or to come in terribly late, and even better, not one of them was likely to be much competition with the boys in the ward.

Diane felt some moments of homesickness, especially when she tried to settle into her lumpy mattress at night, but Terry kept her going in the daytime. Registration, in the Smith Fieldhouse, was a nightmare, and both girls ended up crying more than once, but they finally collected enough IBM cards, with signatures, to be able to claim they had a full-load schedule. Diane didn't have a single class she had wanted, and a couple she ended up with scared her to death, but she really was a college student.

On Saturday evening, Diane went with Terry to the football game. Diane had been hearing all the talk—at least from the guys she had met so far—about BYU sports being on the rise. During the previous year the football team, after being terrible almost forever, had won the league championship and even beaten Utah—for only about the third time in history—and the basketball team had won the National Invitational Tournament. Tonight the team was beating New Mexico, easily, but Diane really didn't care. What she liked was the enormous crowd at the stadium, down on the lower part of campus, and—when she and Terry got tired of football and decided to leave—she liked the way the boys all turned to check them out.

Church, which met in the Harris Fine Arts Center, was especially fun. Diane thought she had died and gone to heaven when she saw all the cute boys in her ward, a lot of them older guys, returned missionaries. And then on Tuesday night her ward held an "opening social." School had started by then, and Diane's professors had piled on a ton of work, but everyone in the ward seemed to show up for the party. Diane loved the atmosphere. Everyone dressed better than they would have at high-school parties, and, of course, no one was drinking or swearing or hanging all over each other when they danced. But it wasn't as "Sunday Schoolish" as some of her friends in Ogden had told her it would be. So many of the kids really were cool—knew what to wear, how to talk. And even though President Wilkinson had established a new rule this year—no more "fad dances"—she rather preferred to dance close with some of these guys, and she loved the Ray Coniff music that was playing.

Diane had been dancing with a tall freshman boy from Las Vegas when another guy, even taller—and *very* good-looking—walked up behind her partner. He tapped the boy's shoulder, all the while looking straight into Diane's eyes, as if to say, "I'll save you from this little kid. A man has arrived."

But that's not what he said when he took her hand and slipped his arm around her back. "I'm Greg Lyman," he told her. "And you're Diane Hammond. I'm *more* than happy to meet you."

Diane allowed her warmest smile, and this guy handled it as though it were nothing new to him. He simply let his own light shine. And he had plenty—straight teeth, tan skin, carved cheekbones, deep-brown eyes. "How do you know my name?" she asked.

"I asked on Sunday, the first time I saw you."

"And who knew?"

"By then, half the guys in the ward."

"People *are* very nice here. They learn your name quickly."

"They learn *your* name quickly."

"So tell me, Greg Lyman—notice that I remembered—where did you serve your mission? Isn't that the question down here?"

He chuckled. "You *are* catching on," he said. Her first take on the guy was that he thought of himself as super cool, but maybe he wasn't *all* show. There was something quite natural about the way he was laughing.

But then a sudden look of concern came into his face. "Oops," he said. "Come with me, okay?" He walked away quickly, pulling her behind him with one hand, not worrying too much whether he bumped the other dancers. They walked from the multipurpose room where they had been dancing into the center court of the Fine Arts Building. "It's a beautiful night," he said. "Why don't we go outside and take a walk?"

"But my dear sir, I don't know you. My mother wouldn't like this."

"I told you, I'm Greg Lyman. Didn't you ask anyone about *me?*"

"I did see you at church. But I only made a mental note."

"Really, you noticed me?" And for the first time, he sounded young, flattered.

"Yes, I did. You're very good-looking. But then, you know that."

He had begun to walk, pulling her a little, but now, just as they stepped outside, he stopped and turned toward her, still holding her hand. "You think I'm cocky, don't you?"

"Yes."

"Everyone does. I don't know why."

"It might have something to do with all that charm you were

spreading around back there." She lowered her voice to imitate him. "'And you're Diane Hammond. I'm *more* than happy to meet you.'"

"Hey, I thought that was pretty smooth. Didn't you like it?"

"It was a little *too* smooth, if you want to know the truth."

"Maybe I am a little cocky," he said, and he began to walk again, down the stairs and then out into the quad. "But I'll tell you the truth. People who seem arrogant are usually just insecure. I learned that in my Personal Adjustment class. So think of me that way—just a guy who's unsure of himself around a beautiful girl and, therefore, putting on a front."

"Oh, brother."

"You don't buy that?"

"No. I think you're an overly confident guy trying to pretend that he's not quite sure of himself, so he'll seem even *more* appealing."

"More appealing than what?"

"You know 'more than what'—more than just good-looking."

"So tell me this: How good-looking do you think I am? In my insecurity, I really need to know."

She let go of his hand and stopped. "Hey, do you ever let up?" she said.

He turned toward her, stood with his hands tucked into the pockets of his tan slacks. He was wearing a brown V-neck sweater that bulged a little over some pretty well-developed chest muscles. She liked that. "Yes, I do," he said. "I'm going to start right now. But don't you want to know why I dragged you out of that dance the way I did?"

"Actually, yes. I was going to ask."

"Someone was on his way to cut in on us. I didn't want that. I figured possession was nine points of the law—or whatever it is they say. By the way, I'm planning to go to law school—just in case you're looking for a man with a future."

"You *don't* lay off."

He laughed hard, in a burst, and then he said, "No, really. I do."

There were lots of stars tonight, a big sky, and the moon, or about half of one, was coming up over Y Mountain. She could see him fairly well, and she liked the look that had come into his eyes. "No more jousting," he said. "I really do want to get to know you. Tell me a few things about yourself."

"You go first."

"No. I'm serious. I want to know who you are."

"My name, you know. I'm from Ogden."

"Actually, I found that out, too. You're a freshman. Your dad's a professor at Weber State, and your uncle is Alex Thomas, the congressman. That much I know already."

"I haven't told *anyone* that. How could you know?"

"Well . . . I did a little research. I know people who know people."

"Where are *you* from?"

"Salt Lake."

"East High, I'll bet."

"No. Olympus."

"Why didn't you go to the U?"

"I did when I was a freshman. But after my mission, I wanted to come down here—partly to live away from home for a while, and mostly so that I would break connections with my old friends from the frat houses. I wasn't likely to be my best self if I fell back in with them."

"They don't have fraternities down here, do they?"

"Not exactly. But they have clubs. Maybe you've heard of the Brickers?"

"I thought BYU ended all that."

"They did. But there's a sort of *extension* of the old Goldbrickers Club, I guess you might call it. It's called the Samuel Hall Society. I'm a member."

"Isn't that just getting around the rules?"

"Yeah, maybe. But it sure is a good group of guys." He laughed. But then he said, "Wait a minute; we were going to talk about you."

"What do you want to know?"

"What do you like to do?" He was still standing in front of her, and she was amazed at how confidently he kept looking into her eyes. She hadn't known many guys who didn't lose a little composure when she met them eye to eye.

"Ski, for one thing."

"Actually, I knew that too. Skiing is not my life anymore, but it once was. I could never marry anyone who didn't ski, or who wasn't willing to learn."

"So is this my interview? Are you trying to decide whether you want to marry me?"

He finally did look just a little embarrassed. "I'm sorry," he said. "That came out wrong. I just meant that as a comment—not quite the way it sounded."

"You must also know that I have a missionary."

"I did hear that, but I had assumed it anyway. Every freshman girl is waiting for a missionary."

"What happened to your girl, while you were gone?"

"You're really very good at this, you know it? That's about three times you've stabbed me right in the heart. I'm not used to girls who know how to do that."

"I've had to learn to play some defense in my life."

"Yeah, well, I can understand that. But the answer to your question, of course, is that she didn't wait. Maybe you don't understand how the system works. Girls wait until they meet a returned missionary they like better than the one they sent off. Then they get married, and the poor guys who get dear-Johned come home and take up with girls who are supposed to be waiting for other guys. It's a good system because girls are always waiting, but they never have to wait the full two years."

"I will."

"That's good."

"You don't believe me, do you?"

"I don't know. It *does* happen every now and then. But you're going to have lots of chances to change your mind."

"I'm eighteen. I don't really see a problem in waiting until I'm twenty."

"I think you're right."

"Really?"

"I do. I'm twenty-two. I've been home a year. I'm glad I didn't get married as soon as I got back. And I'm actually in no hurry to get married now."

"So what does that mean?" she asked. "You're not going to pursue me?"

He smiled at her gently, if coyly, and then he took hold of both of her shoulders. "Trust me. It doesn't mean that," he said. "Consider me, officially, in pursuit."

For once in her life, it was Diane's knees that felt a little weak.

Later, when she went to bed—after answering all of Terry's questions about her "disappearance"—she wondered at herself. Kent hadn't been "gone" three weeks yet, and she was already unsure that he was the only guy she could ever take an interest in.

# Chapter 15

Kathy had spent most of the summer of 1966 in Massachusetts. She had gone home for a couple of weeks right after school had gotten out, but then she had made an "emergency call" to LaRue. "Could I possibly come and stay with you for the summer?" she had pleaded. "It's just not good for me to be at home right now." LaRue had gone one better than that. She had called around and found Kathy a job as a research assistant for a professor on campus. It wasn't a big-paying job, but it had given Kathy the chance to tell her parents that she could earn money and further her education at the same time. The fact was, she could make almost twice as much working in the office at her father's car dealership, but money was not the main issue, and Kathy had the feeling that her parents were almost as uncomfortable with her as she was with them. Kathy's hair had grown long now—long and straight—and she liked the look of long cotton skirts with sleeveless blouses. At work, at the dealership, the other women in the office had teased her about looking like a "hippie"—a word that people were using these days to describe the bohemian types who were congregating in San Francisco and a few other places. Wally kept telling Kathy that he didn't think sleeveless blouses were proper for a Mormon girl. "I'm not a *girl*, Dad," was usually Kathy's response. The tension between Kathy and her parents about language never seemed to end. "They're not *colored*, Dad," Kathy would say. "And they're not Negroes. They want to be called *black*."

Lorraine would try to explain that it wasn't easy to make those kinds of changes, that she and Wally had always been taught *not* to use that word, but Dad would get irritated. "'Negro' is not an insulting word," he would tell her. "I'll try to remember to say 'black,' but if I say something else, you know very well how I mean it."

But the discomfort ran deeper than that, and most of the friction came from debates over Vietnam. It was true that Dad sometimes wondered whether it was wise for America to get so deeply involved in a foreign war. He had listened to Alex, who thought that South Vietnam had to take responsibility for its own war if there was to be any hope of success. But it was one thing to discuss an issue like that in the halls of Congress, or even to question presidential decisions, but it was quite another, as far as Wally was concerned, to march in the streets, shut down traffic, and especially to denounce America. He pleaded with Kathy to work "through" the system, not "against" it, to enter the "public debate." He would watch the news at night and then tell her how disgusted he was with the demonstrators. "They're supposed to be students, but they dress up like gypsies and yell gutter language. What kind of debate is that?"

The truth was, Kathy had been fighting all the previous year to convince her SDS chapter not to be so hostile. But she didn't tell her father that. "Maybe it's the only way the opposition can be heard in this country," Kathy would say. "You can debate all you want and no one pays any attention. But when you march in the streets, you end up on TV."

"Sure. But there are decent ways to behave, and a good Church member ought to know enough to stay away from that kind of behavior."

This, of course, was a warning. Dad had been released as bishop during the previous spring and called as a counselor in the stake presidency. He seemed to feel, more than ever, that he had to take the "official position" on every issue. But Grandpa was even more difficult for her, and it was an argument with him that had finally left Kathy feeling that she had better leave before she made things worse. She had been sitting with her dad and Grandpa Thomas in Grandma and Grandpa's living room after one of Grandma's wonderful Sunday dinners. She had enjoyed the time there and was in no mood to argue. She didn't say a word when Grandpa talked about the good chance he saw for Republicans to pick up some seats in the House that fall. "Maybe we can stop Johnson before he ruins this country," he said. "This bussing of kids out of their own neighborhoods is just about the worst idea I've ever heard." He glanced at Kathy, looking a little wary, but she didn't respond.

A little later, she didn't blink when he said, "I like what Ronald Reagan told people out in California. He said these antiwar demonstrators are standing up for 'sex, drugs and *treason*,' and that's about right. He's going to win that election, and he'll be a good governor."

Dad wasn't saying much, probably because he was waiting for the fireworks, but Kathy told herself that she wasn't going to take the bait this time. But then Grandpa talked about the terrible decisions the Supreme Court had made since Earl Warren had been chief justice. "Those guys are putting handcuffs on the police instead of on the lawbreakers. With this new Miranda decision, a case will get thrown out if the police jail a man, tuck him in bed, and forget to kiss him goodnight."

Kathy decided to say only one thing. "But remember what happened to me in Mississippi, Grandpa. There have to be some restraints on police and judges or they can get away with anything. You wouldn't want someone searching your house without a reasonable—"

"If I have nothing to hide, why should I be worried about it?"

Wally jumped in quickly. "Grandpa's not opposed to police having to get a search warrant, but criminals—hard-core *criminals*—are getting off on little technicalities these days."

"That's exactly right," Grandpa said. He was sitting in his big chair—the throne he had spoken from for as long as Kathy could remember. He leaned forward, pointed at Kathy, and said, "And I'll tell you what else is wrong. This court is leaning over backward to be fair, and in the process is ending up *unfair*. With all this so-called *affirmative action*, a white guy hardly has a chance to get a job these days. And look at the other things Warren and his buddies are doing: taking prayer out of the schools;

ruling that pornography is nothing more than *free expression*. I don't agree with some of the things the John Birch Society is saying, but they're exactly right when they say Earl Warren ought to be impeached."

Kathy wasn't about to defend pornography, and even though she didn't think it really mattered all that much whether prayers were said in school—since that seemed more of a personal matter—she decided it was better just to let the conversation die. She glanced away, didn't say anything.

Grandpa laughed. "Well, now, I know what you're thinking, Kathy. 'My old-fashioned grandpa is spouting off again.' And I guess I am. But, honey, I really am alarmed at what's happening to us. The other night, on the news, I watched one of these antiwar kids light an American flag on fire, and I didn't know whether I felt more anger or sadness. There was a time—and not very long ago—when no one would have *thought* of such a thing."

Kathy nodded. She didn't like flag-burning either.

"I don't want to see you mixed up with people like that, honey. I know you oppose the war, and that's your right, but these kids are going way too far. You've got to agree with me there."

"Grandpa, I don't agree with people doing that," Kathy said. "But remember, that's the thing about America that's great. We all have a right to express ourselves. To some people a flag is just cloth, and by burning that cloth they can shock someone like you. It's a way of getting your attention. It says how serious they are, how ashamed of America they are right now. It's a symbolic way of—"

"That flag is a symbol a lot of people fought and died for," Grandpa said. "Including the uncle you never had a chance to know. Look at what your father went through for that symbol."

"Not for the symbol, for the country."

"To us it's the same thing," Wally said. "When I saw that flag the first time, coming home from the war, I thought I'd never seen anything so beautiful in my life."

"I know, Dad, but I'm just saying, part of what you fought for was the right to free expression. The great thing about America is that a person can do something that's offensive to most of us, and we don't take him out and shoot him for it."

"Maybe we should," Grandpa said. He leaned back in his chair, folding his arms over his big chest, the wide expanse of his white shirt, his brown tie.

"Grandpa, think what you're saying. If you're worried about the flag, you ought to be *really* upset about our pilots dropping napalm, killing children, burning up—"

"That's not our fault. The Communists asked for this fight."

It was the old argument, the old nonsense, as far as Kathy was concerned. Her temper fired, and she struck back hard. "Well then, Grandpa, why don't you start making parts for those millions of tons of bombs we're dropping? You got rich off World War II. Maybe you could get even richer off this war."

"Kathy!" her dad said. But Grandpa only stared at her, unable to say a word.

Later that night, Kathy could find no excuse for what she had said. She apologized soon after she had let the words fly, and apologized again before she left to go home. But she could see what she had done. She wasn't sure that she could ever be close to her grandpa again, that he would allow it. And worse, she wasn't sure, if she stuck around, that she wouldn't do something just as stupid again. The gap between her and Grandpa—and maybe even the gap between her and her parents—had become too deep.

It was while Kathy was on the airplane, flying back to Boston, that she finally admitted to herself that part of the reason for her bad mood, half the reason she had been so cantankerous, had nothing at all to do with "issues." She had known that things had not gone well with Marshall at Christmastime, but she had hoped that something better would happen that summer. Her tendency was to think that she and Marshall were wrong for each other, but Grandma had let Kathy know that he had gotten his mission call to England. He would be leaving soon. It was hard for Kathy not to cling to some little hope that something more could develop when he got back. Maybe she only liked the idea of having a boyfriend, or maybe she only wanted to think that the one guy who had ever kissed her would be eager to see her whenever she got back to Utah. But she hadn't heard from him, not even after Grandma had seen him at church and let him know that Kathy was home. He hadn't called to say hello—or good-bye. What Kathy heard from a friend at the university was that he was going with someone, but Kathy didn't pump the friend for details. She pretended that she didn't care—even pretended to herself. But now, on the airplane, she realized he was gone from her life for good. She thought of the lovely times she had spent with him, and she liked the memories, but she was mortified when she felt a tear drip onto her cheek.

She hoped she would feel better about life once she got back to Northampton, and LaRue, but that also turned out to be uncomfortable at times. Aunt LaRue was willing to think and talk, but she never took any action. She constantly denounced students who were "too young to know much of anything but all fired up to go out and change the world."

"That's because only people under thirty have the guts to make changes," Kathy would tell her. "Once you've gone through the whole system—college, job, family—you lose your nerve. You just go along with everything and you quit *recognizing* what's wrong."

"Tell me again. Just what is so wrong?"

"Americans are a bunch of zombies, walking around in their sleep. They're cogs in a wheel. Corporations tell us we need a bigger refrigerator this year, so we dump the old one and 'buy up.' They tell us our natural body fluids smell bad, so we dab a thousand chemicals on ourselves. We won't even let our natural hair grow on our bodies. We watch TV commercials, see all these perfect models, with perfect skin, perfect teeth, perfect little noses, and we tell ourselves, 'If I don't look like that, I'm disgusting.'"

But LaRue had begun to laugh.

"What's the matter?"

"You haven't stopped shaving under your arms, have you?"

Kathy rolled her eyes, but she couldn't help smiling. "No. But I should. I'm too much of a sleepwalker myself."

~

At least LaRue could make Kathy laugh at herself once in a while, and LaRue did share some of Kathy's feelings: about civil rights, about the heartlessness of too many Americans, and even about the war. What she often did, however, was take the edge off some of Kathy's rhetoric. Kathy would come home from meetings with her friends in the movement, livid over some new issue she had learned about, and LaRue would raise questions, ask for evidence, suggest other factors, and Kathy would find herself coming off her high horse a little. Still, it was that very balance that kept her from feeling quite complete. Some of the SDS people were so clear in what they thought, what they hated, that they never had to search their own souls. They were religious in their commitment, and in that sense Kathy found them much like her Mormon friends. They had a simple, clear point of view and never wrestled with it. What Kathy longed for was some place in her life where she felt that same unity of mind and soul.

When school started in the fall, the SDS chapters at the University of Massachusetts and Amherst were picking up in intensity, and a lot more Smith women were getting involved. The first meeting in the fall, held on the UMass campus, was full of intense emotion. Seventy or eighty members had gathered in a classroom that was too crowded, with all the seats full and people standing against the walls around the room. Robby called the meeting to order and gave a little talk about the need to "turn up the heat" this fall. He was interrupted over and over with cheers and applause.

The buildup in Vietnam was accelerating, and speaker after speaker expressed the theme that Robby had introduced: the only way to stop the war was to bring America to its knees, to stop "business as usual." Working "through the system" only implied that the system deserved respect. It was the system itself that was corrupt, and a powerful movement, especially of young people, would have to turn everything upside down. Average people would accept Lyndon Johnson's lies until they recognized that a massive number of dissidents was standing up for what was right.

Kathy was nervous about almost all of that, and concerned about the actions some might take. She was no longer a freshman, no longer new to the organization, and it seemed time, finally, to let her own opinion be known. She raised her hand and Robby called on her. "No one hates this war more than I do," she said. She felt the shrillness in her voice. She coughed, to hide her tenseness, but as she did, she heard someone whisper, "You *know* what *she's* going to say." At least that angered her enough to give her some power. "If we're going to change the minds of the American people, we cannot offend them so deeply that they won't listen to us. Demonstrations show our disgust with the war, but we have to communicate something more than that. We have to reach parents—at every economic level—who don't want to lose a son on the other side of the world. We have to—"

"Sit down, little rich girl. We've *talked* to people enough," someone called out. "It doesn't work." Others in the room cheered at the words.

Kathy stood straight, waited, and Robby shouted, "Shut up! She's one of us. She has a right to speak. Remember, we're the Students for a *Democratic* Society."

Only Robby could have said something like that and stopped the voices. Kathy appreciated that he would help her.

"There are ideas that ring true to many people in this country," she said as calmly as she could. "We're spending vast amounts of money for a war that common people receive no benefit from. Stokely Carmichael said that white people are sending black people to make war on yellow people in order to defend the land we stole from red people."

"Right on!" a woman shouted. Kathy was fairly sure it was Dee Dee, but she didn't look around.

"That's something blacks in this country are beginning to feel. It's an idea we can build on. Inflation is picking up because of the war, and that's something the average working guy understands. We need to ask him what he's getting for his dollar while the government is spending billions on bombs. Johnson tells us we're fighting Communism, but that's pretty abstract when people have to pay more for gasoline or a loaf of bread."

"Make your point, Kathy," Robby said.

"I'm saying that if we pound on some of those ideas, drive them home, we'll get somewhere. But if we burn flags, or try to—" A shout went up—a deluge of insults. She tried to shout over the noise. "We can't make people so angry that they forget the real issues." But they weren't listening.

Robby called the crowd to order, but then he said, "We understand that point of view, Kathy. It's what we were saying two years ago, even last year. It's a way of thinking that most of us have finally given up on."

This brought a raucous response, cheers and shouts. Kathy sat down.

But Lester was suddenly on his feet without being called on. "Kathy's made the first sense I've heard today," he yelled, his voice so full of passion that he seemed to stun the others. "Don't you see what we're doing to ourselves by creating all this hatred? We're losing our own moral high ground. We're becoming the enemy. People hate *us* so much that they're embracing a war that once meant nothing to them."

Lester paused and the room was quiet. But then, from the back, Kathy heard Dee Dee's voice. "You tell 'em, Uncle Tom. And teach us all how to say, 'yass-suh, boss.' I think you know how to say it just right. You've had practice."

"That's not fair, Dee Dee. You know I—"

"You tell those black folks down in Grenada, Mississippi, to be *polite*—the ones who got their heads busted with ax handles last week because they wanted to integrate the schools, *according to the law*. Or tell it to the parents of that black man who was murdered by the police in Chicago last month. Tell those Chicago folks they shouldn't be putting up a fuss, rioting in the streets. They should ask the police, very *politely*, not to kill anyone else."

Another roar came from the crowd, and Lester was finished too. Kathy knew that the momentum of the movement, not just here but across the country, was far beyond her influence, or Lester's. And she wondered—maybe they were right. Maybe quiet little demonstrations would never make a difference. Maybe this really was war—war at home—and maybe brute force was the only power that could disrupt the country enough to wake the people up.

After the meeting everyone was gathering at Robby's house, as usual. Kathy pleaded with her friends from Smith not to stay too long. She felt out of place now, embarrassed that so many of the members felt that she was some sort of voice for middle-class values. She tried to explain herself to a couple of people who gave her a hard time, but gradually she slipped into the background and chatted only with her closer friends, people who had been on the line with her and respected how hard she had worked.

Everyone was drinking, except for Kathy; and LSD, the drug that had swept through San Francisco and was creating a whole new way of seeing things—new music, new clothes, a new craziness—was finally reaching some of her SDS friends. She was almost sure that the guys who shared

Robby's house, Kirk Zapata and Stu Yates—and a few other people—had dropped acid before the party started. They were acting wilder than they ever had on alcohol or marijuana. The mood of the party was almost frightening to her.

Eventually, though, Robby approached Kathy and said, "Come here. I want to talk to you." He took her by the hand, began pulling her toward the door.

"Come where?"

"Out to the porch, where it's not so noisy."

So they walked outside and sat on a broken-down couch. The house was a big Victorian two-story place, white frame with black shutters. It had probably been nice at one time, but the furnishings were shabby, the carpet soiled. Here on the porch the floorboards were worn, even breaking up. Kathy could hear the buzz of the people inside, but more pressing were the pounding voices of the Troggs, wailing, "Wild thing, you make my heart sing. You make *everything* . . . groovy."

"I've missed you," Robby said. "I've thought about you all summer."

"Do you mind if I don't believe that?"

"Yes. I do mind. I'm not as good a person as I ought to be, but I don't lie. I think you know that."

Actually, Kathy didn't know that. Robby loved the sound of his own voice, and she wasn't at all sure that he was tied to truth as the main arbiter of what he had to say. Maybe he meant the things he said when he said them; she just wasn't sure that he was honest with himself. "What did you do this summer?" she asked, so she wouldn't have to deal with what he had said.

"I went home. That didn't last long. I couldn't stand it. So I moved in with a couple of buddies of mine in Manhattan."

"Did you work somewhere?"

"No. I was bummed out. You know, from all we were doing in the spring. So I just took it easy. I partied too much, smoked too much weed.

Dropped more acid than I ever thought I would." He laughed. "You can't imagine that kind of life, can you?"

"Maybe not. But we're not so different in one way. I went home too, and I didn't like being there. So I came back here. I worked for a professor."

"Always the good student." He turned more toward her, and he leaned back against the end of the couch. He was smiling, looking good. His hair was longer than ever, almost to his shoulders now, but he had shaved his beard as she had always thought he should. There was something new in his dark eyes, as though shaving had given them more prominence, more clarity.

"I was a good student in high school," Kathy said, "but I sort of blew away winter semester last year. My grades dropped like a rock. I've got to study more this year."

"Do you still want to go to law school?"

"No. I don't think so. I'm not going to play that game. I'm thinking about leaving after next year, maybe going into the Peace Corps."

"Hey, we're getting to you. You're starting to change. But what was all that business in our meeting today? You sounded like little Miss America."

But he smiled, looking gentle. She wished she hadn't said anything in the meeting. She was afraid she had sounded like her grandfather. "It's what I feel, Robby. But maybe I'm wrong. I'll have to admit that what we've done so far hasn't changed anything. Maybe we do have to push things harder this year."

The truth was, she wasn't sure what she believed at the moment. But she did feel the need for him to think well of her.

"You *are* something, Kathy. You said what you thought, and said it well. But you listened, too. I keep watching you evolve, right before my eyes. And, oh, I do like what I see." He shifted and then slid toward her. When he slipped his arm around her shoulder, she smelled the alcohol on his breath, but she smiled and shook her head. "Now, now," she said.

"Yes. Now. It's time for me to kiss you."

And he did.

Kathy didn't stop him. She even let him pull her close and kiss her a second time—warmly, not wildly, but certainly more passionately than the kisses she had shared with Marshall. She told herself she was giving him all she would ever give, but she also knew he wasn't thinking that way. She put her hands on his chest, pushed back, and then slid farther back from him. He smiled, as if to tell her that he would let her decide for now, but that he would be back sometime, and she worried about what she had allowed to get started.

"You're a virgin, aren't you?" he said.

"You know the answer to that question."

"I think that's good. Virtue is always good. It's commitment. It's sticking to what you believe."

"Is this your clever little way of trying to get closer so you can take my virtue away?"

"Probably. But don't let me do it. I'll think more of you if you don't. You're the purest person I know."

"*Purest?* That's not what you told me last spring. You said I was a little Mormon do-gooder."

He grinned. "You have a good memory." He turned, faced forward, and looked across the front yard. "Okay, here's the truth. You should *never* trust me. If I try to come at you one way and it doesn't work, I'll try something else. Even what I'm saying now is just another way to manipulate you. It's how I am. It's how I do things. I want you, but probably just for a night, and then I'd lose interest. What I like about you—besides the way you look—is that you don't seem to have any ulterior motives for what you do. You have this innocent quality, like a child. If I were a decent man, I wouldn't want to mess that up. But you're a challenge to me, and I can't seem to stop myself. I'll tell you later on that I was drunk when I said all this, but I'm actually giving it to you straight."

Kathy was amazed by all of this. She was impressed that he would admit so much. "Robby, I know you think I'm too uptight, but you need something to believe yourself. I get the impression you're looking for it."

"I believe what I say about the war and about this country."

"I know. But you need something behind it all—to build a philosophy on."

"I have a philosophy. I'm just not a decent human being. I want what I want, and I go for it—no matter what it does to someone else." He thought about that for a time, and then he added, "Religion isn't the answer. I may be a con man, but religion is the biggest con of all. I think sooner or later, as you get older, you'll know that. It'll become the natural thing for you to break loose from some of that. Then—if that time comes—and you want me for a night or two, and I still want you, I see no problem. What difference does it make?"

"I could never feel that way," Kathy said.

"No. Probably not. But the time is coming when you'll have to choose. I keep telling you that." He patted her hand, like a friend, and then he said, "I'm going to see who's got a joint to smoke."

Kathy stayed on the porch and waited. Peter, Paul, and Mary were singing "Blowin' in the Wind."

---

It was well into the evening when Kathy got back to Baldwin House. She was rooming with Janet Stowe again this year, although she wasn't sure why. But there was no one else in the house she preferred all that much over Janet, and she didn't want to change houses. If she stayed another year she could get a single room; she looked forward to that. The big excitement this fall was that Julie Nixon, Richard Nixon's daughter, had enrolled as a freshman and had moved into the house. Very few of the girls thought highly of Nixon, but they still treated Julie as though she were a celebrity. Kathy was put off by the whole idea.

Tonight Kathy had been glad when she had seen Janet downstairs smoking with some friends on the porch. That meant Kathy would have the room to herself for a while. She still had two chapters of European History to read. She would have to put off a paper for her English class until another day, but her time was running out.

The first thing Kathy noticed was a letter on her bed. She knew from the lightweight airmail envelope that it must be from Gene. She had only had five or six letters from him over the years he had been gone, but she always liked to hear from him. She had to forgive him for some of the things he would say, of course. She told herself that a mission was a "time out of time," and there was no way he could understand everything that was happening in the States now. She forgave him easily, though—because he was Gene. She sat on her bed, opened the letter, and read:

> Dear Cuz,
>
> So how are things back in the USA? It won't be all that long until I'm back. My mission president told me I'd get to come home before Christmas instead of waiting until January. I guess they figure we don't get much done during the holidays anyway, so why not ship us home to be with our families? I'm trying not to think about that, though. Two years ago I would have given anything to have my mission over, but now I'm trying to finish up right.
>
> You probably don't have much idea what things are like in the mission field. I know I didn't, not until I got here. It's something you do for the Lord, and not for yourself, but knowing that is one thing and doing it is another. I'm trying now, in my final months, to do things for the right reason. I don't know whether I'm doing it very well, but I'm really trying. The trouble is, I haven't

> had a baptism for a while, which is hard, and then I get thinking too much about Christmas and getting back to the U winter quarter. You can imagine what those kinds of thoughts do to the spirit I keep praying for.
>
> I don't know whether I'll manage things when I get home or not. Every now and then I hear some of the music that's playing in England and the States now, and it scares me. I don't know how anyone can listen to that stuff and still feel close to God. The other day we were at a member family's home and they were watching the news. I saw all these long-haired American kids throwing rocks at cops and yelling like they were nuts. I just couldn't believe it. What's going wrong with America? I don't know how I'll adjust when I get home.

Kathy dropped the letter onto the bed. She knew where Gene was coming from, knew how he thought. She loved him for how hard he was trying to do the right thing. But still—what was the big deal about the length of someone's hair? Why did that make so much difference to him? And why couldn't he at least allow the possibility that protesters were people who were as idealistic as he was? Could Gene, after his mission, sit down with Robby and talk about their differences, or would Gene take one look at Robby and refuse to listen? Or would Robby be the first to do that?

It was strange to think that both of them were questioning their own motivations, both rather disappointed with themselves, and yet she doubted that either could admit that to the other. They would take their positions and harden them as they talked. Kathy loved Gene, and tonight she had rather liked Robby. Still, she knew, the two could never tolerate each other. Maybe Robby was right. Maybe the day was coming when she would have to choose which side she was on. And maybe it really was impossible to choose both. But she couldn't stand to think that was true.

# Chapter 16

During the years when Hans had longed to escape his country, he had told himself that he could manage to leave his family. Now, however, he was finally away from home—in Magdeburg, at the university—and he missed his parents and Inga every minute. He had never really been away from his family for more than a few days at a time, and he hadn't experienced any other way of life. Now he was almost 200 kilometers away and wouldn't be able to make a trip home until Christmas. What was worse than that was that he knew he would probably never live at home again. His homesickness really was like an illness, weakening him, ruining his appetite, upsetting his stomach. He worked hard, did his homework dutifully—partly because it occupied his mind—but he felt no connection to other students. They thought differently, behaved differently, and they took a dim view, for the most part, of his Mormon background.

Hans was a year younger than the typical first-year student. Most prospective students had to work in a practical field for a year before entering a university, but *Direktor* Knorr had arranged for the government to waive that requirement. He had convinced officials that they should allow Hans's labor during the year he had been away from school to substitute for his practical training. Hans had worried until the last second that the *Stasi* would protest his admission, but he had heard nothing more from their agents. What he didn't have was any assurance that the matter was closed.

Hans tried to be happy that he was finally a university student, but he attended his classes, studied in the library or his dorm room, and stayed on the edges of university life. It was easier not to get to know people so he wouldn't have to explain himself, his beliefs. He even avoided becoming personal with his roommate, Rainer Kuntze.

Hans had stopped asking himself whether he was the cause of Berndt's death. He knew it was something he could never answer, and he had to go on with life. But avoiding the question didn't take the picture out of his head. At odd times, and often in dreams, he would see Berndt's body fall, see his shape in silhouette, and he would hear the gunfire. He knew it was a kind of self-indulgence, something like self-pity, to blame himself, and yet it was a dark spot in his memory, an ugly awareness, and it represented Hans's vulnerability. He could lose what he had gained, his chance to study, at any moment. He never lived a day without wondering whether the *Stasi* would show up.

Even though Berndt had not been a terribly close friend, he was virtually Hans's only friend. Now there was no one. Greta had seemed to fill the void for a time. Her letters had been evidence that she liked him, and his imagination had made her part of his life. He had been able to picture a day when he would sit down to breakfast with her, their children around them. Their lives together would mirror the one he had always known. But now there was nothing. He was surrounded by young men and women who seemed more than pleased with their lives. They worked hard enough in school, but they also got together in the evenings, drank together, laughed. He knew this because he heard them speak of it, and sometimes he walked by a *Gasthaus* in his neighborhood and heard the noise inside. But that was as close to their lives as he ever came. Rainer had learned to stay away from the room most of the time. He had friends, had places to go, and he was satisfied to allow Hans his own life.

Hans did have something of a refuge on Sundays. There was only a small branch of the Church in Magdeburg, but the people were happy to have him as part of their group. There were no young women close to his age, and he was the only university student who was a member of the

Church, but there were several families, and they were happy people, thrilled to have a new young man with them. He had never really liked church when he was growing up, but the services were now the highlight of his week.

One Friday afternoon in October he was happy that the weekend had arrived. He told himself that he would study most of the day Saturday and then take a long walk along the Elbe river. It was something he did love, to walk and look about, and then the next day, he would be among friends. One of the families in the branch had invited him to Sunday dinner, and that gave him something to look forward to.

When Rainer came in that afternoon, he seemed in a rush. "Hans, I'm taking the train home for the weekend." He grinned. "My girlfriend wrote. She says she can't stand to have me away. Out of pity, I've decided to grant her the happiness she deserves."

The little pod they lived in was a room only slightly larger than Hans's bedroom at home. Into it were crowded two narrow beds, two small chests of drawers, and a tiny desk at the foot of each bed. The walls were concrete block, thinly painted, off-white, with not so much as a picture or calendar for adornment. Rainer pulled a little suitcase out from under his bed and then began stuffing socks and underwear into it.

"Don't you have studies this weekend?" Hans asked.

"I'll do what I can on the train. But I need a break. I study too much as it is. I'm certain I study half as much as you do—and you study three times too much. Work the math." He turned around for a moment; looked at Hans, who was sitting at his little desk; and laughed.

"I'm just slow," Hans said. "It takes me longer."

"No, no. Everyone says you're some sort of prodigy. The professors say you're the best of our new class."

"That's something you've invented, surely."

"No. Not at all." He went back to his packing. "One of the engineering professors told it to a friend of mine. I didn't just imagine it. Of course,

I might have been a little drunk at the time. Maybe he said you were flunking out. It was one or the other."

This seemed a grand joke to Rainer. He let his head fall back, and he laughed, hard. At such moments, Hans liked Rainer. But he had no idea how to be his friend. Their paths were always heading in opposite directions.

"So what are you doing this weekend?" Rainer asked, but not with a tone of real interest.

"I'll study tomorrow. Go to church on Sunday."

"Sounds like death on a dinner plate, if you ask me."

Hans laughed. "Some of my church friends invited me for dinner. That should be nice."

"Can you stand all that sermonizing? Don't they tell you that you'll burn in hell?"

"No. Not really."

"That's because you don't sin. I'll do enough this weekend to get thrown into a pit of fire forever. Thank God I don't believe in God."

Hans was not about to comment. The two had talked a few times about Hans's religion. Rainer tried to be respectful, but Hans knew that he found the whole idea ludicrous. Hans picked up one of his fat textbooks.

"Do you believe in hell?" Rainer asked.

Hans was not sure he wanted to get into this. He hated to give Rainer information that would only turn into little ironies, cast back at him later. Still, he answered, if nothing else to show that his religion was not so simpleminded as Rainer might suspect. "No. Not in the way most people think of hell. Mormons believe that the purpose of life is to become more like God, and we believe that we can keep doing that in the next life—by continuing to grow and improve. 'Hell' is a condition—a limitation—not a place. It's the loss of opportunity to move forward. We don't believe in lakes of fire and devils with pitchforks."

"So who ends up with this 'limitation'?"

"Those who drink too much beer and sin on weekends with their girlfriends." Hans had kept his voice serious, but when Rainer looked around at him, Hans smiled.

Still, Rainer seemed to take Hans seriously. "Do you really think it's so bad—a little beer, a little love-making? How can that be evil?"

"I was only joking with you."

"No. Not really. You don't drink. I assume you don't have sex." He grinned. "Or you wouldn't, if you ever got the chance."

Hans set his book back on the desk. "Beer isn't good for the body. That's all. The way we look at it, the spirit and the body work together. Hurting one is hurting the other."

"What about sex?"

"It's for marriage."

"Well . . . nothing wrong with having such beliefs, I suppose. But I think I have the better life." He didn't smile.

"For me, it wouldn't be."

"You don't know that, Hans. You've never *lived*. The only thing you do is hide from life. And I'll tell you something else. You may think I'm corrupt, but I'm not. I may take my little pleasures, and see no harm in them, but I'm as idealistic as you will ever be. I'm not an opportunist who professes Communism for the sake of my career. I believe in Marxist-Leninist theory. It's the only thing that has ever made sense to me. You can have your gods, if you want. What I believe in is a process—men and women standing together to make a better world. During all those centuries when religion was supposed to guide the world, what did we get? Corruption. Caste systems. Exploitation of workers. A world divided into the haves and the have-nots. That won't be the case when Communism triumphs. There will come a time, if you ask me, when religion will become a relic of the past, an idea as silly as any ancient mythology."

"I suppose that remains to be seen."

"You don't dare disagree with me, do you? You think I'll report you for denouncing Communism."

Hans was taking no such bait. He had learned in his life that he could never let down his guard. True believers, and Rainer seemed to be one, felt a duty to stop any talk that could conceivably undermine the cause of the regime. "There's nothing to report me for," Hans said. "What makes our country great is that religious freedom is allowed, and so is freedom to believe in other philosophies. We can agree to disagree."

Rainer laughed. "You've never joined Free German Youth, have you?"

"No."

"You missed so much, Hans. I was the *FDJ* leader in my school. We had great times, and we got good training, too. It gave me a chance to learn leadership, to sort out what matters and what doesn't matter in this life."

"That was good for you."

"You're not listening, Hans. You say that you're religious, but you're not happy. You sit here glum and silent. I embrace life, clear my head of superstition, and don't call natural things sins. I'll probably have more pleasure in this one weekend than you will the rest of your life. You religious people are always the same—worried about little things that don't matter, calling the best things in life sin. Me, I'm forging ahead, concerned for my fellowman, intent on making the world better. That's what religious people have always claimed they were doing—and never have."

Hans looked up at Rainer, who was staring down at him. "I'm not the best example of someone from my religion," he said. "I've had some hard things happen lately, and they've been on my mind. But Mormons are happy people. You should know my parents and my little sister. Or the people who go to church here. They're clear about what they believe, and they give to each other. I agree that there's been a lot of corruption in religion, but I think of my church as a renewal of what religion ought to be."

"So what's troubling *you*, Hans? You never tell me anything about yourself."

"Just some personal matters."

"I don't blame you for not trusting me. You're probably wise not to say too much. But if you study here for four years and never make any friends, never come out of your shell, you'll be miserable the whole time."

"You're probably right. I need to think about that."

"You people who join these strange sects, you make such a mistake. It forces you to feel separated from the rest of us. And what do you get from it, really? Why not accept what is good in our nation, pick up the flag and help carry it forward? It's such a better way to live."

"We have to make choices, Rainer. We have to live by what we believe. Communism makes great promises. We'll find out, in time, whether it does anything more than that."

Hans knew this was on the edge, probably something he shouldn't have said, but it made Rainer smile. "Yes, we will see. And I think your little church will seem insignificant—embarrassingly so—as the Soviet and other great socialist nations change the very nature of life on this earth."

Hans was actually impressed to find that Rainer believed that strongly, but he wasn't persuaded by the arguments. Hans had his own assessment of Communism, and he felt more secure than he ever had about his faith in God. Still, after Rainer was gone, Hans thought about the prediction that his time at the university, all four years, would be miserable. Right now, that seemed a very likely possibility.

---

Saturday turned out to be a long day for Hans. He wished so much that, like Rainer, he could take a train home for the weekend. But the trip was a little too long, too expensive. He simply didn't have the money. What he wanted to do more than anything was to travel to Dresden and visit Greta. He could make his visit seem nothing more than friendly, but then he would see whether there was any chance that she still held some interest in him. His fantasy was always the same: that she would change her mind about the other young man and then turn toward him. As he walked along the river, he found himself running the scenario through his mind. She would write to him and tell him she had missed his letters, and then she would make an admission: she had always loved him and had only realized it lately, since she had compared him to this new friend, who wasn't all that Hans was. He knew it was stupid—pathetic—that he devoted so much time to such fantasies, but it was a little pleasure in a life that offered very few.

On Sunday, however, he felt an immediate joy when he stepped through the door of the church. Little Helga Dürden ran to him and then stopped suddenly and held out her hand. She was eight, newly baptized, and so much like Inga had been at the same age. Hans talked to her every week. He shook her hand, but then he bent and hugged her too. "How are you, my friend?" he asked, crouching in front of her. She was wearing her hair in two long braids, and she had on a pretty red dress, much like a *Dirndl*.

"I'm fine. And you're eating with us today. My sister Elli is very happy about that, but don't tell her that I told you."

"I won't. It will be our secret." Elli was pretty, but she was only fifteen or so.

Sister Dürden walked to Hans, across the little foyer from the coat racks. She was a woman in her late thirties who looked even younger. "Hans, I'm glad to see you. I wanted to ask you, do you like *Schnitzel?*"

"Are you joking? Of course I do."

"Very good. I was able to buy some pork cutlets. Elli waited in line half the day yesterday so we could get them."

"That was good of her."

"It wasn't hard to convince her. Young girls can become very excited when a nice-looking university student comes to visit." She laughed and showed her deep dimples, like Elli's.

But now the branch president was coming over. "Hans, I'm glad you arrived early," he said. "I need to talk to you for a minute."

"Of course."

Hans followed President Neumeyer to his little office, off the foyer. Inside, he motioned for Hans to sit in one of the two folding chairs that sat facing his desk. "I'm hoping that you have the time to help us out a little in the branch," the president said. He was a husky man, with round cheeks, but he had a big smile, all gums, that made him seem a little comic.

"Yes. I would like that very much."

"Wonderful. I want to call you to serve as Sunday School teacher for our young people."

"Which young people?"

"The youth—twelve to eighteen. We only have one class, and usually not more than five or six who attend. But they're good young people, very devoted, and they need someone who has faced all the school problems and come out well. It means a great deal to them to see our Mormon young people accepted at the university."

"But what do I teach them?" Hans asked.

"What you know. We have no manuals, no materials we can offer you. But use your scriptures. You could study the Book of Mormon, if you wish, or maybe the New Testament, or perhaps take a different subject each week, and then employ all the scriptures. Will you have time to prepare?"

"I think so. It will actually be good for me."

"You'll be good for them, too."

"President, you don't know me very well. It wasn't that long ago that I made up my mind to leave the Church. It hasn't always been easy for me to believe in God."

"That's perfect, Hans. All the better. You'll understand these young people. We have one boy who worries his parents terribly. His teachers are causing him to question everything. You can tell him how you answered some of the questions you had to face."

"I don't know that I've faced all my questions, President. But I *have* felt the Spirit. That's what I'm trying to rely on."

"It's exactly what you need to rely on. And it's what all our young members must rely on. Teach them how to do it."

"I'll do my best."

"That's more than enough. What a blessing you are to us, Hans."

Hans looked away from President Neumeyer's eyes. "On Friday, my roommate told me that I profess religion but that I'm not happy. He said it was proof that religion didn't provide what it promised."

"Is that true, that you're not happy?"

"Not exactly. But I'm homesick, and I don't feel part of anything at the university."

"I know the problem, Hans, but I wouldn't shy away from people. Maybe they don't live the way you do, and you can't compromise on that, but if they don't see you the way we do here, friendly and satisfied with life—I don't know how they will ever know what religion can do."

"I know. I've thought about that since Friday. I think maybe I've been feeling a little too sorry for myself." He hesitated, then looked back at the president's eyes. "There was a girl I liked—a Mormon girl. But she didn't feel the same about me. She's engaged now to someone else. I've been a little disappointed about that."

"Only a little?"

"More than a little, I think."

President Neumeyer smiled. He reached across the desk and patted Hans's arm. "It's the greatest hurt, Hans—this disappointment in love. But I'm going to promise you something. If you will be faithful, teach these young people while you're here, and greet the skeptics at the university, the Lord will bless you."

"Will he help me find a wife?"

"Don't be in such a hurry. You're still young."

"No, no. I'm not saying that. But I thought that Greta—the one I cared about—was the right one for me. And now I've lost my hope for that."

"This matter isn't easy in our country, where we don't have so many matches. But there are young women in the Church. You can meet them. You can choose one. And the two of you can make a happy life. Too much is made of all this finding just the right one. We have to find a sister in the gospel, and then we have to make ourselves right. It's the men who are usually the weak ones anyway. More of them fall away." Suddenly he laughed, showing his pink gums again. "That's all right. It gives the faithful boys more of a chance. Better odds."

"That's a good way to think of it," Hans said, and he told himself that he needed to stop thinking so much about Greta. He knew that the president was right about the way he was acting, too. He needed to get to know more of the students, to make some friends.

Hans wanted to talk about Berndt and about his fear of the *Stasi*—wanted to let someone know his deepest worry—but he hesitated to do that. He had promised himself that no one but his parents would ever know about the help he had given Berndt. Hans would never be safe as long as *anyone* knew about it. Perhaps it was wrong not to trust his branch president, but it was probably wise not to say anything—and put President Neumeyer in the awkward position of knowing something he would have to deny, if interrogated.

So Hans said nothing more, but he accepted the calling and actually looked forward to his preparations and to his first experience with his students. At dinner that afternoon, when he told Elli Dürden about the calling, she smiled uncontrollably, her dimples sinking deep, and then she turned red when her family laughed at her. She was such a cute girl, but tiny and young-looking even for fifteen. Still, Hans felt sorry for her. There was something rather sad in this infatuation she obviously had for him. He knew what it was like to be enamored with someone older, only to be ignored.

# Chapter 17

Diane was at the Salt Lake Airport. It was early on a Tuesday morning in December 1966, and she and her roommate, Terry, had driven from Provo so that Diane could say good-bye to Kent. He had finished his LTM training, and now he was headed for Argentina. The only problem was, Terry—the only friend who had access to a car at school—was a little slow getting up, and even slower "putting her face on." Now they were hurrying down the corridor, and Diane was in a panic that Kent might already be on the airplane. But from well down the hall she saw him standing in his gray suit, looking her way, the only elder in sight. When he spotted her, he ran toward her, a camera swinging from one shoulder and a bag with a strap hanging from the other. "I have to board," he gasped when he reached her. "I thought you weren't going to make it." He grabbed her by the shoulders, as though he were ready to kiss her quickly, then turn and run.

"I'm sorry. We—"

"It's okay. You made it." He let his eyes run down her and back up, and then he stared into her eyes as though he wanted to memorize her. "You're so beautiful. God only made one girl like you."

"Actually, I look like I just—"

"Walk back with me. They're mad at me for not getting on the plane." He grabbed her hand and took off walking, hard, pulling her with him. He hadn't even glanced at Terry. "I'm back. Don't worry," he called out to a woman in a blue uniform who was taking boarding passes at the gate.

As they approached, the woman said, "I'll give you *one* minute. Kiss that girl and then get on the plane." But she seemed to be teasing.

Kent turned back to Diane. "I was so scared you wouldn't come. I thought maybe you had met someone already."

"Kent. Come on. I wouldn't do that. Terry was just slow getting ready. I wanted to have half an hour with you, so we could talk. I feel so bad we're late."

"I saw you a couple of times this fall. Sometimes I would walk and just watch for you around campus or at the Wilkinson Center. Twice I spotted you."

"Why didn't you say something?"

"We're not supposed to. Besides, I was afraid I would go crazy. I can kiss you good-bye today—that's the rule—but if I'd seen you at school, I couldn't get within arm's length of you."

"I know. But we could have talked. Every time I saw missionaries around, I looked to see if it was you."

"Really? Did you want to see me?"

"Kent, I've missed you so much. There's no one else like you."

Kent shut his eyes, leaned his head back, and let his breath blow out as though he were trying to launch a prayer at the sky. "Diane, you can't believe how much I love hearing you say that." He set his bag on the floor and took hold of both her hands. "I really know now how much I love you. It's been all I can do to study. You're on my mind every minute. I shut my eyes sometimes and try to remember how pretty you are."

"Well, I'm not very pretty this morning."

"Diane, I could see, when I spotted you at school, how all the guys were checking you out. By the time I get back, the coolest, best-looking guys on campus are all going to have a shot at you. All I can think is that I don't have a chance."

"Kent, you need to stop saying things like that. I've dated quite a few guys this fall, and not one of them comes even close to you."

"Quite a few? Really? How many?"

"I don't know. I mean, I've met a lot, whether I've dated them or not."

"But how many have you dated?"

"I'm not sure. I didn't keep track."

"Have you dated any of them more than once or twice?"

Diane glanced to see where Terry was. She was standing back a few paces, looking amused. Others were watching too. An older couple was sitting in a nearby waiting area, both smiling, as though they thought this was all very cute. "Well . . . yes," Diane whispered. "But it's not like I'm *interested* in anyone."

"How many times?"

"What?"

"What's the most times you've gone out with one guy?"

"Kent, come on. Let's not talk about that."

And now the woman at the gate was calling, "Young man, you'd better stop talking and start kissing. Your time is up."

Kent stepped closer to Diane. He was squeezing her hands so hard it hurt. "I'm sorry, Diane. I didn't mean to question you like that. I'm so nuts about you I act stupid sometimes. I'm not like this usually. Do you know what I mean?"

"It doesn't matter. Everything's fine."

"I love you, Diane. I really do. *Te amo.*" Tears began to drain from the corners of his eyes. "I've wanted to say that to you so many times."

"I love you too, Kent. I do. So don't worry about anything. When you come back, I'll be here."

"Promise?"

But Diane felt herself hesitate. She didn't want to say that.

"I'm sorry. I'm sorry. I shouldn't ask that."

"I'm starting to count down from ten," the woman was calling now.

Suddenly Kent grabbed Diane and wrapped his arms all the way around her as though he wanted to pull her inside his suit coat and take her along. His kiss was pressing, too, and long. And when he finally stopped kissing her, he held onto her, his hands clasping her with such force that Diane wondered what the older couple was thinking. It didn't seem like the sort of thing a missionary ought to be doing.

"I'm going to shut the gate, and you're going to be in very big trouble," the woman said, but she was laughing.

Diane pushed away enough to take a quick look around. Lots of people were watching, smiling. Another missionary had apparently returned to the gate and was standing next to the woman. "Come on, Elder. What do you think you're doing?"

Diane put her hands against his chest and gave him a nudge. "Go," she said. "I'll write you every week. We're going to be okay."

He bent forward, gave her one more peck, and said, "I love you, Diane. I'll *always* love you. For time and all eternity."

This time she shoved hard, and he turned and ran. "Wait. Your bag!"

He spun back, took a couple of quick strides toward her again, and grabbed the strap from her hand, but then he grasped her and kissed her again, hard and quick, "I'll *always* love you," he whispered, and away he ran.

By now the people around Diane were laughing. A man was standing nearby, a big guy in a business suit. "That boy's got it bad," he said in a rumbling voice, and a woman next to him said, "You would too, if you were leaving *her* behind."

Diane looked away from them, felt the heat in her face. At the gate, the airline employee threw up her hands to stop Kent. He jerked to a stop, and his camera swung forward. "I need your boarding pass," she said, laughing.

"Oh, yeah," Kent said. He began searching wildly through his pockets and finally found it on the second try at his inside coat pocket. He handed it to her, spun around, and waved one last time, mouthing the words "I love you."

The woman took the pass, tugged him forward by the lapel, released him, and then gave him a playful little push. She turned back, once he was gone, and shook her head. "That boy's in love," she called to Diane.

Diane shrugged and smiled, but then she ducked her head and walked to the windows where she could look at the airplane. Mostly, she wanted to get away from the stares of all the people in the waiting area. She saw Kent hiking up the steps that had been rolled up to the airplane. He looked back, scanned along the windows until he saw her, and then waved one last time before he disappeared into the airplane. About then Terry stepped up next to Diane. "Wow," she said. "That poor boy—he's a mess."

"I've never seen him like that," Diane said. "He's really a cool guy—normally."

"He had *steam* coming out of his ears. I don't know if he can stand two years away from you."

Diane heard something in Terry's voice that she didn't like. She seemed disdainful, as though she thought Kent was some sort of dolt. "He's really sweet, Terry."

"Hey, I believe you. I wish someone was that nuts over me."

"I think he was just a little shook up because we were so late getting here."

"So it was *my* fault he acted like that?"

Diane didn't voice her opinion, but that was exactly what she was thinking. She had actually been a little bothered by Kent seeming so . . . whatever it was. Desperate? She remembered the confident guy she had met in Virginia. She wondered why he was acting so unsure of himself now. She turned and walked away, hurried through the waiting area, and then started down the corridor. She hoped Terry would try to keep up. Diane was realizing that she had to hurry back, get herself put together a little better, and get to a nine o'clock class. She was not doing very well in some of her classes, and part of the reason was, she had dated a great deal all fall. She had rarely missed going out on a Friday or Saturday night, and she had gone to campus movies or ward socials other nights, football games on Saturday afternoons, and usually to church with someone, or to a fireside in the evening or to someone's apartment for a gathering of friends. Somewhere along the line she really hadn't studied all that much. At the apartment, something always seemed to be happening, and when she went to the library, she usually ran into people she knew—boys, more often than not—who would come to her study table to talk. Maybe she did tend to sit in places where she would be noticed, but even when she got serious and hid away, someone always seemed to find her, and then she would talk more than study.

She was finding, too, that college was hard. She had gotten by in high school without knocking herself out, but professors at the Y were pretty tough on her writing. She rarely made errors in grammar or punctuation, but these professors challenged her logic, tore her up for reaching "unwarranted conclusions." She wondered whether they didn't like her because of her blonde hair and the image she may have projected. She thought at times that she should pin her hair up and wear plain clothes, but she liked to be noticed when she walked across campus, and it hardly seemed worth it to change her appearance for those dull old professors.

"I guess you haven't said anything to him about Greg." Terry was walking next to Diane now.

"What do you mean?"

"You know very well what I mean. You two are together all the time."

"We *are not*. I go out with him sometimes, but I go out with a lot of guys."

"You've been out with Greg at least once a week, all fall, and he comes by to see you, sits by you in Sunday School class, and takes you out for ice cream. If I'd been with one guy that much, I'd think I was *engaged*."

"It's not like that. He knows I'm waiting for Kent."

"I'm sure he believes that—about as much as I do."

"Terry!" Diane stopped walking and turned toward Terry, who took another step and then stopped too. "Don't you believe I'm going to wait for him?"

Terry smiled, cocked her head to one side, and said, "Not a chance." She was wearing too much eye makeup, as always, and too much of the foundation she used to cover up her "blemishes." She was actually a pretty girl, but she dabbed on so much goop every morning that she looked like a clown to Diane. At least her brilliant yellow-green outfit—all double knit—was mostly covered up. She was always cold in Utah, had started wearing winter coats in October, and now she had on a big quilted ski parka.

"Why do you say that?" Diane put her hands on her hips. She really was astounded that Terry would doubt her.

"Let me ask you one question?"

"All right." But Diane realized what was coming, and she knew she had put herself in a trap.

"Have you been kissing Greg?"

What was maddening was that Terry was smiling—very *knowingly*—like that was the whole story. Diane let her arms drop to her sides. "Okay, he has kissed me. I admit that. But it isn't like you think. We're mostly just friends, and for about two months I wouldn't let him get near me at the door, but the last couple of times we've gone out, he's just given me a goodnight kiss—just a short, friendly little kiss."

Terry was nodding, still smiling. "Short, was it? *Friendly*, was it?"

"Terry, it was. I don't even like Greg that much. He thinks he's the coolest guy in the world, but he's not even my type. I'm waiting for Kent."

"Good. Then that's final." She winked. "And if it's not, I'm sure Kent will get over you—somewhere in the course of time and all eternity."

Diane let out a little sigh. "Come on, Terry. Don't do that to me. I'm going to break it off with Greg. I really am. And he's the only one I've kissed. Really. The only one."

"So far."

"No. I'm not going to kiss every guy who comes along. And next semester I'm not going out so much. I need to study a lot harder or I'm going to flunk out."

"Don't worry. You'll get your M-R-S degree. You won't need good grades for that. And Greg's going to be a lawyer. He'll provide for you just fine."

"Be quiet. I want to think about Kent."

"One last time?"

Diane rolled her eyes, but she didn't reply. She headed for the car. The truth was, she was troubled. She really did wish she hadn't let Greg kiss her. He was getting way too affectionate lately, with his arm around her all the time, or holding her hand in church. She really didn't like him, and she needed to break up. But what was lingering with her even more at the moment was some sense that Kent shouldn't have been quite so goofy. She wanted him to be calm and collected, secure—actually, in that way, more like Greg.

When Diane left BYU for Christmas, she vowed that she would spend most of her time at home studying for the finals she would have to face when she got back. She knew she had to come through and save herself—either that or face her parents with her miserable grades. She actually started preparing them almost as soon as she got home, admitting that the first semester had been tough for her but that she had learned her lesson about devoting too much time to her social life. She predicted that things hadn't gone all that well but held onto the hope that some hard study in the next couple of weeks could stave off a disaster. But Bobbi was not pleased. She gave Diane a little talk about the importance of grades, how they followed a person forever, how hard it was to raise a GPA when it started low.

Diane listened and nodded a lot. She did want to graduate, but she knew it would never be with honors, and so she didn't mind getting C's; she just didn't want to end up having to take classes over, and right now she was thinking she was okay in Freshman Comp and World History but that she might be on the edge in her Natural Science class. She hadn't taken her Book of Mormon class very seriously either, thinking it would be more or less like high-school seminary, but she had bombed the first test and had been fighting back from that ever since. She hoped Brother Martin believed in mercy as well as justice.

But on Christmas day she wasn't going to worry about all that. She got clothes for presents—all things she had bought at Clark's in Provo and then brought home for her mother to wrap. It was easier that way, and she got exactly what she wanted. She was excited about a little gaucho outfit she had picked out, with culottes, a vest, and high boots, and a simple, tailored dress with a white collar. She had tried on the tan one but in the end had settled on red. After all, it was the color Gram would have chosen. She was actually expecting no surprises, but her dad gave her an Instamatic camera, which would be fun to have at school. She loved her dad for always doing something a little extra for her.

She wore her culotte outfit to Grandma's house, and all her aunts thought she looked cute. Even her uncles commented. But maybe it was the contrast. Kathy was there in a weird getup. Her hair was halfway down her back now, and she had on a peasant blouse and a long skirt with vertical rows of color, like a braided rug. Diane wondered how she could show up at a family get-together looking like a hippie. All she needed was a bandanna in her hair and a peace symbol hanging around her neck. It was really embarrassing.

But Kathy was still Kathy, and Diane had always looked up to her. So while Grandma was working on dinner, and "her girls" were helping,

Diane pulled Kathy upstairs to Bobbi's old room. "Tell me what's happening back in Massachusetts," Diane said. She sat down on the old wooden chair, by the desk.

"I'm flunking out, I think," Kathy said. She sat on the bed, which was covered with a pretty old log-cabin quilt, done in browns and reds. "I haven't studied the way I should this fall."

"You've got to be kidding," Diane said. "That's my problem, but I didn't think it would *ever* be yours."

"I've just been doing too many other things. I'm really involved with my SDS chapter."

"I guess I don't know what that is."

"SDS?"

"Yes."

"Diane, it's impossible for you not to know that. Don't you read the newspaper?"

Diane was humiliated. There was a tone of disdain in Kathy's voice that Diane had certainly heard before, but not with such harshness. "I guess I've heard of it," Diane said, "but I'm not sure what the letters stand for."

"Students for a Democratic Society. We're the ones leading the way, trying to shut down this obscene war."

"I don't think we have that at BYU."

Kathy flopped on her back, across the bed, and laughed. "No, no. You don't have a chapter. I can guarantee that. BYU students actually passed around a *pro*-Vietnam petition last spring. I think they sent it to Johnson."

"But some people don't support the war. Students at the Y don't all have the same opinions."

"Oh, really? Do you mean to say that *thought* is allowed at BYU?"

Diane didn't answer, and that brought Kathy back to a sitting position. "I'm sorry. That wasn't nice."

"Kathy, some of my professors at the Y are *brilliant*."

"I know. But there are things you'll never talk about at BYU. I'll bet you don't hear a word about Vietnam in your classes."

"I don't take any classes where it would even come up."

"But see, that's the difference. At Smith, all the professors talk about what's going on in the world. Vietnam isn't just part of politics or history; it's our lives. It's the center of the corruption this country has fallen into. A country can't commit atrocities and then go on about life as though its *murdering* of innocent people doesn't matter. Whether you know it or not, it's part of our collective consciousness. We all share in the vileness of it—and the guilt."

Diane had no idea what Kathy was talking about. She knew that some people believed in the war and some didn't—including her own parents—but she had never heard anyone say that Americans were committing murder. All she knew was that the war was supposed to be about stopping the spread of Communism, and as far as she knew, that was good. Both Kent and Greg believed in the war, and both were willing to go there to fight if they were called upon to do so. She admired that sort of attitude a lot more than someone accusing her own country of murder. But she said none of that. She always knew better than to argue with Kathy. What she did say was, "I thought you were mostly concerned about Negroes."

"I *am* concerned about civil rights, Kathy. But blacks are taking on the fight themselves. The big issue on most campuses now is Vietnam." But then she laughed. "Except, of course, for BYU, where the closest thing to a demonstration is a *panty raid*."

"I don't think we're going to have those anymore."

"Of course not. BYU isn't going to put up with such wicked behavior. I read that in the newspaper."

Diane hardly knew what to say. "Well, it is kind of stupid—from what

I've heard. But it's funny, too. Most of the girls just laugh about it. It's not any big deal."

"But Diane, it sounds like something out of high school. Don't the students ever protest *anything?*"

There had been some students upset about the ban on fast dancing, but Diane didn't want to bring that up. "There's been an underground newspaper that—"

"Diane, the administration shut that down. I read that in the paper too—in the same article. They're supposedly 'cracking down.'"

"I guess. But it's not that big a deal." Diane had no idea how to explain what BYU was like, how great it was. "Look, I know things are different at the Y. But I'd rather be there than anywhere."

Diane watched Kathy, saw her stop herself and then just nod.

Diane searched for something else to say. "Do you see Aunt LaRue very often?" she decided to ask.

"Quite a bit. We go to church together on Sundays, and we usually spend some of the day together. Once in a while I stop by her place in the evening, but I'm so busy I don't do that very often."

"What's the Church like back there?"

"It's a little better than here, but not much."

Diane stared at Kathy, trying to think what in the world she meant, and there was an awkward period when she had no idea what to say. But the silence was worse than the embarrassment of asking, so Diane said, "What do you mean?"

"It's not quite as reactionary back there, but you get all the same types. Most of those people, except some of the students, know nothing about the war and don't care. They're fussing about whether drinking Coke is against the Word of Wisdom or whether it's all right to plan your family—while the rest of the nation is trying to decide who we are and what's gone wrong with us."

Diane knew better. She wasn't going to ask again.

"We're sick, Diane. People spend their lives chasing after some American dream that doesn't exist—never did. Madison Avenue runs this country. But some people are looking for a simpler life. In the end, it's the connectedness to other people that counts, the love you have for other human beings, the acts of goodness you've performed."

"I think that's right, Kathy. We talk a lot about that at BYU. In religion class, Brother Martin is always talking about materialism, and how in the Book of Mormon, it always turns out to be a false way to happiness."

Kathy's face seemed to inflate, as though she were about to burst with all she wanted to say. "Diane, how can you say that? Your whole life is about the way you *look*."

Diane told herself to relax and breathe, not to get upset, but she wasn't getting much air. Maybe she would hate Kathy in a few more seconds, but for the moment she was too overwhelmed to know her own reaction. It was what she had always been accused of, what everyone thought of her—including her mother—so maybe they were all right, but it didn't feel that way inside. She had taken the words she had heard in religion class to heart.

Suddenly Kathy was leaping toward her, sliding onto her knees in front of her. "I'm sorry. I'm sorry. I didn't mean it the way it came out. I love you, Diane. You're a better person than I am. You really are." She grabbed Diane's forearms and shook her. "I mean it, Diane. I love you. I think you're a victim. You're so pretty that people always bring attention to the way you look, and it starts to seem more important than anything else. At BYU, everyone is so into clothes, I'm sure it's hard not to go along with all that."

But this was just more of the same. Diane pulled her arms loose from Kathy's grip. "You don't know what BYU is like at all, Kathy," she said. "People do like to look nice. And I don't think that's wrong. I don't know why hippies want to dress up in such weird clothes, but what's the difference? They have their style. They all look alike. Is that better?"

"That's a good point," Kathy said. "It's definitely true."

"Maybe Mormons do like to have nice homes and things, but look how much of their money they give to the Church. How many young people in the world take two years off to go out and teach the gospel? Kids at BYU talk a lot about what's right and wrong, and it's not always about the Word of Wisdom and stuff like that. I know people who want to be really spiritual, and they study the scriptures every single day, even get up early in the morning to do it."

Kathy slumped. She laid her arms across her knees and then dropped her head onto her arms. "I'm sorry," she whispered. And then, after a time, she added, "I have so many problems with Mormon culture, Diane, but I didn't mean to take it out on you. I've loved you since we were little girls together, and I don't ever want to lose that."

Diane was confused. Kathy was a mystery to her. But she did understand this last. She put her hand on Kathy's shoulder, and she said, "Kath, I wish you would come back from the East and finish up at BYU. It would give you another kind of experience that could balance out some of what's happened to you back there. At BYU, we talk about religion in *all* our classes. You get so much support and guidance, and you—"

"Thanks, Diane. I know you mean well. I really do. And I appreciate it. But it wouldn't work for me. It just wouldn't."

# Chapter 18

Kathy decided it would be better to go downstairs and help with Christmas dinner. She was better off when she loved Diane but didn't talk with her about things that really mattered. She was in the kitchen with her grandma and her aunts when she heard the laughing and excitement at the front door. She knew that meant that Gene had come in, home from his mission. His airplane had arrived in Salt Lake the night before, and Alex and Anna had been there, home from Washington, to pick him up. Grandma and Grandpa had seen him briefly, they said, but no one else in the family had had the chance until now. Kathy walked out to the front entrance where all the Thomases were collecting around Gene, taking their turns hugging him.

All the younger cousins rushed for him first, and he grabbed them up in his arms, one at a time, talking to each one for a few seconds. Kathy's little sister Shauna had been only five when he left; she was seven now, soon to be baptized, and Gene talked to her about that. Beverly's kids were all nuts about him, especially Alexander, whom everyone called "Zan." He was nine now, and tall. Gene pretended that the two were almost the same height, laughed, and then hugged the boy. He also took Beverly's new baby—little Beatrice—in his arms and cooed over her like a grandpa. Richard and Bobbi's daughter Maggie had had a crush on Gene most of her life—Diane had told Kathy so—but Maggie was thirteen now and hardly the same girl she had been two years before. "Oh my gosh, Maggie!" Gene said. "Is that you? You're so grown-up."

Kathy watched Maggie react, saw her face color. She was going to be a pretty girl but never spectacular like her big sister. Kathy wondered how well she was managing that, living in her sister's shadow. Maggie stepped toward Gene but stood rather stiff and let Gene do all the hugging.

Kathy stayed in the background, letting the uncles and aunts have their turn. She wanted Gene last, and then she wanted him longer. She wanted to see who he was now. But things didn't work out quite the way she would have liked. Gene had Aunt LaRue in his arms, was laughing with her about something, when he spotted Kathy. "Who's that girl with the long black hair?" he shouted. "That can't be Kathy. I remember Kathy. She couldn't have turned into a *hippie*."

Kathy rolled her eyes and stayed away from him for the moment, but as the family began to take seats at the many "dinner tables," he finally came over to her, wrapped her up in his big arms, and pounded her back. Then he stepped back and said, "Kathy, I shouldn't have said that. I'm just not used to seeing you look so different."

"I'm not different. I'm still way too skinny."

"No. You look good. You're prettier than you've ever been."

"But you don't like my hair."

"I don't know. You always had short hair in high school. That's just how I think of you."

Kathy never liked talking about her appearance, especially not now, since everyone in Utah had decided her "look" didn't appeal to them. "I want to hear about your mission," she said.

"Yeah. We need to talk. Right after dinner."

As it turned out, Gene had been given a seat of honor at the main table, and Kathy was at a card table with Diane and Maggie, and with Beverly's oldest daughter, Vickie, who was now twelve. Grandpa started things out with a little greeting to everyone, and then, before the family prayer, he said, "We're happy to have Gene back with us after serving an honorable mission. He served as a zone leader and saw some wonderful people come into the Church, and I could tell from the few minutes I talked to him last night that he's grown up a great deal. He's a mature young man now, deepened in his testimony and commitment to the Church, and ready to do great things with his life. His brother Joey, as you know, is now serving in the Northwestern States Mission, where he seems to have a baptism almost every week, and Wayne tells me that he's planning to leave on his mission this year, just as soon as he finishes spring term at the U."

It was strange for Kathy to think of her little brother as old enough to go on a mission soon. She had never gotten the impression that Wayne was all that interested in church. She wondered whether he was only going because everyone else did.

"These are great years as we see our grandchildren mature and prepare themselves for the leadership roles they'll be serving in the Church," Grandpa Thomas was saying. "We hope every one of you boys will serve a mission, and maybe some of the girls, too. But most important, we hope we'll be attending lots of temple weddings." He smiled with a self-satisfaction that Kathy had noticed more often in him lately. For the most part, his family was doing what he had always hoped.

"It's the big brood of great-grandchildren *I'm* looking forward to," Grandma Bea said, and she laughed. Her voice seemed a little deeper, rougher than Kathy remembered it. Grandma looked good, healthy and bright, but she was over seventy now, and in the past year or so was finally showing some of the signs of age, the wrinkles around her eyes deepening into creases, even showing up in her forehead.

Grandpa nodded and laughed in that grand baritone voice of his. "I had something like that in mind myself," he said. He put a hand on Gene's shoulder. "I'd like to call on Gene to say our prayer for us, but maybe, before he does that, he could give us just a very short report on his mission."

"Ah, come on, Grandpa, we're hungry," Kurt, Gene's fifteen-year-old brother, called out.

"You need to listen closer than anyone, Kurt," Grandpa said.

But that was awkward. Everyone in the family knew that Kurt had been a handful for Alex and Anna since they had moved east. Recently, there had been an "embarrassing incident" for the congressman's son. Kurt had been at a party that had been broken up by police—a party where a lot of under-aged drinking had been going on. Kurt had apparently admitted to his parents that he had "tried" some beer. He hadn't been arrested, but Anna had told Lorraine that she and Alex were worried about him, especially about his attitude toward the Church.

"Go ahead, Gene," Grandpa said.

Gene slid his chair back and stood up. "I think you'll all be coming to my homecoming next Sunday, so I won't say much now. I'll just say that a mission is a lot different from what I expected—and a lot harder. Germany is not one of those places where people are joining the Church in big numbers, so it's discouraging at times. I did all right with the language, and I tried to work hard, but I don't think I really got it into my head what a mission is all about until the last six months or so. One thing I do feel good about is that I can honestly say I have a testimony now. I'm not sure I was even ready to go on a mission, and I had to do a lot of praying and studying to get to a point where I felt worthy to testify. I wish I had gotten myself better prepared before I went, but it's hard to do that back here where no one ever challenges what you believe.

"But anyway, it turned out good for me. I feel like I grew from a baby to maybe a kindergartner. Now I need to grow a whole lot more."

He nodded, looked around, and then bowed his head. He said a simple prayer that touched Kathy. He thanked the Lord for sending him to such a strong, good family, thanked the Lord for his loving grandparents, uncles and aunts, and cousins. And then he said, "Forgive us, Lord. We have too much, and we don't appreciate it as we should. Help us to look beyond ourselves and use what we have to bless others."

When dinner was over, Kathy helped gather up dishes and carry them into the kitchen, but all the aunts and girl cousins were helping and the room was too full for everyone, so she found Gene, who was talking to his uncles. "Let's talk now, before they start opening the presents."

"Okay," he said. "Let's go for a ride. I drove Dad's new T-Bird over—and I've still got the keys." He smiled.

Kathy didn't know anything about cars. She never had learned to tell them apart. She was just happy to get out of the house and away from all the noise for a little while. When she slipped into the bucket seat of the Thunderbird, however, she did realize that she was in a beautiful car. She wondered what it must cost—how many people in Mississippi could live for a year with that amount of money. She laughed, though, and she said to Gene, "You said in your prayer that we have too much, but you sure seem to like this car."

He looked at her and smiled. The guy was more handsome than ever—still as blond, still those huge blue eyes, like his mother's, but now with more maturity, the bluish tones along his jaw were showing a real beard. "That's just the trouble," he said. "I love cars. And nice clothes. All of it. I wish I didn't."

"But you've changed, Gene. You've grown up a lot, haven't you?"

"I don't know. I'd like to think so, but a mission forces change on a person. I've seen a lot of guys come back and slip right back to who they were."

"I know. But I think your mission humbled you. And that's what you needed."

He started the car, put it in gear, and pulled away from the curb, but he was laughing softly. "You always have had a way of reminding me of my weaknesses."

"I don't mean it that way. I'm just saying that things have always been easy for you, and this was apparently hard. But it sounds like you met the test. You got your head on straight."

"I'm not sure I know what that means. But I did go over there thinking I was a hotshot, and I found out that teaching the gospel has nothing to do with being a good talker. People sense who you are. They know whether you really believe what you're saying—and whether you're a good person. If the right people pick up on that, they'll listen."

"Grandpa told me you had some great baptisms."

"Yeah, but some of them fell away afterward, so it was pretty frustrating. The family we baptized this fall, though—the Schotts—are really great people. The man didn't believe in God when we met them. His wife thought maybe there was a God, but she considered religion nothing more than a *Geschäft*. That's what Germans say. It's like calling it a 'business.'"

"What changed them?"

"I think they just liked us at first. Some people like to meet Americans, practice English, stuff like that. They had some kids who took a liking to us. We took them to Primary and Sunday School. The parents liked the change they saw in the kids."

"And that converted them to a belief in God?"

"It wasn't just that. We kept working with them, and they finally agreed to pray. Nothing came of it for a while, and then we got there one night and everything was different. Brother Schott and his wife had finally tried praying together, and they said they got up from their knees, looked at each other, and both knew that something had happened. After that, they started asking questions like crazy, and they kept praying. They joined the Church, and so did their kids. So it was . . . I don't know . . . pretty amazing."

"Gene, I needed to hear that story. I'm really struggling with the Church these days."

"That's what my mom said."

Kathy hated that—the thought that her mom and her aunts had been talking about "Kathy's problem," the way everyone talked about Kurt these days. But she didn't want to think about that now. She liked what she was feeling.

Gene was driving slowly, staying on some of the little streets in the neighborhood, working his way down toward State Street. There was snow on the ground, on the sidewalks, and piled up in dirty hills by the sides of the streets. "I needed something like that too," he said. "For a long time I was doing everything for the wrong reasons. But for the last six months I tried to concentrate on being a good missionary, and just to forget everything else. I was a zone leader, but that didn't matter to me at the end. The big thing was meeting the Schotts and finding out how the Spirit can work on people."

"Sometimes I think I should go on a mission. Something like that would really help me."

"Do it. You could go, when, next year?"

"I'll be twenty-one next year, but I couldn't go. You know I can't."

"What do you mean?"

She knew what he was thinking, that she wasn't worthy, but that wasn't true. She hadn't done anything so wrong that it would keep her from going. "Gene, I'm too . . . whatever I am. I just don't fit in with Church members anymore."

"The only thing I know is that you don't dress like most Mormons."

"Gene, I don't *think* like a Mormon. I question everything. I come up with different political conclusions. That's not allowed in the Church. We have this unwritten rule that we all have to march to the same drumbeat. We can't have our own opinions."

"Oh, come on, Kathy. That's an exaggeration. A lot of people in the Church have similar viewpoints, but that doesn't mean it has to be that way. Especially when you get away from Utah, you see plenty of members who don't fit the mold."

"Maybe. But there's a lot of the same kind of thinking in my ward out in Massachusetts, and when I come back here, I almost go crazy, just trying to tolerate the stuff I hear."

"What about George Romney? He's a traditional Mormon, but he's liberal on a lot of issues. And the way he's going, he could become president."

"He supports the war in Vietnam, Gene. Almost *every* Mormon does. They think you're anti-American if you happen to believe the war is wrong."

"Look, you told me in your last letter that you had marched in some demonstrations—and I could never do that—but I don't see why—"

"Why couldn't you, Gene? Do you understand what we're doing in Vietnam?"

"Kathy, let's not do that. You were telling me two and a half years ago that the war was a bad idea, and I told you then, I'm going to support my country. As far as I'm concerned, there are two great forces in the world. There's Christ's plan and there's Satan's. And Communism is Satan's plan. We have to stand up to it. If we don't do it now, it will only be worse later." Gene had reached State Street. He turned right and drove north, toward downtown Salt Lake.

"Gene, that's so simplistic. The leaders in South Vietnam are as corrupt as Satan could ever want. This isn't about defending good against evil."

"Maybe. But we promised those people. We can't just cut and run. If we make a commitment to a country, we have to keep it. If that's simplistic, fine. It's also the right thing to do."

Kathy didn't want bad feelings, but it drove her crazy that he would make such blanket statements. "Gene, our government lied to us. The Tonkin Resolution was based on a totally trumped-up attack. It never even happened. Johnson has built this whole war on the 'permission' he claims he got from Congress. What kind of promise is that—all based on lies? Johnson keeps talking about 'winning the hearts and minds of the people in South Vietnam.' If they *wanted* us over there, we wouldn't have to win them over."

Gene didn't respond for a time, and Kathy knew why. He knew

nothing about the politics of the war. She doubted he could point to Vietnam on a map. Finally, he said, "Kathy, I don't want to get into a fight with you. All I'm saying is that I'm loyal to my country. If I'm called on to serve, I'm going to do it. I've always told you that."

"It's easy to say when you've had a religious deferment for the last couple of years, and now you can get your student deferment back. It's the kids who don't have the money to go to college who get stuck fighting this war."

"Look, I want to get on with my education. I need to do that. I could—"

"If you think it's such a great war, why don't you put first things first—go kill some 'Commies' before you go to school. That's what our dads had to do."

"Don't, Kathy. I don't want to do this."

"I don't either, Gene. But you need to do some thinking before you turn this corrupt war into some kind of religious battle for good against evil."

"I do think. But I also listen to the prophet. What he keeps saying is that Mormons should support their country—and that's what I plan to do. I'm *always* going to listen to the prophet."

"Oh, brother. You haven't changed. You used to be cocky; now you're self-righteous. I don't know which is worse."

"Kathy, you're talking your way right out of the Church. If you keep heading the direction you're going, you'll be inactive within a year. It just makes me sick to see what's happening to you."

For a moment Kathy was irate, but the anger passed almost immediately, and the hurt set in. She didn't want to let him see her cry—and give him that victory—but she couldn't help it. And the worst thing was, she had a feeling he was right. She didn't know whether she was leaving the Church or it was leaving her, but the result was the same. She was trying to follow her conscience, and it was that, more than anything, that was making her feel that she wasn't a Mormon any longer. How could that be possible?

Kathy leaned against the door and cried, and part of what she was feeling was regret. She did love Gene, and she had felt so close to him only a few minutes before. But when he reached out and patted her shoulder, said, "I'm sorry," she wondered what he was sorry for. She was the outsider, and he was the glorious returned missionary. Grandpa would never stand before the family and tell everyone how proud he was of his granddaughter who demonstrated against a war she considered immoral. Kathy was an embarrassment to the Thomases and probably always would be.

---

When Gene got home from Grandma and Grandpa's, he felt rotten. He didn't like what he had done to Kathy. He had apologized, and they had talked a little, even said the right words to patch up their differences, but he understood why she had called him self-righteous. He didn't know enough about Vietnam, and it hadn't been fair for him to imply that he and President McKay were standing together—against her. He wished, especially, that he hadn't predicted her apostasy—even though he was afraid he might be right. She was too rebellious, too negative about her fellow members. How long could she carry that kind of spirit around with her and not walk away from the Church entirely?

Gene had something else he had planned to do that night, and he feared it might be another mistake, but he didn't want to let the chance pass him by. He knew that Marsha had left the University of Utah, had gone to a college in California. But she would surely be home for Christmas. He wanted to call her now and see whether he couldn't spend a little time with her before she left Utah again. So he waited until his parents had gone off to their own bedroom, and then he walked quietly to the kitchen. He had never forgotten the number, but as he dialed, he felt the tightness in his chest. "Could I speak to Marsha?" he asked Marsha's mother, but he didn't reveal who he was. And then he waited.

"Hello," he heard, and her voice filled him with memories.

"Hi, Marsha. It's Gene. I got home last night."

"Oh. Well . . . that's nice. Is it good to be home?" Her voice was formal, even tense, and Gene felt his chest constrict.

"I'd sure like to see you while you're home. I was wondering whether I could come over tomorrow and we could just talk for a while—maybe go for a ride or something."

"Gene, I've got some things going on tomorrow. And . . . I think I'd rather just leave things the way they are."

"Okay. But I guess I'd like one chance to talk to you. I feel like I changed a lot on my mission, and—"

"I changed a lot too, Gene. I don't think you would like me."

"What do you mean?"

"I don't know where to start—and I don't think you would understand anyway."

"Try me. Why don't we just spend an hour or two together—as friends—and see what's happened to us."

"Gene, I have a boyfriend in California. He's not in the Church. He doesn't have this male-dominant attitude that Mormon men have."

Gene continued to hold the phone to his ear, his hand clamped so tight by now that his fingers hurt. He could have imagined almost anything but this. "But you're the one who said my commitment to the Church wasn't deep enough."

"Gene, I was a teenager. I thought the sun rose and set on the Mormon church. I had never studied any other philosophies. I've discovered that outside the Wasatch front there actually exists a world, and it makes a lot more sense than the one I left behind."

"What are you saying? Aren't you in the Church anymore?"

He heard a little laugh. "Gene, I understand how you would feel about that, but believe it or not, there are other ways to understand this life. Let's just leave it at that. Good luck to you. I'm sure you'll find a nice girl now, and you'll be very happy."

"Marsha, don't just drop out. If you have questions, maybe I could answer some of them. I've done a lot of thinking in the last couple of years, and I've studied the gospel. I've had experiences I'd really like to tell you about."

There was heat in Marsha's voice when she said, "Tell it at your homecoming, Elder. I don't need your missionary effort. Good-bye, Gene."

Gene heard the click, but he still held the phone to his ear, still tried to believe what he had just experienced. For all these years he had been trying to live up to this girl's expectations, and now she had gone off to some other place. For so long he had prayed that somehow the Lord would give him another chance with her, and even on the airplane, coming home, he had pleaded for one more opportunity. Now, in an instant, she was gone—not just off the phone, but gone. She wasn't even Marsha anymore.

"Oh, I didn't know you were in here." It was Alex.

Gene quickly hung up the phone. "I was just . . . finishing."

"Are you okay?"

"I don't know. I think I've come back to Mars. Are you sure I'm in Salt Lake?"

"What are you talking about?"

"Do you have a minute?"

"Sure. Just let me take my pill first. The doctor has me on some stuff that's supposed to keep my blood pressure down." Dad had gained some weight in the past few years. But more than that, his hair was graying. Grandpa had less gray hair than he did. Alex had turned fifty this year, and the truth was, to Gene he looked even older. The skin along his neck was beginning to wrinkle, and there was something more solemn about him than Gene remembered.

Gene walked into the family room and turned on a lamp. His dad took his pill and then followed him. He sat in his favorite old chair. Gene sat across from him on the couch, in the yellow circle of light from the lamp. "I think the world has gone crazy while I've been gone, Dad. I feel like I've been lost in space for about twenty years."

Alex nodded and laughed. "I can imagine," he said. "It almost seems that way to me, and I've been here to watch it."

"What's going on?"

"Well . . . I don't know. Where do I start? The center of it always seems to be the controversy over Vietnam, but it goes a lot deeper than that."

"What does?"

"All the change. All the new attitudes. I'm in the middle of a whirlwind back in Washington, Gene. So many forces are at work, there seems almost no way to sort it all out. I went back there to take a stand on the things I believe, but the old conservative and liberal split is so confused right now, no one knows what to call himself anymore. Here in Utah, I have right-wingers screaming that I'm selling my soul to the devil, and at the same time, I got rated by a newspaper service as one of the most conservative-voting congressmen. I can't find a constituent who isn't angry at me for something I've done."

"Why is everybody so upset?"

"Some really deep divisions have opened up, rather suddenly. The students across the nation are convinced that Vietnam is wrong, and they've taken to the streets—as I'm sure you've heard. But now they're turning up the heat. It could get violent, the way things are going."

"I don't get it. What good would that do?"

"Well . . . it does bring a lot of attention to their issue, and they certainly have gotten a debate going, but it infuriates my generation. People who fought in World War II look at these kids as traitors—giving solace to the enemy."

"That's right, isn't it? If they don't like the war, they can work within the system, can't they?"

Alex leaned back in his chair and hoisted his foot over his knee. He worked his loafer off. As he started on the second shoe, he said, "I guess I agree with that, generally. But most of these kids know more about the war than the congressmen I deal with every day. The students are raising some legitimate questions. For one thing, I don't think this is a war we can win. I've been saying that from the beginning. We could bomb the whole country into oblivion and declare victory, but what would that prove? One thing the history of warfare should have taught us is that you can't defeat guerillas with bombing raids. The Vietcong just dig in or hide out, and we don't stop many of them. We defoliate forests to flush them out. But how far can you go with that? I sometimes wonder what's going to be left of the country we're over there trying to help."

"So are you known for being against the war?"

"Not exactly. I'm known for raising serious questions about it. A lot of people in this district don't like that. They don't want a debate. It's all this 'my country, right or wrong' business. But I talked to George Romney just the other day, and he's almost to the point of announcing that he opposes the war."

"What does that mean, Dad? Would we just turn around and come home? We've never lost a war."

"I know. And that's Johnson's dilemma. He doesn't want to be the first president to accept defeat."

"What would happen to the South Vietnamese? I've heard there would be a bloodbath if we ever left."

"That's the other big question. I don't know. But I do know that we can't fight this war *for* those people, and I'm not sure the South Vietnamese—the common people—even want us there."

"So what's going to happen?"

"I don't know, Gene. Johnson won't back down, and if he can't drop enough bombs to win, this thing could drag on for a long, long time. All the while, the split in our country gets deeper and deeper. You have to remember, too, that's only one of the issues. We have the civil rights movement going on, and most blacks no longer—"

"Why are people calling them 'blacks' now? I heard someone else use that word—on the news last night."

"That's the word Negroes prefer. They're saying, 'Why should we straighten our hair and try to pretend we're white? We're black, and we're proud of it.' That's why you see them wearing their hair in what they call 'naturals,' or 'Afros.' But a lot of blacks have lost their trust in nonviolence. What it comes down to is that we have another war on our hands, right here at home, and I'm caught in the same position. I support what the black groups are fighting for, but I don't want our cities burned down."

Gene had looked forward to coming home for such a long time, but all of this was frightening to him. He had heard bits and pieces of news while he was gone, but he could hardly believe what he was hearing now. "What I don't understand is this whole hippie thing. Who are those people?"

"I don't know, exactly. I guess they're warmed-over beatniks. But they're tied into the antiwar movement. It's mostly young people who reject almost everything about American life. They don't want to wear ties and go to work in an office. They want a society where love is at the center of everything—communal living instead of competition. A lot of them are really idealistic—young and hopeful about breaking away from materialism. At a certain level, I can agree with some things they're saying, but a lot of them think drugs are the way to reach a higher level of understanding. They wander around in a daze. I don't know whether you heard about the acid tests?"

"The what?"

"Have you heard of LSD?"

"Sure."

"Well, Timothy Leary and Ken Kesey and some other people have been behind this whole LSD movement. It's this idea that the drug opens up all kinds of creative avenues in the brain. They talk about it like it's a religious experience. Kesey has this group called the Merry Pranksters, and here a while back they were throwing these big parties and giving out free LSD. It's all supposed to lead to a gentle new life. They listen to some of these strange new rock-and-roll bands, and they wear outlandish clothes. Some of them are starting to form communes now."

"What's a commune?"

"Little groups of people all living together, sharing everything. Most of them believe in 'free love,' which is just having sex with *anyone*, and babies are coming from that. It's one of those things that starts with maybe some basic truths and turns into chaos. I have a feeling that the whole thing will self-destruct in time, but a lot of people my age are overreacting. I guess I would too if I had a kid in one of their communes."

"Isn't Kathy heading there?"

"No, Gene. I don't think so. She's really smart, and she looks at issues carefully. She's not doing anything wrong—not as far as I'm aware, anyway. Her problem is that she's trying to walk a line that's almost impossible. I'm a lot more traditional than she is about most things, and I'm still trying to walk a delicate line—but it isn't easy. I've had people tell me that I'm not a good member of the Church because I told a reporter we should be careful about committing more and more troops to Vietnam."

"Dad, I think I really hurt Kathy's feelings today. I told her almost the same thing. I said that the way she talked, she seemed to be slipping away from the Church."

Gene saw his dad cringe a little. "Well, I'd talk to her again. She really is negative sometimes. She has a hard time with the whole idea of authority. She feels that it's terribly important for us all to think for ourselves. So the authority structure in the Church rubs her the wrong way." Alex leaned forward. "But I'll tell you what, Gene. That girl can hold my feet to the fire as effectively as anyone I know. If everyone in this country would look at the issues as carefully as she does, we'd be in better shape right now. If you still want to run for some kind of office, you could learn a lot from Kathy. Just don't be as combative as she is."

Gene thought about that. He knew he had never studied political matters the way Kathy always had. "I don't think I'll ever run for office, Dad. I don't know what I want to do now, but I've lost interest in seeking power."

"Then you *should* run. What I long for in Washington are more colleagues who are trying to figure out what we ought to do. Most of them want to run for president. I've met some wonderful people back there, but I've met some who really scare me."

Gene wondered what he *would* do with his life. His mission really had changed him, whether Kathy thought so or not. He just wasn't sure how he could use what he had learned. It was strange to think that so much of what he had worked to become was the result of things Marsha had said to him, and now she was out of his life. "I called Marsha just before you came in," he said. "She went away to college, and now she's telling me that she's grown beyond the Church."

"There's a lot of that going around, Gene. When you start questioning every kind of authority—which is right at the heart of what's happening to young people—religion starts to look way too controlling."

"It all seems like Sodom and Gomorrah, Dad. I turned on the radio today, and the music scared me. When did they stop singing and start screaming?"

Alex smiled. "That's what *my* generation keeps asking." Then he added, "Some of what's happening really is all about self-indulgence: just do whatever you feel like doing, and if it feels good, it must be right. A lot of the kids who hate all middle-class values are living off their middle-class fathers, who go off every day to that office job these kids claim to hate. There's all kinds of hypocrisy out there. But you know what? America is sort of like that. We wrangle and fight and call each other names, and in the process, some of the changes we make are good. If there's one thing I've learned in Washington, it's that democracy is really sloppy. All the same, if you think it's right, I guess you have to ride out a time like this and not try to stamp out the good side of it: the debate, the idealism, the 'seeking.'"

"I don't know if I can handle it."

"You'll be fine. You'll be in school in a couple of weeks, and you can start thinking about all these issues for yourself."

"I think I'm more interested to find out who wins this new Superbowl game they're starting."

Dad laughed. "I'd rather watch O. J. Simpson in the Rose Bowl." But then he added, "The thing is, there's no avoiding some of this stuff. Everyone's trying to figure it out."

"What about Vietnam? Will they start pulling us out of school?"

"That's very possible. And there's talk of doing away with deferments for Mormon missionaries."

"Dad, if I'm drafted, I'll go."

"I know."

"But how do you feel about that?"

"It's my nightmare, Gene. It's my worst nightmare. I fought a war I believed in—still believe in. It was the right thing to do, but it was a journey into hell. I still have bad dreams about things that happened to me—still think about people I killed. I'm never quite sure that my concerns about the war don't come down to that—my fear that you and Joey might have to go, and you'll have to do what I did."

Gene felt something like a chill go through him. It had always been fine to say that he would serve when his time came, but now the reality was setting in. He could go back to college for now, but sooner or later he would probably end up in Vietnam, shooting and being shot at. When he was younger, he had thought of winning medals, the way his father had, but now he wondered. He hadn't known that his dad still had bad dreams. When he tried to imagine himself in those jungles he had seen on television, the idea was unsettling, frightening. But he would go. Maybe his dad—and Kathy—were right. Maybe the politics were complicated. But he was an American, and he couldn't even consider turning his back on what that meant. After all was said and done, he still believed what he had told Kathy. Evil was spreading in the world, and however evil some Americans seemed to him now, at least those people were choosing for themselves. How could he not fight against a system that wanted to steal that right?

# Chapter 19

As Hans walked across campus, he felt the wind pushing him, flapping the collar of his jacket against his neck. It was spring now, March 1967, but it hardly seemed so. The air was full of ice crystals; when he turned a corner and came out from behind a building, the prickles stung his face. He ducked his head, held his old leather briefcase in front of his face, and bucked the wind until he crossed a street and could walk close to another building. When he finally reached his dorm, he was happy to turn into the protected entrance, and then to close the door behind him. What he knew, however, was that once he had been upstairs a few minutes, he would feel the cold inside his room. The building was not well insulated, and the furnace never produced enough heat. He had frozen in his room all winter. Everyone said the only thing that was worse was the heat of summer, without any way to circulate the air.

He climbed the dark stairs and then used his key to open the door to his room. What he didn't expect was to find his roommate there. Rainer was lying on his bed, and for a moment Hans thought that he had fallen asleep. But Rainer wiped his hands across his face and raised his head, then sat up and looked at Hans. Hans was startled to see that Rainer's eyes were red, his cheeks smeared with tears. "What's the matter?" he asked.

Rainer didn't answer immediately. He was swallowing, obviously fighting to get himself under control. "It's nothing," he said. "Nothing that should concern me so much."

"What do you mean?"

"My mother sent a speed letter to tell me that my *Oma* died. But she was seventy-six years old. It's nothing to feel so bad about."

"Had she been sick?"

"No. It came as a surprise. I suppose that's why . . ." But he couldn't finish. Hans saw new tears slip onto his cheeks.

"Were you close to her, Rainer?"

"Yes. My mother worked when I was little. *Oma* raised me more than my mother did."

"What about your grandfather? Is he still alive?"

"No. He was a little older. He died two years ago, or I guess it's three now. But he was a quiet man, hardly said a word to me. *Oma* was . . . *everything* to me." Rainer couldn't hold back. The sobs came, and he covered his face again. But not for long. He stood after thirty seconds or so and said, "I'm going to catch a train home. I'll be back by Thursday or Friday."

"Rainer, is there anything I can do?"

"No. I'm fine. I'll just pack a few things." He walked to his chest of drawers and began to pull stockings and underwear out and lay them on the bed. Hans thought of his own *Oma* Schaller, who had been so close to him when he was little. In recent years he hadn't seen her very often, but it was much the same for him. When his mother had been young and working, he and his parents had lived with *Oma* Schaller, on her farm, and he had spent many long days with her then. She had always been more patient than his parents, more willing to play with him, even when she was tired. He regretted never having known his other grandparents, the ones in America, or his *Opa* Schaller, who had died in the war. Some children he knew had grown up with four grandparents, but he had only ever known one, and he wondered how he would feel when the day came that she was gone from him.

Hans sat down at his desk, at the foot of the bed. He pulled a book from his briefcase and told himself that he needed to study for a while before dinner.

Rainer pulled his old suitcase from under his bed, and then he dropped his clothes into the case. When he shut it, he turned toward Hans. "I'm going to walk down to the train station," he said, "and just see when the next train leaves."

"I'd wear a warm coat. It's cold out there."

Rainer nodded. "Maybe I should." He walked to the corner of the room, by the door, took down his black winter coat, slipped it on without buttoning it, and then grabbed a dark cap. "I'll be going," he said. He came back for his suitcase, then stood close to Hans. "I only wish I could have seen her one more time," he said. "That's what's bothering me."

"Of course. I can understand that."

"I was planning to go home one of these weekends—to see my parents, and to see her—and I didn't do it. I wish so much, now, that I had gone."

"Yes. I understand. But there's no way you could have known."

Rainer shook his head. He looked toward Hans, not into his eyes, and he whispered, "I just hate to think that I'll never see her again—not ever. Do you know what I mean?" His voice had reached the breaking point again.

"Yes. Of course."

"But it's not what you believe. When you die, you think there will be a heaven, and you will see your family and friends there. Isn't that how you think of it?"

"Yes."

Rainer nodded. He set the cap on his head, as though to signal that he really was going now. "You *really* believe that?"

Hans didn't want to say anything that wasn't true. "I *believe* it. I can't say that I know it. Faith has never been easy for me. At one time it was exactly the sort of thing I doubted. But a lot of things have gotten easier for me to believe."

"It seems primitive to me, Hans. It's like believing in fortune-tellers or . . . other nonsense of that kind."

"It seemed so to me at one time too, Rainer. But when I trust in the Lord, my life gets better. Things fall into place for me. So I believe. And then I have to trust that it's true, what we teach about another life after this one."

"I'm sorry, Hans, but that sounds like the worst kind of superstition. How can a man of science accept such simplemindedness?"

"I don't know, Rainer. Maybe *you* can't." Hans didn't want to sound stupid. He thought it might be better to drop the subject.

"But what about you? Do you put science out of your head and just believe things that are nice to believe?"

"No. I don't think so." He wasn't sure he wanted to say anything more, but Rainer was waiting. Hans didn't look up at him; he said, quietly, "My father gave me a blessing once—he holds the priesthood in our church—and I felt something happen. It was as though power was flowing into me. It was something real, as far as I could tell. And there were other things, similar, that happened around the same time. Since then, I've trusted more, and that helps me. Things work out better in my life when I trust in God."

"Work out better? What are you talking about? This girl you cared so much about has turned her back on you."

"I know. But I have to believe that's for the best. I just have to trust in that—or hope that maybe it's not too late, that she'll change her mind. I may go see her, and see whether I still have a chance."

"Hans, think what you're saying. Your logic runs this way and that. I couldn't believe in such things. I have to be consistent. My *Oma* is *dead*. And that's the end for her. Her body goes back to the earth, and there's no beauty in that. There's only *decay*." But saying that was too much for him. He broke again, and this time began to heave with sobs. He went back to his bed and sat down, pulled his cap over his face, and cried into it.

Hans didn't say anything. He thought of going to Rainer and putting his arm around his shoulders, but he knew doing that would embarrass both of them.

Three or four minutes passed before Rainer calmed, but when he did, he asked quietly, "Hans, tell me how you think of it. In your mind, what happens when we die?"

"Our spirit leaves our body, and it's our spirit that goes on living."

"And what is a spirit?"

"It's a body, just like the one we have. But it's made of finer material. There's no blood in it."

"What's God then, to you?"

"He looks like us. He has a body. But he's exalted, all-powerful. He knows everything. He knows our hearts."

"And how do you know all this?"

"God visited Joseph Smith—our first leader. He chose Joseph to be a prophet, to bring truth back to the earth."

"I've never heard such craziness, Hans. You're too intelligent to believe something like that."

Hans smiled. "I suppose I'm not," he said. He waited for a moment, and then he added, "But Rainer, I'm not dishonest." He finally looked directly into Rainer's eyes. "I wouldn't tell you anything that I haven't honestly felt, and I've felt God touch me. I've felt him telling me that I'm going the right way now that I've come back to my church."

Something happened. Something subtle . . . but *something*. Hans saw Rainer's eyes relax, saw a softening in the set of his jaw. Hans was certain that Rainer had been moved, even if only a little.

Rainer was silent for a time. He seemed to be thinking things over. Finally he said, "This learning and getting better—even after death—that you talked about one time, I like the idea of that. It's the one thing you've said that I would really like to believe. But it's what everyone wants—to continue on, after death. We know death is natural, but we fear it. I suppose that's the source of all religion—people making up fantasies that sound better than the terrible reality that we all must die."

"Maybe. Or maybe we lived before this life, and we were with God, and we come to this life with understanding that clings to us. We know we're eternal. And the spirit—what Mormons call the light of Christ—whispers to us that the end is not really the end."

"But how could anyone ever know that—and know for sure?"

"I'm not sure how it would be for you, but when I went back to church and started to live the way I had promised to live when I was baptized, I felt something. It was the same feeling I got when my father blessed me. There was a sense that I was in the right place, doing what I was supposed to do, and God was telling me so, filling me with certainty."

"But I've watched religious people lose all their faith when things go wrong for them. What would you be saying now if you hadn't been admitted to the university? Many religious people are turned down, but you were allowed to enter. If you hadn't, maybe you would be cursing God now."

Hans slid his chair back a little, turned, and looked away from Rainer. He wasn't sure what he dared to say. He couldn't give Rainer any details—he knew that—but he wasn't going to let him think he hadn't suffered. "Rainer, you don't know my life. Many things haven't gone the way I hoped."

"What's been so bad?"

"I can't tell you. There are things that have happened that I can't tell anyone."

"I don't understand that."

"You believe in the party. If I told you certain things, you would feel responsible to report me."

Rainer looked astounded. He leaned toward Hans and said softly, "Hans, I believe in Marxism, but I don't believe in all this reporting on one another that happens in the GDR. I don't care whether you tell me what's happened to you, but I've given you great power over me—by saying this. Now you can use my words against me, if you choose."

Possibly. But Hans knew the other possibility. If Hans said too much, Rainer could report him and then claim that he had made such statements as an opening with Hans, to bring out information that the state needed. It was crazy to take a chance, and yet he had always wanted to know someone, have a close friend—someone outside his family—and Rainer seemed to be inviting that. He told himself he could talk of some things, perhaps—things the *Stasi* knew already. "I tried to escape this country, Rainer," Hans said. "I failed, and the *Stasi* could never prove that I had done it—but some of their agents knew. That's one of the reasons there was a great question about whether I could enter the university. For a long time I thought I couldn't get in. My school director stood up for me or it never would have happened."

Rainer was still sitting on the bed, leaning forward with his elbows on his knees. He seemed in no hurry to leave now. "Yes. I see what you're saying. I'm sure you were frightened for a time. But it came out all right for you. What if it hadn't?"

"There are other things."

"What?"

"Things I can't reveal."

Rainer nodded. "All right," he said, and he stood up. "I must go." Hans felt the distance return, the compromise that had existed between them all year.

"I tried another escape, later," Hans said. "Once again, I didn't make it, but I wasn't caught that time. If the *Stasi* ever finds out, I'll be thrown out of the university. So now you're the one with the power. You could ruin my life in an instant if you told certain people."

"I won't report you. I don't even blame you. I know your life can't be easy here, not with the religion you've chosen. But you're not understanding what I'm saying. You have nothing to fear now. You got what you wanted. I'm saying that you might not believe now, not if things had turned out the other way."

But Rainer hadn't understood. Hans was trying to say something about trust. How could Rainer really believe in Communism and not see that, at least in this country, it was built on a foundation of fear? Rainer had said that he didn't like all the reporting, but the government would have collapsed long ago if the people hadn't feared one another. What amazed Hans now, however, was to feel the freedom that came from admitting the truth, at least to one person. He had never even dared to tell Greta what he had done, and now he had shared his secret with someone very different from himself. He wanted to say it all. "I may still be under investigation, Rainer. I did something else—something that bothers me every day of my life. I tried to help a friend escape. I could have tried to stop him, and that might have saved his life, but I helped him, and he was killed."

"He knew the chance he was taking. He never should have asked you to help. You were taking an even bigger chance to help him and then stay behind."

Hans had always known that, had resented Berndt a thousand times for it, but the boy was dead. Hans didn't want to hate him for what he had asked. "I saw him die, Rainer, and I can't get it out of my head. Without God, I never would have made it through this past year. I don't have a friend in this place. Not anyone. You know what everyone thinks of me."

"I'm your friend, Hans. I promise you that. I'll take your secret to my grave."

Hans nodded. He wasn't sure that would be true. He knew that people meant to keep promises, but they didn't always do it. And still, he felt relieved, just to have been open with someone, once in his life.

"Do you think the *Stasi* is still looking into this?" Rainer asked.

"I don't know what they're doing. They questioned me, and then . . . nothing. But that happened before, and then later I was removed from

*Oberschule* for a time. I was lucky enough to be readmitted, but something like that could happen again, and I would lose everything."

"And *then* would you turn on God?"

"No. Not now."

"And it helps you to have this trust in him?"

"Yes."

"I think it's self-deception, Hans. I really do. But I envy you. If I could see my *Oma* again, knew for certain that I could, it would make a great difference in my life." But he looked stolid now, not hopeful.

Hans stood up. He wasn't sure what to do. He knew he would be too embarrassed to embrace his friend. But he put his hand on his shoulder. He knew the power of hands, of blessings, and this wasn't exactly a blessing, but he prayed for Rainer, silently, and he felt Rainer's gratefulness flow back to him.

~

Diane hadn't spent the entire day with Greg—not exactly. It was "Y Day," and she had left that morning with Terry and Julianne and a lot of other girls—and guys—from their apartment complex. A truck with a loudspeaker had come past the apartments around six o'clock, and Julianne had harped on Terry and Diane until they had piled out of bed, put on their cutoffs, joined their friends, and made the hike onto Y mountain, not far from their apartments. The only trouble was, the students in their group had gotten there ahead of most, and that meant they had had to hike well more than halfway up the mountain. After that, heavy buckets full of whitewash had been passed all the way up the hillside and then dumped onto the rocks that formed the big block letter "Y."

Greg had come wandering up the mountain almost an hour after the others, and after finding Diane, had worked his way into the line, next to her. He did work hard, though, and he let Diane rest a couple of times. Diane was always a little slow waking up, but Greg was funny, and everyone had gotten into the spirit of the thing. She actually did have fun, even though she was tired by the time she hiked back down the mountain. But when everyone walked across campus and on down to the Smith Fieldhouse, where hamburgers were being served for lunch, Greg continued to stay at Diane's side, and somewhere along the line, Terry and Julianne had connected themselves to a different group. By the time lunch was over, Diane was with Greg. They watched some of the bicycle race together, and a flag football game, and then walked back to their apartments so they could shower and change and attend the Men's Chorus presentation that evening.

Diane was struggling to stay awake toward the end of the concert, but Greg talked her into walking to the Wilkinson Center for ice cream. Along the way, he brought up his favorite topic: the life he wanted, the success he hoped he would have as an attorney.

"It's one thing to be an attorney," he told Diane, "but it's another to be a really *famous* one. I want to win huge cases, write books, maybe teach at Harvard Law—stuff like that. I don't want to be good. I want to be the best, with the financial rewards that come with it."

"Does money really matter so much?" Diane asked.

"Hey, Mormons believe in striving for excellence. I don't know any other way to think."

"I thought we also believed in humility."

Greg laughed. "Don't worry. I'll become great and famous and always be just as humble as I am today."

"Exactly."

"Well . . . it's not easy, being me." He flashed all those white teeth, as though he knew that looking at him was a treat.

The weather had been nice all day, but the wind had picked up now, and Diane could feel that a spring storm was blowing in. She hoped the snow was over now, but the cold apparently wasn't. The campus was still busy, though, with lots of students clinging to the last of the little vacation from schoolwork the day had brought. By now, most of the people still out and about were in couples. She wondered what had happened to her roommates. Terry got asked out fairly often—although Terry didn't think it was often enough—but Julianne had gone out only a couple of times all year. Diane hoped the two were still together and Julianne hadn't ended up alone.

The fact was, Diane wished that she had managed to escape Greg today. He was fun at times, but she hadn't liked him tonight. He could be exciting, sort of overpowering, but she was always annoyed when he made it clear just how full of himself he was. She wanted a husband who would make a good living and be able to build her a pretty home—the things she had grown up with—but she didn't need, didn't want, a superstar. She had always wanted nice kids, a job in the Church, a husband who became bishop, not some wheeler-dealer type.

She thought of Kent, who loved her so unabashedly but was also a guy who would do well in his career. He knew how to walk on the ground. Kent was the right one for her, and nothing made her more sure than listening to Greg. But Greg kept coming back, and he clearly considered Diane part of his future. She had told him over and over that would never happen, but he wouldn't listen. One of these days she would merely stop going out with him, but for now he was the person she could relax with most easily.

"You've got to come down here with me in June," Greg was saying. "The NCAA track championships are going to be held in our stadium. Jim Ryun, O. J. Simpson, Bob Seagren—all the great college track stars will be here."

Diane had heard of Bob Seagren. She thought he was the one who had broken some record in the pole vault, but it didn't sound like anything she cared to make a trip to Provo to see. "Jim Ryun could break the four-minute mile at altitude. That's never been done in Utah. I've got to see that."

"I've never paid much attention to track," Diane said. "You were really into it in high school, weren't you?"

"Oh, yeah. I ran the 880 and the mile. I never lost a mile race in my senior year—at least not until I got to the state championship. I finished third at state, but I got this bad cold about a week before, and my whole training schedule got knocked for a loop. I was the favorite, but I just couldn't run that day. You can't believe the guts it took just to hang in there and get third."

Diane rolled her eyes, but not so he could see. "I couldn't run a mile if a grizzly bear was chasing me," she said.

"It's tough. But that's what I like—that kind of challenge. Law school is going to be a lot the same. If I get into a really good school—and I'm sure I will—I'll be up against sharp guys. The only way I can stay ahead of them is to work twice as hard."

"You didn't say 'keep up,' I notice; you said 'stay ahead.'"

"In the mile, I used to run guys into the ground the first two laps, and then I'd coast home. I don't believe in running from behind and sprinting the finish."

They had come to the Wilkinson Center. Greg stepped ahead, opened the door, then used his free hand on Diane's back to direct her through the door. Diane moved quickly, just to resist his control, but then she waited for him to catch up. "You're the most conceited guy I've ever known," she said, "and I've known some bad ones."

Diane was laughing, and Greg laughed a little too, but he didn't say anything for a time. They walked past the candy counters, through the open center of the building, then into the snack bar area. Diane decided she wanted a root beer instead of ice cream, so Greg got root beer for both of them. It wasn't until they had found a quiet booth and sat down that he said, "There's something I want to talk to you about."

Diane feared moments like this. She laughed and said, "I was only teasing you back there."

"I know. But it's true. I am cocky." He took a drink of his root beer. "But I don't think of myself that way. I just want to make the most out of life. At least I admit how hard I'll have to work. It's not like I'm bragging that I'm smarter than other guys."

"But you never doubt yourself. You never think that you just might work your hardest sometime and still come in second."

"I ran third at state, Diane. And okay, I had a cold and all the rest, but I'll never forget the rotten feeling I had when it was over. I don't want to feel that way again."

"Do you think your Father in Heaven thought less of you that day?"

"No. Of course not. He loves the guy who finishes last. He loves lazy bums who don't even give life a good try. But look at the parable of the talents. He wants us to do something with what we've got, doesn't he?"

Diane was rather impressed with the response, but not comfortable. She tried to think how she could tell him what she was thinking. "Okay. Let's say you're running the mile and a little boy runs out on the track. One of the runners crashes into him and then steps on him with those sharp spike things on his shoes. Do you stop and help the kid, or do you keep running? And what would Christ want you to do?"

"That example doesn't work, Di. There would be lots of people around. Someone else could help the kid. The runners would keep going."

"Okay. You're running a cross-country race and you're alone. *You* crash into the kid. Do you stop and help him?"

"Of course I do."

"Even if you lose the race?"

Greg turned in his seat and leaned against the wall at the end of the booth, and then he stretched his legs out across the seat. "No question. I'm not as bad as you think. I want to win, but I know what's right and wrong. I'll never be a crooked lawyer, for instance. And I won't take money to fight for things that are wrong."

"Okay, let me try another question. You're at work, and you have a big case coming up. When quitting time comes, do you come home to help me with the kids, or do you stay at work until all hours of the night?"

"Let me get this straight. You're planning to marry me, and you want to know how I'll treat you?" He smiled and then took a sip of his drink.

Diane knew she had made a stupid mistake. "That was a slip," she said. "I shouldn't have said, 'me.' I should have said, 'Will you come home to help your wife?'"

"But it's an interesting slip, isn't it? It encourages me."

"Answer the question."

"The answer is, I don't know. I think there's got to be some give-and-take in marriage. If I'm on a huge case, I may have to stay late sometimes, and it would be your role to—"

"Your *wife's* role."

"Okay. My *wife's* role to understand on that particular occasion. Another time, my wife is sick and the kids have the measles, and the house is burning down—or whatever—then it's time for me to knock off and run home."

"But only when the house catches fire. Right?"

"I'm just exaggerating. You know what I mean."

"But it's an interesting slip, isn't it? It *scares* me."

He sat up straight, slid back in front of her, and reached for her hand. She pulled it away before he could get hold of it. "Diane, listen. This is no joke to me. I see you trying to picture us together, trying to decide what it would be like. Maybe I am too confident, but I'll always do what's right. What I'll expect of my wife is only that she'll give me the chance to be all I'm capable of being. And I'll try to do the same for her."

Diane liked that more than she wanted to admit. And she liked the gentle way he was looking at her. She let him take her hand.

"And I'll tell you something else. I'll always be home early enough to go to bed at the same time you do. I wouldn't want to miss that—not one single night."

"Miss what? A good night's sleep?"

He smiled. And she did love his smile. She also liked the thought of . . . what he was talking about. He reached with his foot, touched his ankle to hers, and she liked that, too. She tried to imagine sleeping next to him, their legs touching, or her cheek against his chest. Kent was probably a nicer person, and good-looking, but Greg was even better to look at. She wondered how important that was. She only knew that she did like his touch right now.

"Diane, I do want to do some good things with my life. But none of it will mean a thing if you're not part of it. I know that now. Maybe you think I only compete for things I want. But there's more to it than that. I fall in love. And I'm passionate about the things I love. They become everything to me. I know you wonder about me sometimes, but I think I'm going to be a good husband. I'll work at it the way I do everything else—with all my heart."

Diane took a long, deep breath. Maybe he was only talking, but she did like what she heard, did feel softened toward him. She had always loved to be loved.

When they left the Wilkinson Center, Greg took her hand, and then, when they reached her apartment, he kissed her longer than usual. It was a real kiss, not the brief touch she usually allowed him. He kissed her neck, then her hair, and he kissed her lips again. She let it happen even as she was telling herself she wouldn't, but after the second kiss, he stopped before she had to stop him, and he backed away before she did. Then he stood in the dim light and looked at her. "The truth is, I'm the one in danger," he said. "Once we're married, I'm afraid I'll do absolutely anything you say. You're slowly wrapping me right around your finger."

Diane loved the moment, the devotion she could see in his eyes. She also knew that something had changed between them. Their relationship had taken a step forward, and that seemed all right.

When Diane reached her bedroom, Julianne appeared sound asleep, but Terry was sitting in bed with a bed light on and a paperback book in her hand. Diane knew she wasn't studying; the girl was hooked on romance novels. Terry looked up casually, but then Diane saw the surprise in her face. "You've been making out," she said. "You're all flushed and dreamy-eyed."

"I'm not either," Diane whispered—but with way too much force.

"Poor Kent. Greg just finished him off."

"Shut up! You don't know what you're talking about." Diane dropped her jacket onto her bed and hurried into the bathroom. But by the time she got there, she was crying. She *had* betrayed Kent, and the thought of it made her sick.

And yet, when she got into bed, she found she couldn't sleep, and she wasn't thinking about Kent. She was remembering the way Greg had looked into her eyes, and what he had said to her. She thought again of sleeping next to him, the warmth of his body touching hers.

# Chapter 20

When Kathy got to Baldwin House, it was almost ten o'clock. She was so far behind on her studies she hardly knew where to begin. She had already decided, while climbing the stairs, that she wouldn't go to bed that night, that she would stay up and write a paper that was due the next day. It wouldn't be great, written at the last minute, but at least she would get something in and the professor wouldn't flunk her.

When she opened the door, she found Janet and Trisha sitting on the floor, playing cards.

They spent way too much time doing just that, and it drove Kathy crazy. They probably still had homework to do. They never got started until eleven or so, even though they usually sat around downstairs most of the evening.

Kathy stopped, just inside the door. She wanted to ask Trisha to leave so she could settle in and study, but she wasn't sure she dared say anything. Janet glanced up, then looked back at her cards as she asked, "Where have you been?"

"We had a meeting, over at UMass."

Janet raised a clenched fist. "Power to the people," she said. Then she looked at Trisha and smiled.

"I'm sorry, but I don't see the humor," Kathy said.

"You never do."

Kathy was hearing lots of this kind of stuff from her friends lately, and she was sick of it.

"So what was this meeting about?" Trisha asked. "Planning another *march?*"

"Yes, as a matter of fact. Over in Amherst tomorrow afternoon."

Janet laughed. "That's good. One more demonstration. This time Johnson will probably be so frightened he'll just call off the war."

She continued to stare at her cards, but she was grinning, obviously delighted with her own wit. Her hair—more blonde than it had been when Kathy had first met her—was put up in big pink curlers, held by a hairnet, and she was wearing an old pair of cutoff jeans that were so tight the seams were pulling loose.

Kathy took off her jacket and threw it onto her bed. "I'll tell you the irony in that little comment," she said. "If everyone who *claimed* to be opposed to the war would take to the streets, it really would end. Three-fourths of the girls at Smith claim we shouldn't be in Vietnam, and most of them are sitting around like you two—doing *nothing* about it."

Trisha leaned back against Kathy's bed, flipped her hair back with a quick motion of her head, and said, "Kathy, you are so incredibly naive. The inmates in a prison can bang their tin cups against the bars all they want. That doesn't mean the warden is going to set them free."

"Nice metaphor, Trisha," Kathy said. "If you think America is a prison, you're the one who ought to be putting up a fight."

"All I'm saying is that a bunch of students carrying signs and shouting little slogans are nothing more than a joke to the government—and to all the rest of us."

"You're the joke, Trisha. You and Janet, both. You try to act *informed* and *cynical*. You play your Dylan album, or you listen to Joan Baez, and that makes you *with it*. The truth is, you're just a couple of spoiled brats. You don't really care about anything—except *shopping*."

Trisha threw her cards on the rug and stood up. "I can tell you didn't *buy* that little costume you've got on tonight. It looks like something you found in a garbage can."

Kathy didn't answer, wasn't going to. That was hardly the point.

"Don't talk to me about being *spoiled*," Trisha was shouting. "Your dad's paying your way through this place, the same as every other Smith girl. And I'll tell you what my father told me. He said your family made every penny they've got off World War II. They built weapons for this government you hate so much. If there's a hypocrite around here, it's little Miss Utah."

Kathy was stunned. She wanted to find words that would hurt Trisha just as deeply, but nothing came to mind, and it was humiliating to stand there. "I'm leaving this place," she finally said. "I can't stand you two anymore." She walked to her closet, found her suitcase in the back, jerked it out, and began throwing clothing into it. She stripped a lot of things from her chest of drawers and her closet but realized she couldn't get everything in without packing carefully, so she stuffed a few personal items on top and slammed the suitcase shut. Trisha had walked out by then, and Janet was telling Kathy to calm down, that she was sorry, that they could talk this out.

Kathy was trying to think where she was going to go. The only option that came to mind was asking whether LaRue would let her stay a night or two, maybe the rest of the year. She didn't think she could stay at Smith much longer. She was probably going to flunk out anyway—and even if she didn't, she wanted to get away. Maybe she could join the Peace Corps.

She decided it was best to leave without saying another word, so she grabbed her suitcase and headed for the door. "Come on, Kathy. Where are you going to go?" Janet was asking.

But Kathy kept going. She stepped through the door, pulled it shut, hard, and then she hurried down the stairs. She walked as fast as she could up a hill and over a few streets to where LaRue lived. She wasn't sure what LaRue would say about this, but it had to be easier to deal with her than it was to deal with Janet and Trisha day in and day out.

When LaRue opened the door, she looked only a little surprised. She was wearing a flannel robe and house slippers. She stepped away from the door to let Kathy in, and she only asked, "What's up?"

"Could I stay here tonight?"

"Sure. I guess. What's the matter?"

"I can't live at Baldwin anymore. Those girls are driving me crazy."

Kathy saw LaRue's reaction, the little impatient shrug, as if to say, "What a child you are." But she only asked, "What's wrong with them?"

"They hate me. All they do is criticize me for what I'm trying to do."

LaRue was looking Kathy over almost the way Trisha had. Kathy was wearing old jeans, frayed around the cuffs and torn out at the knees, sandals, and a purple tie-dyed shirt. She also had a wooden peace symbol hanging from the end of a macramé necklace, with matching earrings. She knew it was outrageous—the kind of thing she had hated at one time—but she had decided it was time to show her solidarity with the people who weren't going to sit by and let things continue the way they always had. She didn't care if it was a uniform; she might as well be known for the army she was now fighting with.

"Oh, Kathy," LaRue said, and she smiled, "if your mother could only see you now."

Kathy didn't want to deal with anything more tonight. She needed to borrow LaRue's typewriter and get started on her paper. What she only now realized was that she hadn't brought a couple of the books she needed. How could she get around that?

"Kathy, I don't care if you stay tonight, but I have some tests I have to read. I'm going to be busy until pretty late."

"That's great. I have a paper I have to write. I probably won't go to bed."

"When's the paper due?"

"Tomorrow."

"Don't tell me you haven't *started* it." LaRue stepped past Kathy and finally shut the door.

"I haven't. But I've thought it all through. I know what I want to say."

"What kind of paper is it?"

"It's for my sociology class. It's about poverty. I'm going to use some of my experiences in Mississippi."

"Is this a research paper or just an opinion kind of thing?"

"Well . . . it's supposed to involve some research. I checked some books out of the library, but I forgot them when I left so fast."

LaRue took a long breath, then seemed to choose not to say what she was thinking.

"Do you have *The Other America* here?" Kathy asked.

"I'm sure I do. I can probably find it. But Kathy, that's rather old research now. You need current material."

"Do you have anything?"

"Sure. Let's go look. But this isn't light reading. You should have started two weeks ago."

LaRue walked into an extra bedroom that she used as a study. The entire room, every wall, was covered with bookcases. Kathy followed as LaRue walked to a corner near a window and began looking at titles. In a moment she pulled down a thick hardback, which she extended toward Kathy. "How many sources do you need?" she asked.

"There's no set number. I'll use the experiences you and I had down there as my major source."

"Is your professor going to buy that? Who is it anyway?"

"McNally."

"Oh, dear. Honey, she's a tough old nut. You're not going to be able to bluff your way past her. You'll have to know what you're talking about."

"I do know what I'm talking about. We've been there."

But the words turned LaRue around. "You've been in the South once—for two weeks—so you know all about poverty?"

"That's not what I'm saying."

"Kathy, your experience is very limited, no matter what you saw. How many white people did you get to know in Mississippi? Black people are not the only ones who know poverty in this country, you know. You'd better do your homework."

Kathy didn't say anything. She knew. She had been telling herself for two weeks that she needed to do the reading for this paper. But so much had been going on. She had been behind on the reading for her psychology class, with a test coming up, and tomorrow was the biggest demonstration of the spring, followed by a Vietnam teach-in. She had been spending all her time at organizational meetings and preparing herself to do small-group sessions on the history of the Vietnam involvement. She had had to make choices, so she had put the paper off.

"I don't know how you can keep this up," LaRue said. "Are you flunking any of your classes?" She had pulled down a few more books, but she didn't hand them to Kathy. She walked to her desk, sat down, and set the books in front of her.

Kathy dropped into a chair. "No, LaRue, I'm not."

"I don't see how you can pull off this paper tonight and get anything better than a D. Betty NcNally has no tolerance for sloppy thought. And she's a stickler about documentation. You'd better have your footnotes right."

"I will. I need to get started."

"Okay. You can use this desk. If you want my help at some point, and I've gone to bed, wake me up."

"Thanks, LaRue." Kathy was touched. But she understood, too. LaRue thought the worst fate in life was to get a low grade. She had pretended, off and on, to be an activist, but in truth she was an intellectual. To her, education ascended above everything else. Or at least grades did.

"Kathy, I understand what you're trying to do, but you have such a great mind. Please don't waste this experience. You're so lucky to be at Smith."

That was annoying. LaRue didn't need to preach. "Some things are more important than others," Kathy said.

She saw LaRue's jaw tighten. "What bothers me is that the money your parents are putting into your education seems unimportant to you."

So here it was again. "LaRue, I've heard that speech before. I don't have time for it tonight."

Kathy saw the jerk of LaRue's head, the little flash of anger, but LaRue looked at her desk for a time before she said, without looking at Kathy, "When I came east to school, I worked my head off to keep my scholarship. I understood what a great opportunity I had, and I took advantage of it. My dad gave me some financial help, but I carried the major load myself."

Kathy felt the accusation like a slap in the face. "And you must have learned what he wanted you to learn, because you sound just like him."

"I hope that's true. I've never once disagreed with my father about the value of hard work. Or the value of a good education, either."

"LaRue, you're just as tied to the system as everyone else in our family. You're the one who taught me what poverty does to people—and racism—but all you do is weep about it. You don't try to change anything. You 'discuss the war' with all your liberal faculty friends—tell each other what a shame it is—but I don't see a single one of you putting your body in front of a tank."

"Is that what you're doing?"

"If I get the chance, I will."

"Kathy, be careful. You're twenty years old and you think you have all the answers. Maybe you need to 'discuss' a few things with the faculty instead of listening to yourself and your tantrum-throwing friends all the time. Democracy is *about* discussion."

"Democracy! Our so-called democracy is a bunch of generals and business executives sitting down together to decide what's good for us.

We're being sold a bill of goods by a bunch of fat-cat politicians who don't have the slightest concern for the people of Vietnam."

"Well, you've got the rhetoric down. Is that your idea of *thought*—spouting the clichés you've learned from Robby Freedman and his crowd? Kathy, I'm sick about what's happening to you. You were a brilliant kid, with a fantastic future ahead of you, and you've come out here and become a little puppet. You go to church on Sundays and try to keep one foot in your past, but the rest of you is sinking right into quicksand."

Kathy stood up. A decision was in her head, and it had come in an instant. LaRue was right about one thing. Kathy was going to pull that last foot loose—loose from her family and loose from Church members who didn't care about things that really mattered.

Kathy got up. "Good-bye, LaRue," she said. And then she walked back to the living room and picked up her suitcase.

LaRue followed her to the front door. "Where are you going?"

"I need to be with people who don't hate me."

"Kathy, you sound like a baby. You're not leaving this house. Just sit down and let's talk."

"I've heard enough of your talk. You've told me what you think of me."

"Kathy, what I'm describing is what I see you becoming. But I also know what you've always been capable of. Let's see if we can't sort some of this out."

"No. You've helped me decide." She opened the door. "I know where I belong now." LaRue tried to grab the door, but Kathy's temper fired, and she jerked it from LaRue, pushed past her, and then she hurried down the stairs. LaRue was calling after her, asking her to come back, but Kathy kept going out into the damp spring evening. It was cold outside, and she had left her jacket back in her room at Baldwin, but the air actually felt good. Kathy walked back down the hill, past her house, and then down the long Main Street that curved through town. She continued on down to where she reached the road to Amherst. Then she crossed to the other side, put out her thumb, and walked backward.

This was something new for Kathy. She had ridden to meetings with people she didn't know well, but she had never tried to hitchhike. The idea was frightening, but it was one more break with her past. After twenty minutes of watching cars go by, however, Kathy was getting cold, and now that her initial anger had calmed, increasingly nervous. When an old Pontiac finally stopped, she was scared. The driver was a young guy, but a girl was sitting next to him on the front seat. That looked safe enough. Kathy opened the car door and asked, "Are you going to Amherst?"

"Sure," the girl said. "Hop in."

The two turned out to be students at UMass and were anything but intimidating. They even dropped her where she wanted to go: Robby Freedman's house. But once Kathy was out of the car, she knew the step she was taking was bigger than she had comprehended back at LaRue's apartment. She heard LaRue in her mind, wondered about the things she had said—about being a puppet, about refusing to listen to anyone—but she had been answering that accusation in her mind all the way from Northampton. Who were the real puppets? Weren't most people worse than she was? The whole nation was spouting the official government line on the war without even questioning it. And Mormons were usually the worst about that.

Kathy walked to the door, making a fist so tight that her fingers hurt. She waited, thought, then almost backed out, but she couldn't think of anywhere else to go. So she knocked.

There was no reaction for a time, but then she heard a movement inside and the door came open. Robby's friend Kirk was standing there, looking blank, hardly aware of what he was doing. His long hair hung in his face, and his beard was now so dense that he seemed all hair, only eyes and a nose peeking out. "Hey," he said.

"Is Robby here?"

"Sure." He stepped away from the door. "Robby," he called. "You got company."

Robby appeared in a moment, from the kitchen. He was wearing nothing but his underwear—boxer shorts—no shoes, no shirt. Kathy looked away. But Robby didn't seem to worry about it. "Kathy," he said. "What's going on?"

"Can I flop here tonight?"

"Sure. But I can give you a ride over to Smith, if that's what you need."

"No. I'm out of there. I'm dropping out."

"Are you serious?"

"I am." She still couldn't look at him. She had never stood before a boy who was almost naked. Kirk walked down a hallway, leaving the two of them alone.

"Sit down. Tell me what's going on. I was just going to have a beer. You ready for that, too?" He laughed.

Kathy continued to stand by the door. She didn't know the answer to his question. She had never wanted to drink, never been interested, but maybe it was something to do at some point. She had no idea what she might do now. She wondered whether she would take any more of her parents' money. She doubted she could do that, but she had never looked for a job, didn't know exactly what she could do to make enough money to get by. She had been thinking about that since the moment she had walked out of LaRue's apartment, and the idea was frightening to her. She would have to make some of those decisions in the morning, but she told herself she was merely making the first break tonight. "No, thanks," she said about the beer. "You go ahead."

He walked to the kitchen and opened the refrigerator. She heard the hiss of a beer can as he used an opener on it. "Take a load off," he said as he returned. She glanced at the underwear, his bare chest with a bit of hair growing down his breastbone. Maybe she needed to go somewhere else. But he set the beer on a rickety end table and walked to his bedroom. When he came back, he was wearing jeans, as though he understood her embarrassment. She liked that—liked that he respected her feelings.

"What happened?" he asked. He sat down in a chair that matched the shabby couch she was sitting on. "What made you decide?"

"I can't stand the girls in my house. They're all little princesses. They don't care about anything."

"Hey, those girls do a lot of good in this world. They donate their old clothes to the poor—last season's stuff."

Kathy felt some guilt. Most Smith students really were better than he—or she—were implying. But she didn't say that to Robby.

"So what are you going to do?" he asked.

"Work for the movement. I'll have to find a job of some kind. I guess I'll start looking around in the morning."

"You can crash here as long as you want." Then he said, rather carefully, as though to watch her reaction, "I have a nice, big bed."

"Could I just sleep on the couch?"

"Sure. It's up to you. But you know where I am if you ever want to join me. I told you that a long time ago."

That was something to wonder about too. How would she decide such things from now on? She felt an emptiness, something like a stomachache, and she wondered whether she would ever feel at ease again. There was suddenly so much to be afraid of.

Robby talked about the demonstration the next day. "It's time to turn up the heat," he told her. "Some guys think we ought to start bombing buildings, but I don't agree with that. I don't mind destroying some property, if that'll help our cause. But I don't think it will."

"No. I don't think so either." But Kathy wasn't thinking at all. And after a time, Robby seemed to know that. "I'll get you a blanket," he finally said. "I've got a feeling you might not sleep much tonight. You've made a big leap. But I'll leave you alone so you can deal with it."

"Okay."

"Unless you *want* to talk. If you do, I'll sit up all night with you."

"No. That's all right."

So he went off and found a blanket and a lumpy old pillow with no pillowcase. When he was gone, she took her shoes off but left her clothes on, and merely pulled the blanket over her. But she was cold, and she was alone, and he was right: she couldn't sleep. She was starting to wonder how all this had happened. Somewhere late in the night she finally drifted off, but she was awake early and more frightened than ever. The wait until Robby finally got out of bed was perhaps the worst couple of hours of her life. She wanted to get on an airplane, to fly home, to go back to being the Kathy she remembered. She kept telling herself that she couldn't lose her nerve, that she had to accept this discomfort until she figured out exactly what she was going to do. For now, she had teach-in classes to direct that afternoon, important things to say to people who needed to hear the truth.

Robby convinced her not to look for work that morning but to help him with the final preparations for the demonstration and the teach-in. Everything would begin at noon. Dee Dee was going to speak, along with the chapter leader from Amherst College. And then Robby would try to fire people up to come to the teach-in sessions. What was exciting was to see how things had changed on campus. Well before noon a large crowd had begun to gather, and just before twelve, Kathy heard Kirk say that he thought more than two thousand people were there, "and more coming all the time." Then he said to Robby, "I've got the flag, and I brought lighter fluid, so it'll catch and really burn."

A little stage had been built up, made of wooden boxes, and the local SDS leaders were standing behind it, Robby in the center of everything.

Still, he glanced at Kathy. He must have seen the surprise on her face. He stepped toward her. "It's going to get us on TV," he said.

"Don't you think people will just—"

"No, Kathy. We have to stop thinking that way. We have to get to people's emotions. That's the only thing that busts them out of their apathy. When they try to explain to themselves why we're so wrong, they start thinking. Maybe they start looking for some answers. Nothing else works. It's what we have to do."

"They won't think. They'll *stop* listening."

"Kathy, decide. Right now. Are you with us or not?"

"You know I am. I'm just talking about methods. I don't think it's the best approach."

"It's just a piece of cloth."

"I know. But I also know how guys like my dad and my grandpa feel about something like that."

"Then just go home, Kathy. Listen to your old man and your grandpa. Be what they are. Let the war continue. Let this nation go on the way it always has. If you don't have the stomach for this stuff, just admit it to yourself. I really don't care."

She stood her ground, gave her head a little shake. "I'm here," she said. "I'm not going anywhere."

"All right."

But when Dee Dee was speaking, howling her anger, Kathy watched Lester out in front. He didn't applaud, didn't shout. He looked defeated. By the time Robby took the stand, Kathy could see what was happening. The insiders—the SDS people around the stage—were going crazy. As Robby took the stand, they were chanting, "Hey, hey, LBJ, how many kids did you kill today?" And when he began to speak, they shouted their agreement with every angry word. But most of the outer crowd was listening, considering. Many cheered when the war itself was denounced; others stood around the perimeter, as though they were mostly just curious. To draw those people in, convert them, some solid logic, some convincing arguments were probably needed, but Robby did what he always did with a big crowd. He resorted to slogans, to emotional language, even platitudes.

"Bring the troops home!" he shouted. "Peace now! Peace now! Peace now!"

Kathy just hoped she could have her chance to make a real argument during the teach-in. She felt sure that anyone who really understood the history of the war would agree that it was fundamentally wrong. She was thinking about the things she wanted to say, the way she wanted to build her case. And then she heard her name. "Kathy, jump up here. Help him hold the flag."

She responded to the first sentence before the second one registered. And suddenly there she was, in front of the crowd, and Kirk was extending a corner of the flag toward her. Another guy was standing behind Kirk with the lighter fluid in one hand and a cigarette lighter in the other.

She stopped, held back. "Just hold it up until we get it started," Robby said. "I'll light it."

She didn't move.

"Kathy, come on. This is it."

But now she was stepping back. She jumped, half fell off the stand, and took one last look at Robby, who was glaring down at her. "You just made your choice," he said. And then someone else climbed onto the stage.

Kathy began working her way through the crowd. What she didn't know was where she was going. Where *could* she go? What could she do now? She didn't belong anywhere. LaRue had told her the truth, that she wasn't a Mormon any longer, and Robby had told the truth too: she still was. They couldn't both be right, and yet they were. Maybe the truths canceled each other. Maybe she was nothing at all.

# Chapter 21

Gene was working for his Uncle Wally for the summer of 1967, selling cars. He didn't like the job, but maybe what he disliked most was that he was good at it. Selling cars, especially used ones, didn't feel entirely honest to him. He would ask customers to make an offer, have them fill out a complicated set of papers and initial them—so the car seemed almost theirs—and then tell them he had to talk to his sales manager. When he came back, the offer was always rejected, but he would present a counteroffer. The ones who got the best deals were the ones who fought him the hardest, and they were often the ones who could afford to pay more. Nice people, quiet people, humble people—they were the ones who got eaten up by the technique. Sometimes Gene told the ones who weren't very aggressive, "Why don't you try one more offer? I've got a feeling the sales manager will come down another couple hundred bucks." Of course, he knew that the manager would—since the difference came out of Gene's commission—but being so duplicitous bothered him.

What Gene did like this summer, however, was that his family was home. Mom and the kids were staying until school started in the fall, and Dad was flying back and forth to Washington. Gene had lived alone in the big house on Harvard Avenue all winter and spring, had gone to church by himself in a ward that didn't have a lot of people his age, and found himself rather lonely at school. He had expected to be active in Sigma Chi again, but he had lost a lot of interest. He hadn't dropped his membership, but he rarely went by the house, and he didn't attend a lot of the date events. He had expected to date all the time when he got back—so he could find someone to replace Marsha—but the girls he had dated so far hadn't interested him much. Some of them were waiting for missionaries, and he was unwilling to get in the middle of those situations. Others seemed surprisingly worldly. He didn't think of himself as a prude, but the music had turned wild while he had been in Germany, and he could hardly believe the way nice Mormon girls were dancing.

Gene's mission had been hard, and he had been a little "trunky" the last month, but now, at home, he missed the way he had felt as a missionary. Part of what he missed was the respect he had received from Church members compared to the insignificance he felt in his home ward. Even more, he had reached for a higher spiritual level in the latter part of his mission. He had come home feeling that he still had a long way to go, but at home, progress was not just difficult but nearly impossible; the goal hardly seemed to have meaning.

One morning he was eating a bowl of cornflakes when his mother asked him, "Do you want some toast to go with that? I'm sorry I don't fix you kids better breakfasts these days."

"This is all I want," he told her. "I've gained about five pounds since I got home."

"Then cut back on those big, greasy hamburgers you eat for lunch, not on a good breakfast."

Gene looked up and grinned. "It's nice to hear stuff like that. I haven't been mothered for a long time."

Anna shook a finger at him. She was wearing white shorts and a pale-blue knit shirt. She had been out with a friend of hers playing tennis already that morning. She wasn't quite as thin as she had once been, and she was conscious of it. "I'm closer to fifty than forty now," she had told Gene in a wistful tone one day that summer, as though she hated to accept what was inevitable—that she wouldn't always be so beautiful.

"Don't worry, Mom," Gene had told her. "You look thirty—and you need to look a little older anyway now that Dad is fifty." The fact was, he had turned fifty-one that spring.

"I'll mother you just as long as I want," she was telling him now. She came to him, wrapped an arm around his neck, and kissed the top of his head.

"That's fine with me. Could you make my bed?"

Now she thumped him on the head with her knuckles. "That's not a mother's job. Hire yourself a maid." She stepped away. "Where's Kurt? Don't you guys have to be to work in a few minutes?"

"He hasn't come down yet. I woke him up half an hour ago, but I haven't heard the shower yet."

"Gene, what am I going to do with that boy? He stays up half the night, even if I make him stay home, and then he won't get up in the morning."

"He's sixteen, Mom. That's his only problem."

"At sixteen you were so responsible you were scary. I never had to talk to you about doing your homework—and you didn't even *think* about doing some of the things Kurt has done."

"I'm probably kind of weird—you know, a high-strung first son—but Kurt is the one who's normal. Maybe he tried a little beer once, but—"

"It was probably more than once. We just caught him that one time. The worst part is, we know that he's lied to us sometimes about where he's going and what he's doing. He'll say anything to get out of the house, but then he forgets his promises, once he's gone."

"I'd better go yell at him again. We need to leave in about ten minutes." Gene glanced at his watch. He actually had fifteen minutes, or even twenty, but he wouldn't tell Kurt that.

"Gene, would you talk to him?"

"About what?"

"About getting ready for a mission—maybe what your mission meant to you. And about living worthily. Your dad and I have talked and talked, but it doesn't seem to make any difference."

"I doubt he'll listen to me."

"Try, okay?"

"Sure."

Gene walked upstairs, knocked hard on Kurt's door, and then yelled, "Come on, Kurt. Jump in the shower, really quick. We've got to be out of here in ten minutes." He heard nothing for a few seconds and was about to yell again, but then he heard Kurt's feet hit the floor. Gene walked back down to the kitchen. By then he could hear the shower running.

Mom was sitting at the kitchen table. She was eating dry toast and a cup of rose-hip tea—something she had kept a love for since her childhood in Germany. "What's happening with your love life?" she asked. "Did you like that girl you took out the other night—Marilyn, or whatever her name was?"

"Not much. She talks through her nose."

"She's cute."

"Kind of."

"Are you still thinking about Marsha?"

Gene sat down at the table. "No," he said. "I called her last week. She's back in Utah for the summer. Since I got home from my mission, I've just wanted to spend a little time with her, have one good talk—but she still won't do it. She started in on this big speech about Mormon men thinking they can run their families any way they want—because they hold the priesthood. She doesn't sound like a Mormon anymore."

"Gene, you're the last guy in the world who would try to dominate anyone—especially Marsha."

"I know. I told her I had no intention of 'running my family,' and I wasn't sure she could make the same claim." He laughed.

Anna set her tea down and smiled. "What did she say to that?"

"I think it hurt her a little. She said I was right. Then she said she probably never would get married. I guess she broke up with that last guy she was going with." The shower shut off—rather quickly, it seemed, considering it was Kurt. Gene hoped the kid would hurry and get dressed now.

"Do you feel bad about Marsha?" Mom asked.

"Sure I do. But I don't really understand what's going on with a lot of girls these days. It's like they hate guys."

"Well . . . a lot of men do try to dominate their wives. And young women are starting to ask questions about that. That's probably good, but it still scares me. Some women are angry about everything, and I'm not sure where all that will go."

Gene didn't know either. He just knew he wanted someone to love. But he didn't tell his mother that. "I'd better yell at Kurt again," he said. "We've gotta get out of here."

But as Gene climbed the stairs, he met Kurt coming down. His hair was still wet and his shirttail was hanging out over his cut-off jeans, but he seemed in a pretty good mood. So on the way to the dealership, Gene kept his promise to his mother. "Kurt, you're planning to go on a mission, aren't you?" he asked.

"I don't know." Kurt was slumped down in his seat, but he rolled his head toward Gene. "I doubt it'll be my choice." He looked a lot the way Gene had looked at the same age—the same blond hair and his mother's blue eyes. He was a boy that girls would always be enamored with—not just because of his looks but because of his easy manner.

"Why do you say that?"

"Mom and Dad expect me to go. They've never asked me whether I want to."

"Maybe it seems that way, but it will be your decision. And I can tell you this much—if you do go, you'll be glad you did." Kurt didn't respond. He looked back toward the passenger-side window. Gene wondered whether he should let up, not push the matter right now, but he figured this might be his best chance, now that the subject was before them. "The thing is, a mission is really hard. But you grow like crazy, and you learn a lot about yourself. I don't think I had much of a testimony before I went, but after depending on the Lord as much as I had to, I feel like I really have a lot of faith. I think that'll help me more than anything, all my life."

"Did Mom tell you to give me a pep talk?" He was still looking the other way.

"Well . . . sort of. She just—"

"Did she tell you about the beer?"

"I heard about it. I think Dad was the one who mentioned it first."

"So I guess they think I'm going to burn in hell because I drank a little brew." He sat up straight, rubbed his hands over his face. "This family is so straight. My friends back in Virginia just can't believe all the rules Mom and Dad slap on me."

"Maybe your friends need a few more rules."

"Oh, come on, Gene. You were forty years old when you were born. Some guys know how to have a little fun when they're young."

Gene knew he had to be careful. "Hey, I had a great time in high school. I loved sports, and being in leadership positions was great. I liked to—"

"Not everybody is a star athlete. And there's no way I'm going to run for office and win out in Falls Church. I have some good friends, but I'm not one of those 'student government' types."

"That's fine. I'm just saying there are a lot of ways to have fun without drinking."

"And I'm a big drunk now, right? After all, I drank some beer. Now I'm ruined forever."

"Was it really just once?"

Kurt laughed. "You *are* Dad, aren't you? You even know his script."

By then Gene was driving the car into the parking lot at the Rambler dealership. He was still driving the Ford he had bought when he hadn't been all that much older than Kurt. He had worked for Uncle Wally back then, too. He had washed cars and cleaned up in the showroom, washed the showroom windows—the same stuff Kurt was doing this summer. But

Gene had also shown some gumption. He had learned to sell, and he had picked up a couple of nice commissions. Kurt always seemed to do the minimum. He didn't care whether the windows were streaked, whether the cars looked good—and he sneaked into the offices to flirt with the secretaries as often as he could.

Gene parked the car, but before he got out, he said, "Kurt, I'm not trying to get on your back about this. I just hope you'll plan to go on a mission. I think it would be the best thing you could do. And I know I could have prepared better than I did. The more you do to get ready now, the more you'll enjoy the experience, and the better missionary you'll be."

"I don't know whether I'm going, Gene. And I don't want a lot of pressure about it—not from you and not from Mom and Dad. I'm going to decide for myself."

"Fair enough. But as you think about it, don't just ask yourself whether it will be *fun* or not. That's a teenager's way of thinking. It is sort of fun sometimes, but mostly it's hard work. Still, it's the best work you can do. One of these days I'd like to tell you about some things that happened to me over there. You can't believe what it's like to feel the Lord's Spirit working through you, using you as a messenger."

Kurt opened the car door. "I heard your homecoming talk. Don't give it again," he said, and he walked away.

Gene was devastated. He hadn't wanted this. He couldn't believe that he hadn't found a way to say what he wanted without sounding like such a typical RM. He walked into the building and sat down at his desk at the back of the showroom. He wondered what he and Kurt could possibly do together to get a little closer. Kurt had plenty of old friends in Salt Lake, so he spent his evenings running around, jumping at a trampoline center or going boating. He was apparently a tremendous water-skier, and Gene knew he could be a good athlete if he would just get involved. He was a little smaller than Gene had been at the same age, but he was quick. The two played basketball together sometimes, out in back, and the kid had excellent moves. He just didn't practice enough to become the kind of shooter and ball handler he needed to be.

Gene could see Kurt out on the lot, dragging a hose, getting ready to wash cars. Gene had some paperwork he needed to finish, and he stuck with it for a while, but he was struggling to concentrate. He decided to walk out and say something friendly to Kurt, just to ease the tension. When Gene reached Kurt, he was washing a little Ford two-door coupe. "That blue metallic looks a lot better when it's clean," Gene said. "I'll bet it polishes out really nice."

Kurt was running water over the car, rinsing it off. He looked over the roof at Gene. "Uncle Wally didn't say anything about waxing it."

"Oh, no. I'm just saying, if someone buys it and then really shines it up, it'll look good, even if it is a few years old."

"I guess," Kurt said. "I'm sure that's what you'll tell them, anyway."

So now what was he saying? That he lied about the cars? Gene had made a point lately of pointing out to customers everything that was wrong with a car before there was any dickering on the price. "I just meant it's a nice color."

"When I get wheels, I want a Triumph. How much would a TR3 cost?"

"I don't know. More than you can make around here in a summer."

"Dad said he might buy me a car if I'll prove I'm responsi-*bull*."

"I earned my own car down here. But I did some selling. You might think about that. I bought a nice little car for three hundred bucks—and I'm still driving it."

"But then, you knew how to put the *bull* in responsi-bull. You're Mister Klean. You're everything Grandpa ever wanted in a grandson."

At least Kurt was smiling, and Gene tried to do the same. But he had no idea what he could say in response.

"The only thing is," Kurt said. "I'm not sure that you're quite clean enough."

Gene wondered what sort of accusation that was. Kurt was raising the hose, apparently to spray the top. Gene saw him press his thumb over the end and began to step back, to avoid the spray, but suddenly he took a blast straight in the face. He jumped back quickly, but Kurt kept the stream going, drenching Gene's white shirt, his red silk tie. By the time he retreated around another car, the back of his shirt and the seat of his pants were just as wet. Gene's first reaction was fury. He wanted to run at Kurt, to knock him on his back. What did the kid think he was doing?

But as Gene peeked out from around the old white Pontiac he had taken refuge behind, he saw Kurt smiling as though he had just done something wonderful. Gene remembered the impish little boy Kurt had been—able to get away with almost anything. Still, he tried to sound firm when he called out, "Hey, that's enough, okay? I've got to dry off before any customers come in."

"Sure. That's all right." But Kurt was stilling grinning, and when Gene took a trial step from behind the car, Kurt took another shot at him. Gene stepped back as though he were going to withdraw from range, but as he moved around the Pontiac he spotted a bucket of soapy water that Kurt had left at the back of the Ford. Gene darted to it. By then Kurt was squirting him again, but Gene charged anyway, tossed the water, sponge and all. He caught Kurt in the chest, soaked him, then tossed the bucket aside and charged again. He grabbed the hose, and the two struggled, both getting wet, but Gene was stronger, and he managed to wrestle the hose away. Then he turned the water on Kurt, who ran back a few steps, stopped, and turned around. Gene doused him from head to foot, and Kurt only laughed.

Gene finally took his thumb off the end of the hose and let the hose drop to his side, where the water splatted on the blacktop. He knew he was a mess, and he hoped Uncle Wally hadn't happened to look out his office window while all this was going on, but he also felt more relaxed than he had in a long time. He had almost forgotten, during his mission, what it was like to feel this young.

"It doesn't matter if I'm wet," Kurt said. "But you've gotta face the customers."

"I know." Gene wiped his hair back, felt the drips of water down the back of his neck. His tie was probably ruined, and he knew it, but he still couldn't get himself to care. "That means I still owe you. Don't worry. I'm going to get you sometime—just when you least expect it."

"Are you saying this is war?" Gene had never seen Kurt look more pleased. His hair, which was as long as Dad would let him keep it, was wet and hanging into his eyes, but his eyes were alight.

"Hey, no. You can't start doing this to me every day. Really." But he couldn't stop himself from laughing.

"You'd better watch yourself around me, big brother. I'll be waiting and watching—and I could be anywhere, anytime."

"Excuse me. Do you work here?"

Gene spun around. The voice had been pretty, and the young woman was even prettier. She had dark brown hair, almost black, quite short, and a devious little smile, with two very deep dimples. She was wearing a denim skirt, also short, and a bright red shirt.

"Me?" he asked stupidly.

She glanced around. "I don't see anyone else around here. But maybe you have a dry person in the showroom. Do you want me to check in there?"

"No! I mean . . . no. I'd be happy to help you. I seem to have had a little accident involving a younger member of our staff. I plan to take his life, later on, but I'd be happy to help you first."

"Maybe it's not a good idea to hire brothers at the same place of business."

Gene nodded, feeling a little "discovered." "How did you know we were brothers?"

"Well . . . aside from the fact that you look like two wet rats, you also look exactly alike."

"Hey, watch it," Kurt said. "I'm better-looking than he is."

But Gene said, "We're brother rats. And if our uncle rat catches us having water fights out here, we could both get fired."

She let those dimples sink all the way in again. "Boys will be boys," she said.

"He's a boy. I'm a man," Gene said.

"Really. I guess sometimes it's hard to tell the difference."

Kurt walked to Gene and took the hose from him. With his voice as deep as he could make it, he said, "We're both men, ma'am. And we can both help you, if you like. Or even better, I can help you, and Gene here could wash these cars."

She liked that, but Gene had a feeling he had better start sounding like a grown-up before he chased a customer away. He walked away from Kurt—praying that the kid wouldn't blast him again—and then he said, "What exactly did you have in mind?"

She answered seriously. "I go to the U, and I just need a car for driving back and forth. I can't afford much, but I've been working this summer—enough to get a little money ahead for a down payment."

"So I guess you want something economical—good gas mileage and that sort of thing."

She winked. She actually winked. And she said, "No. I want a Corvette, if you want to know the truth. But I don't think a two-hundred-dollar down payment will get me into one. What do you think?"

"We happen to be all out of Corvettes anyway." But then he gave her a piece of information she didn't really need—still, information he hoped she found interesting. "I go to the U too. I drive an old '54 Ford I bought before my mission. But back in the fifties, they built some great cars. That might be the way to go."

"I'm sure that's what I'll have to do. Do you have anything for seven or eight hundred?"

"Maybe. Let's walk down here."

But as he started to walk, she whispered, "You're sloshing. I hope your uncle doesn't hear you, inside his office."

"Thank goodness for our dry climate," he said. "I should dry up in no time at all. My pants are cotton, and my shirt is wash and wear."

"But your tie is silk, and your shoes are leather."

They stopped in front of a car, and Gene turned to take another look at her. "You do notice things, don't you?" he said. She was petite, maybe five-foot-five, with a tennis player's figure. He had noticed her tan legs when he first looked at her. He didn't look again, not standing this close.

"I do. I notice *everything*."

He hadn't realized until now how very white her teeth were. "This car is nice," he said. "It's a . . ." But he couldn't think what it was. ". . . a '58 Dodge, I think. It's—"

"That sign says it's a '59."

"Oh, yeah. They look about the same. But that's even better."

"I don't like green cars."

"Well . . . I can understand that. Should we start with color then, and work from there?"

"Red would be nice."

"It would. But I don't have anything in red that would fit your price range." He couldn't stop himself from smiling, and she was still beaming. "Come this way. Let me show you a car I like." He walked between a couple of cars and was relieved not to look into her eyes for a few seconds. He knew he had to stop all this—whatever it was—that was going on between them. But the girl, in spite of her dark complexion, had blue eyes—vivid blue. How could he think about cars?

They walked to the back of the lot, where Gene pointed to a '56 Chevy, blue-green and white. "You could get into this car for a good price.

It's getting pretty old, but it's a classic. Some people say it's the best-looking car ever built."

"What kind of shape is it in?"

"Well . . . not the best. It needs paint, and it runs a little rough. It may need a valve job. But you could get it at a good price, and then maybe put some money into it. The upholstery is kind of bad, but it wouldn't cost you too much to get some seat covers."

She put her hands on her hips, cocked her head to one side, and said, "You *are* a silver-tongued salesman if I ever heard one—needs a paint job, a valve job, and new seat covers. I don't want a *project*. I want a car I can drive right now and not have to worry about."

Gene tried not to look at her. He tried not to think about her face, those legs. "Well, okay. Do you want to walk around the lot and see if you see anything interesting?"

She seemed to notice that she had just been handed a straight line. She smiled brighter than ever, but she was apparently too classy to say what he hoped she was thinking—and he liked that. What she said was, "Sure. Will you go with me—and point out all the flaws in your other cars?"

"Like you said, I've got a silver tongue."

They walked, and she liked the cars that were much too expensive, and didn't like the ones she might be able to afford. Along the way, Gene took the chance to ask where she had gone to high school and learned it was Bountiful High, that she still lived in Bountiful with her family. She also said that she was a junior, which meant she was probably twenty or twenty-one—maybe a year younger than he was.

"Listen," he finally said, "our selection in these less-expensive cars is really low right now. But we take trades all the time. How about if I watch for something that might fit your needs?" He tried hard to look serious as he added, "Just leave me your name and your phone number."

She was up to the moment. "Of course," she said. "And will you *promise* to call me?"

"I'll call the *instant* we get a good car in." He nodded, in mock seriousness. "Or maybe even sooner than that."

"Now that's what I call service."

"We aim to please."

She gave that cute, coy little smile and let her eyes slide up and away. "I can tell that you do," she said. "Do you have something I can write on?" He couldn't think for a moment what she meant. He couldn't think at all. When she saw his confusion, she said, "For my phone number."

"Oh. Yes. We don't want to forget that."

He pulled a little packet of his cards from his pocket. He handed her two. "Keep one of these," he said, "and write your number on the back of the other one. I'm sorry, but they're just a little wet."

"At least you're a fast dryer. You're coming right along. Too bad your tie is making funny little ripples along the edges."

He looked down at it. "Uh . . . yeah. I may have to run home at noon and get another one."

"You must live nearby, Gene."

He was surprised to hear his name.

"You just gave me your card," she said. "I now know who you are. You must be the Gene Thomas who played basketball for East High and thrilled the hearts of every high-school girl in the state."

"I did go to East. I did play on some of the sports teams."

"Do you have a pen or a pencil?"

"Oh, yeah." He fished a ballpoint pen from his pants pocket.

"My name is Emily," she said as she wrote it. "Emily Osborne. You *will* remember to call me, won't you?"

"Trust me. I won't forget. In fact, maybe we should get together in the near future, and just, you know, make a list of all your automotive likes and dislikes, so I can locate *exactly* what you're looking for."

"That would be going the extra mile. But I would appreciate it *very* much." She handed him the card, and she allowed him one last look at those dimples. As she walked away, he wondered how long he could stand to wait before he called her.

# Chapter 22

Kathy was on her way to San Francisco. After that terrible day at the demonstration, when she had refused to help Robby burn the flag, she had taken a bus back to Northampton, and then she had walked back to Baldwin House. She hadn't known where else to go, but even more, she needed desperately to get back to a place that made her feel like herself again. She had begun by apologizing to Janet and Trisha—who were surprisingly regretful about the things they had said—and then she had gone to Professor McNally, told the truth about what had happened in her life lately, and to her surprise received a week's grace period to get her paper in. She had poured herself into the research and had even gone to LaRue for guidance—and again, to apologize. She ended up receiving a B on the paper, with a full grade deduction for the extra week she had been granted.

Kathy had decided that flunking out of school—or dropping out—was not her answer. It wasn't that she was satisfied with "the system," but a homing instinct in her seemed to say, "Go back to what you're best at." She was not going to stop her fight against the war, but she was going to get along better with the girls in her house, and she was going to keep her distance from Robby. She wasn't sure that burning the flag was quite so huge a thing as her father and grandfather thought it was, but she wasn't going to let Robby decide such things for her.

Kathy finished the school year pretty well. She brought her grades back to a range that was not entirely embarrassing, and she had begun to remember the pleasure that learning had always brought her. Maybe she was more like LaRue in that regard than she had wanted to admit. And yet, when she compared her SDS friends to her family at home, who lived by rules, without much passion for any cause, who were so easily satisfied with things remaining as they had always been, she wondered where the balance was, or whether she could ever find a compromise that worked for her.

Across the country the counter-culture people were proclaiming 1967 the "Summer of Love," and many were heading for San Francisco. Kathy had planned to stay at Smith and work again that summer, but after a month she had become restless to leave. She longed for some change, some emotion other than loneliness. She was living in an apartment that an activist friend of hers had sublet to her for the summer. The friend—a girl named Joanie Peyton but usually called "Sugar"—had written Kathy, told her to let the apartment go and come to San Francisco, where she had decided to stay. "These are the most genuine people I've ever known," she had said. "I've finally found a place where I belong. You need to come." Kathy was curious about that. She knew she couldn't drop everything and go live among the hippies in Haight-Ashbury, but she did want to see what she thought of the atmosphere there. She needed a *place*, a way of life that fit who she was, and she wondered whether some aspects of the life in San Francisco might help her understand what she was looking for.

So much was going on that was confusing to Kathy. That spring 400,000 protesters—mostly young people—had marched to the UN Building in New York, and somewhere around half a million had gathered in San Francisco. It had been a massive demonstration against the war, exhilarating to Kathy. So many important leaders were also announcing their opposition. Martin Luther King had called the war wrong—destructive to the cause of minorities and poor whites. Senator William Fulbright had been holding the administration's feet to the fire for some time, but this year he had published a book, *The Arrogance of Power*, which denounced Johnson's war policies. Walter Lippman, the newspaper columnist, had expressed his conviction that more and more bombing would accomplish nothing, that the nation was being torn apart for a hopeless cause. Even Muhammad Ali had, on religious grounds, refused induction into the military, saying that he had "no quarrel with the Vietcong." He had been stripped of his title and stood the chance of spending many years in prison.

Kathy was excited to see the increasing momentum of the antiwar movement, and yet attitudes on the other side had hardened too. She had heard the talk on the bus, the anger about hippies and long-haired protesters. She had seen the words on T-shirts that people were wearing: "My Country, Right or Wrong" and "America: Love it or Leave It." What worried her even more, however, was that so many young people who opposed the war were also dropping acid, searching for their answers in eastern religions, losing interest in "the issues." Timothy Leary had sounded crazy once, telling young people to "tune in, turn on, and drop out," but now, more and more of them were doing just that. Those same people were listening to the new "psychedelic" bands—the Grateful Dead, Iron Butterfly, Jefferson Airplane—and they were wearing the neon colors and wild patterns that were supposed to be part of the LSD experience. The new Beatles album, *Sergeant Pepper's Lonely Hearts Club Band*, seemed to give overall meaning to these wild, psychedelic impulses, and now the Beatles were saying that even they had taken LSD. A new show on television, *Laugh-In*, was building its popularity on the frenetic mood of the times and the iconoclastic way young people were thinking.

Kathy couldn't help believing that the antiwar movement was going to be lost in all the self-indulgence, and what was almost worse for her was watching what was happening in the Civil Rights movement. Riots had exploded in American cities the summer before, and with a new organization called the Black Panthers telling young blacks to fight the white man, to employ the power that came "from the barrel of a gun," it was hard not to believe that more of the same would be coming this year.

Kathy's heart was still with the movement, but she longed for the days when Reverend King's philosophy of nonviolence had been the guiding force.

What surprised Kathy, in all her confusion, was that she longed to go home. Since that night she had argued with LaRue, the two had "made up," but they hadn't seen each other often. Part of the reason was that Kathy hadn't gone to church. She hadn't rejected her faith entirely, but she had finally recognized that the changes she had experienced within herself separated her from Church members, made her too deeply uncomfortable among her old friends, her old society. She wasn't sure she could ever go back. But she did long for her home, or at least *some* home—a place where she could feel that she belonged.

So Kathy was going to compare. She wanted to go home, but she wanted to experience San Francisco first. When she told her parents she wanted to spend some time with them, they sent her money for a plane ticket, but she had bought a bus ticket instead—to California. She called her parents and let them know she would be getting home a "week or two" later than she had first talked about, but she didn't say where she would be during that time. Wally and Lorraine seemed pleased just to know that she was planning to be home for part of the summer.

Kathy liked the bus trip. She loved the way the hardwood forests of the East gave way to the vast fields of corn and soybeans in the Midwest, and then to the grassy high plains of Wyoming. She was excited when she spotted the mountains in the distance, and again when she began to see sagebrush and cedar trees, to feel the dry air. She liked to think that this land, ugly in its way, and also beautiful, was her land. She passed through Salt Lake without contacting her family, looking at it as though she were a tourist. It was a clean city but seemed smaller than it once had, and the accents of the people who worked in the bus station seemed strange now. She heard what her friends at school noticed in her own speech and couldn't identify: an odd intonation that wasn't as distinctive as a southern dialect, but not exactly like any other speech in America. She heard a man say that he had gotten a "good dill" on a new car, and she realized that her dad had always spoken of "making dills." She had probably said the word the same way herself at one time. She didn't know when she had adjusted to what she had heard in the East.

Kathy liked the friendliness of the woman in the coffee shop at the bus station, but Kathy guessed that she wasn't LDS, or at least not active. She didn't speak with the sweet tones of a Relief Society lady. Kathy wondered about that, about all the people living in Utah who weren't part of the Mormon culture. Could she come back to the mountains and the sagebrush and the sense of home without being part of the Church?

Kathy was glad to cross Nevada at night, to cross the Bay Bridge early, when the water of the bay was still gleaming in the angled light. Sugar was living with some friends in San Francisco, and she had promised that Kathy could crash with them for a while. Kathy called when she arrived, and Sugar told Kathy to take a taxi, that she didn't have a car. The apartment turned out to be a narrow, two-story place, part of a little two-unit building. It smelled of incense but also of mold in the bathroom, and of body odor more than Kathy was comfortable with. There were three bedrooms and a living room, but people slept everywhere, even in the kitchen and on a screened-in back porch. Kathy didn't know who was actually renting the apartment or how many of the residents were "permanent." Different people were there every day, and it was never exactly clear which women were with which men. As far as Kathy knew, no one was married, but there was a lovely three-year-old girl named Lotus whose mother—a woman called "Lavender"—sold jewelry in the streets every day: silver necklaces and exotic earrings, mostly big hoops. Lavender took the little girl with her, and the two sat on a sidewalk on the edge of Golden Gate Park. San Francisco could be very cold, even in July, and the girl was a thin little thing. She took a blanket with her each day, but she came back in the evenings shivering and looking dismayed, tired.

Kathy wandered the streets with Sugar, and she liked much of what she felt. There was so much music, so much that made the neighborhood seem like a carnival. Jugglers and mimes and musicians moved about through the crowded sidewalks, mostly looking for the occasional donation that tourists would drop into their hats or their instrument cases. The streets were like a bazaar, with everything from pottery to drug paraphernalia for sale. And people did seem to be having a good time. The men were almost all bearded and dressed in wild outfits, with tunics and beads, bell-bottoms and headbands. Most of the women wore their hair down, long, and they weren't afraid of color, of long swishing skirts and high boots. Friends met on the street and embraced, laughed and shouted, and almost everyone was young. Kathy wanted to like it all, to believe in it.

On Saturday afternoon, Sugar took Kathy to Golden Gate Park. What Kathy saw there was beyond anything she had imagined. Thousands of people had gathered—the local Haight crowd, teenagers, tourists, even people in Hell's Angels jackets—and then Buffalo Springfield began to play, their music blasting from enormous amplifiers. "Stop, hey, what's that sound? Everybody look what's going down," they sang first. It was their big hit, and the crowd went crazy. People were jumping, swaying, dancing, and Kathy loved the feeling, the wild but happy mood.

Kathy found a place to sit on the grass, but Sugar couldn't contain herself. She told Kathy she wouldn't go far, or if she did, she would find Kathy later, at the same spot, and then she jumped up and moved closer to the crowd. Sugar was no beauty queen, but she was intensely physical, filled with force, with animation. She was wearing old jeans, very tight, and a halter top that was much too skimpy. It embarrassed Kathy to see her dance, but Sugar would throw her head back, letting her long brown hair swing, and she seemed not to know that anyone else was around her. Kathy saw a guy step in front of her, begin to move with her, and then the two took hold of one another, Sugar's arms around his neck, his wrapped around her waist. By the time the music stopped, they were kissing, caressing, his hands moving all over her.

The whole scene was incomprehensible, disturbing to Kathy. She knew what Sugar would say, that it was all part of being free, expressing herself, finding joy in her own body—but the guy was a stranger. Kathy told herself to relax, to allow other people their own way of doing things, but she kept watching, kept hoping that Sugar would think a little about what she was doing. Instead, the two left together, and Kathy wondered when she would see Sugar again.

What Kathy felt more and more, as the afternoon stretched into evening, was that she was the only one there holding back. She did like the music, as band after band played. She was excited to hear Jefferson Airplane sing "Somebody to Love." But as dark came on, people started getting crazier. She heard them speak of "Kool Aid"; she saw people who looked as though they had lost all touch with the world around them. One guy not far from her kept saying, "My skin is turning to velvet. Soft velvet. Rub it. See how it feels." But he wasn't talking to anyone but himself, and he stroked his own arm as though it were a pet he was holding.

Kathy was there to experience this, she kept telling herself, not to judge the way her parents would, and she had promised to wait for Sugar, but finally her discomfort was too much for her. She could stand the language—she had heard it all before—and she could tolerate the playful, rollicking mood that so many were obviously feeling. But there was a certain falseness about much of it, as though the craziness required effort. And something almost animalistic was taking over, revolting her: she saw a man relieve himself while he was holding hands with his girlfriend, and she saw a woman with her top off, dancing and throwing herself about.

Kathy got up to leave, but just as she did, she heard a deep voice behind her. "Hey, girlie, you've got the kind of legs I like." His arms were already reaching around her, his hands grappling at the front of her. She reacted instantly, drove both of her elbows back with all her strength. She heard the guy grunt, felt him fall back. She spun and faced him. He was a little guy with a feeble beard and bad teeth. He was holding up his hands in front of him, laughing. "Don't hit me anymore. I give up," he was saying, and a guy on each side of him was shrinking back, pretending to be terrified.

They were all three wasted, hardly a real threat, but Kathy told the guy, "Don't you *ever* try that again," and she walked away. She no longer worried about Sugar. She found her way back to the house. The radio was on, and Harpers Bizarre was singing "Feelin' Groovy" so loudly that the walls were vibrating.

A guy named Marcus—a big fellow with a black beard—was the only one in the living room. Kathy had talked to him a couple of times and had the impression he had lived there longer than most. Maybe this was his place.

"Didn't you go to the park?" she asked.

"No." He laughed. "I was sitting with a sick friend."

"Really?"

"Well . . . sort of. I've got a buddy named Chester. He's burned his brains out. He's done too much speed, too long. He got himself hurt this afternoon. I took him to the hospital."

"I didn't think Haight would be the way it is," Kathy said.

"Haight is dead," Marcus said. "There was no crime here a year ago. Everyone was cool about what was supposed to be happenin'. Now we got junkies ripping off street people, stealing anything that isn't nailed down, just to get high. And the place has turned into a tourist attraction. I'm getting out. Some of us are going to New Mexico. We're going to buy a farm if we can get some money together."

Kathy was also leaving. She waited a day and said good-bye to Sugar, who had come back to the apartment sometime during the night, but on Sunday evening Kathy boarded a bus once again, and she rode all night.

When she reached Salt Lake the next morning, she took a city bus to her house so she wouldn't have to call her mother and ask for a ride. She had to walk the last several blocks, but she had sent some things home from Northampton by mail, left a lot of her things out there, and she was carrying only a small suitcase. When she got to her house, it was the middle of the morning, and she found her mother in the family room, vacuuming. Kathy was surprised to see her wearing slacks—even if they were rather nice ones. "Hi, Mom," Kathy said.

Lorraine didn't hear her immediately but after a moment seemed to sense her presence and look up. She turned off the vacuum cleaner. "Oh, honey, how did you get here?" She stepped toward Kathy and took her in her arms. Kathy had always known this, that she could come home anytime, from anywhere, and her parents would be glad to have her back. "How did you get home?"

"On a city bus."

"From the airport?"

"No. I came here on a bus." Kathy didn't want to explain.

Lorraine looked confused, but she didn't ask. "Why didn't you call me? I would have come for you."

"The bus was okay. I didn't want to bother you."

Mom stepped back and looked at her. "It's not a bother, honey. I'm just so glad you're going to be home for a while."

Kathy nodded. She didn't know why she was crying. "Do I still have a room?"

"Sure. You can always come here and have your place."

But that sounded just a little too calculated, a way of saying, "Like the Prodigal Son, we'll always accept you."

"Where's Douglas?"

"He's in summer school—just half a day." Lorraine glanced at her watch. "He'll be home in a couple of hours. He's doing so well. He has more confidence than he used to. And guess what? Wayne got his mission call. He's leaving in August. Where do you think he's going?"

"I don't know. He took Spanish in high school, didn't he?"

"Yes. So we thought he'd go to Mexico or South America, but they're sending him to England—and Wales is part of his mission. I can't tell you how thrilled your dad is."

"Is Wayne excited?"

"He really is. Kathy, you won't believe how much he's changed lately. He's been reading his scriptures every morning before he goes to work, and he did so well in college this last year. He never worked hard at all in high school, but he's taking responsibility now. He's so much like your dad, it's hard to believe. He even looks more like him all the time."

"What about Glenda and Shauna?"

"Oh, you know those two. They're busy as little bees. In fact, Glenda's in Beehives now. She goes to MIA. Can you believe that?"

Kathy actually had realized that. On the bus, coming from California, she had thought about the kids, calculated how old they were getting to be, and pictured what they might be doing this summer. But what she wondered most was what they thought of her. How much had been said? Had LaRue talked to her parents, told her that she had stopped going to church? Would there be pressure about that? Would it be easier just to go to the meetings and not create bad feelings?

"Are you okay, Kath? You look sad."

"It's strange to come home now, Mom. I hardly know how to think about it."

"Let's talk, okay? I need to know what you're feeling—it's so hard to tell from your letters."

"Mom, I don't think it's a good idea for us to talk too much. I love you. I love all of you. But when we talk about things, we don't have much that we can agree on."

"We don't have to agree. What I want is to understand."

"First I have to understand myself before I can explain much of anything to you."

Mom touched Kathy's cheek. She looked so pretty. There was a bit of gray mixed into her hair now, but she never seemed to change, always had that kindly smile. "You don't have to explain. Just share with me what you've been feeling."

Kathy actually wanted to try. She wanted to feel close to her mother, but she doubted that it could happen. How could Kathy tell her about her disappointment with the "movement" when Mom hardly knew what it was? How could she explain why she wasn't going to church? How could she describe what she had seen in San Francisco without convincing her mother that all the stereotypes about hippies were true? But she said, "Okay. I'm tired right now. I was on the bus all night. But we do need to talk some time."

"All right. I won't push. And I won't question you. I know I've done too much of that in the past. I just hope we can be open with each other."

"Sounds good. I think I'll lie down for a little while before Douglas gets home."

"Okay. I'll just finish up down here. But I'll call Daddy. He'll want to know you got home. What do you want for dinner tonight?"

Kathy thought of saying "fatted calf," but she didn't want to make fun of Mom. All this was real.

On Pioneer Day Kathy didn't go to the parade in the morning, but she did go to Sugar House Park in the heat of the afternoon, and she managed to get through all the teasing about her looks. She knew that her uncles and aunts and cousins found her strange, but she also knew that to them she was the Kathy of her childhood, and she did like that. Uncle Alex was home, and so was his whole family. Alex, more than the others, seemed to carry a special respect for her opinions. The two of them talked about the war, and the antiwar movement, and he listened to what Kathy had to say. Bobbi came to her too, told her that she shared her concerns about the war. She was only worried about what would happen to the South Vietnamese if American troops merely withdrew. It was the last argument left for liberals—their way of saying "I don't support the war, but I'm not ready to support withdrawal." Kathy had little patience with that kind of logic, but at least she was reminded that she wasn't the only one in the family who raised questions.

Gene was there with a dark-haired girl named Emily. She was pretty, even funny, and she was wonderfully warm to "Gene's favorite cousin," as she called Kathy. But she didn't say anything serious, and Kathy couldn't tell whether she was capable of such a thing. What Kathy could see was that Gene was nuts about her. When Wally got a softball game going, Emily jumped right in, and Gene yelled, "I'll play. But I need to talk to Kathy for a few minutes first."

Grandpa called out, "No one can talk to Kathy for a few minutes. It's impossible."

Maybe that was sarcastic, but at least Grandpa wasn't being careful around her.

Kathy was sitting in the shade of a fat spruce tree. Gene sat down next to her, carefully, probably to avoid staining his khakis.

"So when's the wedding?"

"What wedding?" Gene asked, but that fair skin of his gave away his embarrassment.

"You're *in love*. It's dripping from your pores, like *honey*."

Gene crossed his arms, resting them on his raised knees. "I do like her. But we've only been going out a few weeks."

"You brought her to the family picnic, Gene. That's like a public announcement."

"I have to let her get used to this bunch," he said. "That's a pretty good test."

"Oh, come on. Tell the truth. Every girl in town would like to be a Thomas. We're the upper crust of Salt Lake society."

"No, we're not." She had been joking, but clearly Gene wasn't. "We've done well, but we don't hobnob with the snooty crowd. We're pretty down-to-earth people."

Kathy actually thought that was true. But she wondered about some of her cousins who had grown up with money the way she had. "What about the Washington branch of the family? Are they starting to think they're important?"

"No. They want Dad to lose when he runs for reelection next time—so they can come home. Even Mom would rather be here."

Kathy wasn't sure what to talk about. She didn't want to get into another one of her arguments with Gene. "Tell me the truth. *Are* you in love?"

He laughed, and then he looked off at Emily, who was standing by third base, pounding her glove, shouting "Hey, this guy can't hit." "I'm *dizzy* I'm so in love right now," Gene said, "but I don't know, maybe I'll get to know her better and not feel that way."

"I don't think so."

He grinned. "Actually, I don't either. But I need to give the whole thing a little more time. For now, I'm just happy to keep testing the waters. I think Marsha was good for me at the time. She challenged me, and I needed that. But Emily really likes me. I don't have to convince her."

"Gene, anyone would like you. It's absolutely impossible not to like you."

"Even if I'm wrong about everything?"

"Yup. Even then."

"Well, Marsha found a way to resist my charms."

"Gene, I liked Marsha. But I never did think you two were right for each other."

"That's because she's thoughtful and intelligent—like you—and I'm not."

Kathy actually had thought of it that way at one time. But she felt something from Gene now that she wished she had felt from more of the guys she had known in her life. "Gene, I've always known one thing about you. You're a good person—a genuinely good person. I think at one time I was condescending about that, but I'm not anymore. I don't think there's anything more important."

"I don't know, Kath. I try to be. But—"

"No. That's not what I'm talking about. You probably worry about whether you missed reading the scriptures one day last week, or whether you told some guy that a Rambler is a better car than a Chevy—stuff like that. You worry about *doing* good. But I'm saying you *are* good—rules or no rules. You wouldn't hurt anybody, ever, not knowingly."

He stared toward the players for quite some time, but he didn't seem to be paying any attention to the game. "I told you last Christmas, if I'm drafted, I would never resist. I still feel that way. And now there's no deferment for grad school. So I'm sure I will get drafted."

"And if you go, you might have to hurt people. Is that what you're saying?"

"Yeah." He looked at her with sorrow in his eyes, as though he had already killed just by saying that he was willing.

"You know how I feel, Gene. I don't think anyone should go."

"I know."

"I think it will hurt your soul if you go."

Gene was still looking back into her eyes. "Maybe. I don't know. But I still think God is on our side—not on the side of the Communists. My problem is, I feel like I made some progress during my mission—you know, spiritually. I don't know what the army would do to me."

Kathy pulled up a blade of grass, slipped it out of its root. Then she sucked, for a moment, on the clean, white part of the blade. "I'll tell you what's confusing to me, Gene. Some of the guys who are refusing to go are not as good as they ought to be. And a lot of the kids who are going are good. They love our country, and they think the only way to stand up for it is to shoot Vietnamese. It's the worst thing I can imagine. It's all upside down. The best people, the ones like you, are the ones who ought to say no."

"Maybe that ought to tell you something."

Kathy had no idea what it told her, but she knew what Gene meant, and she didn't want to discuss the subject any further.

"Are you okay, Kathy?" Gene asked, and she could feel that he was sensing the danger too, that they were edging toward one of their fights.

"I don't know. I feel really lost right now."

"It's good you came home."

"No. It's not working all that well. I only came here because I didn't know where else to go."

"Your mom told my mom that you're not going to church."

"Gene, that's not as significant as everyone imagines it is. I'm really not so far away."

"I'm sure that's true. But you need to stay close. It's so easy to get pulled in the wrong direction."

Kathy knew better than to talk about that. She looked up toward Mount Olympus, wished it were the same mountain she remembered from her childhood. But it didn't feel the same.

"What are you going to do, Kathy?"

"I'm not sure. I'm going back to Smith this fall—just because it's the one thing I know how to do. And I'm going to study—mainly so Aunt LaRue won't hate me. But I don't know much about the future. I don't belong anywhere."

"You belong here. To us."

Kathy looked at Gene, saw it in his eyes, how much he meant it. She longed to believe he was right.

Rainer had surprised Hans when he accepted his invitation to a branch party. Now the two were sitting on wooden folding chairs behind the little branch house, holding their plates on their laps and eating as they talked. Hans was trying to explain why the 24th of July was a day to celebrate. "Do you know who Brigham Young was?"

"Yes, of course. He was the man who had so many wives."

Hans laughed. "Yes, yes. But he was also a great pioneer. He led the early members of our church to the western part of the United States—to a place now called Utah."

"What does that have to do with the 24th of July?"

"That was the day the first group arrived at the Great Salt Lake, where Salt Lake City was established."

"Ah. Now I understand. This is *very important* to us here in the GDR—the day a city in the United States was started."

Hans was laughing again. "In Utah, it's called 'Pioneer Day.' I'm not sure how it got started here. Probably our missionaries from America brought the tradition with them."

"I don't think I would mention the purpose of your party to the *Stasi*. Those fellows might not see it as seminal to the Marxist movement."

That was true, of course, and Hans suspected that when President Neumeyer reported on the party to the government, he would describe it only as a social gathering. What surprised Hans, however, was that Rainer would joke about something like that. All year Hans had understood Rainer to be a doctrinaire Marxist. Of course, Hans had often noticed that people in his country were careful around strangers and would express only orthodox opinions until they felt secure.

As odd as anything at the party was the choice of food: *Bratwurst* on a *Brötchen*—a sort of dinner roll. Germans ate both, but they didn't normally make them into a sandwich.

"You know what this is called?" someone asked. Hans turned to see Elli Dürden walking toward them, holding up her plate. She looked cute today with her big, round eyes and her hair recently cut shorter than Hans had seen it before.

"No. What?" Hans asked.

"Hot dog," she said in English, and she giggled. "It means a *Hund* that is *heiss*."

"I've heard of that," Rainer said. "It's curious what Americans call things. This other sandwich they like to eat—they call it *Hamburger*, but no one from Hamburg ever heard of it."

"Who are you?" Elli asked. But then she looked away and said, "Just a minute. Hold this." She handed Hans her plate with the hot dog and some potato salad, and she walked away. People were sitting on blankets on the grass or in little circles, on chairs. It was a warm evening but very nice, the sky still blue even though it was after eight. Elli found a chair that wasn't being used and carried it with one hand, her drink in the other. She placed the chair in front of Hans and Rainer. "Do I know you?" she asked.

"My name is Rainer Kuntze."

"Are you a Mormon?"

"No."

"Welcome. Are you a friend of Hans's?"

"Yes. We're roommates at the university."

"You don't like Hans, do you?"

"Not much. Why do you ask?"

They were grinning at each other. "I only wondered. I don't like him at all. I thought you might feel the same way."

"What's this?" Hans asked. "Why the insult?"

"You're too serious. You come to church with a long face, like a boy who lost his dog."

"His hot dog," Rainer said.

This was a great joke to Elli. She laughed much too hard. She was a delicate girl, in appearance, but she had a strong voice, and her eyes were always darting about, alert.

"I'm not so serious," Hans said. "No more than I should be—at church. I watch you with your little friend, laughing and talking during the sermon. Do you expect me to be like that?"

Elli's mouth was full. She chewed for a time, swallowed, and then asked, "What *little* friend?"

"Lieselott."

"She's not so little. She's taller than I am. And older."

Hans knew he had said the wrong thing. Maybe Elli was young, but clearly she didn't want to be thought of that way. "Excuse me. I should have said 'your immensely large friend.'"

But this made Elli laugh again. "This is why I don't like you. Another reason. You make fun of me."

Hans glanced at Rainer. He seemed delighted by Elli. Maybe he didn't realize quite how young she was. "This isn't right," Rainer said. "We won't help him find that dog of his—the hot one—if he doesn't treat you better."

This seemed the joke of the century to Elli. She put her hand on Rainer's arm and leaned toward him. "We'll cool it off, this dog. I don't think it's comfortable, being so warm."

"Never mind that," Rainer said. "Let's make things worse. Let's heat up his cat."

Hans rolled his eyes. "Terrible, terrible jokes," he muttered, but that only made the other two laugh again. Hans had finished his *Bratwurst;* he decided to get another one. But as he stood and looked toward the serving table, he could see that the meat was gone now. It was always difficult for the branch to buy enough food to put on a dinner. Several members usually had to use their meat quotas to buy what they could get. But now that he was standing, Hans decided to get another cup of apple juice. "Who wants more to drink?" he asked.

The others said they still had some, so Hans walked to the serving table by himself. He noticed as he glanced back that Elli seemed quite taken with Rainer. One more crush, he supposed.

Earlier, Hans had introduced President Neumeyer to Rainer. Now, as Hans filled his cup with apple juice, the president walked over and said, "Tell me about your friend."

"He's my roommate. At first, I didn't like him, but we've become friends, gradually. He has at least admitted to me that he would like to believe in a life after death. But he doesn't believe in God."

"Bring him to church. If he wants to believe, maybe he will in time."

"I'll ask him if he'll come, but he may worry what others think. He's been active in Free German Youth, and he's joined the Party now. He has hopes for a good future."

"I understand. We can only do missionary work very carefully these days—but when someone shows a little interest, we should do what we can."

"I'll invite him."

Hans walked back to Rainer and Elli, who were still laughing. "We agreed not to like you," Rainer said. "Elli doesn't want you to call her friend a little girl after this."

"I won't. I promise. I'll only call Elli one."

Elli stood. "That's not funny," she said. She gave him a hard look—either serious or intended to look that way—and walked away.

Rainer grimaced. "I think you just said the wrong thing," he told Hans.

"I'll talk to her. I don't think it's anything very serious." But Hans did worry about the situation. He didn't want any sort of awkwardness to develop. She, after all, was one of his students in Sunday School, and her family was one of the best in the branch.

Hans didn't get another chance to talk to Elli, however. She avoided him the rest of the day. Then on Sunday she wasn't as talkative as usual during class, and she left quickly when it ended. Still, as Hans was getting ready to leave, Sister Dürden found him and invited him to Sunday dinner. Hans hardly knew what to do. If he turned down the invitation, Elli might be offended, and if he went, that might imply something that just wasn't possible. Surely, the parents had to know that she was too young for him. He had only a moment to think, however, and he decided it was better to say yes.

So he rode on the streetcar with the Dürdens back to their building. They had a small apartment, but it was neat, nicely kept. Elli had an older sister who was married and a brother named Karl who was eighteen. He was in his last year at *Oberschule*, and from all reports, very bright—but entirely silent during the dinner.

Elli was on her best behavior, talking little, letting her parents chat with Hans. He had a feeling that she had made up her mind not to giggle and tease so much.

"Have you been in the Church all your lives?" Hans asked, actually hoping to keep the focus off himself.

"I have," Brother Dürden said. He was a short man with a plump face. "I'm third generation. My grandfather joined the Church before the first world war. He converted my grandmother. My father did the same, converted my mother. When it came my turn, I was able to repeat the accomplishment, but not quite so quickly."

"Or so easily," Sister Dürden said. "He was over thirty when he met me, and I was only nineteen. When he first told me that he was a Mormon, I wouldn't have a thing to do with him. I had heard that Mormons had many wives. I wasn't interested in anything like that."

"The truth of it was, I couldn't find even *one* wife," Brother Dürden said.

"So how did it happen that you finally married?"

"He wouldn't give up. I thought he was too old for me, and I must say, not the best-looking man I had met. I don't know how he managed to convince me. I think, when I finally let him tell me about the gospel, I loved him more for that than I did for anything else."

"It's not bad for a man to be older," Brother Dürden said. "It works out better that way."

Hans nodded, but Sister Dürden looked away, and Elli ducked her head. Hans wasn't sure that Brother Dürden was referring to Hans and Elli, but certainly mother and daughter took it that way, and Hans was suddenly wishing he had never come.

But after dinner Elli said, "Brother Stoltz, I like to take a walk after dinner on Sunday afternoon. I know a nice path, along the river, if you would like to go. It's very pretty."

This was said rather formally, and the "Brother Stoltz" established a tone between them that seemed the proper one. So Hans said he would go, but as the two walked out, Elli hardly seemed herself. She wasn't chattering the way she normally did. "Brother Stoltz, that was interesting today, what we talked about in Sunday School. It was very important, what you said about prayer. I just *say* my prayers and don't think enough about what I'm saying. Half the time, I'm falling asleep when I try to pray."

"When I was your age, I didn't pray at all. I had decided that I didn't believe in God."

Elli walked down some old stone steps. At the bottom was a cobblestone path that followed the curve of the river. Hans could see swans on the water, maybe ten of them strung out along the near bank. "I think it's easier not to believe in God," Elli said. "My friends at school say that God makes no sense. They like it that way. It means they don't have to worry whether they're doing right or wrong."

"The Marxists would say that right and wrong must be a consciousness of the greater good, and in a way, I think that's right. But for me, that never answered the really basic questions about living my own life."

"What brought you back to believing?"

"A swan." He pointed toward the river.

She stopped and looked at a pair of swans on the water, and then she looked back at him. "What do you mean?" There was something lovely in her expression, her big eyes, so curious.

Hans smiled, tucked his hands in the pockets of his trousers, and stood facing her. "I had decided that life had no meaning. But one day I was watching a swan swim against the flow of a river, and suddenly I felt something. I didn't know what it was, but it seemed as though a power outside myself was speaking to me, telling me that I was going to be all right—that I could go against the flow too. I didn't make too much of it for a time, but it kept me going, kept me thinking that maybe spiritual things weren't all nonsense. Since then, I think I've learned to know the Spirit when I feel it."

"I felt it at youth conference last year, in testimony meeting. During some of the testimonies I felt as though I were being filled up with helium. It was like I was going to float away."

"Youth conference helped me, too," Hans said. He turned toward the water and watched the swans. A weeping willow was dangling its limbs almost to the river, and the white of the swans was vivid against the gray-blue river and the gold of the tree. It was a hot afternoon, but a breeze was coming off the water, almost cool. "I met some friends there who had more faith than I did, and that made me think I should keep on trying."

"I've never doubted as much as you did. I've trusted my parents, mostly. I need to try harder, I think, if I want a really strong testimony—like the one you have now."

"Don't make me better than I am, Elli. I'm not nearly as spiritual as I would like to be."

"You're the best person I know. Every week in our class I think how blessed I am that you came here."

Hans didn't know how to take that. Maybe she thought he was an old man—a Sunday School teacher and nothing more. But one thing did seem certain. She was more grown-up than he had thought. Maybe she was trying hard today not to seem so young, but still, he could tell that this serious side to her was genuine.

Hans began to walk again. Elli joined him, falling into the same pace, her shoulder touching his arm at times. Hans knew what he had to tell her. "At one of those youth conferences, I met a girl. Her name is Greta. She lives in Dresden. I fell in love with her. I guess I'm still in love with her, to tell the truth."

"That's good," Elli said, but he heard a change in her voice.

"The only problem is, she doesn't feel the same way toward me."

Hans didn't look at Elli, but he could feel that she was looking up at him. "That's the worst feeling a person can have," she said.

"It is. But there's nothing I can do about it. She's engaged now. She met another man—a member of the Church—and they're getting married."

"How old is she?"

"She's actually a little older than I am." He knew why Elli had asked.

"So you have a broken heart?"

"I don't know. I suppose I do. It's been difficult."

"Does she know how you feel?"

"No. She thought of me only as a friend. I could tell from her letter, when she told me about her engagement, that she thought I would be happy for her."

"Then you have to tell her. You have to go to her and tell her that you love her. If you don't, you'll always wonder whether she might have changed her mind, had she known."

"No. I don't think so. It would only make her feel bad. And it wouldn't do any good."

"You're wrong, Hans. I mean, Brother Stoltz."

"It's all right to call me Hans."

"You're wrong, in my opinion. I think she will like knowing that you love her. And maybe it will change how she thinks about you."

Hans stopped and looked at Elli. He suspected that she was being noble now, sacrificing her own feelings for Hans's. It was endearing, even a little painful. "It's something I'll have to think about," he said. "But I've been trying not to feel bad for myself, and to wish her my best. I think that's the right thing to do."

"If you love her, you can't stop thinking about her."

"How do you know?"

"Hans, I'm not a child—no matter what you think. I know some things."

He smiled. "Like what? Tell me about yourself."

"That's not what we're talking about."

"We are now. Tell me."

There was a bench a little farther up the path. She took the lead, walked to it, and sat down. When he sat next to her, she said, "I'm smart, Hans. You probably think I'm not because I like to laugh. But I am smart—as smart as my brother Karl, even if he doesn't think so. I get high marks in school—especially in math. Karl studies twice as much as I do, and I get the same marks he does. Still, I won't be going to a university."

"Why not?"

"You know how hard it is for a Mormon to get in. But I don't want a career anyway. I want to be a mother and a housekeeper. I'll have to work—the government will expect it of me—but I don't want a career that takes me away from home any more than necessary."

"What do you like to do?"

"Play chess and look at the sky through a telescope."

"Really?"

Suddenly she laughed in the way he had come to expect of her. "No. That's what Karl does. I'm good at science—and I'm interested—but I don't spend my time doing such things."

"So what do you do, really?"

"I like to be with Lieselott. We have great fun together. We like movies, when we can go, and she has television from West Germany. We watch it all the time." She hesitated, then looked up at him. "You're disappointed, aren't you? Now I'm a little girl again."

"No. I never had close friends when I was growing up. I always wanted someone I could spend time with, just to talk and laugh."

"I'll tell you a secret about me."

"Good. What is it?"

"I'm in love too."

"You are?" Hans was afraid what might be coming.

"Yes. I'm in love with Brian Wilson."

"Who's that?"

"He's American. He's one of the Beach Boys."

"I don't know what that is—Beach Boys."

"It's a singing group. Rock 'n Roll."

"It's something I never listen to."

"You should. It's easy now. The government doesn't even stop us. If you heard 'Good Vibrations,' you wouldn't be able to stand still. You'd want to dance."

Hans was relieved. The girl was in love with a singing star—not with him.

"But I'm not *really* in love with him. I like his music and I think he's cute, but he's not what I want."

Hans decided not to ask.

"I want a good man who believes in the Church." She laughed. "But cute, too. And I want someone who will be a good father."

"Maybe there's no one like that. It may be too much to ask."

"No, Hans. There is someone like that."

She wouldn't look at him now, and she seemed relieved when Hans changed the subject. After a time they got up, and they walked again. But Hans felt bad. He had only made things worse, and that was obviously clear to Elli, as much as to himself.

When they returned to the Dürdens' house, Elli's parents invited him to stay a little longer and then take the streetcar to sacrament meeting with them, but Hans made an excuse, saying he had to run back to his dorm room first.

"Would you like to come again next Sunday?" Sister Dürden asked.

"Oh, no. You won't want to put up with me again so soon."

"That's not true. You could eat with us every Sunday if you like. It would be nice for us and maybe get you away from your dreary room a little more."

"It wouldn't be fair to my roommate. I leave so long on Sundays as it is."

This was an utter lie. Rainer always had things to do on Sunday. Hans virtually never saw him that day.

Maybe Sister Dürden sensed that this was a mere excuse. She didn't press. She only said, "Perhaps another time though?"

And Hans said, "Yes. That would be nice." But he saw Elli looking at the floor, maybe embarrassed, certainly disappointed. He felt terrible when he left, but he knew it wouldn't be wise to go back again. What he did think about on the way back to his dorm was the suggestion Elli had made. Maybe it really was wrong never to tell Greta how he felt. Maybe he should talk to her.

~

That night, after sacrament meeting, Hans decided to walk home. It was a warm evening, and he was in no hurry to get back to his lonely room. He was also not anxious to stand at the streetcar stop with Elli and her family. So he took his suit coat off, draped it over his shoulder, and walked slowly, trying to take in the air that had begun to cool a little. He had gone a couple of city blocks when he decided he wanted to get off the busy street and enjoy the quiet of a neighborhood. It was only then that he realized that a man was walking behind him, and that he had crossed over the same street and continued in the same direction. Hans had been on guard for so long that it was only natural to check behind him, but he was surprised by the sudden fear he felt. He had begun to believe that his worries about the *Stasi* were over.

At the next corner Hans took another turn, to his left, and then hurried ahead. Halfway up the block, he stopped and looked in the window at a little bakery. He saw the man come to the corner, begin to turn, then spot Hans. He changed his path, crossed the street, but continued on the opposite side in the same direction as Hans. So Hans doubled back and returned to the corner he had turned. He rounded the corner, crossed the street, and then hurried into an alley. No one came for a time, and Hans began to breathe more easily.

But then, there he was again.

Hans stepped back into a doorway and let the man pass the alley. He was a young fellow, it appeared, not wearing a suit, not really looking like any *Stasi* agent Hans had ever known. But the *Stasi* hired informants. This could be someone paid to follow him, report on him. That made Hans wonder. Had he been followed other days? Had he done anything that might be considered suspicious? Suddenly this whole situation seemed stupid. Whatever *Stasi* agents knew, they would learn nothing new by following him.

So Hans left the alley. He would simply walk home and let the fool enjoy the nice evening, the same as he was doing. When he glanced back, however, he couldn't see anyone. Hans continued the route he had been taking in the first place, walked through a neighborhood and entered a park. But he would soon be home, and he knew how hot his room would be. He decided to sit on a park bench and watch the children play at a little playground.

He had only just seated himself, however, when he saw the man again, cutting across the grass. He was coming directly toward Hans, apparently dropping all pretense. Hans waited, but he could hear the sound of his own blood rushing in his ears.

The man was smiling. He walked straight to the bench and sat down. Without looking over, he said, "You had me lost there for a few minutes. It was pure luck that I found you again."

"I'm not sure what you mean," Hans said. He wasn't going to be drawn in by this guy. He would admit to nothing.

The man finally turned toward him. He was not more than twenty-five, Hans thought—a neat young man with short hair, the sleeves of his white shirt rolled up, no tie. "I'm not what you think," he said. "I was good friends with Berndt Kerner."

Hans didn't respond. This was a dangerous game, and this fellow seemed good at it.

"I don't blame you for not saying anything. Don't. I'll just tell you some things."

Hans didn't so much as nod. But his heart was still pounding.

"I was in on the planning for the escape. I made a promise to Berndt. I told him that if something went wrong, I would try to help you. I would get you out of the country, if that's what it took. I've assumed since then that you're all right, that the *Stasi* has lost interest in you. But I also know that agents have long memories. They could still come for you if they decide you were involved. And now I'm planning to escape myself—we have another group going out."

He waited.

"I don't know what you mean," Hans finally said.

"You're right not to trust me. Don't commit to anything. But let me tell you one thing. You can go with us if you want. If I leave without you, I can never keep my promise to Berndt. For my own peace of mind, I'd like you to go along. If you want to, there are ways that you can let me know—and I have ways that I can prove who I am. I'm going to start by giving you a letter. It was written by Berndt."

He placed an envelope on the bench between them. Then he stood. "Don't say anything. Just read the letter and think about it. I'll contact you again. If you want to go, I'll tell you what the next step will be."

"If you're talking about leaving the country, I have no interest. I'm not certain why you think I would."

"Yes. That is what you should say. You've handled this well. You'll hear from me again."

"If you do, I'll have to report you. I don't know what you're up to, but you're talking to the wrong man."

The man smiled. "Very well done," he said, and he walked away, across the grass again, in the direction he had come.

Hans was still breathing hard. He didn't like anything about this. He picked up the envelope and walked quickly from the park. Along the way, he pulled the letter from the envelope and scanned it quickly. It was a letter from Berndt; he knew the handwriting. It was addressed to someone named Wolfgang. But it seemed to be nothing more than a friendly letter. What did that prove? The *Stasi* could have confiscated it from someone. This whole thing was a process of winning his trust and getting him to say something. Or maybe the offer was real, and that was just as bad. Hans could be spotted with someone from a group that was getting ready to escape, and once they were gone, he could be implicated again. There seemed no way to escape the trap he had set for himself when he had first promised Berndt that he would help him.

When Hans reached his room, he was surprised to find Rainer there ahead of him, sitting at his desk. When Hans stepped through the door, Rainer looked up from the book he had been reading. "What's wrong?" he asked.

"Nothing."

"Something is. You're white. You're sweating."

"It's warm outside. I've been walking."

"Hans, what's wrong?"

Hans took a breath. He might as well tell Rainer. "Someone was following me. He made contact. He might have been *Stasi*. I'm not sure." Hans tossed his coat to the side, then sat down at the foot of the bed, across from Rainer.

But now it was Rainer who looked frightened—more than Hans would have expected. "What did he say?"

"He said he was a friend of Berndt's. He offered me a chance to escape with him. It might have been a *Stasi* trap."

"Don't tell me any more."

"Why? You already know."

Rainer shut his book, then sat with his elbows on the table for a time. Hans had no idea what was going on. Finally Rainer said, "Don't trust anyone, Hans. Including me."

"What are you saying?" Hans stood, suddenly frightened again.

"Sit down." Rainer motioned with his hand, and Hans did sit down. "I need to tell you something. I've thought of telling you for quite some time. Last fall, not long after the school year started, a *Stasi* agent approached me. He told me to get to know you, to gain your trust and learn what I could about your past. He has checked with me every month or so, and I've always told him that you were silent, that you've told me nothing."

"Rainer, I've told you *everything*."

"I know. But I don't believe in reporting on people. I've told you that."

"Is that what you're saying to gain my confidence? Are you lying to me now? I don't know anyone I can trust anymore."

"No. I'm not lying to you. If I had told the agent what you told me, you would already be gone. You know that."

"Maybe you're gathering more information. Maybe they've asked you to wait, so you can implicate others."

"No. I'll never say anything. I've promised you that. But don't talk to anyone else—especially not this man who approached you today. You're right to think he's with the *Stasi*. The agent told me that he knew you were guilty of things—he didn't say what—and that he would apprehend you, sooner or later. But remember, Hans, I'm in as much danger as you are. If they catch you, and they break you, you'll tell them that you talked to me. Then what happens to me?"

"And if they decide to put more pressure on you, what happens to me? How can I ever be sure you won't give me up?"

"You can't. And I can't be sure either. That's just the way it is."

Hans tried to think. What were his options? But he had none. His life was in Rainer's hands, and in the hands of these *Stasi* agents, maybe in the hands of this man who had talked to him on the park bench today. What hope did he have?

# Chapter 24

It was a Saturday morning in September, and Gene was with Emily at the Hogle Zoo. He hadn't been to the zoo since he was a kid, but he had great memories of the place. Now that he and Emily were standing in front of the big monkey enclosure, however, Emily had just admitted that she really didn't like zoos.

"I've never heard of that," Gene told her. "How can you not like a zoo?"

"The animals always look miserable, like they're bored out of their minds. And, frankly, I don't like the smells."

Gene laughed. Actually, he had kind of felt the same way today. When he was younger, the place had seemed more exciting. "So how come you let me drag you up here?"

She turned to him and took hold of his hand. "It's Saturday morning and I'm with you. If you had asked me to take a tour of the city dump, I would have said okay."

"Why?" He smiled at her.

"Because I *love* . . . garbage. That's why." She gave him a little punch in the stomach.

"I think you *love* me. I'm so charming, I can make the dump seem like a little heaven on earth."

She leaned close to him and whispered in his ear, "Gene, if it helps you to believe that, go right ahead." Then she stepped back and smiled at him, impishly.

Gene liked this playful side of her. She was never one to pour on too much syrup, but he also liked what she had said first—that she wanted to be with him on a Saturday morning, no matter where it was. He felt the same way. He worked at the dealership on Saturday afternoons, and sometimes those afternoons stretched rather long, so it was not always easy to take her out for a full evening. But he had always loved something about Saturday morning. It was the laziest time of the week for him, the one morning that he felt he had time to relax. He loved to think up excuses to be with Emily.

Gene and Emily had spent a lot of time together all summer. Neither one had talked about a future together, but they both seemed to know that's where all this was going. Sometimes, without meaning to, one or the other would say something that would imply that they both expected it. What Gene was well aware of, however, was that he had a lot of school ahead of him. It hadn't been part of his plan to meet someone quite so soon. He had told himself that he would "date around" for a couple of years, get close to graduation, and then start thinking about someone seriously. But with graduate school ahead—he was thinking either law school or a master's in business—he really didn't want to marry all that soon.

And there was something more ominous than that—something that worried Gene all the time. What about Vietnam? When he was younger and he had thought of the possibility of war, he had imagined himself winning medals for valor, distinguishing himself the way his father had. But he hadn't thought so much about leaving a wife behind—also the way his father had. Gene didn't remember those days when his father had been gone and he had been a baby. Now, seeing all this from the other point of view, as the one who would be leaving, he hated the idea. What he also realized was that giving up more of his life, right during these years when he was trying to get his education, would be more than inconvenient. It could change his whole future. In some ways he was a better student now than he had been before his mission. His mission had required a lot of study; it had taught him more discipline than he had ever had before. But what would the military do to him—especially the war? He didn't want another long interruption now. Still, every time he got to that point in his thinking, he felt rotten for even telling himself such things. His dad had served a mission and then been away at war for four years. And he had still accomplished more than most people.

Something else was also on Gene's mind. His dad had been in extreme danger many times, and yet he had survived. Gene figured that he would too. But Dad had sometimes spoken about horrors that he didn't want his sons to experience, and Gene wasn't entirely sure how he felt about that. He knew he didn't want to kill anyone, and he didn't want to be mutilated in battle. But Dad had experienced some evil, some abomination, that plagued him still. Gene wasn't sure he wanted to know something that still darkened his own father's mind after all these years. What he wished was that the atmosphere was more like World War II, when everyone was involved in some way, and for a soldier, it was simply a matter of joining others and doing what had to be done. This time, he knew that some would have to go, would have their lives changed, and others would stay home, continue college, continue life. It was hard not to hope that he might be one of the ones who would stay, marry Emily, if that worked out, and get on with his goals.

"So have you had enough of the zoo?" Gene asked.

"I'm fine. Are there other things you wanted to see?"

"Yeah. The snakes."

"Fine. I'll stay here, and you go into that dismal building and look at those nasty little creatures."

It was a pretty morning but a little cool. Emily looked cute in her red "Utes" sweatshirt. She was planning to go to the Utah football game that afternoon with some friends, but Gene couldn't go since he had to work. The truth was, he didn't care all that much. He had never liked to watch football as much as he liked to play it, and when he did watch, it sometimes reminded him how obscure he was, sitting in the crowd, not being on the field. He played on his ward basketball team and enjoyed that, but it was a ragtag bunch who knew next to nothing about running an offense. He missed the days of being part of a real team. This time after his mission had often seemed empty, and part of it was just that—not being connected to so many people the way he once had been. What he wanted was to marry soon, to have Emily with him, to start a family. But that thought always brought him back around the same circle, the same probability: Vietnam.

"We've still got some time," Gene said. "What would you like to do?"

"I'll take you out for a treat. I tried something the other day that I think you'll like."

"What's that?"

"It's a secret. Just drive out to the Cottonwood Mall and I'll introduce you to something new."

Gene had no idea what she was talking about, but he had only been to the new mall once since he had been home from his mission, so he rather liked the idea. When they reached the place, what Emily bought for him was something called an Orange Julius. It was a new kind of drink made with oranges but rather creamy tasting. Gene did like it. As the two drank, they walked along the mall and looked in some of the windows.

When they stopped in front of a women's shop, Gene said, "Look at that outfit—that's almost exactly what you had on the first time I saw you. A denim skirt and a red blouse."

"I had on a denim skirt and a red top, but it wasn't like that."

"Well, kind of. Maybe the skirt was a little shorter." He smiled. "Man, I looked at you, and I thought, 'That's the prettiest girl I've ever seen.' You *do* look good in red. And I might add, in short skirts."

"Hey, I was a customer." She leaned close, took hold of his arm, and whispered in his ear, "You shouldn't have been thinking things like that."

"You knew *exactly* what I was thinking."

She stepped away and let her eyelashes flutter. "I was thinking a few things myself."

"Like what? What did you think of me that day—all soaking wet?"

Emily began to walk, slowly; she didn't answer. But after a minute or so she said, "Gene, I have to tell you something. It's going to haunt me forever until I do."

"What?"

"You might hate me."

"I kind of doubt it." But Gene wondered what in the world she could be talking about.

Emily stopped and waited for him to turn toward her. People were walking by, and the two were in the stream of things, so she pulled him more to the center of the walkway, next to a planter with flowers in it. "I'm a devious person, Gene. I mean, not usually—but I did something really *calculated* that day."

"I was the one calculating. I hadn't looked at you for ten seconds before I made up my mind I was going to get your phone number somehow."

"Oh, Gene, you're just a baby at this. You have no idea what I was up to that day, do you?"

"You were flirting—right from the beginning. I knew that."

"But it's worse than you think." She wouldn't look at him. "I wasn't looking for a car that day, Gene. I was looking for you."

"You knew I worked there?"

"Yes." She stared directly into his yes, as if to watch for his reaction.

"But you didn't know me."

"I know. But I wanted to. I saw you play basketball against Bountiful one time, back when I was in high school, and I had this *huge* crush on you. I kept telling my friends I was going to find a way to meet you. And then this girl I know called me one morning. She'd found out from a cousin of hers who lives over by you that you were back from your mission and you were working for your uncle. I staked out the place and watched for you. I was down there twice before that day I finally found you. Then I saw you get in that water fight with your brother, and it just seemed like the perfect time to tease you a little. But I had to lie. I had to tell you I was looking for a car. If I hadn't, I wouldn't have had an excuse to be there."

Gene was laughing by now. "I can't believe this," he said. "What a little con artist you are. I never even thought of that."

"Didn't you wonder why I stopped talking about getting a car after we started going out?"

"You made up some excuse. You said your dad was letting you use his car."

"I know. But I was using it all along. That's how I got down there that day. Didn't you even think of any of that?"

"No. I was just happy I met you."

She looked at him innocently and put her hand on his arm, and for the first time he realized that she really was worried. "Are you still glad?" she asked.

"Sure I am."

"But Gene, I went after you like a hunter or something, and I tricked you into asking me out. I've been feeling guilty about it all summer. I was afraid you would find out somehow."

"It was more like fishing. You put the bait in front of me, and I swallowed it—hook, line, and sinker."

"Is that okay?"

"No. I'm caught. The hook is in my lip, and I can't shake it loose. Don't I look like I'm in pain?"

"Is there anything I can do?"

"You could kiss it, to make it better."

"I don't think so. Not at the mall."

She turned and started to walk. Gene was still trying to think about all this. The girl really had deceived him; he was amazed that he had never suspected anything. "You knew how good you looked in that short skirt and that red blouse, didn't you?" he asked.

"It wasn't a blouse. It was just a little—"

"But you knew how good you looked."

"Gene, I tried on about ten outfits. I admit that."

"And you flashed all those cute little smiles, showed off your dimples every chance you got."

They were walking toward the glass doors of the mall now, and Gene opened the door for her. "Sure I smiled. I was flirting."

"But you know how cute your dimples are, don't you?"

"Can I take the fifth on that one?"

"You don't have to. I know the answer. Tell me this: Did you have that whole story all worked out? You made it sound awfully real."

"Yeah, I sort of did. But I had to ad lib quite a bit. And when I saw you and started talking, flirting with you was sort of natural. You know—because you're *sooooo* cute."

Gene was still laughing. When they reached his old Ford, he opened the door for her and then walked around and got in. "Emily," he said, "the more I think about this, the more it bothers me. I really hate to think that you're such a conniving person."

"I'm not really. Not usually. Honest."

"I'd probably be more upset, except that I have something I also have to admit."

"What?" She turned to look at him, and she did look rather worried.

"At this very moment I'm doing some of my own calculating and conniving."

"What do you mean?"

"I'm slowly working my arm around behind you so that I can try to make a move on you."

"Actually, I knew that. And that's why I've been gradually leaning a little closer to you."

"But, Emily, I have *designs* on you. I'm planning to *kiss* you."

"And if you do, I'll give you just one minute to stop—or maybe two."

And so he folded her in his arms and kissed her. It was not the first kiss, but it seemed as though it were. This was something of a new person now that he understood what she had been up to all along. But the truth was, Gene rather liked the whole idea. It was flattering.

When the kiss ended and he moved back from her a little, he said, "You know, one of the things I liked about you that day was that you seemed to be interested in me without knowing who I was. You know—that my dad was a congressman and all that."

"I know. And that's exactly why I hated to tell you. All that stuff *was* in my head that day. You were always such a superstar in high school, and every girl wanted to meet you. But now that I know you, I don't think about that. I know *you*, and I love who you are."

"Say that again."

"What?"

"What you just said."

"I know you, and I love—"

"Stop right there!" He touched his finger to her lips. "Now—just say, 'you.'"

"Gene, I do love you."

"I love you, Emily. I do. Thanks for going fishing."

He kissed her again, felt the lovely softness of her lips, liked the way she fit in his arms. It crossed his mind that he had never been quite this happy, ever.

---

Hans was on a train to Dresden. He had written Greta to say that he wanted to visit her, and she had responded with excitement. He could stay at her home, and her family would be pleased to have the chance to meet him. She spoke also in the letter of her wedding plans, of Jürgen, her fiancé, and of her happiness. Hans had almost backed out and written to her to tell her so. But what he sensed was that he needed to do this. He needed to wish her well even if he never dared to tell her what he had been feeling for her all these years. He needed to end the hopes in his own mind and then move on with life.

Sometimes it seemed that life for Hans had always been on delay, that his choices had led to an inevitable, eventual disaster, and that his narrow escapes were only tricks of fate—nasty little tricks that tantalized him with hope for a happiness that would never be his. Weeks had gone by and he had heard nothing from the *Stasi*, nothing from the man who had talked to him in the park. What did it mean? He tried to tell himself that another little danger had visited him and slipped by, that once again he had been spared. But it was just as likely that the end was near for him. As Rainer had told him, *Stasi* agents had long memories.

A gloom had come upon him, there on the train. He saw a young couple, perhaps not married long themselves. They were sitting just up the aisle from him, and he could watch them as they sat together, touching, holding hands, laughing, talking seriously. He wondered what it would be like to love someone that way, to be so close to someone, to share everything, even difficulties, and always to exchange those affectionate touches. He watched the young woman smooth out her husband's hair after he had slumped for a time and drifted off to sleep. The little act was lovely to Hans. It was kind and at the same time sensual. No woman had ever owned him that way, felt so easy about touching him. He had held Greta in his arms once when she was wet and warm from swimming. He had felt himself drift into something like euphoria, just having so much skin and softness against him. He wondered whether he would ever find anyone he could love that completely, someone who would also love him.

When Hans's train pulled into the station, he was happy to see Greta waiting on the platform for him. But he didn't know what to do as he approached her. He was glad she took the lead. She threw her arms around him, in a friendly, happy gesture, and then she pounded his back just a little too hard, as though she wanted to distinguish her hug from the kind that a girl might give to a boyfriend. Was she aware that she had to be careful with his feelings?

But she didn't seem careful when she began to talk. She asked him about everything as she led him to the streetcar stop, and then, on the streetcar, she told him in detail all about the wedding she and Jürgen were planning—even though the date was still almost six months away. "We hoped that we could get a visa to go to Switzerland, so we could get married in the temple," she told him. "But there was no chance. We're too young. They let older couples go to the temple sometimes, hoping, I think, that they won't come back, and the government won't have to pay them a pension. We were told, over and over, that our case would be considered—our 'religious ritual'—but I doubt they ever took a second look at our application."

Hans was sitting next to her, facing the same direction, but he kept glancing at her, watching her hands, the slim line of her legs. He even liked that her elbow touched his sometimes. He could hardly believe how much he loved the sound of her voice, her enthusiasm, even though none of it was directed toward him.

"Tell me about Jürgen," he said. "I really don't know much about him."

"He's really wonderful, Hans. In so many ways, he's like you. He and I can talk about anything—and when we're together, that's what we do. I have the feeling that we can talk the rest of our lives and still not feel that we know everything about each other. He's not afraid of honesty—not afraid to tell me things he's never told anyone."

"How old is he?"

"He's almost an old man; that's what he tells me. He's twenty-eight. But that's good. He's ready to be married. He's finished with all his training, and he has a decent job. He'll never be a professional, the way you want to be, but he's a glazier, and a very good one. There's enough building going on now that I think he'll always have plenty of work. You know how life is. We won't have much—especially not at first—but we've applied for an apartment, and we may get one by the time we marry. If not, we might have to work something out with my parents, or sublet a little room somewhere. I don't worry about that, though. I just want to be with him all the time. I'm so tired of his only coming to see me every other weekend."

"I thought he lived here."

"No. He came here on a temporary assignment, to complete a building project, but he's back in *Karl-Marx-Stadt* now. That's where we've applied for an apartment. I just feel certain that God sent him here to meet me. I was beginning to think I would never find anyone—that no one who was a member of the Church would ever take an interest in me."

Hans could hardly believe what he was hearing. He turned and looked at her, trying to let his eyes ask the question. And maybe she noticed. She did look away. Surely, she had to know.

Greta didn't say anything for a time. The streetcar turned, the wheels screeching around a corner. But then she talked again about Jürgen—the kind of man he was, his family background. It was all expressed with the same excitement, the same gratefulness for how well her life was turning out.

At the end of the ride, as the two got off the streetcar, Greta took Hans's arm and walked with him as though they were the best of friends, but by then Hans was sorry he had come. It was all too much for him. He knew now that he would not tell her. He might have tried had she not told him that God had sent Jürgen to her, but how could he bring up his own selfish interest in her now, after she had borne that testimony?

So he met her family, ate dinner with them, and afterward sat and chatted with them until it was late enough to go to bed. Her parents went off to their bedroom, and Greta gathered some bedding to make a place for Hans on the living-room couch. The two were standing at opposite ends of the couch, stretching out a sheet, when Greta asked, "So tell me, Hans, have you met any girls in Magdeburg—anyone you like?"

"No."

"Is there anyone your age in the branch?"

"Not really. I teach some nice young people in my Sunday School class. There's a nice girl in the class, and she's become my friend. But she's only sixteen."

"That's not so young. By the time you're ready to get married, a few years from now, she might be just the right age."

Hans knew it was true. There was no way he could marry until he finished his studies, and even then he wouldn't have much of a salary in the beginning stages of his career. It was difficult for a man in the GDR to get married before his middle or even late twenties. All that made it very clear how Greta thought of him. She had always known that he was far from an age when he could marry. "Perhaps. But I don't think I could ever think of her that way," he said.

"And there's no one back in Schwerin?"

"No."

She picked up a feather tick from the floor, and he helped her stretch it over the couch, as they had done with the sheet.

"Hans, tell me what's wrong. You're not happy. I've felt it from the moment you arrived."

He nodded. "I guess that's true. I'm not very happy right now."

"You don't seem to like your life at the university. Is that the problem?"

"I don't know. Maybe it's loneliness. I wish more than anything that I were a few years older and I could get on with life."

She came toward him and put her hand on his arm. "Hans, I wish you were older too. It was what I wished so much at youth conference, that first time I met you. I've always wished it."

So she did know. She did understand. "I wished it then too. But I didn't know it would be so important."

Hans was glad she had told him how she felt, but he could hardly stand the pain he felt. He turned his head and slipped his hands into his pockets, trying not to make a fool of himself. "You know what you said about the girl in your branch—that you like her, but you know she's too young for you. That tells me you understand. Sometimes you meet someone you like, but you become brother and sister to each other—because of the circumstance. It just can't be helped."

He nodded but still didn't look at her. "But one of the persons may love the other forever, in spite of all that," he said.

They stood for a long time, Greta still touching his arm, and Hans not looking at her. "Hans, I'm sorry," Greta finally said.

"There's nothing to be sorry about. I'm happy for you."

"Thank you for that. I think it's true."

But she had to know it was only partly so, and in the morning, after Hans had lain awake on the couch all night, he found reasons not to stay very long. He took the train back to Magdeburg, feeling as though his very skin hurt, feeling that life had been designed never to work out for him. What seemed to lie ahead was only more loneliness.

But he only indulged himself so long, and then he began to pray, to tell the Lord that he was sorry for so much self-pity. He was blessed to be a student, blessed with a good family, blessed by his chance to serve in the Church. He could worry about finding someone to love when the time was right. He was feeling a little better as he walked from the train station to his building. He would pour himself into his studies now and finally be free from longing for something he couldn't have.

He walked around the corner of his building, hardly conscious of the world around him, and then he saw them—two men in dark suits, waiting at the door.

His impulse, for a moment, was to run. But he couldn't do that, and as he realized that he had no options, he actually felt relieved. The other shoe had finally dropped. At least he would know something now. He walked straight toward them. The taller of the two, a man with a dour, thin face, watched him approach, seemed willing to let him go by, but then said, "Are you Stoltz?"

"Yes."

"Come with us."

"May I go inside first? I have my suitcase, and I—"

The man took hold of his arm. Another man, older and seemingly less interested, stepped up to Hans's other side, grasped the other arm. "I'll carry your suitcase for you," he said, with no apparent irony.

The men led Hans to a car, an old but polished Mercedes-Benz. They didn't say another word to him. The younger man drove, and the other sat next to Hans. After ten minutes or so, the driver parked the car in front of a gray building, opened the back door, and waited. "Get out," was all he said, and then the two agents led him inside, took him to a little room. "Sit down," the same man told him. Hans took a seat, the only seat in front of a small, metal desk. The younger man left, and the other stood behind Hans, still not saying anything. The room smelled of body odor, maybe from the agent behind him, or maybe just lingering.

It was perhaps twenty minutes before anything happened, and Hans had plenty of time to consider what might be coming. He hoped that it was another interrogation. He hoped the *Stasi* was still just fishing. But that didn't seem likely. There had been plenty of time to develop a case against him. It even seemed likely that Rainer had told them all they needed to know. So Hans gave up, and there was relief in that, too. Nothing good was likely to happen to him from now on, ever, but at least the waiting was over.

A man in shirtsleeves and a loose brown tie finally came into the room. His sleeves were rolled up a couple of turns, and Hans noticed thick, black hair on his forearms and hands, even his fingers. He didn't introduce himself. He didn't sit down. He stepped behind the desk and said, "Stoltz, we know you were involved in the escape attempt in Berlin last year. You drove Kerner and Heidt to Berlin, and you waited to cover their escape tunnel. It was you who ran from the scene, after the border guard shot your friends." He waited for a moment, with his hands on his hips, and then said, "What do you have to say about that?"

"I deny it." Hans knew better than to give the agent anything he could use.

"Yes. Of course you do. But it's true. And you are going to prison. You have a long history of enemy activity against the state. You started young, and you show no sign of remorse or change. You have deceived good men into supporting you, and the government actually granted you the chance to study at one of our fine universities. But all that is over now. You can expect fair but appropriate punishment."

Hans felt as though he had stopped breathing, yet he was amazingly calm. There was nothing to hope for now. The game had been played out, and it had reached its logical conclusion. He thought of praying, but for the moment, the absence of hope seemed preferable. For Hans, hope had always ended in disappointment. There seemed no reason to expect anything different this time.

# Chapter 25

Diane was sitting in the Skyroom at the Hotel Utah, looking out at the temple. Temple Square was decorated for Christmas, the trees all filled with lights. "It's beautiful, isn't it?" Greg asked her.

"It is. Especially from up here," Diane said.

"You know, this is the first year of my whole life that I haven't felt like I wanted to go home for Christmas."

Diane laughed. "I hate to tell you," she said, "but you *are* home."

But Greg didn't laugh. "You know what I mean. I just want to go back to Provo and stay there during the break—and be there with you."

Diane was always hesitant when Greg became so intense, or whatever it was. She could now admit to herself that Greg might actually end up her choice—when she could finally compare him to Kent—but she still wanted to give Kent a fair chance. Earlier that week she had gotten a letter from Kent, and he was doing well, serving a good mission. He had been excited about a recent baptism, and he was committed to his work, but he had also asked her, as he often did, not to let someone steal her away before he got back. He had said it jokingly, but she wondered what he knew. Someone surely must have written Kent to tell him that Diane was dating Greg.

"I'm coming to Ogden during the break. How about a date every day—for about sixteen hours?"

"You'd be tired of me by the end of the break."

"I never get tired of being with you, Di. Really."

Diane smiled at him. Sometimes Greg's tenacity was the trait she found hardest to resist. He was like an avalanche at times, a force she didn't know how to hold back. "You need to spend some time with your family," she said. Then she looked at the Christmas lights again. She just wanted to have a pleasant evening. She didn't want to think about the future.

A waiter had arrived, and Diane realized that she hadn't decided what she wanted to eat. "What do you recommend?" Greg asked the waiter, and Diane watched him move into his "man of the world" style. Greg's father was a wealthy, powerful man, and Diane had watched him take control of situations exactly in this same style.

"I love the trout almondine," the waiter said. "We get fresh trout, even in the winter. But I'd have to say, our grand meal is the lobster tail."

"That's just the thing," Greg said. "What about it, Diane? Wouldn't you like lobster?"

She thought of the night she had eaten lobster with Kent. It had been on that perfect weekend when he had invited her to Provo for the prom. She still couldn't imagine a happier time, a better memory. "I think I'll have the trout," she said.

"Why don't you bring us the stuffed mushrooms as an appetizer," Greg was saying, "and garden salads for each of us." He stopped and looked at Diane. "Is that what you want?"

"Sure."

"All right, then. And do you have a nonalcoholic champagne, or something of that sort?"

"We do, sir. It's a sparkling white grape juice. Very nice."

"Bring that, too. And we'll think about dessert later on, but I've already spotted someone eating chocolate mousse. That's one little treat I can't resist."

The waiter was a young fellow, a little on the stout side. "I can't resist it myself," he said. He patted his middle. "I guess that's obvious."

Greg laughed in a style that didn't seem quite natural, as though it was the manner he used for "these occasions." Diane wondered about that, but she liked the fact that he was comfortable with the way the world worked. Some college boys were like high-school kids, nervous and worried about the cost of everything.

Diane did like the trout, even though the portion seemed small. It was one of the few times, at a restaurant, that she actually could have eaten more, but she made up for that with a hot-fudge sundae. Greg also convinced her to try some of his mousse, and she had to admit, it was tastier than she had expected.

She watched Greg take care of the bill and then leave a three-dollar tip—more than she could imagine her father ever leaving. As they rode down the elevator Greg said, "Let's just walk over to Temple Square and look at the nativity scene." But Diane had a funny feeling about that. She sensed that this evening had been a little more extravagant than usual, and maybe it had been building toward something. She had heard her mother's story about her first fiancé, the one who had proposed at Temple Square.

Diane wrapped her scarf close around her neck and buttoned her car coat before she walked out into the cold, and then she took Greg's arm. He was wearing a camel-hair overcoat that made him look like one of the wealthy businessmen she had sometimes seen in downtown Ogden. He was the only college boy she had ever known who owned such beautiful clothes—except maybe Kent.

They walked to the nativity scene, where a little crowd had gathered, and they listened to the music for a couple of minutes. Then Greg led her to a rather secluded spot south of the temple, where there was a little bench. "Let's just sit down and look at the temple for a minute," he said.

"It's cold, Greg. Maybe we'd better just—"

"Just for a minute."

Diane was starting to panic. She couldn't let this happen. She sat down, but then she said, "Are you guys starting to practice for Song Fest yet? I think we're getting started right away." Diane had joined Chi

Trielles, the elite of the BYU women's clubs, and had been very involved this year. She had learned, through the grapevine, that she was going to be nominated for Snow Queen, at Winter Carnival. She wanted so much to win, and then, perhaps next year, have a chance for Belle of the Y. That's how college was supposed to be. She hadn't planned on all this seriousness.

But Greg ignored the question, sat for a moment, and then said, "Diane, I've been doing a lot of praying lately. I've had some important questions, and I felt that I had to get some answers."

"Greg, I don't think—"

"Diane, just let me tell you this. All right?"

"Okay."

"I'll be graduating in the spring. You know that. And then it's off to law school somewhere. Maybe far from Utah. What I've *felt* all fall is that when I leave I want to take you with me. I want us to get married. But I know your . . . how shall I say? . . . your *concern* about that. And I do understand. But that's why I feel that we shouldn't make the decision merely by thinking about it, considering the pros and cons and all that sort of thing. We need to get an answer from God. He knows exactly what we ought to do, and he'll certainly let us know."

"I believe that, Greg. But there are things to *think* about too. The Lord expects us to use our own brains. I'm not ready for marriage yet. I'm only nineteen. I need to grow up some more before I even start to think about marriage. And I want to graduate from college."

"Why do you need college, Diane? It's not really what you love, and you know I'll always make a good living for us."

"But it would be better—"

"Diane, listen to me for just another minute. I've been praying every night for weeks, and last Sunday I had my own fast. I didn't mention it to you, but remember when I didn't want anything to eat that afternoon?" Diane nodded. "Well, I was fasting. And this is what I want to tell you."

He twisted toward her, pulled her hands from her coat pockets, and then took hold of them. He was wearing leather gloves. "Diane, I got my answer. I know you have to get your own, and I want you to do that. But I have mine. I know now—beyond a shadow of a doubt—that you're the one I'm supposed to marry. The Lord doesn't want me to leave BYU without you. He wants me to take you with me when I leave for law school."

"Greg, don't ask me, okay? I'm not ready."

"I'm not proposing—although I am asking you a couple of things. First, I'd like you to take my Samuel Hall pin. I want us to spend a lot of time together this winter. And I don't want to deal with these other guys who keep asking you out. I want you to be able to say you're pinned. And then I—"

"Greg, I can't do that. What if Kent found out? It would kill him. I can't commit to anything right now."

"I know. It's just a way of having some exclusive time for each other—a testing time, so you can really have a chance to know who I am and whether I might be the one you would choose. What I would ask you to do this next semester is pray about us every day, maybe have a fast with me. God wants both of us to find the right person. He's given me an answer, and I know he'll give you the same one—if you just ask."

"I'll pray, Greg. Of course I will. I've already been doing that. But I want to wait another year or two before I start getting serious about *anyone*. I didn't promise Kent, but I promised myself I wouldn't get married until he got back."

"And maybe that's *exactly* what you should do." He lifted her hands and kissed each one. "I'm not trying to put pressure on you, Di. All I'm saying is, I believe it's time for me to get married, and God has verified that for me. He told me to marry you. All I want you to do is ask and see whether you don't get the same answer. Will you do that?"

"Yes. I will."

"I love you, Diane. There's never going to be anyone else like you for me. This *has* to happen. There just isn't any other possibility."

"Please don't say that. You just told me that I have to get my own answer."

"I know. Forgive me. But I know exactly what God is going to tell you."

Diane looked down at his hands, her hands. She wondered what she was going to do. Somehow, she had to take control of the situation.

"Diane, I don't know Kent. And I don't know the thousands of other men who would like to marry you. You'll always have all the choices you want. But I know this: No one ever will, ever could, love you more than I do. And no one will give you a better life. It's not just that I'm going to make a good living—which I do think will be nice for both of us—but I'm also going to give our marriage my complete devotion. My dad's been very successful, but I grew up hardly knowing him because he was gone so much. I'm not going to let that happen. I'm going to raise my kids *with* you. And I'm going to be a tender, loving husband. I'll put you on a pedestal and worship at your feet. That's how much I love you, and it's how much I'll *always* love you. I'll give you *everything*, build you the house you want, take you on the vacations you want to take, and keep you in the clothing that will always make you beautiful. But more than that, I'll give you *me*. I'll be there when things are tough. I'll stand by you through *everything*. My life's goal will be to become the best husband any girl ever had."

Diane felt herself soften, felt her breath catch in her chest. She wanted to keep her head, wanted to keep him at arm's length, but she had never heard anything so beautiful. She could picture the life he was talking about, the way they would live, and she knew he was telling the truth. He treated her so beautifully. She had no doubt he always would. She had worried at one time that he might put his work first, but clearly he now understood that she wouldn't stand for that.

"Will you at least take my pin? Will you make that much of a commitment, to grant us some exclusive time—so we can both know for sure what we should do?"

"I don't have to take the pin. I'll just start turning down other dates. We could do that, couldn't we?"

"I'd just like to take a little first step, so we know we're . . ." But then he stopped. "No. That's not fair to you. I'm trying to sell you on something you really don't want. Never mind. This has to happen at your pace. I'm not going to push you anymore. Where we go from here will be entirely up to you."

She looked up at him. His cheeks were red from the cold, but she could see tears brimming in those wonderful, warm brown eyes of his. She had always hoped to be this loved by someone so handsome, so good. Why was she making everything so difficult? "I'll take the pin, but let's not say anything to anyone. I'll turn dates down, but the pinning will be something just between the two of us."

"That's perfect. I can't tell you what it means to me that you would do that. I'll pin it on you now, but when you get home, put it away, wherever you want, and it will be something that only you and I know about."

So she opened her coat, and he put the pin on her pretty cranberry-colored dress. Then he buttoned the coat for her, hiding it away. And after he had wrapped her muffler close around her neck, he pulled her to him and kissed her with almost delicate tenderness. She felt herself seem to merge into him. She knew she was letting go, loving him, and wondering why she had held back so long.

❧

Diane finished packing the next morning, and then she waited for her ride back to Ogden. But now she hardly wanted to go. She hated to think of seeing Greg at home, where Mom and Dad would ask him all their usual questions. When Terry came wandering out to the living room, still half asleep—in spite of the fact that she didn't have long to get ready either—it was all Diane could do not to tell her that she had taken Greg's pin the night before.

"Did you and Greg have a nice time last night?" she asked.

"Yes, we really did. We ate at the Skyroom, at the Hotel Utah."

"Wow. How come all the guys who take me out think that fine dining comes 'with fries'"?

Diane laughed. "Greg really knows how to do things right. You should have seen the coat he had on last night. Camel hair."

"Poor Kent."

"What?"

"You know what I'm talking about. Kent doesn't have a chance. You've got him in the grave. All you have to do is throw a little dirt on him."

"That's not true, Terry. Not at all."

"Yeah, right." She walked, rather aimlessly, back to her room.

But Diane was suddenly upset with herself. She had gone to bed basking in all that had happened with Greg, but Terry's accusation was a slap, a wake-up. She had to set Greg straight and get this whole thing back where it belonged. She even thought of calling him right then, but she couldn't do that with her roommates around. Maybe she would write him during the holiday. In fact, that was the perfect answer. She wouldn't have to look at him then, and she could explain herself clearly. One thing was certain: whomever she married, the wedding wouldn't happen for at least a couple of years.

~

Diane reached Ogden early that afternoon. Her parents weren't home, but Maggie came in before long, and the two chatted for a few minutes. Maggie was almost fifteen now, and she seemed to change a little more every time Diane saw her—even if only three or four weeks went by. She was still not very mature physically, but she was finally finding interest in clothes, and, although she wouldn't admit it directly, in boys. She wanted to know what the girls at BYU were wearing, what was fun to do there, but she also wondered about the guys Diane was dating and what they did on dates. She had gone to a couple of school dances—without a date—but she told Diane, "I don't think I'd like being with a boy, just me and him. Most of the boys I know are pretty stupid. I can't even think what I would say to them."

"But there are some cute ones too, huh? Some you like, I'll bet. At least one."

Maggy was sitting on the floor in the family room, leaning against Dad's chair. She wouldn't look at Diane. "Cute, yeah. But he's still stupid. The only thing he knows anything about is sports."

"Oh, a sports star. Is that the kind you go for?"

"I don't *go* for him. I just think he's cute."

"And what does he think of you?"

"He thinks I'm as interesting as the blackboard in our home room—when there's nothing written on it."

"You need to get his attention."

"How am I supposed to do that? His only interest is Sharalee Neuberg, the cheerleader."

"And I guess she's got all the right equipment."

Maggie's face reddened immediately. "She looks like you did when you were in ninth grade. She's got blonde hair, down to her waist—and these long, long, thin legs."

"All that won't matter when you get to college."

"I don't think I believe that."

"I just mean that all the girls are more mature by then. Some girls who look like kids in ninth or tenth grade are the ones who really blossom in college."

"I'm never going to look like you." She slid down, rested her head in the seat of the big chair, and folded her arms. "The high-school guys in our ward still want to know when you're going to be home next time."

"Oh, Maggie, why would you want to look like me? You look like you, and you look great."

Maggie got up. "You don't have to say that," she said. "We both know the truth. It's not like I'm ready to kill myself. I just know how things are."

Diane tried to think what to tell her, but she knew that anything she said would sound wrong. Maggie was cute, would probably look great in time, but for now, she really wasn't someone the boys were going to go crazy over. What Maggie didn't know, Diane thought, was that that wasn't such a bad thing.

"Anyway, I'm glad you're home," Maggie said. "Could we maybe do some stuff together while you're here?"

"Yeah. I'd really like that. Maybe we can go to a show. I haven't seen much of anything lately."

"I want to see *The Graduate*. It's going to be here next week, I think. It's supposed to be really good."

"Maggie, that's not what I've heard. I don't think it's the kind of movie we ought to go to. There's supposed to be some really bad stuff in it. The one I want I want to see is *To Sir, with Love*, with Sidney Poitier. My friends keep telling me I need to see it."

"Okay. I want to see that, too. It's already here."

"It's a deal, then. Maybe we can go tomorrow." Diane decided she might as well get unpacked, so she carried her suitcase to her room, which fortunately was still hers. She had things pretty well put away when her mom showed up with Ricky. He was four now, and more than a handful. Mom still taught a couple of classes at Weber State each quarter, and a sister in the ward looked after Ricky. But he was an indulged little boy, in Diane's opinion. He seemed to know that he could get away with almost anything. "Diane!" he shouted, and ran to her arms.

Diane picked him up and hugged him, realizing how much she had missed him. She hadn't been home since Thanksgiving, and really, only a couple of times in the fall. This second year of college, she hadn't come home as often as she had the first. But Ricky didn't want to be hugged very long. He squirmed and Diane set him down, and then he charged out of the room.

"He must have something he wants to tear down," Bobbi said. "He gets uncomfortable when the house is all in one piece."

"Don't you think we all need to be a little more strict with him?"

It was the wrong thing to say. Diane saw it immediately. "Maybe so," Mom said, but only with control. "So how is school going?"

Mom had an instinct for these things. How did she know? "I'm not sure. I'm doing okay in my religion class, and probably in English. But I had tests in physics and human physiology on the same day last week. I don't think I did very well on either one of them."

"Did you study?"

"Yes, Mom. I did."

"But did you study enough?"

"I guess not." And then there was quiet.

Bobbi stepped closer and took hold of Diane's arms, at the wrists. "Honey, I'm sorry," she said. "I shouldn't start in on you like that."

"You didn't have to. I knew when I walked out of those tests that I hadn't been prepared. I've never really learned how to study."

"I teach a freshman orientation class sometimes, and we deal with study methods. Would you like to talk about that while you're home?"

Diane didn't want to, not at all, but she said she did, said she would, and at least that was over. But Mom touched the other nerve. "What's happening with you and Greg?"

"Don't you mean Kent?"

"I know what's happening with Kent. He's preaching the gospel. It's Greg who's down at good ol' B-Y-Woo trying to make time with Kent's girl."

"Mom, that's not fair. Greg never pressures me. He just . . ."

"I think you'd better finish that sentence."

Diane was hanging up the last of the dresses she had brought home. Now she walked from the closet to her bed and sat down. "Mom, I don't know what to do."

Bobbi sat down next to her. "What do you mean?"

"Greg's really in love with me, and he's ready to graduate this spring. He wants to marry me before he goes away to law school."

"I thought *you* wanted to graduate."

"I do. I guess."

"Oh, Diane, think about it. You're nineteen. Why get in a hurry to get married?"

"I'm not in a hurry. But does it really matter that much if I don't graduate? Most girls don't. Almost everyone I know gets married before they graduate, and then they help their husband through school."

"I know a lot of girls do that. But I thought you and I agreed that it was silly to get in a big hurry. College is a great experience, and a degree is something you may wish you had someday."

Diane never knew how to talk with her mother about things like that, but she decided to try. "Mom, Greg has been trying hard to get an answer from God about what we ought to do. He's been praying, and he even had a fast. He received an answer from the Lord that I'm the one he should marry—and that I should go with him when he leaves for law school."

Diane waited for a reply. She could feel how stiff her mother was, next to her, and she knew exactly what she was thinking. "Honey, be careful. I never trust these guys who tell you they've gotten themselves a revelation about what *you* ought to do."

"But Mom, you've taught me all my life to pray and try to get answers about things like this. All Greg wants me to do is pray about it and see whether I don't get the same answer."

"That's fine—nothing wrong with that."

"But what?"

"I don't know. It just sounds manipulative." She hesitated for a moment and then added, "Diane, I'm not sure what kind of husband he would make. He seems the type who's always going to say, 'I'm the guy with the priesthood around here; we're going to do it my way.'"

"No, Mom. That's not true—not at all. He's really kind and tender. He'll do anything for me. He promised that he would be like that all his life."

Mom exhaled, and the sound was annoying.

"You don't like him, do you?"

"It's not that, Diane. I just . . ." She stopped, waited for a rather long time, and then said, "No, I don't like him. I know that's going to make you mad, but I didn't warn you about Scott, and afterward you told me I should have."

"How can you compare those two, Mom? They're nothing alike."

"I'm not sure that's true, Diane. Maybe this is the worst thing I could do, but I think I ought to give you my impression of him, for what it's worth."

"That's fine. That's what I want you to do." But it wasn't. Diane didn't really want to hear any of this.

"I find Greg too *slick*. He knows exactly what to say, how to handle himself in every situation, but he's like a salesman or a public relations rep. I can almost see the wheels spinning in his head when I'm around him—as though he's calculating every word, understanding exactly what kind of impression he's making."

Diane nodded, trying to seem at ease with that assessment. "I know what you mean, Mom. At one time I sort of had that impression, but now that I know him, I don't feel that at all. Maybe he sort of does that with lots of people, but around me, he's really himself."

"Okay. I'm probably wrong. Maybe he just feels some pressure around your dad and me. But I will say my instincts are pretty good. When I met

Kent, I thought he was young, but I also thought he was good. I've never felt that from Greg. Kent may not end up making as much money, and he may not be quite as smooth, but I just have the impression that he'll be a better man to spend eternity with."

But that wasn't fair. "Mom, you don't really know either one of them very well. You've just met them a couple of times. I'm the one who's spent a lot of time with them. Greg is good. Much better than me, if you want to know the real truth."

"All right. That's good to know. I do trust your judgment. And if you marry Greg, I'm sure I'll learn to love him as much as you do. I just don't think it would hurt anything to get another year older and wait until Kent gets back. I don't have to tell you—one more time—how important I think school is."

"Mom, I'm not a very good student. I never will be. Greg's dad is going to pay for law school, and he'll give him a job with his law firm, if that's what he wants. I don't think there would ever be a time when I would need to work."

"Honey, you don't know what might happen in life. And besides, don't you think college is about other things—not just job training?"

"I don't know, Mom. I only know that I don't even know what I want to major in—and I hate most of my classes. I could probably read things I'm interested in and learn more by doing that—while I'm raising my kids."

"Oh, Di. You won't have time to sit and read once you start having babies. You might get a few things read, but you'll never have another chance to concentrate completely on learning. And you *are* smart. I've been waiting all your life for you to realize that—and really come into your own. If you drop out now, you may never do that."

Diane hated every word of this. It was the conversation they had been having since Diane was in junior high: "You're smart; you need to apply yourself; start studying harder. School is really interesting—honest."

"I'm making the same old mistake. Right? The more I put Greg down, the more you'll think he's the right choice. The more I push college, the more you'll hate it."

"No, Mom. But it's something I have to decide for myself."

"I agree. Just let me say one last thing, and then I'll shut my mouth forever on the subject." She wrapped her arm around Diane's shoulders. "We had a guy come to our home and try to sell us on an investment. At some point along the way, he told us in so many words that we could trust him because he was a high priest and a temple worker. Your dad got rid of him just as soon as he could, and then he said exactly what I was thinking: 'When a guy starts using the Church to make a sale, I get leery.' As it turned out, this guy got away with a lot of money. He was basically a crook. So when I hear someone say, 'Marry me because I've prayed and got my answer—you can trust me on that,' I wonder about it. I think maybe the guy is trying to sell you on something and has to rely on his supposed spirituality to convince you."

"That could happen, I guess. But he should be praying, shouldn't he? He should be trying to get an answer. And he got his answer. How can I not pay attention to that?"

"I didn't say you shouldn't. But I would test his answer very carefully, not let him force his on you. And I would ask myself whether, after you got married, he wouldn't tend to pressure you into doing things on that same basis."

"But Mom, when Lehi got answers in the Book of Mormon, we wonder what was wrong with Laman and Lemuel, and sometimes even Sariah, that they didn't get in tune with the Spirit."

"I know. It's not an easy matter. Just be careful."

"I am being careful. He knows I plan to finish school before I get married."

"Is that what you still plan to do?"

Diane thought for quite some time before she said, "I don't know for sure. That's what I'm going to pray about." But what she was feeling was the unfairness of her mother's accusations. Mom didn't know Greg, didn't know how sincere he was or how careful he had been not to pressure her. Diane had been missing Greg all day today, actually more than she ever remembered missing Kent. That had to mean something.

# Chapter 26

Gene made a right turn and then drove all the way into Emily's driveway. It was a cold evening in March 1968. He stopped the car in front of the garage, alongside her house, and then turned toward her. "I need to talk to you about something," he said.

"Something's wrong, huh?"

"What do you mean?"

"You've been quiet all night. I could tell you were thinking about something."

Gene and Emily had gone with some friends—four other couples—to eat dinner at the Athenian, a Greek place that even had belly dancers, and then they had gone to Butch Rowland's house afterward. Butch was an old Sigma Chi friend, but like Gene, he had lost a lot of interest in the fraternity after his mission. Everyone had danced and listened to music, and Gene had tried to teach Emily to play pool. But it was true that Gene had had something on his mind all evening, something he had been thinking about for a long time, and he felt that he had to bring it up now, before the two of them got any more serious.

"Emily, I'm just thinking that maybe we're spending a little too much time together. I don't know if that's the best thing right now."

"Why? Because of school or . . . what?"

"No. Not exactly. I just don't know whether the timing is right. Maybe we ought to start dating other people and just keep things sort of fun between us for now."

Gene saw Emily react—noticed a kind of hardness in her mouth that he had never seen before. She stared at him for several seconds before she said, "Why do guys always do this?"

"Do what?"

"If you want to break up, just say so. Don't give me this 'We ought to date other people' stuff."

Gene took hold of Emily's forearm and waited for her to look at him. "I didn't say anything about breaking up. It's just so difficult, the way things are. When we start kissing, I don't want to stop. But it's going to be a long time before we could think about—"

"Who is it you want to go out with?" She pulled her arm away, turned, and leaned back against the door, folding her arms.

"Emily, really. That's not at all what I want."

"Gene, I may have played my little game to get to know you, but I've always been straight with you since then. I haven't held anything back. You know how much I love you."

"Emily, I love you too."

"Don't do that. That's the very worst. 'I love you but I want to go look around—date some other girls.'"

Gene didn't know how to do this. The last thing he wanted was to lose Emily, but he also knew that things were moving too fast. What he really wanted was to marry her—the sooner the better—but that just wasn't possible. "Emily, what I hope is that we'll end up together. But it's going to be a long time before we could think about marriage, and I don't see how we can keep spending this much time together with so long to wait. I just think we ought to back off for a little while."

"Fine. See you on campus sometime." She twisted around and opened the car door. "Have you already chosen the other girl you want to go out with, or are there quite a few that you still want to check out? It pays to shop around, you know."

"Emily, that's not it. Honest."

"You forgot to cross your heart." She slid out of the car. "Good-bye,

Gene," she said as she shut the door, and then she ran around the back of the house.

Gene jumped out too, called after her, then hurried to catch up, but he was too late. By the time he got around the corner of the house, he heard the back door slam. He stood for a time, trying to think what to do. He thought of going to the door and ringing the doorbell, but he didn't want to create a big scene and wake up the whole family. What he told himself, as he walked back to his car, was that maybe this was right. Maybe this was what had to happen. He knew that he might lose her, but he saw no alternative. He had thought about their situation from every angle, and he was certain that he had to slow things down.

But it was one thing to do the right thing, and it was quite another to begin living with the decision. As he drove home he felt empty, actually sick to his stomach. He felt worse than he had when Marsha had sent him his Dear John letter. Emily was here, she loved him, and he had just hurt her. He hadn't wanted anything like that. He really had thought it might be possible to step back a little without ending their relationship. Now he didn't know what to expect. He could try to talk to her again, but what was he supposed to say?

By the time he got home, he was almost sure he had done the wrong thing. He sat down in the family room with the lights still out. Even more than usual, he hated being alone in this big house. Tonight it seemed to symbolize what his life would be like if he stopped seeing Emily. Maybe he would call her in the morning, tell her he was sorry, tell her that he wanted to take everything back. But that didn't solve the problem. There was no way the two of them could just keep dating, perhaps for years. What would happen to them during their separation if he ended up in Vietnam?

When the phone rang, he was not entirely surprised. In fact, he was relieved. At least he could talk to her tonight, maybe do a better job of explaining. He moved over to his father's chair, sat down, and picked up the receiver. But he *was* surprised when it wasn't Emily's voice that he heard on the line.

"Mom? What's going on? How late is it out there?"

"After two."

"Is something wrong?"

"I don't know. You tell me. I've been worried about you. You haven't written to us for almost three weeks, and every time I call, you're not there. I tried all evening, and the later it got, the more worried I got. I couldn't sleep."

"I'm fine, Mom. I've just been on the go a lot." He leaned back and stretched his legs out.

"You don't sound fine. You sound like you're about to cry."

"I probably was crying. I'm not sure."

"Why, honey?"

"Emily and I just broke up."

"Oh, Gene, don't tell me that. Why?"

Gene took a breath, then slid down in the chair a little more. "Mom, I messed things up. I told her that we ought to start dating other people, and she got the wrong idea. She thought I was saying that I didn't want to go with her anymore."

"Of course she did. What would you think if she had told you that? She was expecting you to give her a ring one of these days."

"I can't do that. That's just the problem."

"And why can't you?" Anna's voice had a way of tightening, becoming more German when she was upset. She sounded disgusted right now.

"I can't get married for *years*. You know that. How could we get engaged and then not get married for such a long time?"

"Why can't you get married?"

"You know what's going to happen next year, just as soon as I graduate. I'll be drafted, and then I'll be heading to Vietnam. There's no way that won't happen. They don't give deferments for graduate school anymore. And there's no way the war is going to end. Since that Tet Offensive this winter, no one believes the Vietcong are weakening."

"So you've got it into your head that you can't get married until you get back from the army?"

"Of course."

"Why, Gene? I don't understand that."

Of all people, Gene thought his mother would understand. There was some moonlight tonight, the windows in the family room casting angled rectangles across the carpet. But clouds were scudding by, and the room suddenly went black as the clouds covered the moon. He hated all that darkness. "Mom, I've heard about you and Dad all my life, what you went through when he was gone to war and you were alone with me. I don't want that to happen to Emily. What if I go over there and get myself killed—the way Uncle Gene did? I don't want her to be left alone, married for eternity to me, and I don't want to leave a child for her to raise alone."

"Oh, Gene, you're not stupid, but sometimes you can be *so* dense."

"What's that supposed to mean?"

"Do you really think I would have traded that time with your father—before he had to go back to the war—or traded you for *anything?* What would have been my consolation? Being all alone?"

"Emily won't be alone. If something happens to me, she'll meet someone else. That's what you would have done."

"She wants *you*, Gene. And she wants you for all eternity. If she loses you in this life, she'll know she still has that."

"But what kind of life would that be?"

"Gene, think about it. You can't start by assuming that you'll die—no more than anyone can. We all *could* die anytime. If you've found the right girl for you, you need to move ahead, get married, start your life together, and then make it through the hard times together. The day will come when you're closer to each other because of what you've gone through. It doesn't work the other way. You can't protect against the bad possibilities."

Gene had thought about all this so many times. Sometimes he had told himself the same things his mother was saying, but when he got that far, he always saw the difficulties: another year of school, then off somewhere for training, a hitch in Vietnam—almost for certain—and then back to grad school. For so many years Emily would be left alone or dragged about the country, living in military housing or dinky apartments close to base. It simply wasn't how he thought about life. He wanted to give her a home. Emily lived in a beautiful house in Bountiful, had never known anything else, and she hated being alone. She had stayed at home while she was in college mostly because she disliked the dorms and the sorority houses, the separation from her family.

He had also thought of the other possibility: that he would leave her behind and she wouldn't wait for him. It seemed the most likely thing to happen, considering how pretty she was, how fun she was to be with. But still, it might be the best thing for her. In his own mind, he had been doing something noble tonight.

"Mom, what kind of life can I give her? I've still got so much school ahead. It will be *years* before I can buy her a home and give her what she's used to."

"I take it back. You are stupid."

"Why? What's wrong with asking that?"

"Gene, her parents didn't *start* with their home. We didn't either. One of the joys of marriage is working for the things you want. When you get as old as your dad and I, you'll know that so much of love is nothing more than shared experience. You grow old like two horses pulling the same wagon. You fall more and more into step with each other. You understand what it means to let up a little when you have to and feel the pull on the other side, and then to take a little more than your own share when that's what's needed. Life isn't good because it's easy; it's good because it makes us pull so hard."

Gene had begun to cry, and he wasn't sure why. Maybe it was the relief. Maybe it was because he thought his mother was giving him a better answer. "What should I do, Mom?"

"Go to her."

"Okay. I'll call her in the morning, and I'll—"

"You numbskull. Do you really think she's asleep? The girl is lying on her bed, crying. Her heart is breaking. Don't make her go through that all night. Go to her now."

"Should I call her, or—"

"No, Gene. Go back to Bountiful. Take her in your arms and hold her, and tell her you'll never *ever* hurt her like this again. And you'd better not, either. If you do, you'll have me to deal with."

"Do you like her, Mom?"

"Like her? Honey, I love her. So does your father. She doesn't analyze; she just loves. And she's *crazy* about you. She'll make you very happy."

"*Ich liebe dich, Mutti.*"

"*Also, tu was ich Dir sage. Nach* Bountiful *mit Dir. Und gerade jetzt.*"

"Okay, okay. I'm going. Thanks. I'll write you tomorrow. Honest."

"Good. This phone call just ruined my budget for the month."

Gene said good-bye and hung up. Then he walked to the bathroom and washed his face. He wasn't so sure that his mother was right about Emily's still being awake, but he hoped it was true. He got in his old Ford and drove back. And all along the way, he tried to think what he could say to her, how he could tell her he was sorry. He drove over Capitol Hill and out Beck Street, then stayed with Highway 89 into Bountiful. When he reached Slim Olsen's giant gas station, he turned and headed east, toward the foothills where Emily lived. By the time he reached her house, he was scared. He didn't want to ring the doorbell and wake everyone, and he didn't want someone to think a prowler was coming around, so he decided he would slip around to the backyard and try to get Emily's attention by tapping on the window. If the girl was actually sound asleep and didn't hear him, he wasn't sure what he would do.

What he had forgotten about was Emily's dog, Merle. He was a black Labrador, and much too affectionate. But as Gene opened the gate at the side of the house and tried to creep past the screened porch, he heard Merle rouse, growl tentatively, and then begin to bark. Gene stood stiff and still, but the barking continued. He thought of calling out to the dog, reassuring it with a voice it knew, but that seemed unlikely to work. It was a big ranch-style home, and Emily's parents slept at the other end, far from the dog. Gene had to hope they wouldn't hear. He decided to hurry to Emily's window and reassure her that he wasn't a burglar, and then maybe she could go calm the dog. But Merle must have heard Gene move. He began to jump against the screen door, pounding with his big paws and scraping the screen. By now the whole neighborhood was probably waking up. So Gene ran. But he realized he wasn't sure which window was Emily's. There were two bedrooms on the back side of the house, and a family room. He ran to the shrubbery, close to the back of the house, then tried to think how many windows from the end Emily's bedroom would be, but Merle was going wild. Gene was locked in place, unable to think what to do, when the light in the screened porch came on. A moment later he heard Brother Osborne's raspy voice. "What is it, Merle? What's the matter?"

Gene hoped maybe Brother Osborne would not be too concerned and would maybe take Merle inside. But the old lab was still barking hard, and Brother Osborne was saying, "Okay. Show me what it is. I'll let you out."

Suddenly Gene found his voice. "Brother Osborne, it's me. Gene Thomas. I'm in the backyard."

"What?"

"I needed to talk to Emily, and I was trying to find her bedroom."

"*What?*"

"What I mean is, I didn't want to wake you up by ringing the doorbell. I was going to tap on her window."

"What time is it?"

"I'm not sure. Maybe one o'clock. Something like that."

"Gene, this isn't like you. What's so important that you have to—"

"It's all right, Daddy. I'll talk to him here on the porch." And then in a louder voice, she called, "Come here, Gene. Merle won't quiet down until he can sniff you and hear your voice."

Gene wasn't at all sure he wanted to let the dog that close to him, but he walked back toward the porch and stood at the door. It was Brother Osborne who opened it. "I don't see why this is necessary," he mumbled. Gene stepped a little closer and waited for those big jaws to clamp down on his leg. It seemed only right to let him do it at this point.

"See, Merle. It's only Gene," Emily was saying. "You know Gene. You like Gene. Pet him, Gene."

So it was his hand he would have to sacrifice. But Merle seemed to respond to the touch. He suddenly went from barking to loving. He jumped on Gene with both front legs, almost knocking him over. Gene didn't mind dogs, but he had never liked to be slobbered on. Still, he stood his ground and took his licking.

"I'm going to leave Merle here," Emily's dad said. "Just in case."

This seemed to be some sort of joke, and Gene tried to laugh, but Brother Osborne never bothered.

"Don't be long, Emily," he said. "Your mother is going to be upset about this."

"I'm really sorry," Gene kept saying. "I won't be here ten minutes. I just had to talk to her about something. It's really important."

And then the door shut, and Gene was standing in front of Emily. She had a silky robe on. Her hair was a mess. Her arms were folded tight across her middle. Gene realized how cold she must be. "I'm sorry. Were you asleep?"

"No."

Merle was still nervous, still prancing about, twisting as he walked back and forth between them. "I don't want to break up," Gene said.

"You said that before. You just want to date other people."

"No, I don't. I don't want to date anyone but you, ever."

"What's going on, Gene? I don't get this." She grabbed Merle's collar. "Sit," she said, with command. Her tone frightened Gene a little. She was not in a good mood.

"As soon as I graduate, I'll be drafted."

"I know that. We've talked about that before."

"I thought it wasn't fair to you, if I had to leave for a long time and maybe go to war. I thought we would have to wait too long to get married—and that wouldn't work."

"One thing at a time, Gene."

"What do you mean?"

"Do you want to marry me? You've never actually told me that—not directly."

"I know. I felt like I shouldn't bring it up, not with all these years we might have to wait."

"But do you want to marry me?"

"Yes."

"So are you proposing?"

"I don't know. I guess I am."

"You sure know how to be romantic."

"I mean, no. I'm not proposing right now. I'll do it right, okay? We'll go out, and I'll have a ring and everything. But I'm just telling you, I do want to marry you."

"When?"

"Emily, I don't know. What if I have to go to war?"

"Then you'll go. But when do you want to marry me?"

"Now. I *want* to marry you right away. But I'm not sure that's a good idea."

"What about June?"

"This June?"

"Yes. This June."

"Okay."

"You have to ask me. I haven't even said I want to marry you."

"Do you?"

"Yes, I do."

"In June?"

"Yes."

"Well, okay."

"No. It's not okay. We can't get engaged like this. Not out here with Merle, and me in a robe. You make me furious sometimes, you can act so stupid." She wasn't smiling. She really did sound angry.

"That's what my mom said."

"I don't blame her. She's right."

"So should I leave, and then—you know—ask you another time?"

"Yes."

"Okay then. I guess I'll go." He turned toward the screen door.

"Gene, what are you thinking?"

"What do you mean?"

"You're going to ask me to marry you and then just walk away? You haven't even kissed me."

"I know. But I thought I wasn't supposed to ask you yet."

"But you did."

"So did it count?"

"Kiss me, okay? At least I want to have that much. All my life I'll have to remember this sorry little scene out here." She still sounded mad.

"I wasn't going to do it like this, Emily. I'm sorry. I really am."

She stepped forward, and now he could see her face better, with the moonlight coming through the screen. "It's okay," she said, and finally she smiled. "Let's just not tell anyone, and then we can still have an engagement night, the way we want."

"Okay."

"Is there anything else you wanted to tell me?"

"No. I don't think so."

"Wouldn't it be a rather good opportunity for you to mention that you love me?"

"I do, Emily. I do. It felt like I was going to die after I left before—when I thought I'd lost you."

"I've been crying ever since you left."

Mom was right.

Gene finally took her in his arms and held her. She was shivering from the cold, and he wanted to envelope her, protect her, but it was he who felt restored to life. He decided not to worry about all the other things he had been telling himself. He kissed her, and he would have held her much longer, but Merle was either concerned for Emily or jealous. He began to bark again, and Gene decided it was a good time to get out of there—before Brother Osborne came back.

# Chapter 27

Diane had spent a lot of time with Greg all winter. It was late March now, and she still hadn't made a decision about her future—not consciously—but her commitment was changing, and she knew it. Kent was a wonderful boy, and she would always remember him with fondness, but Greg made her feel secure. She felt that she was moving from a teenage romance to a grown-up relationship with a man of confidence and authority. Diane had always loved her father more than anyone else, but sometimes she had wished that he would be a little stronger, a little more in control. In that way, maybe Kent was a little too much like her dad. But Greg never would be.

Diane tried to convince herself that she was still considering, still praying, but she knew the truth: she was delaying. Once she committed to Greg, she would have to write to Kent, and she dreaded doing that. Kent still wrote her loving letters every week, always pledging his love, but at least his letters had gotten shorter as time had gone by, and he seemed less desperate about keeping her. Maybe distance and time were having their effect on him; maybe he was becoming more realistic about how these things usually turned out.

In February Diane and Greg had been chosen to reign over Winter Carnival as Snow King and Queen. They had been introduced at a BYU basketball game, at halftime, and they had attended all the events, from ice carving to the ski races. The big dance had been held in various halls, throughout the campus, and she and Greg had dashed about to each, just to make an appearance The two had even had a chance to meet President David O. McKay, who was ninety-four years old now. He and Sister

McKay had teased them about being such a "cute couple." It was a perfect week for Diane, something to remember forever, and even though she hated to admit it to herself, one of her hesitations about getting married was that she still dreamed of being named Homecoming Queen or Belle of the Y, and she would have to stay single and stay at BYU for that to happen.

Diane had only gone home once during the winter—for semester break. Bobbi had taken the chance to question Diane about her feelings for Greg, and Diane had certainly made it clear that she was leaning in his direction. She didn't want her parents to be taken by surprise when the decision came. Mom didn't say anything negative about that; she merely listened. But she looked concerned, and Diane knew that she still had her doubts.

Even though Diane hadn't announced her decision, those close to her at BYU, especially her roommates, obviously sensed what was happening. Terry constantly reminded Diane of her promise not to get married until Kent got home.

"I didn't ever promise to wait for Kent—not exactly," Diane told Terry one April afternoon. She had just come back from her last class of the day, and she had promised herself that she was going to study for the entire evening, not waste a minute, since she was so far behind in all her courses.

But Terry had come in not long after Diane, and she had plopped down on the couch, across from where Diane was sitting in a chair—a stiff, uncomfortable one that was supposed to keep her from falling asleep. "I can see what's happening," she had told Diane. "You've sold poor Kent right down the old river."

"What I told Kent," Diane said, "was that I expected to be single when he got back, that I didn't want to get married until I graduated from college. I didn't *promise*." Actually, Diane knew she had been a little more direct than that, but she wasn't going to admit that to Terry.

"When Kent comes home, I'm going to throw myself at him," Terry said. "I only saw him that one time, but he was *so* cute, and *so* nice."

"I thought you were going to marry Jean-Claude Killy." Terry had talked of little else since the Olympic Games that winter.

"Well . . . that may not work out. Kent's my second choice."

"Yeah, right. You made fun of him at the airport. You thought he was a nut case."

"He was. But it was cute, the way he acted. I'd love to have someone that bonkers over me. I think you're crazy to dump him."

"Who said I was *dumping* him?" Diane was holding a psychology text. She closed it but kept a finger between the pages to mark her place. She wasn't going to let this conversation last long.

"Don't give me that. You and Greg are like Siamese twins now. I never see one of you without the other."

"You see me *now,* and he's not around."

"Yeah. For how long?"

"I'm not seeing him tonight. I'm going to study." She opened her book again, but Terry had stretched out across the couch now, and she was laughing in that shrill, irritating voice of hers. Diane couldn't concentrate. She was still thinking about Terry's claim that she was going to "throw herself" at Kent. Terry would, too. She was a forward girl, and she would get her claws into poor Kent just as quickly as she could. The idea of it was infuriating. Terry was all right, in her own strange way, but Kent deserved better.

"What's your hurry to get married, Diane? Why don't you at least give Kent a chance? He'll be home next fall."

"What are you talking about? Who said I'm in a hurry to get married?"

"Diane, when a little stick goes over Niagara Falls, it doesn't take a genius to know that it's going to end up in the river, down below. Greg's got you hanging over the edge, and you're about to go with the flow."

"Greg doesn't make my decisions for me. I'll decide what I want to do."

Terry was laughing again, making maddening little grunting noises.

"Shut up, okay? Just shut up."

"Fine. That's what I'll do." She hesitated for a couple of seconds, and then she sat up and waited for Diane to look at her. "Except I want to say *one* last thing. If you dump Kent and marry Greg, you're making the biggest mistake of your life. *Everyone* can see it."

"What do you mean, 'everyone'? Who's been talking about me?"

"We're not talking *about* you, Diane. We love you, and we hate to see you make a mistake you'll end up regretting forever."

"Who's saying that?"

"Everyone who knows you. Everyone who knows Greg. And that's our whole ward."

"That's not true. I don't believe you."

"Just a minute." Terry got up and walked to the bedroom door. She knocked. "Julianne, are you in there?" Julianne was great for staying up late at night, but she came home almost every afternoon and took a nap.

After a few seconds there was a muffled response. "What do you want?"

"Come out here. I need you."

At least a minute passed before the door opened, and all that time, Diane was getting angrier. What gave all these people the right to judge Greg? No one knew him the way she did.

Julianne was wearing cutoffs and an old sweatshirt, with white socks, no shoes—her usual attire around the apartment. Her hair was a scattered mess. "What?" she said.

"Tell Diane what you've been telling me about her and Greg. She needs to know."

"Terry, don't get me into this."

"Tell her now, while it's not too late. Someone has to say it to her."

Julianne rolled her eyes, then looked off across the room as she said, "I just think you would be better off to wait until Kent gets home before you—"

"You don't even know Kent."

"She knows *Greg*," Terry said. "Tell her what you think of Greg, Julianne."

"Terry," Julianne said, "I don't want—"

"Just tell her what you think of him. If we don't say anything, someday she's going to ask why we didn't."

Julianne stared away again and said quietly, "Diane, I don't like to judge people. You know Greg better than we do. But some things about him do bother me—and I guess some other people too."

"A *lot* of other people," Terry put in.

"Like what?" Diane asked.

But it was Terry who answered. "He's too calculating, Diane. He gets what he wants, whatever it takes. He uses people."

"What are you talking about? Give me an example."

"Okay, I will," Terry said. But then she looked at Julianne, who was edging back toward the bedroom. "Don't leave, Julianne," she said. "Come over here and help me." Julianne rolled her eyes, but then she did walk to the couch and sit down at the far end from Terry. "Here's an example," Terry said. "Greg was assigned to home teach Jane Ann and Melinda and—you know, the group down below us. They apparently aren't up to his standards or something, so every month he reports that he visits them, but he doesn't. He went once, at the first of the year, and he's never been back."

"A lot of guys don't do their home teaching like they ought to."

"Maybe so. But do they lie about it?"

"He probably sees them at church and figures that's good enough."

"That's right. That's how he would think." Terry glanced toward

Julianne, as if for support, but Julianne was hunched forward, looking at the floor.

"I just don't think that proves anything, Terry. You don't like him, so you—"

Terry clapped her hands against the sides of her head—with her usual flair for the dramatic. "Why would I have anything against him? I just watch him operate, and I think, 'That's the kind of stuff Diane will have to put up with all her life.' If he thinks people have the right sort of connections, come from good families—like Brent Westover, whose uncle is an Assistant to the Twelve—he treats them fine. But anyone he considers a nobody, like me, he hardly looks at. Don't you know that the first thing he liked about you was that your uncle is a congressman? He thinks you're a good connection. He said as much to his roommate."

"Said *as much?* This is all just rumor and backbiting, isn't it? It makes me sick. You don't know how generous and good he is. It wouldn't surprise me if he weren't an important Church leader someday."

"I'm sure he has hopes to work his way up to that."

"I'm not going to listen to any more of this. It's all unfair."

"It's the truth, Diane." Terry turned to Julianne. "Isn't it?"

"I don't know," Julianne said. "I think so. But Diane is the one who has to decide."

"You're so chicken," Terry said. She looked at Diane. "You ought to hear her when she's being honest. She can't stand Greg any more than I can. No one trusts the guy."

"Are you finished now?"

"I guess I am. I just wish you were listening."

"I have listened. But I don't want you ever to talk this way again. I'll make up my own mind." She ducked her head again and pretended to study. After a time Julianne got up and walked back to her room, and Terry left the apartment entirely. But still, Diane couldn't study. What troubled her was that she did know what Terry was talking about. There had been a time when she had had a similar impression of Greg. She asked herself now whether there was any chance that her first impression had been right. But that was unfair. She knew him better now, better than Terry ever would, and it was only that style of his—which did come across as rather cocky—that gave people the wrong idea about him.

❧

The next couple of weeks were difficult for Diane. She wasn't concentrating on school the way she needed to, and she knew it. Her grades were headed in the same direction they had gone every semester. She didn't want to believe what Terry and Julianne had said about Greg, or what her own mother thought of him. But she was noticing again some things Greg said about people, some of his attitudes about himself. It was enough to worry her—enough to make her ask herself again if it would hurt anything to wait for Kent to get back in the fall. If Greg went away to law school, maybe the separation would serve as a good test for them.

Greg now knew that he was heading for Seattle in the fall. He had been accepted to the University of Washington law school. He had hoped to get into Yale or Harvard, but he hadn't made it. Still, Washington had an excellent law school, and Greg was excited. Sometimes when Diane listened to him, she got excited too. An escape from college actually sounded nice. She could work somewhere in Seattle, help Greg get through school, and just forget about having to study all the time. She had been to Seattle once when her mom and dad had attended a conference there, and she loved the place. She remembered the green hills, all the water and bridges. The thought of being married, living there, really sounded good. At the same time, she didn't want to get married when she was feeling any vestige of doubt. It had to be her whole heart or nothing.

That's why she found herself a little nervous when Greg asked her out on a Friday night, early in April. Samuel Hall Society was having a party, so that was ordinary enough, but he told her he wanted to take her out to dinner first so she ought to wear a nice dress. Greg knew Salt Lake better than Provo—and there were many more nice places to eat there—so he usually drove to Salt Lake when he wanted to do something special. Diane was almost sure that he was going to propose, and so she was careful, as soon as she got into the car with him, to say, "Next week, I'm going to spend a whole lot less time with you. I'm going to study like I've never studied before. I've just got to save my grades."

She sensed before he spoke what he was going to say. "You know, Di, college is great, but maybe for some people it isn't the most important thing."

She was ready. "Maybe. But I'm not stupid. I can do better. I think I've just played around too much. A lot of people do that their first couple of years. But I'm going to salvage what I can from this semester, and then next year I'm really going to settle down. I've made up my mind about that."

That was her declaration. She hoped he got the point.

But Greg did know when to pull back; she had heard him do it many times. "Well, I think that's the right way to look at it," was all he said.

At dinner, at the Paprika, she saw that Greg was trying to put together a perfect evening. He ordered for her, as he liked to do, and chose the most expensive dishes on the menu. He told her how beautiful she looked with the soft light of candles on her, and he told her, "Diane, I've watched you grow so much these last two years. You came to BYU as a high-school girl, and I've watched you blossom into a woman. When I first met you, I think I was so dazzled by your looks, I hardly thought about anything else. But you're strong-willed, and you've got a sharp mind. You're really a very exciting woman to be around."

Diane wasn't sure that anyone had ever called her a woman. She liked the way that made her feel. Maybe Greg was pouring it on a little thick, but not many people respected her for being able to do anything but look good. Greg really did seem to believe in her, to recognize what she was capable of.

He waited until they had eaten, and then he said to the waiter, "For dessert, we'd like to share that little cake you have on your menu."

Diane hadn't noticed cake on the menu, but she didn't think much about it. Greg always knew what was good. And she loved the old-world elegance of this restaurant. He couldn't have chosen a nicer place. The only problem was, it was too perfect, too obvious what was coming.

"Diane, there's something I want to talk to you about."

Diane tried to think what to say. She needed to change the subject. She avoided what he had said and told him, "I really love the atmosphere in this place. The food is really good, too."

But he ignored all that. "I know I kind of pushed things when I talked to you in December about getting married. I'm glad you had the good sense to put me off a little, because I think our relationship has deepened in the last few months. I did ask you, though, to pray about it and see whether you got an answer about us. I haven't wanted to press you, but I've been praying all this time myself, and I can promise, I'm more certain than ever that we're right for one another. Tell me if I'm wrong, but what I sense from you now is that God is guiding you closer to me, not farther away."

"That might be right, Greg, but I keep feeling that there's no rush. I just turned twenty. I think another year or two would be good for me, and you could start law school without worrying about anything but your studies."

"Diane, if I go to Seattle alone, I hardly know whether I can stand it. I don't think you understand how deeply I love you. I don't want you to be out of my sight, ever. I want you to be there when I come home from a day at law school. I want you to sit with me in a cozy little apartment while I study. I want to go to bed with you every night, hold you in my arms, and wake up with you all warm and soft against me in the morning.

I want to take care of you—to give you a simple but good life now and then spoil you terribly as I begin to prosper. I want to have babies with you—kids as beautiful as you are. I want to sit in church with them on my lap, and you next to me. I want to teach the boys to throw a baseball and let the little girls wrap me around their little fingers. I want *us*, Diane—always us—to be the center of our own little universe. I want success, Diane, but I can live without it. I want to make a good living, but I can live without that too. What I need is *you*—to have and to hold forever. All I want is a nice little home, a beautiful family, a chance to serve in the Church, and you. I want a life of knowing that I married the one girl in this world who was chosen for me by God."

Diane felt herself fighting this, holding back, but it was so beautiful, his picture of things. It was what she had always wanted. She watched the candle on the table, the flame illuminating the glass around it. She could see her reflection in the glass, fluttering in the flame, and it almost seemed symbolic: the warmth of the flame, lighting her, filling her up. "Are you *sure* you have your answer?" she asked.

"Beyond any shadow of a doubt. And I'll tell you something else. I know you have your answer too. I feel you trying to fight it—probably because you told yourself a long time ago that you would finish college before you married—but when we're together I feel your love, and I know you've chosen me the same as I've chosen you. We've been guided to each other by the Lord, Diane."

It was something Diane had thought about. They had ended up in the same ward when she had come to BYU, and they had met at the very first ward function. It did seem as though they had been dropped into each other's paths.

"Let me assure you about a couple of things."

Diane nodded, waiting. She was feeling a bit of shame. She had always been the one to hold back while Greg had worked so hard to make their relationship work.

"First, you *will* finish college. I'll see to it. I wish you could do it now, but I just feel so sure that this is the right time for us, and we would be making a huge mistake to let it slip away. But wherever we are, whatever we're doing, the season will come for you to finish your education, and you know what? You'll be a better student. You are smart, but you're also right that you haven't really settled down yet. Marriage will do that for you."

That did seem to make sense. Diane knew that she was always resolving to study, but she couldn't seem to do it now. Maybe the maturity that would come with marriage and children would lead her back to college someday. It was something she could tell her mother, too.

"And here's the other thing I know you worry about. You didn't promise Kent that you would wait, but you told yourself you would be single when he got back. I understand that, and I can see why you want to hold to that. From a purely logical point of view, that makes sense. But that's why we have inspiration. That's why we pray to God for guidance. We use our own minds, but we also have to ask sometimes when we've gone as far as we can with the reasoning capacity we have. And here's what I know: God wants us together, and he wants it to happen now. He knows how much I need you. He also knows that a right time for marriage comes, and going past that time can ruin a relationship."

Diane felt suspended in a kind of haze, the flame still flickering behind her reflection, her breath shallow. She looked up at Greg, and she saw the devotion in his face. A vibration passed through her, seemed to confirm everything he had been saying. She was certain that he would always give her and her children what he promised: guidance and warmth and security. Her friends were *so* wrong about Greg.

Greg was smiling now, and he reached across the table and took her hand. He held it for a few seconds, and then he looked across the room and nodded. A waiter crossed the room, holding a little round cake on a platter. It was beautifully decorated, all white, like a little wedding cake.

The waiter placed a knife alongside the cake and said, laughing a little, "I hope you enjoy it." Greg smiled back, and Diane knew what this meant. But it was okay. She no longer wanted to fight what was happening.

"You cut the cake," he said, as she knew he would.

So she picked up the knife and tried to slice it in half, but she wasn't surprised when she hit something hard. She looked at Greg and smiled. "What's this? There's something in my cake."

"Should I send it back?"

"No, Greg. Let me see what it is first." They gazed at each other for a moment, and Diane was extraordinarily happy—happier than she had ever been in her life. This *was* right. So she separated the halves of the cake with her knife, found the little velvet box in the middle, and pulled it out. She licked some frosting from her fingers and was about to open it when Greg said, "Diane, will you marry me?"

It crossed Diane's mind that she didn't want the question put to her in a room full of people. She even noticed that the people at the next table had noticed what she was doing and were looking at her. But she opened the box and saw the immense diamond—certainly more than a carat, in a marquis cut. It was what she had once told Greg she preferred. "Yes," she said. "Yes."

He took her hand. "August, before I leave for Seattle? Would that give you time to plan the greatest wedding ever?"

"I think so. Yes." She couldn't think. She didn't know how much time that was. But she was ready to move forward, not look back. This was surely right.

"I want to kneel at your feet and ask, before I put it on your finger. And then I want to kiss you. So let me settle the bill, and then we'll settle the rest."

Diane glanced at the older couple at the next table, who were smiling at her, both delighted. She didn't like that, felt embarrassed, but she waited while Greg called the waiter over and asked for the check. And then they quietly ate a little of the cake. Greg told her how happy he was, that this was the greatest moment of his life. By now, however, Diane was thinking of her parents, and she was feeling tense again.

"Are you going to talk to my father?" she asked.

"Oh, I'm sorry. I forgot to tell you. I did. And I received his blessing."

"When?"

"Last weekend. On Sunday, I told you I had a meeting. But really, I drove up to Ogden and talked to both your parents."

"Were they okay about it?"

"Well . . . yeah. Your mom really wants to see you finish college, and I promised her that you would. So I can't break that one. But they both said it was up to you—that if you wanted to marry me, they would support your decision."

"Were they mad?"

"Mad? No. Your mom seemed—I don't know—a little unsettled about it. But you know how parents are. They always think their little girls are still their little girls."

"Were they nice to you, though?"

"Oh, yeah. No problem. We're going to get along great."

Maybe. Diane wondered.

Greg had everything planned. He took her to his own home, and outside, in the fresh, cool air of spring, he knelt and asked her, formally, to marry him. "Yes," she said again, but this time with a little nervousness, and then he slipped the ring on her finger, and he kissed her rather briefly but held her for a long, long time. That's when she realized that he had started to cry. "I can't believe how happy I am," he kept saying.

He took her inside, and they told his parents, who were wonderful, very warm, and as always, Diane felt the money in their style, saw it in their home, their furnishings, even their choice of casual clothes. It was something she had always liked, had a feel for, and it was somehow comforting to know that they would always be so tasteful, know how to handle themselves socially, and that her children could learn by watching them. Diane's parents had some money too, perhaps, but they would never understand the truly elegant life.

Everything did seem right, but maybe a little strained at the moment, and Diane felt it even more when Greg walked her to the kitchen and said, "Honey"—he had never called her that before—"we won't have time to run up to Ogden tonight, not if we're going to make it back to the party. But why don't you call your parents and tell them?"

Diane would have liked to have done that alone, but there was something a little more safe about telling her mom, "I'm here with Greg, at his parents' house," before she announced the rest.

Mom was very careful, as it turned out. "Diane, are you absolutely sure this is what you want?"

"Yes, Mom. I've prayed and prayed about it." She glanced at Greg, who nodded.

"Is there such a hurry that you couldn't get some more college behind you first?"

"This is the right time, Mom. Greg is leaving for school, and I want to go with him."

"Have you set a date?"

"Not a day, yet. But sometime in August. Will that be okay?"

"Yes. That should give us enough time. But I'm not very good at these things. I guess you know what you want for a reception."

"I've imagined it a thousand times. And Greg is really good at anything like that. We'll talk it all over. I'll try to get home next weekend."

"Diane, don't forget school. Don't mess up this semester and lose your credits. You need something to start with, if you ever get back."

"I am going back someday, Mom. Greg and I have already talked about that."

"All right. Here's your dad." She hadn't said anything about being happy. But Dad did, and he seemed to mean it. "Now that you've chosen, honey, we'll think of him as our son. We'll give him all our love."

"Thanks, Dad." But why had he made it sound like a commitment—the right thing to do—instead of something he was excited about?

Greg drove back to Provo then, and he took Diane into the Samuel Hall Society party, where he asked for everyone's attention. After he made the announcement, he took Diane around to all his friends, showing them the magnificent ring, and Diane watched the eyes pop. It was fun, but it was a little uncomfortable, too—for reasons Diane wasn't sure she understood. As much as she liked nice things, she probably would have chosen a little smaller diamond.

It was late when Diane got back to her apartment. No one was up. She was happy about that. But she knew what she wanted to do. She had to get it taken care of before she could relax and really enjoy this change in her life. She took out some of her nice stationery, and she sat down at the kitchen table. "Dear Kent," she wrote. "This is the hardest letter I've ever had to write."

# Chapter 28

Hans had been accused of treason, but fortunately he was actually convicted of a vague and less serious charge: "Actions against the State." His term was set for three years, but the lawyer who had represented him thought that might be shortened by a year or more. Hans had spent a few weeks in the Hohenschönhausen interrogation prison, near East Berlin, but then had been moved to a work camp at a uranium mine. He worked long, tiring hours; slept in a guarded old barracks; and got up each day to repeat the routine.

Hans used the little time he had to himself—an hour or two in the evenings and an occasional full day off—as best he could. He hadn't been allowed to take a Book of Mormon with him, but he had a Bible. He had never read the Bible from cover to cover, but now he was studying the book, not just reading it, working his way carefully through every chapter, every verse, connecting doctrines, comparing them, trying to understand what the book told him about his own life. He wasn't happy, but he was, at least at times, thankful for some changes he felt within himself. There was a kind of purity in the way he lived now. He felt humble, dependent on God, mostly free of selfish desires.

Every week he received mail, which was a big help to him. His parents wrote, and so did Inga. Both his bishop in Schwerin and the branch president in Magdeburg wrote from time to time, as did some of the other Church members, including Elli. But everyone spoke carefully, clearly aware of censors, and he learned almost nothing about the world outside. He had to find what pleasure he could within himself, and so he spent his days of drudgery contemplating the scriptures he studied each night. He tried very hard *not* to think of the future.

Hans shared his quarters with nineteen other men. One of them was older than most, a man probably in his sixties but worn down so he seemed much older. Hans had heard the men call him Gustav, but he knew nothing else about him. One night Gustav sat down on the bunk next to Hans's, then waited until Hans looked up.

"I notice that you read the Bible every night," he said. His voice was as dry as the skin on his face, which was cracked more than wrinkled, like old leather.

"Yes," Hans said.

"This is not good for you. It will go in your report."

Hans nodded. He had worried about that, but not enough to stop.

"You're wiser if you get the words in your head and keep them. But don't let them see you read. And don't talk to me. Not again, after this."

Hans looked at Gustav more closely, saw the yellow cast in his eyes, the cloudiness, and still, a surprising urgency. "Why not talk to you?"

"They think I'm dangerous." A hint of a smile came into his eyes. "They're right, too. I wrote pamphlets against the state, passed them out openly. And when they call me in, to review my case, I'll tell them I'll do it again if they let me out."

"Then why do you tell me to be careful? You're not."

"It doesn't matter to me. But you're young. You need to get out of here."

"What good will that do? I'll never have a chance for a decent job. I'll be doing the same kind of work I do here."

Gustav nodded. He looked at Hans's chest, not into his eyes. "Maybe some things will change, in time. Maybe they'll give you a chance for something better."

"Do you believe that? Do you think they will?"

Gustav looked into Hans's eyes again. "No," he said. "No, I don't. But I hope I'm wrong. And still, it's better to get out."

"Yes," Hans said. He did believe that. But he wasn't going to give up his Bible. It was the only thing that kept him going now.

Gustav got up and walked back to his own bunk, at the far end of the room. Hans watched how slowly he walked, how bent he was, and he wondered whether he was seeing his own future. He thought of the months, maybe years, he would continue here, and then he tried to picture the life that might follow. What he knew was that even if he got out, he would always be watched, and every opportunity for advancement would be stifled. What he felt was that life was too long; his brightest hope was centered on the next world. Only a few weeks before, he had been looking at a professional life, a decent salary, the hope of a wife and family. None of that seemed feasible now.

But he couldn't do this. He couldn't think beyond the present; he had learned to control his pain that way, by filling himself with the image of Christ, by concentrating almost fanatically on the higher meaning of mortality. Gustav had pushed him out of the safety he tried to build around himself, and so he did what he enjoyed most. He walked to the near end of the barracks and through the door. There, in a half-lit room, were four rusty toilets, sitting in the open, only two of them actually functional. But Hans had watched, and he knew that no one was there now. He entered the room, let the door shut behind him, and then hurried to the corner, where he knelt. He prayed often, almost all day, but he felt best when he could kneel, with no one watching. "Help me," he begged the Lord. "Help me get through another day." In the beginning he had cried when he had prayed for help. Now, he hoped for the welcome numbness that kept him from crying.

---

It was April 4, 1968, and Kathy was in the Neilson Library at Smith, researching a paper she wanted to do on congressional resolutions. She was convinced that President Johnson had overstepped his bounds in using the Tonkin Gulf Resolution to justify all that he was doing in Vietnam. It was one of those subjects she believed the entire nation needed to understand, and yet, lately, when she tried to discuss such matters with her friends in SDS, she got little interest. Even the brightest of the members was likely to let loose with a barrage of profane abuse on Johnson, more temper tantrum than argued response. But Kathy was convinced that the Tet Offensive in January and February had changed the national mood, and many more people were willing to listen to those who opposed the war. The Vietcong had made one thing clear: after three years of fighting, their forces were as strong as ever. All the bombing and all the buildup of troops hadn't accomplished anything. Even Walter Cronkite had announced on his nightly news show that he no longer believed the United States could win the war. George Romney, a hero to many Mormons, and for a time a candidate for the Republican presidential nomination, had also changed his mind. He had announced earlier that year that in his previous trip to Vietnam, he had been "brainwashed" by the military, and he now saw that the war was a hopeless cause, not worth the cost in American lives. His comment about being brainwashed had created so much controversy and bad press that he had withdrawn from the presidential race, but he hadn't changed his mind.

More recently, in March, "peace candidate" Senator Eugene McCarthy had run against Lyndon Johnson in the New Hampshire Democratic primary and received 42 percent of the vote—an unthinkable number against an incumbent president. Four days later, Senator Robert Kennedy, an outspoken critic of Johnson's war policies, had entered the race. A week after that, Johnson had shocked the nation by announcing that he would not run for reelection. Richard Nixon was arguing that those who wanted "peace at any price" were willing to destroy America's standing and influence in world politics. He promised that if he were to be nominated and elected, he would bring "peace with honor." Kathy was not sure what that meant, but what she saw was a country weary of the war and looking for a way to end it. Now seemed the time to reach the people, to give them arguments they could comprehend. More and more middle-class families were afraid that their own sons might be lost, and they were finally asking questions that went beyond the old clichés about stopping Communism.

Kathy wanted to be active in the cause, wanted to get the truth out, so she continued her connection to SDS—even though the disdain Robby and the other members felt for her was obvious. She feared the rhetoric at SDS meetings, the increasing justification for bombing and occupying buildings. Some politicians were saying that the antiwar movement was prolonging the war, not ending it, and she wasn't entirely sure that that wasn't true. She simply didn't know where else to carry on the fight. What she concluded was that it was best for her to research, gather facts, and then feed that information to the members so they would make sense, be accurate when they wrote and spoke out against the war. She thought maybe she could also do some publishing, get her information to people of influence.

She was looking through the library stacks, searching for a call number, when she heard a woman say, "They don't know who shot him. There's not even official word that he's dead."

Kathy heard the anguish in the woman's voice, and she felt that sick reaction she remembered from the day John Kennedy had been shot. She stepped around the corner of a bookshelf and saw that the woman, a librarian, had been talking to a student, but now she had her hands clasped to her cheeks, and tears were dripping onto her fingers.

"Who is it?" Kathy asked. "What happened?"

The student turned around, her face white. "Martin Luther King," she said.

Kathy felt a wave of nausea, felt the weakness strike her knees. "No," she said. "No. They aren't sure, are they?"

"I think they are," the librarian said. She was clasping her fists to her breastbone now, hunching a little forward, but Kathy wanted to shout at her not to spread such rumors, not to say what she couldn't know for sure.

Kathy spun around, walked quickly down the stairs to the main floor, and looked for someone who might know more. She hurried to the reference desk, to a woman she knew. "What have you heard? Is he all right?" she almost shouted.

"No. They just said it on the radio. He's dead."

Kathy ran. She banged into the electronic gate at the exit, had to step back to let it release, and then hurried outside. It occurred to her in some distant way that she had left her books upstairs, all her notes, but she didn't go back. She stood in the cool air and tried to let it seep into her. She couldn't think what to do next. She could only think of Lester. Did Lester know? What would this do to him?

At least the thought provided some focus. She had to get to Amherst; she had to find Lester. And so she ran. She cut across campus, between College Hall and Hillyer, and then burst onto Elm Street. But she was breathing too hard to keep running. She cut across the street, stored up some breath, and then ran again. But this was going to take forever. She didn't have time to catch a bus. When she spotted two guys, college age, getting into a car, she stopped. "Are you going to Amherst?" she asked in a gasp.

"Yes," one of the guys said.

"Now?"

"Yes."

"Could I ride with you?"

"Sure."

But they were staring at her. She had been crying, she realized, and she must have looked wild. "They killed Martin Luther King," she said. One of the guys nodded. He was older, maybe a grad student at UMass, she thought. He had long sideburns and a mustache, but he was wearing a button-down-collar shirt and cotton slacks. She didn't think he was a radical. It was so hard to tell these days. She pushed by him and headed for the back door of the car. "Could we go now?" she asked.

So they all three climbed into the car, and the other guy drove, the one in an argyle sweater. "This is really bad," the boy said as he backed the car from the parking spot. "There'll be riots everywhere."

Of course, Kathy thought. Wasn't that the point? Why did they think she was crying?

But she didn't talk to them, and the two listened to the radio, to the talk. No one had been arrested. Reverend King had been on a balcony at a motel, standing with some other leaders. Shots had rung out and he had fallen. The reporter said that he had died almost immediately.

Kathy cried all the way to Amherst. The boys dropped her off close to the dorms, and Kathy ran again. Lester was in his room, but Dee Dee was also there, and the girl was going crazy. Kathy heard her from outside, screaming, "This is how things are, Lester. This is how it always turns out for us. Do you finally understand?"

Kathy knocked, and it was Dee Dee who swung the door open. She stared at Kathy for a couple of seconds, her eyes wide with rage, and then she said, "Get out of here. We don't need your white guilt. We don't need *nothing* you want to say."

But Lester's hand appeared. It grasped the door and pulled it away from Dee Dee. He stepped around the door and said, "Come on in."

Kathy could see the tears on his face, the red in his eyes. She wrapped her arms around him. "I'm sorry, Lester," she said. "I'm so sorry."

"It's all over," Lester said. "Nonviolence is dead."

"No. We have to keep trying. He'd want us to try." But Kathy wasn't sure that she believed her own words. Behind her, she heard Dee Dee laugh, and she wondered—maybe Dee Dee was right. But she held Lester in her arms, felt his body shake, listened to him sob, and she thought his was the better response.

~

In previous years Kathy had not gone home for spring break, but when her parents offered to fly her home this year, she decided she wanted to go. She wanted to spend some time away from everything. She had a private room this year in Baldwin House, but it was austere, always too hot or too cold, and never really home to her. She also thought she wanted to talk to her parents. She had begun to feel that she needed that. She needed to rebuild something that had been slipping away from her for three years now—or maybe much longer than that. And yet, when she got home, she couldn't find the things that she wanted to say to them, and her mom and dad were painfully careful with her. Both were sick about Martin Luther King's death, and for the same reason as Kathy—at least verbally. They had liked what he had stood for: the struggle for "Negro rights," and the moderate positions he had taken. He had, after all, dreamed of a world where whites and blacks got along. He hadn't been like the Black Panthers, in California, who strutted around in black clothes and black berets, always carrying weapons.

But Wally and Lorraine clearly didn't feel the pain that Kathy felt, and that was frustrating to her. It was all words to them, political talk, abstraction. Kathy had heard the Reverend speak. She had been knocked down by the blow of a nightstick, and in her mind that had won her the right to a deeper level of understanding than most white people would ever have. She found it equally frustrating to hear people in Utah—especially her dad—talk about their disillusionment with the war and then argue that the military ought to be set free to bring the north to its knees. "You can't fight a war halfway," Dad would say. "No one has the will to win this thing."

Kathy couldn't deal with that. She believed that the United States had no right to be participating in this war, taking sides in a civil conflict. An American officer had recently claimed that he had had to "destroy a village in order to save it." Did America have the right to destroy the whole nation? Would it then be "saved"? She couldn't talk about such ideas without rage, and so she stayed in her room, trying to see her future, but she saw little that made any sense.

On Easter Kathy decided that she would go to church, and it wasn't because she knew her parents were hoping she would go. When she didn't think, just let herself respond, she knew she still believed in God, still believed in prayer, and when she thought of Joseph Smith and his simple story, she knew it was part of her, something she hadn't denied.

Back in her old ward she felt something she had almost forgotten—how good these people were. They seemed to care about each other, and about her. It was good for her to remember that. As some of the older brothers and sisters in the ward embraced her, laughed with her, asked her about her future, she recognized a spirit of kindness and goodwill that she liked immensely.

The sacrament was passed by boys she had known as babies—little twelve- and thirteen-year-old guys who looked like children but who held themselves erect as though they understood the importance of this act they were performing. She liked that, too. But she didn't take the bread or the water; she passed them on to her mother, who certainly had to feel disappointed that Kathy wouldn't take part. Kathy did listen to the prayers, however, the promises, and she was touched by the idea of them as she never had been before. She wanted the Spirit "always" with her. She thought of the day she had been baptized, when she was only eight, and everything had seemed simple and right. She remembered her Grandpa Thomas placing his hands on her head and confirming her a member of the Church. She couldn't recall now what he had said, but she remembered him hugging her afterward, smelling of Old Spice and feeling like wool. She had seen the tears in his eyes, too, and had known how much he loved her.

After the sacrament, the ward choir sang. Kathy had loved choir in high school and had always taken a dim view of the off-tune, warbling old ladies and the flat tenors, always outnumbered and trying too hard. But she found room in her heart to forgive them today. "He Is Risen," they sang, and she knew that she had never stopped believing that. If only she didn't have to listen to those same people at testimony meeting, spouting so many opinions that drove her crazy. She wanted the music, and she wanted Christ. Couldn't she survive the rest somehow? She really didn't know. What she did know was that she had lost something. Maybe it would be, finally, some fairy tale that she had to give up, like Santa and the Easter Bunny, but it didn't seem so. It seemed as though she had drifted away from something that she needed back. She wished it were as simple as grasping the iron rod again, but she wasn't sure she could do that.

After the meeting her family went to Grandma and Grandpa Thomas's house. Aunt Beverly was there, with her kids. Kathy found herself watching Beverly, noticing how tender she was with her children, how trusting she was of everyone she loved. There was something in that, too—maybe the spirit that people were looking for in Haight-Ashbury and failing to find. Maybe there were things back home that were right. And yet, Beverly was as naive as a child, uninformed about her world and about the things that were so deeply wrong. How could that be an answer for Kathy?

Gene and Diane were there. Gene was going to be married in June, and Diane in August. But Gene's fiancée had gone with her family to visit relatives in Idaho, and Diane's boyfriend would be coming over later. Kathy saw the chance to be alone with them and invited them out to the porch, where Kathy sat with Diane in the old love seat they had liked to sit in as little girls, and Gene—everyone's favorite cousin—sat on the chair across from them. Grandma wasn't letting the little kids out yet. After dinner they would be set free, as they were every year, to hunt for Easter eggs in the yard, but most of the eggs were candy, and no one was allowed to start eating chocolate before dinner.

"Remember how we used to hate waiting until after dinner?" Diane asked Kathy and Gene.

"Hey, I didn't," Gene said. "I'd get out of the car and make a mad dash into the backyard. Dad would come after me, but I'd usually pocket a couple of eggs before he could catch up."

"See, you always came out ahead of us," Diane said, "no matter what we did."

From there the talk was all about being kids, coming to Grandma's, listening to Grandpa's lectures. But eventually Gene said, "I was just thinking—it was over six years ago the three of us set those ten-year goals. Do you feel like I do? Like I'm hardly the same person now?"

"Don't you want to be president anymore?" Kathy asked. She watched Gene shake his head, smile, and she did feel the difference. He wasn't so sure of himself anymore, or at least not so quick to make claims. "What *do* you want to do, Gene?"

"I don't know for sure. That's the problem. I've got to decide right away, too. I still might go to law school. Or maybe get an MBA. The trouble is, it doesn't make much difference what I plan. The army's going to get me when I graduate."

"But you can apply for officer school, can't you?" Diane asked. "Greg hurt his knee skiing, really bad, back before his mission. The army won't take him now. But he always says that if he did have to go, he'd rather go as an officer."

"Yeah, you can do that. But you have to stay in longer. If you go in as a grunt, you're finished in two years. That's what I keep thinking, that I want it over as fast as possible so I can get home to Emily and get back in school."

Kathy saw his glance, and she sensed his concern that their old argument was about to start again. But Kathy wasn't going to do it.

Gene was the one to say, "Kathy, I'm gradually starting to think you might be right about Vietnam, in one way. Maybe we never should have gotten involved. But I don't see how we can leave. There'll be a bloodbath if we do that. There's no way we can drop our commitment over there and just let the Communists overrun the south."

"I think you're right, Gene. We should kill off thousands more of the Vietnamese, and thousands more of our own boys, and *then* come home. That'll be a lot more honorable."

No one spoke. Somewhere in a nearby tree, sparrows were chirping, making quite a racket.

Some time passed before Diane said, "Let me go on record as saying that I'm about to reach *my* goal. I told you two that day that I wanted a good husband and a nice family. I've got the husband on the hook, and we don't really want to wait for children. By this time next year, I should have a baby on the way. I'm getting everything I've always wanted."

"That's good," Gene said. He leaned forward and rested his elbows on his knees. "I don't know what to do about that. If I have to go, I don't want to leave Emily home, expecting."

"Why not?" Diane asked. "That might make her happier than anything."

The two talked about that, but Kathy was struck by the difference she felt in herself. She had no desire to get married for a long time. She wasn't suited to be married now, and she wasn't sure she ever would be.

"Kathy, what are you thinking you want to do with your life now?" Gene asked.

"I don't know."

"You used to say that you wanted to change the world."

Kathy nodded. "It's harder than I thought," she said.

"What happened to that boy you dated, just before you went to college?" Diane asked.

"He'll be home from his mission this summer."

"Have you been writing to him?"

"No."

"What happened?"

"Nothing. That's what always happens between me and guys. I think I talk too much." She laughed. "No. I *know* I talk too much."

"Have you really given up?" Gene asked. "Won't you keep fighting for all your causes?"

Kathy looked at him for a long time. She didn't think she had given up. "I'm going to do some things," she said. "First, I want to finish college. I messed up my grades for a while, but I've been doing a lot better lately. After that, I think I might join the Peace Corps."

"That sounds right for you," Diane said.

"You seem sad," Gene said. "Are you still feeling bad about Martin Luther King?"

"Still?"

"Well, I mean—"

"I'll *always* feel bad about Martin Luther King. I keep reading that talk he gave in Washington a few years ago—the 'I have a dream' talk. And I keep telling myself I can't give up on that. I just don't know what to do to make it happen."

Again there was a long pause, the sound of all those sparrows. Then Gene said, "Kathy, you need the Church. You can do more good through the Church than any other way."

"The Church doesn't want me," Kathy said. "I don't fit."

"That isn't true."

"Be honest. I have to change if I'm ever going to be part of a ward again. And I don't know how to change. I am who I am. I believe what I believe. Sometimes I try to run back to my family and become the old me again, but it never works."

"Kathy, I don't believe that," Gene said. "The Church is a bunch of people. But the gospel is a lot more than that. If you believe in the gospel, you can find a way to fit in with the people."

Kathy wanted to believe that was true. She thought about the choir that morning, singing "He Is Risen." She had liked all those people, at least for the length of that song. Maybe she had even loved them.

The old screen door came open with a squeak, and Kathy looked up to see Grandpa step out to the porch. "Grandma told me to round everyone up," he said. "Dinner's about ready."

Gene stood quickly. "I'm about ready myself," he said, and he laughed. Kathy stood too, and Diane.

But Grandpa stayed in the doorway. "I love you three," he said. "And I'm awfully proud of you."

Kathy's thought was that he actually meant the other two, but he was looking at her, not at them. "I'm sorry, Grandpa," was all Kathy could think to say.

"Sorry for what?"

"You know—the way I am."

Grandpa stepped forward and took Kathy in his arms. "Kathy, I need you," he said. "I know how I *pontificate*. And most of the family just humors me. But you make me think—and that's not a bad thing for an old man. It's good for me to question my opinions every now and then." Kathy liked to hear that, was touched, but then he added, "But honey, don't question the Church. That's the only thing I worry about, that you'll wander too far away and never find your way back to us."

Kathy took in some air. She didn't think he was wrong; she just didn't think he could ever understand.

The dinner was wonderful, as always: baked ham, potato salad, green salad, Jell-O salad, green beans, and lots of Grandma's freshly baked rolls.

And for dessert Grandma served freshly baked cherry pie, with ice cream. Afterward, Kathy told everyone to sit down and talk; she would do the dishes. It was a little gift she wanted so badly to give. But Grandma came into the kitchen anyway. She helped load the dishwasher, and then, as Kathy washed the pots and pans in the sink, she stood next to her and dried them.

"Lorraine tells me you went to church today," Grandma said.

"I did."

"Was it nice to go back?"

Kathy laughed. She was dipping a saucepan in hot rinse water. She let the water run off for a time, and then she set it in a drying rack. "Grandma, church is complicated for me. But I did like it more than I expected. I liked the music, and I liked seeing my old friends. I liked the sacrament, too—even though I didn't take it."

"Why, honey?"

"I'm not worthy. I'm not faithful enough."

"Don't be too hard on yourself, Kathy. You told me yourself you haven't been going to meetings, but you aren't doing anything wrong."

"We all do things that are wrong."

"Of course we do, but I'm just—"

"Grandma, my heart isn't right—it hasn't been for a long time."

"No one's heart is always right. I sit through church half the time, wishing it were over. I get so tired of people saying the same old things the same old way. But that's when I listen with my head. Other times, when I'm in the right spirit, all I feel is how much I love the speakers, no matter what they're saying."

"I tried not to listen to the speaker today—because I get so irritated with the things people say—but I can never really shut off my brain. I come out of church angry most of the time."

Grandma picked up the saucepan now, caressed it against her apron as she dried it, as though drying were an act of love. It was what Kathy always felt from her. "What about Grandpa? Did it bother you what he was saying about Hubert Humphrey during dinner?"

"Not really. I've lost faith in all the politicians. I usually agree with him now when he talks about Democrats. It's just that I think Republicans are even worse, if that's possible."

Grandma laughed. "I feel a lot the same," she said. "The best things happen in neighborhoods, not in Congress."

"I know. But some things can't be done over the back fence."

"Maybe not. But when one person loves another person, something very important is happening. And that's what we need more of. Everyone's *screaming* right now. Everyone's angry. That just isn't doing any good."

"You sound like a hippie, Grandma. That's what the kids in San Francisco say."

"Maybe I should become a flower child." She smiled, and those lovely dimples of hers appeared.

Kathy laughed, but tears had filled her eyes. "You're not a flower child, Grandma. You're a flower."

Kathy wiped her hands on her apron, and then she took her grandma in her arms. Kathy was tall enough that they fit together more like a mother and child, but Kathy knew who the child was, knew what a giant her grandma was, and she also knew that if anything in this world was genuine and true, it was her grandma. She clung to Grandma Bea as though she were the last hope in the world.

# Author's Note

Since I published *The Writing on the Wall*—the first book in this series—a number of people have mentioned to me that it "feels" different from my *Children of the Promise* books. That's true, of course, and the difference is in the eras the books portray. World War II, however difficult, tended to bring people in America together. But the sixties were divisive. Generations discovered a "gap" that had never seemed quite so important before. People divided along the lines of race, gender, political opinion, and "lifestyle" choices—and no one spoke softly. The Civil Rights movement, the war in Vietnam, changes in popular culture, the women's movement, the hippie experiments, the use of drugs—each of these set off strident arguments, but all of them together created a cacophony of angry voices that set the age apart from any other. Some of those arguments are still unpleasant, even frightening to remember.

It was not a time without fun, however, and maybe we can now laugh at the outlandish "mod" clothing, the dance styles, even the "revolutionaries," who, as often as not, grew up much more like their middle-class parents than they ever expected they would. But important debates did occur, and some profound changes were brought about. Most of us are now thankful for the beginning of change in attitudes about race and gender, for instance. At the same time, many of us feel that something was lost during that time, that the survival of the family became all the more difficult. Many of the simple values we associate with the fifties were rejected by a large percentage of the people. For Latter-day Saints, the challenge of raising a family and holding to honored truths became harder than ever before.

Many young people, during the sixties, denounced religion as part of what was wrong with the world, and they looked for other answers. And yet, this was the same era when the LDS missionary force grew faster than ever before. Committed members of The Church of Jesus Christ of Latter-day Saints felt that the gospel had never been more important as a guide for living. The result was another kind of "gap": Latter-day Saints feeling ever more estranged from the societies they lived in. What was even more difficult, however, was that members of the Church had to deal with all the same issues, and members' families were often torn by divided attitudes.

So here again, in this series, I'm interested in the challenges that the Thomas family must deal with. It's one thing to worry about your child who has gone to war; it's another to worry about your child who wages war against *you*. I use my characters to represent the many directions of thought that were pulling at people. What I don't mean to do is imply that any one character has all the right answers. Looking back at the debates of the sixties, I would hope that the reader would honestly ask, again, the important questions that were raised. How can we live together as a people—or as families—and what are the values that we can depend upon? What I believe is that the teachings of Christ will always work, that they can get a family through any difficulty. But that doesn't mean that specific answers are always obvious or automatic. Part of the reason for living is to face struggles, deal with them, and grow stronger in the process.

Perhaps the tendency of the sixties was iconoclastic, but some icons need to be challenged, and certain questions deserve to be asked by every generation. Latter-day Saints are not immune from the issues that lead to troubled times. As you look back, I hope you will feel some of the fun, along with the strain, of the sixties era, but that you will also take an interest in answering certain important questions all over again. Even if we always get the same answers, there is worth in the very act of asking.

*Troubled Waters* is the second book in the *Hearts of the Children* series. My plan is, once again, to write five books in the series. Outlines have a way of "morphing" as one writes, but five would appear to be the right number.

As always, I'm reading lots of good books in order to understand the time I'm writing about. When we live through an age, our experiences are limited and our understanding skewed by that experience, so I'm reading books that help me comprehend the bigger picture. In my last volume I suggested a number of overview books. Let me add one more: *The Columbia Guide to America in the 1960s*, by David Farber and Beth Bailey (Columbia University Press, 2001).

Let me also recommend some titles that are helpful on some specific issues. In trying to understand the Vietnam war, along with Stanley Karnow's classic book *Vietnam: A History* (Viking, 1993), I have used *Vietnam and the United States: Origins and Legacy of War*, by Gary R. Hess (Twayne, 1990); *The Soldiers' Story: Vietnam in Their Own Words*, by Ron Steinman (TV Books, 1999); *The Vietnam Reader*, edited by Stewart O'Nan (Random House, 1998); and *Stolen Valor: How the Vietnam Generation Was Robbed of Its Heroes and Its History*, by B. G. Burkett and Glenna Whitley (Verity Press, 1998). Another book that is surprisingly helpful, in spite of its title, is *The Complete Idiot's Guide to the Vietnam War*, by Timothy P. Maga (Alpha Books, 2000). *War Letters: Extraordinary Correspondence from American Wars*, edited by Andrew Carroll (Scribner, 2001), is also a fascinating and often touching book that contains a section of Vietnam letters.

I've continued to study the German Democratic Republic. Regina and Oliver Schreiber have been willing to answer specific questions, and I have read *GDR Society and Social Institutions*, by G. E. Edwards (St. Martin's, 1985); *Spymaster: The Real-Life "Karla," His Moles, and the East German Secret Police*, by Leslie Colitt (Addison-Wesley, 1995); *Inside East Germany: The State That Came in from the Cold*, by Jonathan Steele

(Urizen Books, 1977); *East Germany: A Country Study*, edited by Stephen R. Burant (Federal Research Division, Library of Congress, 1988); *Spy Trader: Germany's Devil's Advocate and the Darkest Secrets of the Cold War*, by Craig R. Whitney (Random House, 1993); and *Germany East: Dissent and Opposition*, by Bruce Allen (Black Rose Books, 1989). A newer book, which benefits from the opening of records in the GDR since its collapse, is *The Anatomy of a Dictatorship: Inside the GDR, 1949–1989*, by Mary Fulbrook (Oxford, 1995).

I had great fun looking through *Banyan* yearbooks from BYU in the 1960s. I also read Ernest L. Wilkinson's history *Brigham Young University: A School of Destiny* (BYU Press, 1976) and Gary Bergera's account in *Brigham Young University: A House of Faith* (Signature, 1985).

My family continues to read my manuscripts and gives me lots of help, and I'm especially thankful that my wife, Kathy, who has become busier than ever, still finds time to read not just one but several of my drafts.

This book is dedicated to my father-in-law, William Daly Hurst. He's one of my heroes. He's more than halfway through his eighties, and he's never stopped learning and thinking. Most of us have a tendency to develop a set of ideas at a fairly young age and then stick with them, no matter what life tells us. But Bill is always reading, listening, and thinking, and as a result, he is also always adjusting and growing. He's pleasant, interesting, and kind-hearted, and I'll always be thankful that my children and their children have him as a role model in their lives.

# About the Author

Dean Hughes has published more than ninety books and numerous stories and poems for all ages—children, young adults, and adults.

Dr. Hughes received his B.A. from Weber State University in Ogden, Utah, and his M.A. and Ph.D. from the University of Washington. He has attended post-doctoral seminars at Stanford and Yale Universities and has taught English at Central Missouri State University and Brigham Young University.

He has also served in many callings, including that of a bishop, in The Church of Jesus Christ of Latter-day Saints. He and his wife, Kathleen Hurst Hughes, who has served in the Relief Society general presidency, have three children and nine grandchildren. They live in Midway, Utah.

If you liked this book, you'll love the *Children of the Promise* series by Dean Hughes!

What was life like during World War II? How did the war affect the lives of those who fought and those who kept the home fires burning? Find out in *Children of the Promise*, the carefully researched and beautifully written story of a family living through those turbulent years from 1939 to 1947. Meet the characters readers have come to love: Alex, who served a mission to Germany and returned to fight those among whom he had preached; Bobbi, a Navy nurse with a divided heart; Wally, a young rebel who finds his true path in the trials of a prisoner-of-war camp; and many others. *Children of the Promise* will touch your heart in an unforgettable way!

Volume 1: *Rumors of War*

Volume 2: *Since You Went Away*

Volume 3: *Far from Home*

Volume 4: *When We Meet Again*

Volume 5: *As Long as I Have You*